THE
DEMON
GABRIELLA

BY

RACHEL CALISH

Bella
BOOKS

2015

Bella Books, Inc.
P.O. Box 10543
Tallahassee, FL 32302

First Bella Books Edition 2015

Editor: Katherine V. Forrest
Cover Designer: Kristin Smith

ISBN: 978-1-59493-443-8

Other Bella Books by Rachel Calish

The Demon Abraxas

Acknowledgments

This was one of those stories where the characters took over and I had a blast hanging on for the ride. My first thank-you goes to the unseen forces who inhabit my characters (and my brain) from time to time. You lot are beyond wonderful.

I have a great community of people who beta read for me, listen to me ramble, help me think through plot points and character issues, and generally keep me as sane as a writer should be. Thanks to: Alia Whipple, Kim Albee, Shuvani Roma, Lin Distel, Jane Wisdom, Kim Nguyen, Sara Bracewell, Wendy Nemitz and all the women of Ingenuity Marketing Group. Thank you also to Kristin Smith for continuously turning my crazy ideas into beautiful book covers.

Special thanks to those who've taught me about magic and meditation. The magic that Sabel and the witches use is inspired by Rachel Pollack. (If you have not read her novels, put one on your list: www.rachelpollack.com.) The teachings of Abraxas are inspired by Craig Lindahl-Urben and Reggie Ray. (You can find meditations from Reggie online at www.dharmaocean.org.)

Thank you to Katherine Forrest for the best editor letters in the whole world and for writing "good scene" after that one scene I was going to cut. Many thanks to Linda Hill, Karin Kallmaker and everyone at Bella Books for making this book and so many others a reality.

And finally my deepest thanks to everyone in my household —I'd be lost without you.

About Rachel

Rachel Calish lives in the Twin Cities area of Minnesota because it's so cold you just have to sit inside and write novels. After growing up on mythology and fairy tales, she obtained her Master of Fine Arts in Writing by writing stories about sexy demons. A fan of games of all kinds, you can find her playing anything from the latest video game releases to checkers with half the pieces missing. Under the name Rachel Gold, she writes LGBTQ Young Adult fiction. You can read more about Rachel at: @rachelcalish on Twitter and www.rachelcalish.com.

Dedication

For Rachel Pollack
who is also from the future

CHAPTER ONE

The eyes glaring at Ana through the upstairs window were varicolored red with slit pupils, like a snake's. A passing car's headlights outlined the dark, misshapen head. Fear and adrenaline spiked through her, pushed on a rising wave of anger. She jumped up from her meditation cushion and threw the window open. A semitransparent black body scuttled up the side of the house like a crab.

Call Lily, the familiar voice of the demon Abraxas spoke into her mind.

"You call Lily, I'm going after it," she snapped back.

Sure, she let a demon live inside her body, but that didn't make it okay for snake-eyed creepers to look in on her at all hours of the night. Plus she wanted to test the enhanced strength Abraxas gave her.

Ana leaned out the window and grabbed a bracket of drainpipe and a bar of the decorative wood siding. Hauling herself up, she kicked out a leg and pulled herself onto a narrow ledge. From there she ran two steps, gripped the edge of the roof, and swung around and up onto the deeply slanted, shingled surface.

The little demon crouched at the far end of the roof, eyes widening with surprise. It fled up over the peak and she followed.

She spoke to Abraxas internally, in case one of the neighbors had an open window. *How can I be strong enough to pull myself up onto the roof and still have a belly?* she asked him as they ran.

Your body is a complicated metabolic organism, he replied.

What?

Too many carbs, Abraxas said. *Lily is on her way.*

The little demon scampered up the next roof and Ana jumped across the few feet between houses without effort. A light wind from the south carried the smells of sweet pine, juniper and lemon that mixed with the gray scent of wet pavement from a light, early evening rain.

Six months ago, she'd been a corporate publicist whose biggest challenge was asking out the professor who made her guts feel like molten lava. Restless and too curious by half, Ana had stumbled into a murder and been captured by a group of demon summoners. She'd let Abraxas into her body to help her escape.

She hadn't realized she'd end up sharing her body with a demon full-time.

Ana went up and over four more roofs, paying close attention to her footing. Her agility hadn't increased with her strength. The fleeing demon was gaining a longer lead, it jumped from the last gabled roof down to the flat roof of a store as they approached a larger street.

She sped up and leapt after it, absorbing the impact by making a quick roll across the flat surface and letting her momentum carry her back up to her feet. Some of the effects of sharing her body with a demon were upsetting, to put it mildly, but she liked how much more resilient he'd made her. And his lessons in demon magics were pretty sweet.

Does Lily know the direction we're going? she asked Abraxas.

He answered with a wordless affirmative. He was probably still in the process of sending her their location. Half-demon,

Lily was the best banisher in San Francisco. Ana had met her that first week with Abraxas, when she was still trying to get rid of him. Lily helped them fight the stronger demon, Ashmedai, who wanted to kill Ana and bind Abraxas to him instead. They'd been friends since. More than friends when it came to Abraxas. Somehow he and Lily were carrying on an intimate relationship despite the fact that he had no body of his own.

The little demon scurried down the side of the two-story flat-roofed building and ran for the four-lane street. It was the size of a large dog and would be mistaken for one—if people could see its black form at all. Most humans couldn't see demons.

There were few cars this late and it dashed across with only a moment's pause. Ana held the edge of the roof, let her legs dangle and then dropped to a ledge at the one-story level.

She dropped again, caught that ledge for a moment and then let go. Her legs hit the sidewalk with minimal impact. She pivoted and sprinted across the street toward where the demon was climbing the wall of another shop.

She couldn't scale the two-story wall, but next to it was a shorter building. With a quick prayer that she had enough speed, she ran two steps up the side of the building and threw her arms up as high as she could reach. Her hands closed over the edge of the roof. She pulled up hard and scrambled with her feet against the bricks until she was up on the roof. On the side of the taller building, not facing the street, were pipes and brackets and a myriad of handholds that made it easy to climb to the higher level.

Did you see that? she asked Abraxas, though of course he had. *I'm like a ninja!*

A long sigh of exasperation crossed her mind in reply.

The demon wasn't even halfway across the higher roof. It had slowed, thinking she had only the strength of an average human and no way to chase it up the wall. Seeing her, its black-veined, red eyes looked around furiously, seeking escape. It turned to run but hit the side of a protruding metal vent and staggered sideways.

Wait for Lily, Abraxas warned.

This was too perfect and she didn't want to chase this thing over another block of rooftops only to have Lily bind it before she could get her hands on it. The little shit had been staring in her window and she wanted to be the one to punch it in its lopsided, toothy mouth. Then Lily could have it. Not that Ana could punch a mostly-incorporeal demon, but Abraxas could. And he could bind it well enough if they could grab it. She ran forward and dove at it.

As soon as she got her hands on it, she felt it begin to dematerialize. Like many of the small demons used as servants, it didn't have a physical body and could only pull the barest amount of solid matter around it so it could function in this material world. Holding it was like trying to enclose a biting, struggling cloud. For Abraxas to bind it, she had to get her arms around it in a circle. She stepped forward and to one side, trying to get a better angle.

Under her skin, Abraxas moved to help her contain it. She felt his energy flow through her arms, but so did the little demon. In a desperate effort to escape, it popped out of the material world. Ana's arms tightened on air. Overbalanced, she tripped forward, hit another vent, stumbled and saw the edge of the roof coming up too fast.

She caught it one-handed. Her momentum carried her over the edge and she felt a painful twist and jerk in her shoulder as her body's full weight snapped down under her. Her fingers lost their hold. She fell the rest of the way to the pavement.

Abraxas tried to break the fall by putting the loose cloudy form he sometimes wore between her and the concrete. That didn't stop her from slamming into it with enough force to knock the air out of her lungs.

Gasping and coughing, she tried to feel through the mass of pain in her back, arm and head to see if she'd really injured herself.

Nothing broken, Abraxas told her. He could scan through her body faster and more completely than she could. *Torn muscles and tendons in the shoulder. Get ice on it and I'll see what I can do.*

He could encourage her body to heal itself more quickly than normal, though hardly at a superhuman level. She wouldn't be bouncing up off the pavement and shaking herself back into place.

If you try to lecture me about this, I'm going to tell Lily that you ogle other women when she's not around, Ana told him.

Just because you let your anger lead and forgot that it could banish itself? That's not enough subject matter for a full lecture. And you should think about that ogling accusation, considering that you're in control of our eyes.

Ana was still working on a retort when Lily drove up in a sporty matte silver crossover. Sometimes Ana thought Lily would be driving a sports car if she didn't need to carry so much magical stuff in the back. Lily worked the hip soccer mom look, probably because being half-demon, she appeared to be midforties but was closer to midnineties. Her thick, wavy, dark brown hair was pulled back and she wore a loose sweater with yoga pants and oversized slippers. If she'd arrived midchase, Ana knew Lily would have those slippers off in a second because her taloned eagle feet were much better for running over rooftops than anything that came standard on a human body.

Ana had managed to get herself sitting and pushed with her feet and good arm until she was leaning back against the wall of the store she'd fallen from. Lily crouched in front of her.

"I heard you had a misstep. Do you want to go home or to the hospital?"

"Home," Ana said.

Abraxas moved so that part of his being was outside of Ana, beside her, also crouching like Lily. His form looked made of mist, and anyone standing more than a few feet from them wouldn't see him at all.

"Before it dematerialized, I touched it," he said. His voice, outside of Ana's head, could sound like anything from wind and sand to a thunderstorm. Right now it was at the quiet end of that spectrum. "It was from Ashmedai."

"He's not—" Ana started, then had to cough, which sent pain shooting from her shoulder across her chest. She bit back a groan and tried again. "Not allowed in the city."

"I don't like this," Lily said. "He must be gathering allies. At least one who can summon demons in the city for him."

"Sick of this," Ana said. "It was looking in my window while I was trying to meditate." She didn't add that she'd been relieved for the distraction and an excuse to stop sitting.

"If we catch the next one, I can try to get it to tell us who's doing the summoning," Lily said.

"I don't want to keep chasing the little ones. This is the third one I've seen around my house this month. We have to find a way to get to Ashmedai, before he gets any stronger."

"We're working on it," Lily said, meaning the larger group of protector demons that she and Abraxas were part of. "Do you want me to call Sabel?"

Ana sighed slowly so the motion wouldn't jar her shoulder. It had turned out that the hot professor was part of an ancient order of witches and way more clued in about this magic stuff than Ana had been. She and Sabel had been dating for the last three months and she wanted nothing more than for Sabel to come over and sit with her while she iced her shoulder, but that wasn't fair to Sabel.

"Let her sleep, she's teaching this week. I'm okay, really, I think. But can we pick up a bag of ice on the way?"

She let Lily help her up and into the car, wondering if Sabel was in bed already and if so what she was wearing. Sabel had the best collection of lacy undergarments and things that were allegedly pajamas but that Ana thought weren't meant to be worn for more than five minutes. But she saw them rarely and almost never got to take them off Sabel because of the centuries-old feud between the demons and the witches.

How much of her impatience to get rid of Ashmedai came from simply wanting to be closer to Sabel? And did it matter? Ana had defeated Ashmedai once and if she could just get rid of him for good, they'd all be happier and a heck of a lot safer.

* * *

Careful of her sore shoulder, Ana leaned back and to the left in the small, hard chair. Two days after the fall from the roof, she thought it shouldn't still hurt that much, but it did. She was glad for the distraction and happy to watch from the back of the classroom while Sabel lectured her class. Sabel wore a soft gray boat-neck top with a small string of pearls. Her black hair was pulled into a loose braid, exposing her slender neck.

Sabel was saying, "According to Jung, 'Everyone carries a Shadow, and the less it is embodied in the individual's conscious life, the blacker and denser it is.' One way the Shadow appears to us is by our projections onto others—what you hate in others, you hate in yourself."

Ana could think of plenty of things she hated in other people that had no connection to how she was, but she was afraid if she brought that up to Sabel later in private, she'd get argued out of thinking that way. Sabel stepped out from behind the desk and Ana saw that she was wearing a dark gray tweed skirt that ended just below her knees. Her calves looked bare, though they probably weren't, and her feet were in sleek black pumps with low, skinny heels.

Ana wanted to cradle one of Sabel's calves in her palm while she slipped off the shoe and then run her hands up under that skirt. But she couldn't. Not just because of the strained shoulder, but also because Sabel wore an invisible, magical device that was supposed to protect her from demon possession.

The leash, as they called it, was hypervigilant. It tended to also protect her from Ana, since her body hosted a demon—Abraxas—and was therefore shot through with demon magic. They could kiss and sit close, but the hotter things got, the more energy the leash registered, and the more likely it was to trigger and start to constrict painfully around Sabel's ribs until she lost consciousness.

"This weekend, look for one incident in your life where a person makes you angry or upset," Sabel told the class. "Then explore it to understand how it's connected to a factor in yourself that you can't stand. We'll discuss that on Monday along with chapters three through five."

Scattered groans rose from the students and Ana gathered that chapters three through five must have a lot of pages. Sabel disconnected her laptop from the projector and closed it while the twenty-odd students shuffled notebooks, tablets, papers, pens and sundries into their bags and backpacks. Like a flock of birds they rose, turned, massed into a roughly triangular formation and funneled through the doorway to the hall, leaving Sabel alone at the front of the room and Ana in the back.

It took her a minute to realize Sabel was standing with her hands on her hips regarding Ana with a bemused smile.

"Don't tell me you have a teacher fetish too," Sabel said.

"No." Ana licked her dry lips. "Just you. That's a really nice skirt. Did you tell yourself from the future that I was coming to visit?"

Sabel laughed. "You'll only know the answer to that if you see what's under the skirt."

Ana tried to get up from the unsteady chair and managed to knock it over and nearly fall the other way before she caught herself on a desk. She straightened up with as much dignity as she could, which wasn't a lot.

"We'd better go to my office before you break something," Sabel said.

"Lead the way," Ana told her with a grin.

"Uh-huh," Sabel replied, but she was smiling too.

She dutifully turned away from Ana and preceded her out the door. Ana mostly tried not to stare at her neck and hips and legs as they left that building, crossed a corner of campus, and navigated the narrow halls to Sabel's office. As an adjunct professor, Sabel had been awarded an office that was about the size of a supply closet. It held a desk, two chairs and two bookcases with enough space to drag in a third chair if necessary and if no one needed to get out the door in a hurry.

Ana paused inside the door with her hand on it and looked at Sabel; she couldn't remember if Sabel had office hours now or not. Sabel nodded and Ana shut the door.

"Abraxas?" Sabel asked.

"I dropped him off at Lily's; they're working on—"

Sabel grabbed the lapels of Ana's jacket and kissed her. Ana's arms went around Sabel, pulling her close as Sabel's lips opened to her. She couldn't resist sliding her palm down from the small of Sabel's back to stroke the curve of her ass under the tweed skirt.

Sabel broke the kiss with a breathless laugh, but she didn't move away from Ana. Her fingers touched the sides of Ana's face and played with the short hair at the back of her neck. "I like the new jacket," she said.

"I'll wear it to bed if you'll wear the skirt," Ana said, more to make Sabel laugh again than as a real suggestion.

She'd rather see the skirt come off. What she'd most like to see come off was the leash the other Hecatine witches had put on Sabel. Most of the time they could barely touch each other without her hurting Sabel.

At least now Abraxas could travel farther from Ana and Lily had made him a golem body he could use at her place so that he could spend time there. When he was outside of Ana, it was easier for her and Sabel to touch. Still, they'd had enough close calls in which the leash nearly rendered Sabel unconscious when they tried to have sex that they were stuck in a terribly frustrating stalemate.

Sabel had been appealing to her mentor, the witch Josefene, to have the leash removed. But since it had already worked once to prevent a demon from using Sabel's powers against others, the witches seemed reluctant to remove it.

"Is Josefene…Did you talk to her?" Ana asked.

"She wants to meet Abraxas."

"Huh?"

From everything Ana had heard, the witches, including Sabel's mentor Josefene, were strongly opposed to the Sangkesh demons. The Sangkesh were the demons sworn to protect humans against worse demons. Lily was one of them, as was Abraxas. Ana swallowed against the guilt rising in her—if she hadn't chosen to keep Abraxas and let him use her body as his home base while he gained strength, the leash wouldn't be an issue.

Sabel said, "She says if she can identify him as a Sangkesh who's not harmful, then she has evidence to offer the others for why the leash should come off."

"That's not a firm yes," Ana said.

"I think she's on our side," Sabel told her. "And if I hadn't been wearing the thing, Ashmedai could have used me to kill you."

Ana had the sinking feeling that until Ashmedai was long gone from this world, the other witches weren't going to take the leash off Sabel and allow her and Ana to interact freely. For weeks, she'd been talking to Abraxas about ways to draw out Ashmedai and trap him, but they had yet to come up with a workable plan.

"Maybe Abraxas can teach you to be unpossessable the way he's teaching me," Ana suggested. "Then you wouldn't need the leash."

Sabel pulled back and stared at her.

"I can't tell if you're horrified or just offended," Ana said.

"That kind of depends on how you expect him to do the teaching," Sabel replied.

Abraxas did deliver most of his lessons from inside her head, Ana realized. "By talking, not putting him in your body or anything. That would be weird."

Ana paced the two steps to the door and back. She hated this feeling of impasse. Sabel leaned back against her desk and crossed her arms.

"What's the deal anyway?" Ana demanded. "You say the Sangkesh demons are pissed because the witches did something ages ago to limit their power, and Abraxas won't even talk to me about it. Shit, every time you invite me over to your place he suddenly has something magical he has to try over at Lily's. He won't even go into your apartment."

Sabel's eyes narrowed with thought. "You're right," she said. "He's never come with you. Not that you come over often. Is that why we always end up at your place? Is he influencing you?"

"He wouldn't. Not like that, without my knowledge."

But Ana wondered if he wasn't doing it consciously. There were times when his preferences became hers and vice versa. She felt that her place was just more comfortable: her TV was newer, her kitchen was bigger, her couch was more broken in.

But maybe she felt that way because Abraxas also felt that Sabel's apartment wasn't...what?

Sabel must have seen the question in her eyes because she said, "There's a standing circle at my place. When you come over, you're inside of it. I wonder if he can't cross it."

"Did you make it to keep out demons?"

"Among other things," Sabel said. "But why didn't he just say something? I can let him in. I'd have to let him in anyway for him to meet Josefene."

"I feel like I'm being asked to meet your parents," Ana said sullenly.

Sabel shook her head. "No, that would be worse."

"Seriously?"

"Josefene wants me to stay healthy and learning. My parents don't have the same goals."

Ana raised her eyebrows but Sabel made a dismissive gesture. "I'd rather tell you about the Sangkesh and the witches," she said.

Ana nodded. She understood not wanting to talk family history. She'd told Sabel a few stories from her own childhood, but most of them she didn't want to revisit. Sabel knew all the important facts about Gunnar, her favorite brother, and if she never had to think about her brother Mack shoving or hitting her again, it would be too soon. She turned her attention back to Sabel's story.

"The witches have kept an archive for thousands of years," Sabel was saying. "The amount of knowledge in it—mind-blowing. But it used to also house a tablet with instructions that allowed us to create and control certain kinds of beings called the galla. The galla protected the archive and the witches who kept it.

"In the year eleven thirty-eight, the Sangkesh attacked the archive and destroyed it, and they either destroyed or stole the tablet. Most of us think they must have destroyed it because no one with power over the galla has surfaced since then and even the Sangkesh can't keep a secret like that for so long. They killed most of the keepers of the archive, including the head of the archive. Without the tablet to control them, the galla turned on the witches…on us."

Sabel stopped and took a long breath. She was looking down, away from Ana, her eyes distant.

"They hunted us for hundreds of years. The galla murdered thousands of witches and then, when they ran out of real witches to kill, they worked with the demons to whip up the frenzy that became the Inquisition and witch hunts among nonmagical humans. Thousands of innocents…" Her voice trailed off.

Ana put her arms around Sabel.

"All those people who had no part in it and died," Sabel whispered. "Many of them gifted, magical, if they could have been found and trained…but we had nowhere to teach, nowhere to be safe. A few of the galla stayed loyal and tried to save some of the archive. They were safe, the other galla wouldn't kill them. That's how we rebuilt."

"Are there still galla who hunt witches?" Ana asked.

Sabel shook her head. "Galla are a specific kind of being that must be created with magic and the secret to creating them was destroyed with the tablet. No new galla can be made. As the centuries pass there are fewer and fewer of them. Now the ones who aren't in the new archive are all in a compound somewhere, defended from the rest of the world while they try to figure out how to make more of themselves. I pray they never find out how."

"Abraxas and Lily both say the Sangkesh are protectors. Why would they attack the witches' archive?"

"They protect humans, not witches," Sabel said. "Even if we are human, mostly. We never got a good answer—at the time the ruling princes of the Sangkesh denied that they were involved at all. They said the attack came from the Shaidan demons, the adversaries, but our magic showed a Sangkesh prince leaving with the tablet. We assumed it was a splinter group inside the Sangkesh who decided we were a threat, but the princes of the Sangkesh weren't willing to find that group and turn them over to us, and anyway we were too scattered the first few hundred years to do anything even if we had them."

"You talk about it like you were there," Ana said.

"I went back and saw some of it," Sabel confessed. "We all do, it's part of training as a Hecatine witch. But it's so hard to watch it and not be able to do anything."

Ana held her tightly and didn't say anything for a long moment, but then she had to ask, "If you can go back, can't you just see the demons who attacked the archive?"

"There are times you can't see into," Sabel explained. "It's like geography: there are places it's easy for you to go and places you can go with some effort, but there are also places you just can't get to. Like you can climb up a mountain, but you can't climb through a mountain. The more dense a time is with emotion, the harder it is to get into. The attack is one of those places you can't travel into."

Ana didn't know how to reply to that, so they stood together for a while until the feeling of Sabel in her arms and the light coconut smell of Sabel's hair made her think about getting under Sabel's skirt again. She was trying to decide if it would be worth the resulting frustration to start kissing Sabel, when her phone buzzed.

She pulled away and looked at it: a message from Lily that Ana could come by any time to pick up Abraxas.

"Are you coming over later?" she asked Sabel.

Sabel's blue-gray eyes brightened. "Want me to keep the skirt on?"

Ana thought that what she really wanted was to lock the door and pin Sabel to the desk, but she managed a cheerful, "Of course!" and fled.

* * *

Ana drove over to Lily's shop feeling uncomfortably like a parent about to pick her kid up from band or soccer practice. Lily answered the door and they went upstairs to her apartment, where Abraxas was sitting on the couch in the clay body he and Lily had made for him. In the colors of orange, red and gold that made the room feel warm and inviting, the tan clay took on a ruddy cast, as if blood ran under its constructed skin.

The body looked like a medium-sized man, hairless, with handsome Middle Eastern features. The gray surface of his skin etched with words and interlocking symbols that showed a faint golden glow. When Ana entered the room, Abraxas poured himself out of the clay body and into her with a sound oddly like a sigh of relief.

Lily wearing you out? Ana asked him inside her mind.

He laughed. *Lily is a joy. That body, however, is heavy as stone.*

But you have superpowers.

Tired super powers, he said. *Very tired.*

Ana sat on the far end of the couch from the motionless clay body while Lily went into the kitchen to pour her a cup of tea. She looked around. The apartment hadn't changed much since the day she'd first staggered up here, an unwitting host to Abraxas, both of them hunted by the summoners and the demon Ashmedai.

The late sunlight was too weak to illuminate the front room that held the summoning circle where Lily could have removed Abraxas from Ana's body. He would have been much weaker outside of her and when it came down to it, she chose to keep him. Now lamps around the living room brought out the ruddy colors in the wood of the glass cases that lined one wall of the room. Paintings, bookcases, side tables and plentiful pillows on the chairs and couches made the room feel full without being crowded or messy.

Lily handed Ana a mug of tea and curled up in her armchair, tucking her clawed feet neatly under her. Half demon, Lily could pass as human if she wore her boots and the caps on her teeth, but her demon blood made her long-lived and gave her the knowledge and drive to be the city's best banisher.

"Can I ask you something?" Ana asked.

Lily raised an eyebrow.

"It's not about your sex life. I know too much about that already," Ana told her.

She didn't add that she felt pretty envious that Abraxas and Lily at least had some kind of sex life, even if the bulk of it happened in dreams. How a person had sex with a clay golem, she really didn't want to know.

"It's about the demons and the witches," Ana said. "You're up on all the history. Do you know why the Sangkesh attacked the witches' archive in eleventy-whatever years ago?"

"Eleven-thirty-eight, common era," Lily said. "It wasn't the Sangkesh. Did Sabel say it was?"

"She said it was a splinter group or something, that the guys in charge denied it."

Lily sighed. "It was the Shaitans and the galla. Believe me, Ana, the Sangkesh looked through their ranks to see if anyone was involved. With what happened afterward—anyone who caused that, we would have brought to justice."

"But the witches said they had evidence that a Sangkesh took that tablet."

Lily nodded. "In the records it says they brought the signature of that demon to the Sangkesh—demons have an energy signature that's like a fingerprint—but it didn't match any of the princes."

"Could someone have faked it?"

"We don't know how, but yes, that's what we assumed happened. But the witches were adamant that it had to be the Sangkesh."

Lily paused and looked at the clay body on the couch and then back to Ana. "Did Sabel tell you what the galla are?"

"Just some kind of being. Are they like bound demons or something?"

"They were constructed," Lily said. She motioned toward the clay body. "A little like that but not using clay. Using a human body, a whole human person turned into a demon-like creature that has to feed on other humans to survive. The witches used them as slaves—immortal creatures bound to serve the witches generation after generation."

"Oh."

That Sabel didn't know that seemed unlikely. Perhaps, like so much in this struggle, the witches had a very different perspective. They saw the Sangkesh as brutal attackers and the galla as willing allies, while the Sangkesh saw the galla as slaves and felt themselves unfairly blamed for the destruction of the archive. What a mess.

Ana switched topics. "Abraxas, Sabel says that her mentor, Josefene, wants to meet you. This could help her get them to take the leash off. She says she can do that at her apartment."

He answered in her mind: *I can't do that.*

"What the hell? Why not?" Ana replied out loud so that Lily could hear.

I can't, he said.

"That's not an answer," Ana snarled and then to Lily, "He said he can't. Screw that, Abraxas, I've gone six months hardly being able to touch Sabel and you can't do this one thing?"

Lily said, "Ana, you have to understand that he basically fought his way back from the dead. You have no idea what that takes. Frankly, I thought it wasn't possible. It could be years before he's regained his former strength and you're asking him to expose himself to an enemy."

"She's not going to hurt him, she just wants to get a look at him."

You have to trust me that this should not be done, Abraxas said.

The hard part was that she did trust him, completely, and he knew that even without her saying it. But the situation with the leash was more than aggravating.

Perhaps now is a good time to begin studying the energy of emotions, Abraxas suggested.

She didn't bother to respond, since her emotions on that point would be abundantly clear to him. She got up and gave Lily a quick kiss on the cheek on her way to the door. That was a compromise between the lingering kiss Abraxas wanted to give her and the parting wave Ana preferred.

Her life had been so much easier before she hosted a demon. But so dull.

CHAPTER TWO

Late in the evening, after an effortful, deliberately light-hearted dinner with Ana, questions tugged at the back of Sabel's mind from their earlier conversation. She felt the heaviness of thought that preceded an epiphany. Standing in front of the bookshelves in her dining-room-turned-office, she pulled down one tome and another. What was it about the attack on the archive that bothered her? She'd studied it in depth about ten years ago when she first learned of it, when it first horrified and drew her, but then she'd become curious about more modern social disasters.

She stood over the table and opened a large book to an architectural drawing of the old archive. There was a new archive now, bigger and better defended, with all the modern conveniences like electricity and flush toilets. But the old one had been spectacular for its time. In another book, she found the recorded accounts of the witches who said they'd seen or felt a Sangkesh prince leaving the archive carrying both the tablet and the witch who ran the archive. The head of the archive had been found dead the next morning and the prince's energy signature was also taken from around her body. The tablet was gone.

The tablet.

She opened her laptop and logged into the external, electronic version of the archive, searching until she found a complete listing of what the tablet contained. Of the few galla alive—if they could be said to be alive—outside of the compound kept by the renegade galla, one of those was the head of the archive. She looked at the time; it was late enough for Devony to be awake now. Sabel sent her a quick message through the archive's secure messaging system and a moment later her phone chimed.

Devony's voice was warm and lightly accented as she said, "Sabel, you have an interesting question. Especially because you *know* the answer is lost. So why do you ask?"

"I was talking to a friend about the Night of Ruin at the archive and it got me wondering."

"The friend with the demon? You should bring her to meet me. I'm so curious how it feels to host someone like that."

"First vacation we get," Sabel said. "Someone must know roughly how the spells on the tablet worked, even after the tablet was lost."

"I do," Devony told her. "But tell me first, what will you use the knowledge for? You're not trying to make more like me, I trust."

"There aren't any more like you," Sabel said. "I don't know that I'm going to use it for anything. It's just bothering me and, you know, 'knowledge is love...'"

Devony laughed and finished the quote, "'...and light and vision.' I see. This is what I know: the galla power is taken from the patterning and time powers. It includes the ability to reset something to a specific pattern based on a chronological trigger—so that every evening the galla have reverted to what they were when they were made."

"Ageless," Sabel said.

"Precisely. But there is a second part to it, so that we can learn. If we were changeless in this changing world, we would quickly become useless. To keep us both ageless but able to learn and grow, the spells include a bridge across life and death. We die and are renewed every day, and that is the key to both our immortality and, one hopes, our wisdom."

"A bridge across life and death," Sabel repeated and the words came out with more breath than sound.

"Does that mean something to you?"

"It might. I have to think."

"Ah, from you that means I'll get another call in about five years."

"'Time is the father of truth,'" Sabel quoted.

"And the mother of a great deal of mischief," Devony replied. "Be well, clever one."

Sabel put down the phone and stared at the open books. A bridge across life and death. The words scared her but she couldn't see why.

She went up to her meditation room and opened herself to contact with her mentor, Josefene. The connection sprang into place almost instantly and she felt Josefene standing beside her, a few feet to the right of her arm. Josefene looked like a shimmer in the air, a heat mirage in the shape of a person.

"Do I really need to get Abraxas over here to prove he isn't a threat?" Sabel asked without preamble. "It's been six months."

"You know how short a time period that is," Josefene said. "And he's not the threat I'm worried about."

"Ashmedai isn't a threat," Sabel protested. "He's incredibly weak. Abraxas and Lily have both said no other high-ranking demon will work with him now."

"There are more forces at work in the world than demons," Josefene said. "And he retains access to his wealth."

"His company is being audited."

"But his personal finances are not," Josefene countered. "Are you confident that he went through the body of Simon Drake so quickly and disposed of it so unexpectedly that he didn't arrange to have access to that money?"

Through a particularly nasty aspect of demon magic, Ashmedai had kept a pair of brain-dead brothers so that he could use their bodies as he needed them. When the first one died, he transferred his consciousness, and his legal assets, to the body of Simon Drake. He had to leave that body to escape San Francisco without being destroyed by Lily and the protector demons, but they had no way of knowing how much money he might have under other names that he could still access.

"No," Sabel admitted in a small voice. "But he's not allowed back in the City of San Francisco. Lily and the Sangkesh demons here made sure of that. Ana is safe as long as she stays in the city and so am I."

"You're going to leave the city." Josefene sounded certain of this fact, but not pleased about it.

"If you mean that vacation I've been thinking about, it's really far off in the future," Sabel said. "You could take the leash off and put it back on if that becomes a reality."

"Listen to me," Josefene told her. "You're going to get an offer to leave the city with Ana. We want you to take it."

This wasn't the first time Josefene had given her information about the near future, but it always surprised her. It had been like this when they sent her to watch Ana's former boss who was involved in demon summoning. When Ana's boss died, the summoners decided to use Ana instead. If Sabel hadn't been there, hadn't been sent to watch over the situation, would Ana have survived?

Sabel wondered how the witches could see that Ana's boss would be in danger but not that Ana would be too. Or maybe they did see the latter and just discarded it as irrelevant at the time. Working with time and information was as much about knowing what to pay attention to as it was about getting access in the first place.

How much danger was Ana in now? Would Josefene know what to look for to even be able to answer that question?

"Ana won't leave the city," Sabel told her. "She knows she's only safe here."

"You're going to encourage her to take this trip."

Sabel paused and inhaled slowly. Working with a mentor who could see more of the future but couldn't reveal it went beyond frustrating at times. "I can't see why I would do that," she said.

"You'll see that the act of leaving the city with her is part of the series of actions that lead to the leash coming off you."

"So it does come off?"

"Of course it does," Josefene said. "It was never meant to be permanent, you know that."

"When?"

"You know better than to ask. I can't tell you the answer."

Josefene was right—communication about the future was terribly difficult. You could rarely receive information about exactly when something happened. It had to do with probabilities, uncertainties and the way the timestream preserved its integrity.

In the past when Sabel insisted, Josefene had tried to tell her information that the timestream wouldn't permit. Sabel had been unable to hear it. The ghostly image of Josefene's mouth had moved and no words crossed to Sabel's mind. She wasn't going to insist they try that again.

But Josefene was also implying that if Sabel could get in touch with one of her future selves at a time where the information was allowed, that self would verify that Sabel had to leave the city with Ana for the leash to come off.

"What happens if we don't go on this trip?" Sabel asked.

"You do go, one way or the other. I think you'd prefer to go in the way that gives you the most power."

Sabel sighed. This was also true. From the perspective of the past, the future could be infuriating. But then from the perspective of the future, she didn't want the past to have been regrettable. And this was one of the reasons her order of witches, the Hecatines, trained in iron self-discipline. It took a lot of will to know you might be walking into a bad situation and do it anyway because the alternative was worse or simply impossible.

"Any more good news?" Sabel asked, mixing irony with genuine curiosity.

"Not that I can tell you," Josefene said, a touch of humor creeping into her voice. "Leash aside, how is it going with Ana?"

"I really like her. And if you can see anything in the future where I get my heart broken, don't you dare tell me."

"I never would," Josefene said. "Not one way or the other. Do you think she feels similarly?"

"I think…yes. I hope so."

"Good. It's high time you had someone with magic in your love life."

Sabel didn't know what to say to that, but by the time she'd run through and discarded a half dozen snappy responses, Josefene was gone. She sat for a while longer playing with the loose pieces of a pattern her mind couldn't assemble: the tablet, a bridge across life and death, the knowledge that they would leave the city, her feelings for Ana. Nothing made sense except that last part.

* * *

Sabel made meditation look so easy (and graceful and beautiful). But after months of practice, Ana could sit for only a few minutes without fidgeting. She'd put her practice off all day, and now that it was evening, she'd gotten sleepy and that made it harder. She was sitting the best she could on the cushion in her office, which meant fidgeting about every one-point-six seconds.

Voices from downstairs made a beeline for her office, slipped under the door and into her ears, muffled in their words but not their tone. Lily and Abraxas were talking in the living room. In the house it was easy for him now to project an image of himself a few rooms away, though he remained connected to Ana.

She peeked at the clock again and stifled a groan. Twenty more minutes to go when she would have sworn she'd been sitting for the full forty-five already. Ana shifted back slightly, pulling her spine straighter around the column of energy Abraxas had taught her to feel just inside her spine. Some days she could meditate more easily, settle onto the cushion and float inside herself. But more often she bounced around the inside of her mind like a hyperactive kid on a rainy day.

In the fight with the demon Ashmedai, Abraxas had to leave her unprotected to get help for Sabel. Ana had used what he'd already taught her, about putting her awareness outside of her ego, to survive Ashmedai's assault on her mind and to weaken him until he had to flee.

Now Abraxas wanted her to practice holding her awareness outside of her ego until it became second nature. It would make her virtually impossible for another demon to possess and set her up to do greater magics. Considering how useful his lessons had been to date, she persisted even when she was mind-shatteringly bored. He was also teaching her something about emotions: perceiving them as pure energy, he said. But she didn't know what that meant yet.

So much had happened since Abraxas came to reside in her. Although they'd defeated Ashmedai, he'd done his damage to the company she worked for and the executives had had to sell to a venture capital company, which had come in with its own PR people and put her out of a job. Ana's boss made sure she had a very nice severance package and, combined with some freelance work, it meant that she wouldn't have to look for a full-time job for a few more months, maybe longer.

The problem was that she was starting to get bored and antsy, especially since she couldn't spend all her spare energy in the relationship with Sabel. During the days Sabel was busy at the university and the evenings tended to be almost as frustrating as they were fun.

For the first few weeks after the fight with Ashmedai, Ana had been content to sleep and pick through the tatters of her memories to piece together what she could. Then she wanted to pretend her life would go back to normal. But normal had changed.

Fifteen minutes to go. Breathe into her belly. Downstairs the doorbell rang and she jumped. Her legs tried to unfold themselves, but she forced herself to be still. Abraxas wouldn't say anything to her for ending her meditation early, but she knew he wouldn't like it. She'd rather sit through a few more minutes than have to put up with his silent displeasure—or was that only her guilty interpretation of his silence?

To her surprise, footsteps came up the stairs and Lily pushed the door open, its lower edge brushing across the carpet with a hiss. "Ana?" Lily whispered. "It's Gunnar. He says it's important."

Ana stood up, feeling relief mixed with worry, and went down the stairs. Her brother Gunnar had also been the target of

Ashmedai's attacks, but the Sangkesh demons that ran the city assured her they could keep him safe. Lily stayed on the second floor, presumably to give them some privacy, since the whole first floor was an open plan with archways between rooms.

It was late in the afternoon and Gunnar still had fine black-gray smudges on his hands from his jewelry-making and repair work. He was three inches taller than her, putting him just over six feet, lean and curled forward in the shoulders like a question mark. He had the same broad jaw as Ana, but his close-cropped brown hair gave his head a square look she hoped never to emulate. While Ana's eyes were a muddy brown, he had their mother's hazel eyes, framed with fine lines from anxiety and years of spending more time outside than in. Another decade and he'd look like one of those faces carved out of tree bark, but wearing wire-frame hipster glasses.

Ana could look at his hands now without flinching, even though the jagged knife scar across the back of his left hand was her doing. At fifteen, when Ana tried to stop the abuse from their older asshole of a brother, Gunnar got caught in the middle. She'd been swinging the knife wildly, but she still felt sick at the memory of putting the blade through his hand. Back then she didn't understand that he was trying to minimize the damage to all of them.

After the fight with Ashmedai, and after Sabel had saved Gunnar from becoming another casualty, they'd really talked for the first time about their screwed-up childhood. They'd forgiven each other. And she thought maybe someday she'd be at the point where she could completely forgive herself.

"How are Erica and Sunshine?" Ana asked. Gunnar's wife Erica had delivered their baby girl just a week after Gunnar's brush with death. They gave her a traditional Californian name, which Ana was sure drove their South Dakotan parents crazy. Not that she'd talked to their parents, nor did she plan to call them to find out.

"Sunny's an easy baby. Sleeps through the night mostly," he said with a lopsided grin, but the look faded quickly. At least the flash of a smile indicated the problem wasn't with the baby.

"Want a beer?" she asked. "Then you can tell me what's up."

"Thanks."

Going into the kitchen, she pulled two bottles out of the fridge. She sat on one of the stools by the cutout window between kitchen and dining room and he leaned against the dining room table. Gunnar never sat when he could lean.

"Mom called me," he said and took a long drink of beer. Ana waited for him to say more. He'd never been a big talker, though he said more to her these days than he ever had. "Dad's in the hospital and it's bad."

She shrugged, but her heart twisted painfully. Her feelings for her father were never clean-cut. Sure, he was her father and he'd done a fair bit of good for her, but he'd also let her other brother, Mack, abuse her even after he'd known. And he'd set an early example by hitting any of the kids if he thought they were out of line. Her feelings for him weren't't free and clear of that terrible burden.

"How bad?" she asked.

"He's dying. They don't think he'll last the week. I'm going out. I thought you'd want to come, to say goodbye."

"What is it?"

"Cancer, in a few places, but its got his liver and that goes fast. All that drinking, probably."

"Mom called you?"

He answered her other, unasked question. "I think she's afraid to call you, afraid you won't come."

"Well, shit," Ana said.

She got off the stool and walked down the hall to the living room, where she could pace in front of the fireplace. Her eyes caught the clock on the DVR and she wondered if Sabel would be here soon too. She'd said she had errands to run that afternoon but that she'd stop by for dinner.

On the one hand, despite the alcoholism and the crushing poverty, he was her father and he'd tried to keep all three kids clothed, fed and housed. He made sure they got to school, even in the depth of winter, and he pushed Ana and Gunnar to do their homework, even after he gave up on Mack, resigned to letting him flunk out and take odd jobs.

On the other hand, she certainly never wanted to see Mack's face again and where her father was, so was he. She didn't feel a strong pull toward her father as a person. A phone call might be enough to say goodbye if it meant she didn't have to be in the same room as Mack.

And then there was the matter of Ashmedai and the fact that she was only protected from him while she was inside San Francisco. She didn't understand quite how it worked, but apparently the good demons had power in some cities and not others. Since they "owned" San Francisco they could take care of her while she was in the area, but not if she left.

Was it worth it to put herself in danger from Ashmedai just to go see the father she'd barely talked to for the last fifteen years? Still, she wasn't about to be cooped up in San Francisco for the rest of her life just because some demon prince had it out for her. Ashmedai had had time to get stronger the last six months, but so had she and Abraxas.

Gunnar had followed her down the hall and leaned against the archway to watch her pace and think. When the doorbell rang again, he opened the door to Sabel.

"Hi Gunnar," Sabel said. "Good thing I brought extra." She held up a large brown carryout bag.

"Hey," Gunnar said. "Not staying long."

Ana crossed the living room and hugged Sabel hard. When she stepped back, Sabel was looking at her with tiny lines of worry across her forehead.

"What's wrong?"

"My father's dying." Even as she said the words, Ana couldn't quite believe them. She'd made it to thirty with only one significant loss in her life, and none of her college friends had yet lost a parent. It didn't seem real that those figures who had both guarded and plagued so much of her life could crumble.

"I'm so sorry," Sabel said.

Ana waved the apology away. "Gunnar's going to say goodbye and wants me to go with."

"Oh." The word sounded light, but Sabel's expression darkened. Ana couldn't tell if it was anger or confusion, but it seemed out of proportion and that usually meant that Sabel knew something. Sabel turned away before Ana could ask for details, and carried the brown bag down the hall to the kitchen.

"Be careful," Lily said from the stairway. "I'm sorry to intrude, but Abraxas just told me to get down here. You can't leave the city. It's too dangerous. We don't know how much power Ashmedai still has. We don't know what his resources are. For all we know, he could have hired people to kill you as soon as you leave the area."

"Well shit," Gunnar said.

"You shouldn't go either," Lily told him.

"With all due respect, that's my father dying," he said. "And no demon's coming after me." He walked down the hall into the dining room and leaned against the wall there, hands tucked deep into the pockets of his low-slung canvas jeans. His left shoulder hunched forward, curling in to protect his old scars.

"Ashmedai *will* come after you," Sabel told him from the kitchen.

Lily came the rest of the way down the stairs and walked into the dining room, Abraxas's body of smoke gliding behind her. She sat at the far end of the table from where Gunnar leaned against the wall, Abraxas to her left.

"Does your magic tell you that?" Lily asked Sabel.

"Just logic. Ashmedai kidnapped Gunnar once and tried to kill him. And now he's pissed. Of course he'll go after him if he knows he's left the city. It's the easiest way for him to get to Ana."

The voice that came from Abraxas's smoke body sounded stormy and dark. "There are ways to mask his leaving the city," he said. "Ashmedai would have to use human channels to discover the journey and since he doesn't know when to look, that's less likely."

"Are you sure it was your mother who called you?" Lily directed the question at Gunnar.

"You think Ashmedai would try to trick Gunnar into leaving the city?" Ana asked. She'd followed everyone into the dining room/kitchen area and leaned against the cutout doorway between the two rooms.

"And bring you with him? Yes," Lily said.

"It was her," Gunnar confirmed. "We talked a while."

"Could he have made my father sick?" Ana asked.

Lily looked up at Abraxas.

"Unlikely," he said. "His powers don't run to disease. If your mother confirms it, we had best assume human causes."

"Like forty fucking years of drinking?" Ana suggested.

Abraxas nodded slowly and Ana felt a moment of warmth for him. He'd been practicing his human gestures.

"Ashmedai is powerful when it involves lust and destruction," Lily explained. "Nothing as slow as disease."

"So as long as Gunnar can get out of the city without being noticed, he can go visit Dad and I'll stay here," Ana said. She crossed her arms in an effort to keep from grinding her teeth.

"Fine," Gunnar said curtly.

Sabel shook her head. She wasn't looking at anyone in particular and Ana wondered what internal conversation she was having. Looking across at Gunnar, she asked, "You're going alone, then?"

"I'm taking the family. Dad has a right to see his first grandkid before he passes, I figure. It's what I'd want."

"How quickly can Ashmedai move if he discovers that Gunnar is vulnerable?" Sabel asked. "Can he get to Gunnar and his family faster than we can if Gunnar calls for help?"

Her face was unreadable to Ana still, but that mix of anger and something like pain or grief was back. Sabel's most common expression was one of curiosity; Ana couldn't remember if she'd seen this tight frown on her forehead before. She'd seen plenty of expressions of pain though, every time the damned leash tightened up on her just because Ana was nearby, and her energy read too much like a demon's now.

If Ashmedai were no longer a threat and if she and Abraxas showed that they could handle themselves, that they could keep Sabel safe, would the other witches finally relent and take that leash off her? They'd have to.

"Wait," Ana said. "How badly was Ashmedai fucked up in the fight with me? How strong can he be now?"

"Not as strong as he was," Abraxas said.

"I'm less worried about his personal power and a lot more concerned about his finances," Lily said. A wavy lock of hair was loose from the knot at the back of her neck and she pushed it behind her ear. "He doesn't need to use magic to overpower Gunnar if he can just hire a bunch of guys to do it."

"But if he thinks Gunnar is going without me..." Ana was thinking out loud. "He's not going to need that many guys. And if we're ready for him..."

"You want to set a trap," Abraxas said and she saw a flash of fire in his eyes.

"Exactly."

The room fell silent, as if everyone was holding their breath at the same time.

"That's not bad," Sabel said. "Lily, if you have time to prepare, you can create a vessel to bind Ashmedai, can't you? If he's weak from moving from one host body to another too often?"

"Yes, I can make a vessel. I'm not sure I can get him in it. He's still a prince, and that means a lot of raw power."

"What if we could add power to the binding?" Sabel asked.

"How?"

"My Voice, the *marevaas* power. What if I speak the binding?"

Ana felt a burst of excitement and hope. Sabel's magic included the ability to use what the witches called "the dangerous voice," which could give commands people had to obey. Combined with Lily's magic, would it be enough to bind Ashmedai for good?

Lily's eyebrows rose in appreciation. "That could work."

"Can you do that part of the magic here?" Ana asked, looking at Sabel. "There's no point in both of us being in danger."

"I'm coming with you. Period. If you're setting a trap, you're going to need all of us."

"A witch, a couple of demons and me—is that enough?" Ana asked.

"I hope so," Lily said. "It depends what he's been up to these last six months. I wish I had more resources to find out. But I only trade in information and no one owes me any favors now. I used them all years ago…" Her voice trailed off and her face reddened.

"You know someone?" Ana asked, curious about this reaction in Lily.

"There's a chance she could at least delay or distract him and probably siphon off a lot of his power. But I couldn't ask her to come here. It's not safe for her in this city. She'd have to meet us on the way."

What could possibly make San Francisco unsafe for any friend of Lily's? To Ana's mind this was now the safest place in the world. Lily was part of some supersecret organization of demons and half demons who ran the place. How could they protect Ana but be a danger to Lily's friend?

"If it's awkward, I'll ask for you," Ana volunteered. "Who is it?"

"My daughter," Lily admitted.

"You have a daughter? How old?" Although Lily looked to be in her forties she was closer to ninety and it was her demon parent who gave her lingering youth.

"She's almost twenty-eight."

"So she looks how old? Like twelve?"

Lily laughed but the sound came out edged. "No, thank the gods, she looks like she's in her twenties."

"And she's some kind of demon ass-kicker? Wouldn't she be only about a quarter demon?"

"She would," Lily said, "if her father had been human, but he wasn't. She's more demon than I am and she has the strength of a full-blood."

"And born with a body?" Abraxas asked. "She could certainly hold Ashmedai for a time. Will she meet us there?"

"Getting Brie to want to travel won't be the hard part," Lily said but didn't elaborate. Ana figured it was mother/daughter stuff. What kind of mother/daughter conflicts did you get when one of you was half-demon and the other all but full-blooded?

"You named your daughter Brie? Isn't that a little modern for you?"

Lily clicked her tongue behind her teeth. "I named her Gabriella, but she likes Brie. What airport are we flying into?"

"We can fly into Minneapolis and rent a car to drive into South Dakota; that's usually easiest," Ana said.

Gunnar nodded. "What I planned to do."

"When and how long?" Sabel asked. "I'm only teaching a few more classes next week but I can tell the department to find a sub."

"I was planning to fly out Sunday," Gunnar said.

Ana put her hand on his arm and he nodded to her.

Then everyone moved at once: Gunnar was giving her a rough hug and saying goodbye while Sabel got plates for the food she'd brought. Lily had her smartphone out and was checking flight times while Abraxas looked over her shoulder. Ana walked Gunnar to the door and afterward met up with the others in the living room so they could eat and plan the details of the trip.

Quickly the conversation turned to planning the trap for Ashmedai and Ana couldn't follow the kinds of magic Lily, Sabel and Abraxas were discussing, so she just ate slowly and watched them. Lily looked worried, but that was hardly surprising. Sabel's face was expressionless and from the depth of her eyes, her thoughts were a million miles away.

Abraxas's expression wasn't exactly happy, but he did seem focused and upbeat. Through their connection, she could feel an eagerness. He wanted to face down Ashmedai and teach him a lesson, show him he couldn't harm the humans under Abraxas's protection and get away with it.

CHAPTER THREE

They had two days to prepare for the trip, so Sabel spent most of the first day giving instructions to the teaching assistants who would take over her class for the next week. After that another professor taught the final weeks of the term. She had erred on the side of taking more time off than she thought she needed—and then wondered if she actually knew how long this was going to take and just wasn't aware of how she had that information.

Often when information came from the future, particularly from her future selves, it felt like an intuition or a good guess. The times she literally heard her own voice across time she could count on one hand. Much more frequently, she just had a hunch that turned out, when she had lived into the future, to have come from herself.

The other hunch she had right now was that she should take Ana shopping, though that might have been more wishful thinking. She knew Ana was being careful with her money since she'd left her publicity job. From where Sabel stood, it looked like being inhabited by Abraxas and knowing there was magic throughout the world made it hard for Ana to fit herself back into a corporate role. She also knew that Ana had a lot of pride, so she didn't say "shopping" when she invited her out to lunch at one of their favorite places—the restaurant where they'd first had mussels together. It was in an expansive mall and it would be easy for them to eat and then happen to wander past the shops.

Lunch was unusually subdued. They sat and exchanged the usual brief updates about their lives since they'd seen each other a day and a half ago. Sabel loved that Ana was always curious about what she was teaching and she talked about the current segment for her "Good, Evil and Personal Responsibility" class. But then Ana fell silent, picking at her steak salad.

"You're worried?" Sabel asked.

Ana shrugged and hunched back in her chair. Sabel got a flash of what she must have looked like as a kid: suspicious, angry, defensive.

"Mack?" she asked.

"I don't want to see him again," Ana said. "Ever."

Sabel moved a green bean from one side of her plate to the other and waited. She didn't look up at Ana's face, but watched her hands clench and unclench next to her plate. Ana didn't talk about the abuse from Mack, but Sabel could imagine how bad it had been if it was enough to make Ana turn on both him and Gunnar, whom she seemed to genuinely care about.

"They send me pictures every year—a Christmas card, Mom and Dad with Mack all smiles. I used to burn them." She gave a humorless laugh. "Till the year I lit the whole trash can on fire, then I started shredding them. I kind of look forward to it now, getting the card with his smug fucking smile on it so I can tear it to shreds."

She was silent again for a while and then sighed. Sabel imagined that Abraxas had said something to her about anger and she was contemplating it. Ana had told her that Abraxas was working with her on emotions and usually when anyone said "working on emotions" they didn't mean the ones like love and joy.

Demon magic was more at home in the emotional sphere than witch magic, and some of the Hecatines theorized that most demons worked purely with the raw energy behind emotion. What would it be like if Ana learned to channel that energy? Could she employ it the same way a demon would?

"I'd never go except for Gunnar," Ana said. "He always had this silent thing with Dad, even when things were bad. He'd just go sit with Dad and they'd work on something together. He's more like Dad than Mack, except for the drinking, thank God."

"Your father doesn't still drink?" Sabel ventured.

"No, he sobered up a few years ago, six or seven maybe. He got really sick and ended up in the hospital. I want to think he's changed a lot, but I don't even know where to start and every time I think about it all...I just can't."

Sabel reached across the table and put her fingers on Ana's closed fist. Ana uncurled her fingers and wrapped them around Sabel's, holding on to her so tightly it hurt. Sabel gripped her back in return, hoping it conveyed everything she felt.

Ana smiled grimly. "Maybe it's good, Gunnar making me go say goodbye. Wish I could do it without Mack, but I'm different now too. Maybe Abraxas will let me beat his face in." She shook her head thoughtfully and muttered, "Yeah, I know."

Then, looking up and meeting Sabel's eyes, she asked, "Can you see how this turns out? Are we okay?"

Sabel suppressed a sigh. She knew better than to wish she could see the future. "You know I don't see the future," she said gently. "It just reaches back to me more strongly than most people."

"You can't tell me if we're going to be alive in a month?"

"No."

"But you said your future self communicates with you," Ana said, her face puzzled.

"She doesn't call me on the phone. She could be communicating from anywhere—"

She made herself stop talking. She didn't need to tell Ana that her future self could be dead or born into another life and still communicating, or she could be on the edges of time or in a place where time moved differently. Time magic was one of the simplest and most complex of all.

Sabel started again, "I'm going to do my best to make sure we have everything we need to get through this. And speaking of that, I think we should take a walk through the mall when we're done, do some shopping."

Ana gave her a bemused, head-shaking look. "You're such a girl," she said.

"You like it." Sabel grinned at her and took a bite of her salad before asking, "The teachings about emotions that Abraxas is giving you, do they help with this situation with your father?"

"I wish," Ana said. "I don't think I'm getting it. I'm supposed to get in that space of grounded openness that's consciousness outside of ego but then think of something emotional so I can feel the emotion as energy. But the problem is that I just get distracted by it and then I'm sitting there thinking about my dad and Mack and getting pissed and Abraxas is all 'feel into the heart of your anger' and I just want to tell him to piss off."

"I'm sorry you have to see Mack again."

Ana wrinkled her nose. "It was bound to happen someday. I guess it's better with friends and allies and stuff."

They finished eating, split the bill and then Sabel led the way into the colonnade. She knew that Ana had grown up without much money, so it wouldn't be appropriate for her to come home for a funeral wearing something ostentatious. But there was a class of clothing that looked simple and felt expensive, and that would be perfect.

Since she first left home for college, Sabel had been using clothing to remind herself that she was not like her family and didn't have to obey their wishes. In her case, that generally meant taking a step down in price and wearing the most lascivious undergarments she could find, but for Ana she thought that taking a few steps up and feeling a higher grade of cloth next to her skin could remind her how far she'd really come from where she'd been born.

"It's colder there, isn't it?" she asked Ana.

"Yeah, mid-twenties, maybe low thirties if we're lucky."

"My future self is telling me you're going to need a jacket."

"For real?"

Sabel pursed her lips. "Are you questioning my magic? Plus we didn't do much for the holidays. Let me get you something."

"I have jackets," Ana said.

Sabel touched her arm, curling her fingers gently around the elbow, and pulled her into a little boutique. She didn't mention that she'd been there the weekend before looking around and thinking about presents. Ana didn't need to know the extent of her planning. Casually she walked them around one side of the store so they ended up at a rack between the fitting rooms and the jeans.

"Try a pair of these on," she suggested, pointing at the jeans.

"How can they cost that much?" Ana asked.

"Just try them on. Humor me."

Ana sighed, but she let the saleswoman who had joined them pick out a few pairs. Ana took them into the fitting room. When she came out, she had a stunned look on her face.

Sabel grinned. "Not your usual jeans, right?"

"Okay, it really is like a second skin. How do they make it feel like this? But still, these are almost two hundred dollars, that's beyond insane."

"Sometimes beautiful clothing is the best armor," Sabel told her. "Leave those on and try this jacket."

She plucked the jacket off the rack and held it out to Ana. It was a color between olive and pine, a subtle, rich green with a fair amount of warm gray in it. It suggested an army jacket but with an extreme elegance to the way it was cut. Plus the fabric was a durable and supersoft denim. The collar was midway between a traditional collar and a mandarin collar, so that it stood up and folded over itself tightly.

When Ana came out of the dressing room again, Sabel admired the way the jacket enriched the golden colors in her hair and the warmth of her tan skin. From a distance, she might look like a thick, well-built woman in blue jeans and an army jacket, but up close the fine tailoring was obvious. And she knew that outfit had to feel even better on the inside than it looked on the outside.

"Do you love it?" Sabel asked and the light in Ana's eyes was all the answer she needed.

"It's too much," Ana said firmly.

Sabel shook her head as Ana walked back into the dressing room to change into her clothes. She didn't know how to explain to Ana how far down her list of concerns money ranked. As long as her family perceived her as a respected scholar at a good university and didn't know about her real work with the Hecatine witches, money came to her. She never needed for much. She'd started doing her diversity training work just to meet people who didn't live in the ivory towers of academia. Maybe that angle would work with Ana.

"Think of it this way," she said when Ana came out of the dressing room and Sabel took the clothes from her hands before she could try to put them back on the rack. "I'm just spending on you the money your old company paid me for the diversity training."

"You should be replacing the suit of yours I ruined instead," Ana told her.

"I already did," Sabel said with a grin. "I love that suit."

She didn't add that she loved both versions of it: the new one and the one painted with Ana's blood from the night she'd been kidnapped by demon summoners and allowed Abraxas into her body so they could escape together. The latter suit wasn't something she'd ever wear again or even admit to keeping, but it was in the back of her closet.

She stepped closer to Ana so that her breast pressed the side of Ana's arm. "Let's get two pairs," she said. "And they're not just for you, they're for me. The way those jeans fit makes me think about slipping my hand down them."

"Oh? Yeah, okay," Ana said breathlessly.

Sabel headed for the register and paid for the jacket and two pairs of jeans before Ana could recover.

Whether Ana could admit it to herself or not, wearing fine clothes was a kind of armor. And if Ana had come out of her childhood with visible scars and Sabel from hers with money, that didn't seem fair at all. She'd balance the scales where she could.

* * *

They flew out in the late morning and were scheduled to arrive in Minneapolis at dinnertime. Ana was surprised at how innocuous the three of them looked—four if you counted Abraxas, but no one could—and no security measure could scan him inside her body. The hardest part had been getting Lily through the checkpoint because once she took off her boots it was obvious her feet weren't normal. She'd worn two pairs of thick socks, but even so, her heels looked narrow and elongated, and the front of her foot overlong. Under that thick fabric, Lily's feet were talons, like an eagle's claw the size of human feet, three long clawed toes off the front, and one short toe on the back. Walking behind her, Ana watched the guard at the metal detector; he glanced down her body, winced at the apparent deformity of her feet, and waved her through.

Ana let out her held breath as Lily sat in a molded plastic chair to put on her custom-made boots again. The leather of them had been thickened and thinned as needed, so when she had them on the effect was gothic rather than small-woman-with-big-feet. Lily snapped closed the shining buckles on the front of the black leather.

"I asked if he could make sandals," she said with a shrug.

"I'd like to see that!" Ana told her, but later when she kicked off her own shoes under the airplane seat somewhere in the second hour of the trip, she looked over at Lily with a pang of sympathy. Lily never seemed to mind the limited choices in footwear or the caps she wore over teeth that were all pointed, but they had to bother her at times.

Because of the boots, Lily chose outfits with lots of black and dark colors that brought out the richness of her skin. For their day of travel she had on dark pants that formed to her thighs and fell loose around her ankles, and a burgundy sweater over a black shell. She had heavy kohl around her eyes and dangling garnet earrings, looking for all the world like a goth who'd gone into the corporate world. Ana wondered what Lily's daughter would look like next to her pseudo-goth mom.

Ana settled back against the seat and napped for part of the flight. She had to admit the jeans and jacket Sabel bought her were the most comfortable clothing she'd ever owned. She rested her hand over Sabel's and closed her eyes. Inside her chest, she felt a sinking sense of dread and under that a jittery fear.

Breathe into it, Abraxas suggested.

She sighed but deepened her breathing. It didn't help. The fear radiated out from the center of her chest.

Now what? she snarled at him mentally.

What's in the middle of all that fear? he asked.

Years of getting hit, she said.

That was long ago, what's there now?

How would I know?

Look and see, he said.

She didn't want to. The middle of that pulsing mass of jagged energy was the last place she wanted to be. It made her want to jump out of her skin just to get away from it. But she was a little curious. If Abraxas said there was something in the middle of it, there must be. And the fear wasn't as bad as the presence of Ashmedai had been when he'd tried to take over her body.

She edged toward it and then took a mental deep breath and dove into the jagged, buzzing, terrifying mass. At first she just felt more fear and the justification for that fear. It was completely valid to want to crawl away from Mack any way possible. The fear held a protective quality. It was there to take care of her and seeing that allowed her to go further into it. The fear wasn't there to make her uncomfortable; it was there to bring her energy she might need—and that realization put her through to its center.

The center of her fear was piercing white and brilliant. It was like pure adrenaline. It was a tiny star of power that could give her the energy to pay attention, to run or fight if she needed. It was so intense she could only perceive it for a moment and then she had to open her eyes and look at the airplane seats and re-orient herself in the world.

"What is it?" Sabel asked, looking up from her e-book reader.

"I think I got what Abraxas was trying to show me, just for an instant."

"Good," Sabel said and at the same time in Ana's mind Abraxas said, *That was good.*

"Jinx," Ana said and Sabel gave her a puzzled look. "You and the big guy just said the same thing. Someone owes someone a Coke."

"He owes me," Sabel said with a smirk and went back to her book.

After they landed, they went to get sandwiches while they waited for Lily's daughter, Brie, to arrive on a flight from Boston scheduled an hour after theirs did.

"Does she dress like you?" Ana asked as they walked to her gate.

"No," Lily said.

Ana watched the passengers coming off the plane and wondered if she could pick out Brie. There was a girl all in black, but she was too young and had her mother with her, and then a woman of the right age in jeans and sandals, but she walked by. Then a short, brown-haired model walked off the plane and made a beeline for Lily. A woman of such beauty that Ana couldn't remember how to close her mouth. She scanned the woman's body for some sign of her demon ancestry. Lily had told her all demon/human offspring carry some mark, like Lily's talons and teeth. Some had horns or tails or claws for hands, patches of fur—all carefully covered up when they walked in the human world. This woman had none of those.

She was shorter than Sabel, maybe an inch taller than her mother, and only her smallness of stature would have kept her out of a career in fashion magazines. A mass of curly cinnamon-brown hair spilled over her shoulders in loose ringlets, setting off a face with full lips, large chocolate-colored eyes, and glowing copper skin.

"Abraxas, Ana, Sabel, this is my daughter Gabriella," Lily said.

Brie shook hands and the touch of that hot skin across Ana's palm started to pull her out of her surprise and into something much more immediate. She suddenly wanted to touch Brie a lot more. She felt Abraxas move down her arm and touch Brie through her. He jerked back at the same time that Brie dropped her hand.

Brie's garnet lips parted over pearly teeth. "You have him inside you," she said, smiling brilliantly. "How cool is that?"

Ana filed Abraxas's response away to ask him about later. Brie seemed innocuous and Ana didn't understand how this college co-ed was supposed to stand up to Ashmedai, but Abraxas's reaction carried shock and the taste of alarm, even fear.

"It's not bad," Ana said after a pause, not sure if Brie's question had been rhetorical.

Brie turned from her to Sabel and her mouth opened, eyes gleaming with amused wonder. "What is *that*?" she asked.

"Excuse me," Sabel said and took a half step away from her.

"Those bands under your skin. May I touch?" Brie asked.

"No," Sabel said.

"What do they do?"

"They keep demons out."

"Really? Would they keep them *in* too?" Brie put her carry-on bag down and walked a full circle around Sabel, who looked annoyed at best. "I want one."

"No, you don't," Ana assured her.

Brie looked over at her, back to Sabel, back to Ana and her eyes lit up with understanding. "Oh, brilliant," she said, sounding delighted. She picked up her carry-on and didn't elaborate on her comment, but the mirth remained in her expression.

Lily took Brie's arm and steered her toward the baggage claim. "You're not hungry are you?" she asked.

"Oh Mom, of course I fed before I came. I'm not going to eat your friends."

Sabel fell in next to Ana as they followed at a moderate distance.

"What do you think she eats?" Ana asked.

"I'm pretty sure it's people, one way or another," Sabel said. "If I'm not mistaken, she's one of the Gul, the demons who feed directly on humans."

"But Lily's a protector, a Sangkesh. Wouldn't her daughter be the same?"

"Depends who the father is," Sabel said. "And that would explain why Brie isn't safe in a Sangkesh-held city."

"Well, if that's true, maybe I can offer Mack to her as a late-night snack." The thought eased the heavy pain that had begun pressing on her heart as she came ever nearer to her childhood home.

It was a four-hour drive from Minneapolis to Sioux Falls where her father was hospitalized, the closest major medical facility to the small town where she'd grown up, farther west by nearly another hour. The car ride started out with strained silence between Lily and Brie in the backseat. Ana drove and Sabel sat next to her, looking at the map.

In the time she'd known Lily, despite the nearly fatal struggle with Ashmedai, Ana hadn't ever seen Lily this edgy. Panicked, yes, and furious, but not this mix of slow-burning anxiety and frustration.

CHAPTER FOUR

The Sioux Valley Hospital was a gleaming amalgam of metal and glass, shining brightly in the early evening. Ana found its modern architecture comforting because nothing in her hometown had this clean look. When she visited the streets of her youth tonight, she'd see busted windows, broken shingles, cracked streets, fading siding, everything dull with dust and dirt. The only reprieve was that her parents had been able to buy a new house ten years ago on the good side of town.

The hospital smelled at first like meatloaf and gravy from the cafeteria and then as they went farther in, like astringent cleanser and the acidic edge of panic. Lily and Brie had insisted on accompanying them, pointing out that they wouldn't be much good as bodyguards if they weren't near Ana's body. Brie had changed out of the low-cut cami and jacket she'd worn on the plane into an outfit more like her mother's loose pants and sweater, but the wool clung too tightly to her full breasts, which seemed simultaneously heavy and yet gravity-defying. It was hard to look at her and not want to touch her skin just to know if it felt as flawless as it looked.

Pieces fell together in Ana's mind and she asked Abraxas silently: *She's some kind of demon of lust, isn't she? It's because she has a similar power to Ashmedai, that's why Lily thinks she can stop him.*

Very good, he said, followed by a pause fertile with ideas about how demons matched each other and fought. *We'll talk about it again later.*

They'd come to the third-floor waiting room, where Ana spotted Gunnar and his family. Gunnar stretched out in one of the small chairs, his body so straight that it made a slope from where his shoulders rested on the back of the chair to his heels on the floor. He surged up when he saw her and pulled her into a rib-creaking hug.

Then there were introductions to make. Gunnar glanced from Brie to Sabel as Ana introduced her and then raised his eyebrows at Ana, who shook her head at him. He introduced Erica and six-month-old Sunshine to Lily and Brie. They already knew Sabel from the many visits she'd made to their house with Ana over the last few months.

"She seems like an easy baby," Lily said and Erica started in on Sunny's birth and sleep habits.

Gunnar pulled Ana aside. "Mack's in there," he told her. "Doesn't much leave. It's hit him pretty hard."

Neither of them needed to speak for Ana to know that Gunnar's thoughts were running along the same lines as hers. Mack and their father had the most screwed-up relationship of all of them. Most of the time, Mack was the beloved first son who could do no wrong, and so his cruelties to the younger kids had been overlooked. But he had a tougher time living up to their father's standards and bore the weight of their father's retribution for that. He was also the one unable to break free from the generations of addiction and abuse. As far as Ana knew, Mack was still an alcoholic and probably using other drugs as well.

Mack had beaten both of them more times than they could remember, but he'd saved the brunt of his rage for Ana. Then one sticky summer afternoon he'd threatened and cajoled Gunnar into holding a knife and accompanying him on his attempt to rape her. She'd gotten hold of the knife and cut them both, but it was Gunnar she'd hurt worse, the brother who tried to take care of her and who went with Mack more to stop him than to help.

They'd both carried the hurt and guilt of that day for the next fifteen years, until Ana's confrontation with Ashmedai brought it fully to the surface of her memory as he made her relive it over and over. He hadn't counted on that experience, with Abraxas's help, desensitizing Ana to the incident. It had done wonders for her relationship with Gunnar, but she still carried the banked coals of hatred in her heart for Mack.

After the attack, she'd been sent to a residential psych facility that turned out to be less shitty than she expected and actually gave her some decent help toward getting her schoolwork sorted out and making a plan to get into college and away from her family. Mack went into the army and by the time he came back, in his early twenties, Ana was well away. She hadn't seen him since then except in photos, where he looked as hard and mean as ever.

She took a long breath and made herself blow it out evenly. Internally she felt the brambles of fear uncurl in her chest and reached down into them to feel the raw power nestled there.

"Let's do it," she told Gunnar. "I have to see him sometime."

Sabel touched her hand, eyes questioning, but Ana shook her head. She didn't want to expose Sabel to Mack just yet. She knew Sabel could handle herself, but if Mack decided to pick on his sister's girlfriend, Ana didn't want that fight to happen at her father's deathbed. And it would be a fight.

If Lily was going to protest Ana and Gunnar leaving the rest of them, she looked at Ana's face and swallowed her words. It had to be safe enough to go down the hall more or less alone. After all, she still had Abraxas inside her, silent but warming, like sunlight on her back.

Gunnar led the way, and Ana tried to prepare herself for the changes to her father's body. Her father had always been a strong man, six feet tall and corded with lean muscle. She got her height from him and some natural athleticism.

She barely recognized the form in the bed. He looked like a badly formed papier-mâché model of himself, small and withered among the sheets. In the last few years his face had grown deeply lined, but now every line was dark, his cheeks hollow, the skin ashen and with a yellow cast. His eyelids looked thin as tissue.

Ana's mother sat in the chair beside the bed. Her wheat hair was more gray than gold, pulled back in a neat coil at the base of her neck. She had a longer face and a strong nose, like Gunnar, whereas Ana and Mack had inherited the wide cheekbones of their father.

Standing in front of the window looking out was Mack. He still had that lean, powerful build, a shorter copy of their father's physique. His oily brown hair had been tied carelessly into a short ponytail with a red rubber band and his T-shirt was afflicted with wrinkles. Ana doubted he'd been home in the last day. He turned at the sound of the door and stared at her with eyes like two chips of dirty ice.

"Now you turn up," he said, sucking his cheeks and squinting at her.

"Mack, don't," Gunnar said. "We're here to see Dad."

"I wasn't—" he started, but Ana's mother stood up from her chair to kiss her cheek and Mack fell to silently staring out the window again.

Ana looked at his back while her mother kissed Gunnar. Mack seemed just a shade smaller than she remembered. If it came to it, she probably could take him.

"He's been sleeping a lot," her mother said and gestured to their father. "But I told him you were coming and he was all smiles."

Ana pushed back welling tears. For all her father's faults, he was unfailingly proud of her. She didn't know if wanting to cry came from seeing him like this, or the feeling that she'd missed so much of being really parented, or some mix of all of it. Abraxas was silent on the subject. She felt him inside her skin, warm and solid, making himself known and available to her, but not intruding on the moment, and she touched him lightly with her mind, using him to steady herself.

Softly, she filled her mom in on the details of the trip, where they were staying, that they'd brought friends who wanted to help if they could.

"This isn't no party," Mack growled from the window, but Ana didn't rise to the bait. He had to be falling apart inside, she told herself. Their father had been his anchor.

"We'll have a dinner at the house tomorrow then," her mother said. "Do they eat chicken?"

"Yes Mama, that'll be great. Do you want me to come early and help?"

"Oh, no, Joyce down the road will come. She's been a great help to me this year." She sounded like she was going to go on about Joyce, but Ana's father's eyes fluttered and opened.

Her mother moved out of the way and Ana took the chair where she could lean into the bed and hold his papery hand. Gunnar moved in next to her so their father could see both in the same glance.

"Hey Pop," Gunnar said, rough and quiet, sounding more like himself as a kid than Ana had heard in years. "We came to tell you we love you and thank you for all you've done for us."

Ana leaned her head against Gunnar, willing him to feel her gratitude that he'd said the perfect words and the ones that wouldn't come to her tongue. She had a lump in her throat she could hardly breathe around and a hot line of tears down one cheek. The mass of fear and anger, pain and longing, and love in her was too complicated to even look into.

"You look good," her father said, his words thick but well voiced.

"Well, that we got from Mama," Gunnar told him and they both chuckled, echoes of each other. "But you made us strong, Pop, and I'm good with my hands like you. I just won another Best of Show."

Ana tried to muster her voice. She made her breathing slow and even, the way Abraxas had taught her, and pushed her awareness a little beyond the boundaries of her body, so her mind seemed to expand outside of her grief. Her vision split so that while she could still see the hospital room perfectly clearly, she also saw glowing figures superimposed on that image. At the head of her father's bed stood a golden man-shape, ten feet tall and looking away from them, and over by the far wall were two more shapes, less human in form but of that same sunlit color, waiting. Her father was dying and they waited for him.

"Dad," she said and took a long breath. She wanted to say *I forgive you* and at the same time she wanted to ask him why for all those years he let Mack treat her the way he did. She knew the power of forgiveness, but only in the context of Gunnar, who was so uncomplicated. For her father, the words weren't there yet. She made herself honor the tone Gunnar set.

"You made some really good kids," she managed and he smiled at her, squeezing her hand.

"I did, didn't I?"

Without a word, Mack turned from the window, stomped across the room and through the door, managing to slam it without making a sound.

"It's hard for him," their mother said.

"Mack's got his own way," Gunnar said. "Remember that time he took apart that old lawn mower and put it back together with that bike engine so he could run and mow?" And with that, he turned the hurt in the room into humor.

After a moment, he excused himself and came back with Erica and Sunshine. Her dad beamed at his granddaughter and Ana wondered if he'd ever looked like that for her.

She stepped back from the center of the action and let Erica talk about every cute thing Sunshine had done for the past six months. When she realized she was standing by the window in the place Mack had been, she moved away from it and wedged herself in next to the television.

* * *

In the visitors' lounge, Sabel picked a seat as far from Brie as she could without being actively rude. This meant taking a chair in the middle of the room with her back to the door, but Lily could see the door clearly and Sabel trusted her to raise the alarm if anything warranted their attention. She pulled out her phone and checked her email—not that she had anything important in there, but she wanted to make sure that Brie was settled and not trying to talk to her before she looked up what she really wanted to know.

Lily and Brie got to chatting about the restaurant where Brie worked, and Sabel flipped from her email to the app that let her query the archive. The Hecatine witches were more advanced technologically than just about any organization she'd worked with, thanks in large part to Devony's leadership at the archive.

She texted her question: *What do we have on the demon Gabriella Cordoba, called Brie, daughter of the Sangkesh demon Lily Cordoba?*

It was too early for Devony to be up and about, and some other archivist would be the one answering her question. The answer came in bursts as the person on the other end accessed various sources and gave her the highlights. Devony had been talking about programming an AI to do this, but Sabel liked that she could still rely on another human being to synthesize the answer.

Gul, the answer said. *Embodied succubus. Two known kills. Hunted by the Sangkesh. Last reported location: New York City.*

After a pause, the words continued: *Possible third kill. Recent. See linked article.*

Sabel typed back, *Embodied succubus?*

Most are noncorporeal, fairly weak. Having her own body makes her many times more powerful and unable to be banished or bound. You in danger?

I'm safe. Just curious. Thank you.

She followed the link to an article in a Boston daily paper about a strange death at a frat party. The frat had a bad reputation and last summer a local student had accused two of its members of drugging and raping her, the charges dismissed due to insufficient evidence. Then, during a party, one of those two frat members died mysteriously. The other member said a woman had poisoned him, but no trace of poison was found in his body and the woman was never located. The coroner ruled his death natural, cardiac arrest, possibly brought on by all the recreational drugs and alcohol in his system.

It did sound like a demon kill. And it made her fear for Ana. For herself, she wasn't worried. As much of a pain in the ass as the leash could be, it should also protect her from being fed upon—but could Abraxas do the same for Ana?

She felt an abrupt, painful need to see Ana, to touch her. A flush of warmth spread up her body and something about it felt too sudden, alien.

Sabel looked up from her phone. Brie's chair was empty. She stood and spun around. Brie was standing behind Sabel's chair, hands held up in a warding gesture.

"I just wanted to touch it a little," she said.

"It's *inside* my body. In what world is that appropriate?"

"Bad personal boundaries?" Brie asked with a little smile. "I'm sorry. I thought...I mean, you're wearing it. It's just like a jacket or something."

"It is *not* just like a jacket."

"Yeah, I figured that out when I touched it, but then I was already kind of there. Doesn't it hurt sometimes?"

"That's what it's designed to do," Sabel snapped.

"I guess if you're into that."

The remark stung, hitting close to the mark, but Sabel regarded her coolly. "You're goading me on purpose. Is that conscious or is it an outgrowth of how you feed?"

Brie took a step back. Her beautiful face looked worried now, no less beautiful, but tight around the eyes and mouth.

"Passion and anger are similar energies," Sabel continued. "If you can't evoke the one, do you just naturally go for the other?"

Brie recovered enough to say, "No, you're pissed off all on your own." She walked out of the room.

Sabel glanced over at Lily, who'd been watching them. "I can't imagine her as a teenager," she told Lily.

Lily shook her head. "I missed those years. It wasn't safe for her to be with me."

"The Sangkesh would really come after your child?" Sabel asked.

"Of course they would."

Lily turned back to the book she was reading and Sabel understood that topic was closed. In some ways, the Sangkesh demon-hunters had a lot in common with the Hecatines. Sabel wasn't sure if it would be better or worse if the two groups ever surmounted their differences.

CHAPTER FIVE

The sullen brother was a real piece of work. Brie could taste him from where she sat across the long picnic table. Years of addiction and rage had layered Mack thick with energetic blocks that called out to her to punch through. She tried to settle herself. It didn't help that he was staring at her with undisguised longing. She made a mental note to avoid hospitals wherever possible; the threat of death made people horny and desperate. Only two days ago she'd sated herself in her usual haunts on the eastern seaboard but now if she wasn't careful all the emotional energy swirling around would draw up her hunger again and she'd have to try some of the local stock.

She shouldn't have messed with Sabel like she had in the hospital that morning, but it was so hard not to. Sabel was the precise opposite of Mack and that made her just as appealing. Everything in her was so under wraps and on top of it she had that beautiful latticework around her body caging her in. Who wouldn't want to spring the lock on that? Not that she knew how. She'd been able to circumvent it briefly by using the lower life force pathways of Sabel's body, but any direct touch to the structure would surely trigger it.

Sabel was clearly avoiding her now and Ana kept looking over at her with confusion. Brie made no effort to talk to them and instead checked out the people at the party, the food and the surroundings.

Apparently Ana had grown up on the wrong side of the tracks. Though Brie had trouble discerning the right side in this town. She herself had grown up in San Francisco, spent a short stint in the Midwest, and moved to Boston after high school, so she'd never been outside a large city and the evenly spread poverty here shocked her. This house was their "new" house, bought in the last few years. It held three full bedrooms and two baths and half of the interior was still crying for fresh paint, carpet that wasn't worn down, uncracked tiles. Granted, the man of the house had been sick for months, but even Brie's college apartment had been in better overall shape. These people seemed like well-versed do-it-yourselfers, so the house must have been a real disaster when they bought it.

Due to the warm, spring day, dinner was being served in the backyard on a long table, comprised of a picnic table with a card table at either end, all covered in thin plastic with a checkered tablecloth pattern printed on it. Ana's mother and her friend Joyce must have been cooking since lunchtime to turn out such a mass of fried chicken, greens with bacon, rice, potatoes, peas and carrots, and pasta casserole. The chicken was fantastic and ruined her for store-bought fried chicken for the rest of her life.

About twenty people arrived for the dinner, half of them somehow related to Ana's family. Brie was good with names and relationships; she'd have them all sorted out in under an hour as long as the conversation stayed lively. There was less crying than she expected and out of curiosity she let her attention wander through the emotional space of these people. She couldn't read all emotions; generally only the hotter ones because those made it easier for her to tap into a person's energy.

She found some anger, but mainly the simmer of longtime grudges, and no small amount of lust: the bulk coming from

Mack, a little from each of the other males around her, and a fair trickle from Ana. That was understandable since Ana couldn't connect energetically with the witch the way she should and that gave her a lot of excess heat in her system.

Speaking of sexual energy, Mack slid around the table to the bench beside her. In his mid-thirties, he had a smaller build than Gunnar but looked stronger with all the wiry muscle that corded his arms. He had small eyes and a narrow chin under his wide cheekbones so his face was all pinched angles. What saved it was his mouth: full lips, almost feminine in shape, but nearly the same color as his sepia skin. If he hadn't been related to her mother's friend, she'd have taken him in a heartbeat. She loved to consume violent men.

"You a model or something?" he asked.

She gave him the demure smile. "Oh, no, thank you, that's sweet of you. I work in a restaurant since I graduated." She waited just long enough for him to develop a fully formed image of her waitressing in a Hooters T-shirt, then added, "Since I got my MBA I found this great spot as the business manager for an organic restaurant on the ocean."

He blinked with such confusion that she felt a pang of guilt for walking him into that one. She hadn't wanted to make him feel stupid, only to screw with his limited ideas of what pretty women did.

"What do you do?"

"This and that," he said. "I rebuild bikes mostly."

"You must be really good with your hands," she cooed and then mentally kicked herself for flirting. It was like breathing to her, but she was supposed to be on her best behavior here. She'd promised Lily.

"Oh yeah." He colored a dark red under his sun-baked skin. Ana came from one of those creamy pale families that could tan but never got darker than Brie was naturally in the dead of winter. She liked that color, but of course she liked all colors, all shapes, all genders and most ages; that was part of her peculiar gift.

"You'll excuse me, won't you?" she purred. "I really must compliment your mother on her chicken. It's extraordinary."

"Hurry back," he suggested and she wished she could.

Brie made her round of compliments and slid up next to Lily, who was hotly discussing some academic point with Sabel. She put a hand on her mother's arm.

"Come walk with me?" she asked.

Lily did. Of all the people here, she was the only one who would understand why Brie might need a walk away from this group. They went up the block, looking at the houses. Every sixth house or so had been cared for better than the others, a neighborhood trying to come up after a long financial drought. Here was a recently-stained fence, there a house with new siding, and another one that had been freshly painted.

"Mack's a piece of work," Brie said when they were far enough away to talk. "I wish I could do something for him."

"Brie, honey—"

"I won't try it," Brie interrupted. "I know better. I just had to get some distance before I got too flirty."

Her mother fished out a crumpled piece of news clipping and held it out to her. As soon as she saw it, Brie knew what it was. She didn't take it. She knew it by heart. In the days after it happened, she'd read it dozens of times, wishing it would be different each time.

"Put that away." The words came out in a harsh whisper. Her mother had never correctly understood the correlation between Brie's own emotions and her need to feed from others'. Just to look at the picture on that page would fill her with anguish and, on the heels of that, a ravenous need.

"I thought you were doing well out east," Lily said.

"I am! I love the restaurant and they understand me there. I stay away from anyone who would be dangerous and I only go into the city twice a month. That was..." She stopped and hugged her arms around her chest. "They slipped me a roofie."

"What?"

"One of the guys at the party drugged my beer to make sure I'd be up for the 'fun' they had planned. I didn't realize...the drug really kicked in midway. They hadn't assumed I'd be that willing; they were trying to rape me. The drug shut down my ability to stop myself once I started to feed."

Brie wanted to be able to tell her all of it, to curl up in her mother's arms and cry about the man she'd killed accidentally and whose memories she'd eaten with his life. She couldn't be taken by force or raped, but this was the most violated she'd ever felt because they'd prevented her from not killing. It helped only a little that the one who drugged her was the one who died. But she couldn't say much more about this to Lily, who was nearly as upset as she was.

"Why didn't you tell me then?" Lily asked.

"I wasn't ready."

"It's not about being ready."

"What could you have done? You would only worry about me and whether or not you needed to tell the family or try to get me to run."

Lily shook her head. "They know, or at least Suhirin and her people do. She wants you as one of her demon-hunters."

"How could that be possible?"

"I don't know of a way to do it," Lily admitted. "It's hard to protect humans when you feed on them. Maybe if you consumed fear or anger instead of life energy…I wonder if there's a way to channel that…"

"The demon-hunters probably only accept those of us who never kill people," Brie said bitterly. It wasn't that Sangkesh never killed, because they did plenty, but they could choose when and whom.

She couldn't make the covenant to protect humanity because if she did and then slipped up again and killed an innocent by accident, she would be destroyed by the condition of her own oath. They would make sure of that. They would make her take the strongest oath, the one that turned the power of the Sangkesh against the oath-taker if they broke covenant. So Suhirin was willing to gamble with Brie's life for the distinction of having one of her rare kind in her family, but Brie wouldn't take that gamble. She could neither join the Sangkesh nor be safe from them until she knew without a doubt that she could control her feeding under any circumstance.

"You should think about moving," Lily said. "Maybe South America. They're going to find you."

"I'll be more careful. And I'll move if I have to. I'll keep moving. I won't let them chain me up again and starve me. But Mom, I love where I am right now. I'll drive farther to hunt, I'll avoid parties. I can make this work."

Lily let out a long sigh, the skin around her eyes tight. She wouldn't say it, but Brie knew that she had been a worry and a disappointment to Lily from the day she had been born perfect. Among demons, that kind of flawlessness meant only one thing: it was a survival trait for hunting and feeding off humans. All the Sangkesh had their flaws and markers: the claws, teeth, tails, horns, hooves and a host of other oddities—most easy enough to conceal in this modern age. Only the Gul, and only a very few of them, were more beautiful than humans.

"Do you think the witch would let me explore that magical corset she wears?" Brie asked.

"I don't trust her," Lily said. "The way she let the other witches bind her—what else would she do at their bidding?"

"I've been looking at it and I like the way they made it. It's really fine work. I think if I could make myself something like that, maybe it could stop me from killing anyone ever again."

"Ask her," Lily suggested.

"She looked pretty alarmed in the airport when I mentioned it."

"That's because you'd only just met and you sounded crazy."

"Thanks, Mom."

"Ask nicely."

Brie stared up at the darkening sky. She could be polite, charming, seductive, but it was hardest to ask for the things she needed most.

They'd made full circuit of the blocks around the house and returned to the party. Voices were louder now as some of the men were on their fourth or fifth drink, and Mack in the middle of them. Gunnar said his goodbyes and got his family into the car and away, and Brie watched Ana doing the same, making the round of the relatives for a last good word and then preparing to flee the storm. Mack must have caught it too.

"You running again?" he asked Ana loudly, voice carrying over the other conversations. "Come pay your respects and run back to your fancy city 'cause what's here isn't good enough for you."

"Mack, leave me alone," Ana snapped back at him.

"What'd I ever do to you?" he asked, belligerent.

"You know what you did," she spat.

Brie moved in closer, not sure that she could help anything, but drawn to the anger like a fly to honey. After the talk with her mother, she wanted to drag him to her and let his energy blot out her pain.

Mack's voice dropped low enough that only those closest to him and Ana heard him say, "You always were a whore and always will be."

"You piece of shit," Ana spat back at him.

Brie felt Mack's violent swing start before anyone could have seen it and she moved as fast as her demon reflexes allowed. She might be five foot six in shoes and slim, but when Mack's fist swung hard for Ana's nose, she knocked it aside and pulled him along with his momentum so he stumbled and fell with her. Hopefully she'd choreographed it well enough that it looked like she'd tripped into him.

She rolled onto her back and flicked her hair out of her eyes. Sabel and Lily each had one of Ana's arms, holding her back. Their body language was casual, but Sabel's forearm quivered with the force she was applying to keep Ana from lunging at Mack.

"I don't like to see fights happen," Brie said lightly. That was a lie, but she went on. "Make love, not war, you know."

She met Ana's eyes as she talked and pushed emotion into her body. Brie couldn't exactly push comfort, that was too far from her core abilities, but she could do something close to affection—on the amorous side of it. She kindled that feeling in Ana and the fiery presence of Abraxas under her skin allowed it to rise through Ana's body.

Then Brie turned to Mack, who was picking himself up from the ground. As she rose next to him, she put her fingers on his bicep and whispered in his ear, "Baby, you're really strong."

He grinned at her and forgot all about Ana and his bruised pride. Pushing emotion wasn't an exact skill, so the desire she inflamed in him was also rising in a few of the other men nearby and the affection from Ana was spilling into Sabel and Brie's mother. General affection for Brie wasn't out of place in Lily, but Sabel's eyes narrowed at her. Sabel seemed to shudder on the energy level and throw off Brie's influence. Later she needed to know how Sabel could do that.

Mack rested his hand on the curve of her ass and Brie let him, but the clock was running in her mind, the five minutes she had before something else stupid was going to happen one way or another. She caught Lily's eye and mouthed, "Let's go."

Miraculously, Lily got them all bundled into the rented car and delicately excused them from Mack's many offers to accompany them. In the car, Brie rested her head on the back of her seat and tried to quell the fire in her belly. At a stoplight, Ana turned around in her seat and looked back at her.

"Thank you," she said. "That was about to get ugly."

Brie managed a smile. She didn't want these people to know the kind of self-control she had to exercise to swim in those emotional currents and expend that power. In her own city it would be easy—she could go out at night to a part of town that didn't know her and find a guy, lonely and possibly drunk, show him the best time of his life and when he reached his climax, drink the energy out of him until she was sated, but not to the point where he died. Brie wasn't comfortable when she didn't know where her sexual outlet lay. But she also wanted to belong, to have some people who just knew her as another person, and she was going to try to make this work.

"He's a bully with a moderate sadistic streak," Brie said. "I can taste it in his energy. I'm sorry you had to grow up with him."

Ana snorted. "Me too. This would be a lot easier without him picking on me because he doesn't know how to express his grief." She fell silent then, her eyes looking inward and Brie wondered if she was talking to her demon guest.

Lily apparently was dating this demon, or whatever her mom and a 2500-year-old disembodied guy would call their relationship. Brie wondered how they had sex: was it only in dreams, or did the demon borrow other people's bodies to do it and if so, how did her mother feel about the bodies she'd slept with? At least this was one of her mother's lovers she'd never need to worry about kindling desire in; Brie's abilities to work up lust in others didn't extend very strongly to those without bodies, probably because her interest didn't cover many non-humans.

* * *

The hotel room was shit for pacing. Ana made four angry steps between the television and the bedside table and turned around. Sabel sat in the chair on the far side of the room and watched her with a grim expression. They had adjoining rooms so that Sabel could sleep away from Ana and not worry about the leash triggering and waking her up in pain, but Sabel had returned with Ana to her room after the dinner.

"You should've let me hit him," Ana said.

"I thought about it," Sabel told her. "But it didn't seem like the right time."

Ana growled but the sound was half agreement and appreciation that Sabel didn't automatically tell her violence was wrong; right now it didn't feel wrong. But she could see that the time to beat the crap out of Mack wasn't in front of her mother and the neighbors. Her mother would have to live with that scene for a lot longer than Ana would.

Still, she was shaky inside from wanting to hit something, and from fear, from the long-honed panic that was Mack's gift to her. She'd never have agreed to come back here and see him again if not for the chance to catch Ashmedai and end him. Maybe if she played it right, she could get Ashmedai to beat the tar out of Mack first. She curled her hands over the back of the desk chair just to have something to clench but after a moment she felt the thick plastic start to crack and let go.

She was a lot stronger than she had been before Abraxas came to live in her. Mack might not realize how she'd changed. Just let him try to hit her again and he would get a stunning revelation right in his asshole face. Lily and Sabel had only managed to keep her back because she didn't want to hurt them by tearing free of their grip, plus Brie seemed to have him well in hand. As a bodyguard, despite her small stature, she wasn't turning out to be a bad choice.

She altered his emotional energy, Abraxas answered her unvoiced question.

"What did he say?" Sabel asked. She'd gotten good at knowing when he and Ana were talking, and Ana hoped this didn't mean that she had a stupid look on her face every time she listened internally.

Abraxas flowed out of her and formed in the other empty armchair in the room. He said, "Brie changed the course of his energy from anger to desire and, as best she could, the other warm emotions like caring."

"I felt that too," Sabel said. "But I couldn't see it. Was she altering everyone?"

"Primarily the brother and Ana," Abraxas said. "Her use of power is very undisciplined, so it spills around."

"That's dangerous," Sabel said.

"She stopped a fight," Ana pointed out. "How bad can it be?"

Sabel looked up sharply, her blue-gray eyes shifting toward the stormy end of the spectrum. "She manipulated you," she said. "She changed how you felt and you don't even realize it."

Ana remembered being furious at Mack and barely able to keep from tearing free to go after him until Brie had looked her in the eyes. Then she'd realized what a good thing Brie had done for her and how she didn't want to screw it up, and she realized that she could be hurting Sabel, which had reminded her of how much she cared about Sabel and pulled her further out of her fury. That hadn't come from inside of her? It was something Brie caused?

"Wow," she said. "That's what she does?"

It was hard to feel upset about it because it had been the right thing at the time. Could she get angry on principle? Sabel was clearly upset about it, but then she'd never actually been possessed by a demon, so she didn't know how much worse it could be. Compared to losing control of her body or her memories, having someone decide to make her a little happier seemed like a great idea.

"That's not all she does," Sabel declared. "She's already killed at least two, maybe three people, by accident. She can't even control her powers well enough to go around without killing. That doesn't seem to me to be the best person to keep you safe."

"She seems pretty nice," Ana protested.

"How do you know you really think that?" Sabel asked her. "How do you know it isn't her manipulating how you feel?"

"How do you know she isn't manipulating you?" Ana responded.

Sabel just stared at her with a look that implied the question had been so stupid that she couldn't begin to figure out how to answer it.

"There's more than one way to know," Abraxas intruded on the silence. "You can use an information lattice, as Sabel does, to know when the information held in your nervous system is changed. You can also open your consciousness more completely at the level of emotional energy and you would feel it directly."

Ana had to laugh, though the sound came out more angry than amused. "You can turn anything into a lesson, can't you? That's part of what you've been trying to teach me."

"It's a good next step after learning not to be possessed," he said. "Now you must learn to identify when you're being influenced."

"See, it's good Brie's around so I can practice," Ana told Sabel.

"Don't defend her!"

"Don't snap at me about Brie when I have to put up with my shithead brother!"

Ana crossed the room and grabbed her jacket off the hanger. She slammed the door open and went down the hall quickly. If she stayed, she was going to say something stupid and she didn't want a fight with Sabel; she just wanted to get through the next few days and say goodbye to this shit town.

"Don't you fucking tell me to get inside my anger either," she snarled under her breath to Abraxas, who had snapped back into her body when she'd left the room.

He didn't respond but she felt his steadfast presence within her.

She walked for a few blocks, but she didn't want to see any more depressing storefronts or crappy two-story apartment buildings. In a bare, one-block park, she sat on a cold concrete bench and tried to cry, but the tears wouldn't come. She sat until the chill seeped through her jacket and the back of her jeans. On the way back to the hotel she stopped at a gas station and got a pint of ice cream and two plastic spoons.

When she opened the door to the hotel room, Sabel stood up from the desk and opened her arms, head bowed. "I'm sorry," she said.

Any remaining tension in Ana's body dropped away. Looking at Sabel, her whole stance arranged as a beautiful apology, warmed her and made it easy to open up in response. Sabel gave her nothing to fight against here, and that was exactly what she needed. She set her plastic bag on the dresser and put her arms around Sabel. They stood together for a long time.

"I'm sorry too," Ana said, though she wasn't sure what she was apologizing for. "Let's just eat ice cream and watch a stupid movie."

"I'd like that," Sabel told her. When Ana stepped back from her, Sabel climbed onto the bed and started arranging the pillows for them to sit together, while Ana opened the ice cream and joined her.

* * *

Ana woke suddenly in the middle of the night, convinced someone was in the room. It was her father, she realized, and pulled the sheet up to cover more of her bare shoulders. He laughed soundlessly, not from a human form like the one she knew during his life, but the tall, golden figure she'd seen at the head of his bed in the hospital room. This view of him was so different from the stiff, damaged, alcoholic man she'd grown up with.

"Dad?" she whispered.

He moved across the room and kissed the top of her head, a droplet of warmth resting there for a moment, and then he was gone. Really gone. She knew he had died.

Ana pulled on her robe and sat in the room's armchair, watching the shifting flecks of gray that danced in her vision in the dark room. She let her breathing turn deep and slow, and her awareness move a little outside herself, floating in that peace. After a while she got back into bed and sleep came again.

The phone woke her a little after dawn. It was Gunnar calling to tell her the news that their father had died in the middle of the night.

"I know," she told him. "He came by my room last night to say goodbye. He was laughing."

"I'm glad," Gunnar said. "They're having the wake tomorrow afternoon and the funeral on Friday, since we're all here."

"What are we doing today?"

"I don't know what to do. Maybe take Erica and Sunny to look at some baby toys since they're going to have to sit through a lot."

"Good idea."

She knocked on the door between her room and Sabel's and filled Sabel in on the contents of the call, leaving out her late-night visitor until she'd talked to Abraxas and knew what to call it. Was that her father's ghost, spirit, soul? She didn't want to sound stupid, still smarting from Sabel looking at her like she was an idiot yesterday when she'd asked how Sabel knew Brie was manipulating her emotions.

Sabel went to get them coffee and Ana was going to shower, but found herself sitting on the bed looking at the diamond pattern of the carpet.

It was his soul, Abraxas told her.

She had a thousand other questions about souls and death and life, but she didn't want any answers right now; she just wanted to hang in this nonspace.

Thanks, she said.

You need to grieve him.

I don't know how. How can he be so big and golden like that and been so screwed up as a person? I feel like if I start crying, I won't stop. Not just about him but about all of us.

You can trust your emotions.

Oh, right. When have my emotions done anything but get me into trouble?

She expected a lecture for asking that question, but he only replied, with a note of humor, *Go shopping with Brie.*

What? Aren't you supposed to go on about emotions and the ego and blah blah? What kind of response is that?

You said yourself that you'll learn more about the emotional field by having her around to influence you, Abraxas told her. *And I want more time to study her. Plus you didn't pack a funeral outfit.*

When did you become my fashion assistant?

Two seconds after you began to anticipate my lectures with a mind toward ignoring me, he said, but he sounded more amused than hurt.

CHAPTER SIX

When Ana went down to the hotel's common room to eat breakfast with Sabel, she wondered if Abraxas's suggestion about shopping had been for her or for Brie. Brie was sitting at a small table staring at an untouched plate and looking like she'd slept less than Ana. Even in a plain white long-sleeved T-shirt, with dark smudges under her eyes, she was beautiful. Ana sighed and put her plate next to Sabel's, but didn't sit. When Sabel looked up, Ana gestured toward Brie. Sabel rolled her eyes but nodded.

Brie was pushing the end of a sausage around her plate listlessly when Ana walked up to her table. "Come join us," she said.

"Are you sure?"

"I'm just inviting you to breakfast," Ana replied.

"Oh rats, I totally thought you were up for a threesome," Brie said with heavy sarcasm, but she picked up her plate and followed Ana back to the other table.

"So what's on the agenda for today?" Brie asked after an awkward silence.

Ana kept her voice bright and upbeat. "Are you a good shopper?"

Brie raised an eyebrow. "I took a bronze medal in mall shopping in the last Olympics."

"I'm short an outfit, something in black."

"I like black," Brie said.

"Do you want to go shopping?" Ana asked Sabel.

Sabel looked from Ana to Brie and back again. "I'll stay, I've got a few things to work on."

She didn't seem to want to look at Brie, which was an anomaly in a room where everyone else appeared to have trouble not looking at her. Two of the guys in the room had actually moved their chairs around so they could watch her.

While she ate her own breakfast, Ana watched Brie out of her peripheral vision. She didn't seem to be doing anything unusual, but was Brie manipulating her feelings even now? She mainly felt fatigue from all the emotions of the last few days: relief that her father's death had been peaceful, and dread that she'd have to see Mack again tomorrow. None of those seemed like emotions that would particularly interest Brie.

Lily joined them without reacting to the thick tension between Sabel and Brie—maybe because she expected it by now.

"Eat that," she told Brie as she sat down. Brie had been pushing food around but there was still most of two scrambled eggs and two sausage links left on the plate.

"Mom," Brie sighed.

"You still have a human-like metabolism. You need to take care of yourself." Then, turning to Ana, she said, "Make sure you're named in the obituary. We did what we could to hide your departure from San Francisco, so we have to make sure Ashmedai can tell that you're here."

Ana's grin showed more teeth than amusement. "Can he get here in time?"

"With the wake tomorrow and the funeral on Friday? He should have no trouble being here by then."

"You think he'll wait until after the funeral?" Brie asked.

"That's easiest. He doesn't know where Ana is staying and he can't move on her at the funeral itself," Lily said.

"Because it's in a church?" Ana asked.

"The people," Lily told her. "They'll limit what he can do. Especially in a setting like a church, where belief is exceptionally strong. If it were me, I'd follow you from the funeral and wait until you set out for Minneapolis again, then try to take you on the road when you're away from help."

"And that's what we want to happen, right? Because when you say it that way, it sounds kind of like the setting for a horror movie."

"That's what we want," Brie said. "He should think he has the advantage so he's overconfident. Then we take out the... whatever you're going to bind him in..."

"It's a book," Lily said. "We decided that was the most portable container of power."

After breakfast, Ana and Brie took the rental car and drove to the nearest clump of decent stores. Abraxas was silent in her mind, but she had the impression he was watching Brie with interest. Still, he was easy enough to ignore and for the first time in a few months, Ana felt like she was in some semblance of her former life, just hanging out with a friend and being silly.

"That's a beautiful jacket," Brie said as they pulled into the parking lot, indicating the deep olive jacket Ana was wearing.

"Sabel bought it for me, late holiday present."

"How'd you and Sabel meet?" Brie asked as they chose the store they wanted to start with and parked.

"She did a series of diversity trainings at my company. Oh, and then she saved me from a group of demon summoners."

Brie laughed. "That's a good start."

"I'd have asked her out eventually without the whole summoner business. I have a thing for girls with brains. What about you, do you have a type?"

"Breathing," Brie said with a snort. "Men, women, anyone out of puberty...No, I take that back. I have trouble with anyone who's depressed or seriously ill. I can't draw enough energy from them."

"That's a really wide range. You don't have a boyfriend or girlfriend or anything?"

"I can't," Brie said.

"Emotionally or logistically?" Ana asked.

"The second," Brie told her and turned to walk through the racks of clothing.

Ana watched her moving with the grace of a gazelle, completely unself-consciously, or at least it appeared that way. She looked like she'd stepped out of a magazine with her hair falling in perfect waves of dark brown highlighted with a warm, ruddy tone and her skin airbrushed. She wondered if Brie even had to put on makeup. As she walked through the store, other people reacted to her and most looked like they didn't know they were doing it. They'd just turn a little to watch her, or pause in the middle of a sentence when they saw her and then resume talking after she passed.

Since Brie didn't seem to want to talk about it, Ana tried to curb her curiosity. She knew what it felt like to want everything to seem normal. They went through a few stores and then stopped for coffee.

"How many of you are there?" Ana asked, hoping to come at the topic from another angle.

"Of me?" Brie laughed. "There's only one of me. People who are part demon and part human, there are thousands, and those who are a quarter blood or less, probably tens of thousands."

"And the pure demons?"

"Not as many as humans. They really aren't legion," she said with a small smirk. Then her mouth straightened in a tight line. "You know what the witches did to us, right?"

"The archives thing?"

"No, that was way later," Brie said. "Back when Solomon was teaching the demons how to make human-like bodies, and how to breed with humans, the witches asked him to make it hard for embodied demons to reproduce with each other. They said embodied demons were too powerful and if he let them reproduce like humans they'd take over everything."

"Is that true?" Ana asked.

"Who can say? Hard to argue with a group of witches who say they can see probabilities from the future, but that doesn't mean they weren't lying," Brie said. "So now if you get even two half demons or quarter demons, they probably can't have kids. Mom had been trying to have a kid for decades before she had me, but most of the guys she was with, it just wouldn't take. Now in terms of the demons without bodies, they can reproduce like rabbits, but the young ones tend to die off, so if you're thinking demons older than a hundred years who still have some interest in interacting with humans, not more than a few million."

"That's still a lot."

"It's even worse when you try to track all the allegiances. Imagine trying to do the genealogy of the State of California."

"Why is all that so important?"

"You should really ask my mom. She'd dig being able to give you the whole lecture. It's kind of like getting an inheritance along with a really complicated system of trading favors and obligations. Oh and ranks. There's ranks."

She took a long sip of her mocha, watching the shoppers walk by. Ana tried to focus on her own emotions to determine if Brie was influencing her in any way. Mostly she just felt happy and more light-hearted than she had in days. Was that weird? Was it genuine? She wanted to ask Abraxas but she felt that would be like cheating on a test.

She did feel, fairly strongly, that she could go on watching Brie talk for hours. This was a much better way to absorb all the demon history lessons that Lily tried to teach her. Brie was still watching the people pass by and Ana hazarded another question.

"If you could feed on anyone here, who would it be?" she asked. "Or is that really rude of me?"

Brie laughed. "I'd feed on you," she said. "Or that guy over there."

"The really big guy in the Hagrid trench coat? Why?"

"He's kinda sad and angry, be really easy to feed from and it'd make him feel better. Plus he's probably got a bit of demon blood like you, runs hot."

"You can tell that by looking?"

"Nah, it's a guess," Brie said. "And Mom told me about you."

"Oh, great. Why feed on me?"

"Honestly? For one thing, you've been pissed off the last few days and I like how anger tastes, and then feeding on you would piss off Sabel and maybe I'd get her in the bargain."

Ana gave her an amused grumble. "You're kind of a tramp."

"No kidding."

"Do you have an upper limit?"

"Four or five, usually."

Ana winced. "I regret having asked that."

Brie sat back in her chair, her eyes wistful, a little smirk still on her lips. "You want me to go back to the lecture? Hang on." She cleared her throat and then started in on a passable impression of Lily: "There are positions and ranks that have to be filled because of certain balances put into play long ago, and if you have the rank, you get all the power associated with it."

Her voice softened and she continued in her normal tone, "For example, Ashmedai—if you look historically there's been a demon named Ashmedai since at least 500 BCE, but it hasn't always been the same demon. Particularly since you've got him named Ashmedai in one place and Asmodeus in another—that often happens when a role gets too big for one person and needs to be split. So there's a role or position called 'the Ashmedai.' The current holder of it might have killed the previous Ashmedai and taken his seal of office, or maybe the other guy got sick of the job. He probably killed him. With the seal and being the Ashmedai, he can do a lot more than he could before he held the office of a prince."

Ana asked impulsively, "Does that mean there's another Abraxas right now?" She could have asked him directly but he got evasive about the demons 'and witches' history and she wanted an outsider's perspective.

"There has to be," Brie said. "Roles like that don't stay open."

Why not take it? Ana asked Abraxas.

I'm not strong enough, he said. *And the office of the Abraxas will have changed since I left it.*

Like the new guy came in and moved all your furniture, metaphorically?

The dry wind sound of his laughter echoed in her mind, but he didn't add anything. Brie was back to watching the people walk by in the mall.

"You don't have a rank or title or anything?" Ana asked.

Brie shook her head and rubbed her hands up and down her arms like she had a sudden chill. "The kind that I am, we rarely do. We're the bottom of the heap."

She got up from the table and Ana followed her. Brie headed for the department store at the far end. They'd already picked up a pair of black pants, so Ana just needed some kind of black shirt and they'd be all set.

"Sabel doesn't like me much," Brie commented as they walked.

"She's just cautious because you can change people's emotions and all."

Brie nodded. "I thought she caught that. My stepdad can feel it too sometimes. He's a witch like her, but I figured he learned how to sense emotion-pushing from being around me." She paused and looked at Ana. "I don't push him, at least not since I was a kid."

"When did he and Lily split up?" Ana asked.

"She sent him away with me when I was seven. The Sangkesh over in Europe came after me—they wanted to study me—so Aran brought me to San Francisco where we hid out for a while until…"

She trailed off and Ana waited. In front of the department store Brie stopped walking and said very quietly, "Until I killed someone. Then we had to run again. It was an accident. I don't go around killing people if I can help it."

"But sometimes you can't help it?" Ana asked cautiously.

Brie nodded. "That's why no girlfriend or boyfriend. Plus when I feed off someone they tend to get hooked on me for a while. They'd want me to feed off them again and the more I do it with the same person, the harder it is to control."

"Can't you just have sex with them without feeding?"

"No." Brie looked down at her feet. "It's automatic. They climax, I feed."

"That's why you asked if Sabel's leash would keep a demon in as well as out," Ana said with a rush of understanding. "That's a good idea."

Brie smiled up at her. "I see what she loves about you."

"Um," Ana started.

"Oh, hush," Brie said. "Do you think she'd let me examine it if I told her the reason why? It's the first magic I've seen that might be able to keep me from accidentally killing anyone."

"Do you want me to ask her?"

Brie stepped forward and kissed her on the cheek. A flare of hot emotions rippled through Ana. Was Brie manipulating her or was she just lovely and vulnerable and in need?

But there was a deeper, dark undercurrent in Ana's mind as well. She couldn't imagine what it was like for Sabel to have to carry around inside her body something that in an instant could hurt her or render her unconscious. Just thinking about it made the skin between Ana's shoulder blades prickle with disgust. She'd never have been able to accept such a limitation and yet Sabel had agreed to it in large part because of her. She wanted it gone.

"If Sabel says yes and you can figure out how it works, can you get it off her?" Ana asked.

"I hope so."

Brie turned and walked into the store and again Ana found herself watching her move and turn heads. What was it like to be wanted everywhere and unable to actually keep anyone?

* * *

Sabel was kicking herself for not going shopping with Ana and Brie because the longer they were gone, the more she worried. How stupid was it to let your girlfriend wander around town in the company of a demon of lust? She made herself focus as well as she could and shored up her own magical defenses. Then she went to the hotel's tiny gym and worked out, showered in her room and tried to settle down to some reading.

When she heard Ana moving around in the next room, she jumped up. Ana knocked on the adjoining door before she even got to it. Sabel opened it from her side, though it hadn't been locked. Ana kissed her hard, but then stepped back after a moment so she wouldn't trigger the leash.

"You need to find another time eddy," Ana said. The one time they'd been able to make love had been when Sabel knocked them both into a place that was, briefly, outside of time and therefore outside the reach of the leash.

"No kidding."

The trouble wasn't really finding one; it was the power to get into one. Sabel could get herself into them, but she was starting to think she couldn't take Ana with her unless the situation was life-threatening.

"Good shopping?" she asked.

"It'll do. I'm only going to wear this once, so I didn't go fancy."

"Brie behaved?"

"Sabel, she's not a bad person, er, demon, whatever."

"Don't tell me you got your nails done together and now you're best friends."

Ana held out her hands and her fingernails were as uneven as they'd been when she left.

"She's in a tough situation," Ana offered. "Kind of like ours in a way. She can't have sex with anyone without feeding on them, but the more often she has sex with them, the harder it is for her not to lose control."

"And kill them," Sabel added, emphasis on the word "kill."

"She's trying to find something she can count on to stop her and she's been thinking maybe the leash could be that thing. Would you let her look at it?"

Sabel glanced down at the carpet so she could think without watching Ana's face. Her first reflex was to say no. Certainly whoever made the leash wouldn't want a demon looking at it closely. But she also understood the request Brie was making. She knew what it was like to carry around a power that could kill a person.

Her own innate power, the *marevaas*, the "Dangerous Voice," could kill as quickly as thought. She could give an unbreakable command to a person to stop breathing or even stop their heart beating. That was the reason she agreed to the leash in the first place. She'd never let a demon use her Voice to kill. Was it similar for Brie?

At the same time, Brie and Ana had been together for hours, which was plenty of time for Brie to influence Ana's emotional state to a considerable degree. She could have lied to Ana. And yet. If Brie could alter the leash, maybe she could put it more under Sabel's conscious control. If it became a tool that Sabel could turn off and on at will, then she could be with Ana whenever she wanted—and oh, how she wanted that—and still be protected from demon possession whenever she needed.

Ana's fingers brushed her cheek. "It's okay, whatever you say," Ana told her.

Sabel turned her face toward Ana again. "Let's ask Lily. If she thinks it's a good idea, then yes."

They went across the hall to the room shared by Lily and Brie. It was an hour before dinnertime and they were both there: Lily reading and Brie napping. She did seem more tired than she had three days ago and Sabel wondered how often she had to feed—and what happened if she didn't.

Abraxas separated himself out from Ana and went over to stand near Lily. He rested an immaterial hand on Lily's shoulder and she smiled up at him. Brie was lying in her bed on top of the covers on her side with her face turned away from the door.

"We have a question," Ana said.

At the sound of her voice, Brie rolled over and sat up in her bed. "Hey," she said.

"Go ahead," Lily told her.

"Do you think Brie should be able to examine the witches' leash that Sabel has on?" Ana asked.

Sabel nodded to show that she thought that was a fair phrasing of the question.

"Assuming Sabel's amenable?" Lily said. "Then I'd appreciate it. Until she can completely control her power, she's in danger from the Sangkesh demon-hunters. She's on their list already. It's only a matter of time before her name gets to the top and the best hunters go after her."

Lily's voice was even, but her eyes tightened with pain as she talked. It had to be impossibly hard to know that her own people would hunt down and kill her daughter.

Sabel met Brie's otherworldly eyes. "If you trigger it, it will knock me out."

"I'll just look," Brie said. "If I can't figure out how to get around the trigger, I won't touch it."

"You think you can figure that out?" Sabel hated to admit it, but now she was really curious.

"I was born into this body," Brie said. "I have a wider range of abilities than most demons. Without a body, they can only manipulate forces and emotions. I have access to all the magics you do from having a body, but with the power of a demon."

"That can't be possible," Sabel protested.

"Ana might be like that too someday if Abraxas keeps teaching her, only without all the succubus effects," Brie said. She got off the bed and stood carefully next to it. "Do you want to come over here?"

Sabel crossed the room. Ana sat on the other bed and Sabel felt relieved to have her nearby.

Brie walked around her, a slow repeat of her behavior at the airport. "That's really elegant," she said.

"It doesn't feel elegant."

"May I touch you?" Brie asked. Her voice was so small that Sabel pitied her. She dipped her head in agreement.

Cool fingers traced a path around her throat near the base. Sabel held her breath and from the utter stillness in the room, everyone else did too. Brie stepped in front of her and touched her solar plexus and then ran her fingers down to the soft area of cartilage below it.

Sabel made herself breathe slowly. The leash hadn't triggered yet and not breathing wasn't going to help. Brie's fingers dropped until they were two inches below her navel.

Then they continued down to the top of her pubic bone. Heat swirled around the floor of her pelvis and she gasped.

"Triggered?" Brie asked.

"No," Sabel answered. The word came out breathless.

"You can tell me to stop any time," Brie said. She moved around behind Sabel again and she felt a firm pressure of fingertips against the base of her spine.

The swirl of energy between her hips heated up again and moved throughout her lower belly. It felt like being aroused but without any object to her arousal—like being turned on but not by any particular person.

The fingers of Brie's other hand touched her back behind her heart and a very weak pulse traveled from her belly upward. The leash tugged.

Sabel flinched.

"Triggered it?" Brie asked.

Sabel nodded.

"Bother. You okay?"

It had only tightened by one invisible notch, so she could still breathe well enough. Later she'd need to be alone to go through the ritual Josefene taught her to make it release completely, but for now she was all right.

"Yes," Sabel told her. "It's not too bad and it stopped moving."

"I want to try something else, but it's more...intense."

"We can try," Sabel said.

"You're going to want to sit down," Brie suggested.

"I am?"

"Trust me."

"You know I don't," Sabel admitted.

That was more than true, but she trusted her own magics to be able to handle anything Brie could do to her. The leash was only the top layer of her defenses, a crude barricade only against a certain kind of demonic intrusion. Below that she had lattices of information and trapdoors she could escape through into the Unseen World, from which she could also mount a defense if it came to that.

Brie laughed. "Good enough, but do it anyway. Sit here." She patted the middle of the bed. "And look out the window."

"Why?"

"You'll figure it out."

Sabel climbed onto the bed and sat cross-legged facing the window. She heard Brie say to Ana, Abraxas and Lily, "Talk amongst yourselves, this might take a while."

They started up a quiet conversation that Sabel didn't pay attention to because she was abruptly focused on Brie, who'd crawled onto the bed. Brie sat directly behind her, putting Sabel between her open legs.

"Um," Sabel began to say.

"I'm not making a move on you, this is how my powers work. Just breathe."

Breathing was one thing Sabel was extremely good at. Breath control made a lot of other techniques easier. She lengthened and deepened her breathing to the level that put her in a light, open trance. Behind her, Brie matched her breathing. She felt their chests rising and falling together.

"You have a safe word?" Brie asked softly from next to her ear.

"I thought you weren't hitting on me."

Brie chuckled. "True. 'Stop' will work."

"Am I going to need to use it?"

"You tell me," Brie said.

She fell silent again and her breathing matched Sabel's and then abruptly there was heat and pressure against the bottom of her pelvis. The base of her energy body flared open and the pressure rose. It felt almost exactly like being fucked hard and suddenly.

"Oh gods." She rocked back against Brie, who wrapped her arms around Sabel's middle and steadied her.

The dense heat pushed up into her. She gasped for breath.

"Triggered?" Brie asked.

"No."

"Stop?"

Sabel shook her head. She didn't trust her voice. It's just an experiment, she told herself, to help someone out. But the rest of her body wasn't listening to her mind just then. She felt stretched open from the inside and filled with pleasure in a thick line inside her spine from its base up to her solar plexus. It rose higher and when it reached her heart, she felt obliterated in a wash of white-hot ecstasy.

It wasn't like an orgasm exactly; it was like every nerve in her body radiated bliss with no center and no sense of time.

When she came back to her normal awareness, she first felt Brie's arms tighly around her, breasts pressed against her back, and realized she'd tipped her head back so it was resting on Brie's shoulder. She heard the absolute silence in the room. And then she felt the leash—it was reset to its normal position, not the tightened band it had been minutes ago.

"Reset," she breathed and then had to tip her head forward and clear her throat so she could speak normally. "You reset it."

"Sweet." Brie's voice held the resonance of a broad smile. "I was hoping that worked. Still can't figure out how I'd get it off you and on me, but I've got the basics of how it closes and opens."

"I think we did enough for now," Sabel said and her voice only wavered a little. She realized she was gripping Brie's legs above the knee where they rested on the outside of her legs and she let go.

Carefully, she crawled to the side of the bed and stood up. The room wavered around her and she put out a hand. Ana caught it and steadied her. In the lamplight of the room, Ana's face was luminously beautiful. Sabel looked back at Brie and saw that she, too, was glowing. She rubbed a hand over her eyes but the effect didn't go away. Looking at Brie on the bed, she also realized that while she was sitting in front of her, facing the window, no one else in the room could see her face. Was that why Brie put her there? Did she know what that was going to feel like?

"You okay?" Ana asked.

"Dizzy," Sabel told her. "But the leash is reset, which is amazing. And I feel...strange."

"You need to eat something," Brie said. "With a lot of protein and fat in it."

Sabel thought what she really wanted to eat was Brie, and Ana, preferably at the same time. She rubbed her hand over her eyes again, harder.

"Gods, this is why I avoid demon magic. Total mind-fuck. You're going to tell me what you did, right?"

"I will," Brie said. "But you have to go walk around and eat something. You're higher than a kite right now. That went a little too well. I didn't expect all your inner stuff to be so well organized."

"Witch," Sabel said with pride and thumped her chest with her index finger. The gesture set her shaky balance off again and she wavered on her feet. Ana put a strong arm around her waist.

"I know," Brie said and then looked at Ana. "Seriously, go order her a steak and some ice cream and she'll turn normal again, I promise."

Sabel let Ana lead her out of the room. She felt a pang of loss walking away from Brie, and a flash of anger that she'd been made to feel that way. Ana kept her arm around Sabel and as they stepped into the hallway, she leaned against Ana.

If Brie could reset the leash, she wondered, could she and Ana be more physical with each other now? It didn't quite work out in her mind because all she could imagine was passing out in the middle of sex and Ana having to ask Brie to come reset the leash while Sabel was naked and unconscious. She didn't want to be unconscious for that. No, not unconscious—she didn't want to be naked. Right? That's how it was supposed to be.

CHAPTER SEVEN

Brie laid low for most of Wednesday. She was good at staying out of the way when she had to. It was clear Sabel wasn't ready to talk to her yet. She was itching to play with the leash again, but doubted that would happen in the next day or two. She'd entered Sabel's energy system the one way she knew wouldn't trigger the leash, which was through the base of the major channel that ran up the inside of the spine. She thought she would put some energy into the system, follow it up and see if she could take it out again without causing trouble. While she'd expected it to feel sexual, because it always did when she put energy into someone that way, she hadn't counted on how quickly and completely Sabel's system could take up her energy, translate her intention, and make use of it.

On the bright side, she hadn't made Sabel black out from the leash. But the experience was like opening a door she thought was going to lead to a hallway and instead finding a cathedral. She'd essentially gone skipping up the central aisle and then took back not only the bit of her own energy, but some of the tremendous excess Sabel created when sparked like that. It was so hard not to. Sabel's energy system was beautifully tended. It had to be, considering the destruction it was built on top of. Brie could spend days just running sparks through it, but Sabel would probably kill her if she tried it.

The wake for Ana's father started midafternoon and went until after dinner, but Ana decided they should arrive on the early side, before Mack was able to drink too much. She wore the black pants they'd bought but paired them with the olive jacket for this event. Sabel had on loose gray pants and a matching jacket with a black shell. Brie picked a long dress from the outfits she'd brought, figuring everyone would benefit from her looking more vulnerable rather than less at this point.

Their party was one of the first to arrive. Brie settled at a table near the back with Lily while Ana went up to the casket and talked to her mother and Gunnar.

Brie eyed the table of food with hopeless longing. Nothing she could eat there would stop her hunger. The energy she'd taken from Sabel was a stop-gap measure and in a way it only made her craving worse. She had enough in reserve that she could make it through a few more days, but with the news Lily brought of certain Sangkesh being onto her, it was actually safer to hunt in this little city in the middle of nowhere. If they were going to face Ashmedai soon, she wanted plenty of energy in reserve. Tonight she had to find a way to sneak out and feed.

Mack approached her as she stood by the buffet table looking at the dishes she had no desire to eat. He was already halfway to drunk, smelling of alcohol and anger.

"Where'd you come from?" he asked.

"Out east," she told him and picked up a plate from the end of the buffet. She walked along, piling it with proteins: chicken wings, roast beef, baked beans. At the end she turned and handed it to him with a fork. He looked puzzled but let her lead him to one of the small tables set up around the room, where he sat and dug into the food.

"She didn't never come home to visit," Mack said. "And Dad talked about her all the time. Her fucking brains and how she got herself through school and got some fancy job. Then Gunnar goes and follows her, leaving me here to take care of 'em 'cause who'd want a fuck-up like me."

Brie watched him chew over the meat and his words, both going bitter in his mouth. He washed it down with a swig from the near-empty beer he'd been carrying. He expected her to protest or correct him, but she didn't need to. She didn't really know any of these people and right now she was only interested in him.

"Where'd you come from?" she asked him in a soft voice.

He looked up, his eyes hard with pain and the need to fight against something. "Hell most likely, to hear them tell it." He waved his hand in the direction of the room at large.

"I don't think so," Brie said. "Not that I've ever been there, but I've heard some descriptions based on reputable accounts."

He barked out a laugh. "No one gave me a second look once Gunnar and Ana came along. Gunnar the athlete and Ana…little bitch could read before she even started school. And me, well, I was good at fighting, I tell you. But I coulda been something if they hadn't taken all the best of everything."

He hunched over the plate and ate in silence. The fork in his hand rubbed up against calluses on his fingers and a muscle in his arm jumped as he gripped it too tightly. He wore a faded, sage-colored oxford shirt that looked uncomfortable on him and Brie had to fight the urge to turn down the side of his collar that was standing up.

He wouldn't talk about his father here, and she wasn't about to ask. The anger was a wall against the pain. He'd looked up to the man, even more so in recent years with the two younger children moved away and them working together to fix up the new house. She'd heard from someone at the wake that even as his father got too sick to work on the house, Mack would set him up where he could see the work Mack was doing and they'd chatter away as if nothing was changing.

She let herself taste his energy. He wasn't psychopathic, he had poor impulse control, was very kinesthetic, overly aggressive, somewhat sadistic and lacking in empathy. He also had a strong, frustrated creative bent. If she had the time and permission to work him over, could she change him? Free up that creative energy and drain away the anger?

Brie excused herself and went outside to stand in the cool air where she tried not to gasp like a fish on land.

They left the wake just before dinnertime. Mack was by now obviously slurring his words. There were enough people around that Ana had managed to stay away from him so far, but Brie could see she wanted to err on the safe side. Brie suggested they have dinner at the small restaurant across the street from the hotel, and Lily took her up on it. Ana and Sabel opted to go back to their rooms.

"You want to go to a movie or something?" Brie asked when she and Lily got back to their room after dinner, hoping her mother would decline.

Lily looked up distractedly from the notes she was laying out on the bed. "Is it that early?"

"Sevenish. I figured we could walk around a mall and catch the nine o'clock show."

"If you go out alone, are you going to get into trouble?"

"I'm not sixteen anymore. Though I do want to see that new ensemble romantic comedy. I really think those are better the more characters they have. I mean why follow one couple's story when you can follow three or four, right?"

"I wish you were joking," Lily said.

"Last chance to come with me."

Lily shook her head. "If you get dessert, bring me some, and try not to stay out so late that it scares me."

"Right, I'll be back around midnight."

Brie flew out the door determined to enjoy her few hours of solitude for all they were worth. If she hauled ass to the mall, she might catch the 7:25 show and have a few hours after to trawl the bars before she had to get back to the hotel and pretend she wasn't misbehaving.

In her day-to-day life, she'd gotten good at maintaining a cheerful, easy persona, really her natural personality, while protecting it from the other side of her life. She went to work during the week and spent time with friends who did not want to sleep with her; she had very gay male friends. On weekends she'd amuse herself around the house, but every other weekend she turned to the side of her closet with the trampy little outfits and went out hunting in one of the big cities of the eastern seacoast.

She did go to the movie because she'd need to be able to talk about it if Lily asked. Then she beelined for the sleaziest bar she'd been able to locate in this town.

It was only by the grace of God that she didn't see Mack until after she'd fed herself. When she was out doing utility feeding, she generally picked men instead of women. She didn't have a strong preference, but men tended to be easier to talk into a back room, back alley or bathroom for a quick blowjob. Plus when she suggested it, they generally looked like they'd won the lottery.

She was coming in through the bar's back door when she saw Mack slumped over a table. The man in the alley behind her was temporarily too weak to try to insist that she come home with him, but she planned to be out of that bar in a few minutes before he recovered. Still, she couldn't leave Mack like this. He was drunk out of his mind, unable to stand, and crying like a little boy lost in a department store.

"Hey baby, you look rough," she said, leaning down to his shoulder.

His red eyes struggled to focus on her. "You," he mumbled. "Wanna beer?"

"No, and neither do you. Let's get you home, big guy. I'm going to help you up, okay?"

"Sure, yeah, home's good."

She pulled his arm around her shoulders, ignored his groping at her breast, and levered him up out of his seat. He was heavy and leaned most of his weight on her. Brie could carry him out if she had to, but that would be hard to explain, so she made it look like he was holding himself up as she dragged him out to the rental car.

"If you're going to puke you'd better warn me," she told him. "Now, where do you live?"

It turned out that he lived only a few blocks from his parents' house, which Brie took as a sign of painful co-dependence rather than touching soft-heartedness. She pulled, levered, cajoled and shoved him up the front walk. He tried to kiss her as she fished in his jeans pocket for his keys.

"Too damned drunk, baby," she told him, unlocking the door. "No pleasure in that."

"Not too drunk," he slurred blearily.

"I rest my case."

The house was a tiny one-bedroom, the bedroom opposite the kitchen. She sat him on the bed and let him fall back. He was snoring almost before he landed. For amusement, she undressed him. Let him wonder how his clothes had come off, if he could even remember in the morning who'd brought him home. She pulled his feet up onto the bed so he lay serenely down one side, looking for all the world like he'd gotten into bed with a partner. Then she sat back and looked at his lean body.

He'd been an athletic man five years ago, before the drinking started to do serious damage. His body showed signs of work and wear. She ran her hands down his flat chest and belly, over the thin ridges of his hips. Even in a stupor, his cock stirred, rising toward her. Oh she wanted to take him in, to drain that violent temper and leave him with an exhausted longing and, she could dream, more respect for the women he might run across in his small circles.

"Bad idea, baby," she told herself. "You don't eat friends' relatives. You just don't. Now cover up the naked boy and walk away."

The sound of her own voice here in this shabby room made her laugh, and she flicked the blanket over him. Before she left, she pulled out her lipstick, covered her lips freshly and kissed his bathroom mirror. Let him wonder.

She stepped into the cool night feeling unusually free—until she smelled the other demon.

Hot iron and pepper scents stung the inside of her nose. It had just enough substance to allow it to see in this world and it was perched, like a small, dark cloud, on Mack's garage roof. It had seen her enter and now leave. Would it follow her? Brie got in her car and rolled the windows down so she could still taste the air. There was more than one now, another had flown up, possibly called to follow her so the first could stay with the house. That was a bad sign, as it hinted at organization and size and goal-directed behavior, plus the fact that Ashmedai was already here with a number of lesser demons.

There was no reason she could imagine for a demon sentry to be hanging around Mack's house other than Ana. Brie wasn't about to lead the one ghosting above her car anywhere near their hotel. They weren't ready to spring their trap yet and she didn't want to give Ashmedai any kind of edge.

She drove to another part of town and pulled into the lot of a Best Western. In the lobby she picked a seat far from the front desk, hoped they'd give her a few minutes in case she was waiting for a friend, and used her cell phone to call Lily's hotel room.

Lily had clearly been sleeping, answering on the third ring with a drowsy, "Hello?"

"Mom, it's me. I'm being followed."

"Ashmedai?"

"A little demon, probably a spy for him."

"How did it find you?"

Brie winced because what she had to say next was going to sound like a lie and implicate her in all sorts of trouble. "I ran across Mack in a bar and took him back to his house. It was there, only one when I arrived, but another came as I left and tailed me."

There was a long pause and then Lily asked, "Where are you now?"

Brie waited for her in the hotel bar. Strange as it seemed to her, it wasn't even midnight yet. She sipped ginger ale and tried to distract herself with a day-old newspaper. After twenty minutes, Lily came in through the back of the hotel.

"I had the cab drop me off a block away and snuck in," Lily said. "This was a good pick."

When they came out of the hotel together it would seem to their watcher that Lily had just come out of her room. What worried Brie was how many watchers might be called to Mack's house and where they may have followed him. They weren't ready to take on Ashmedai yet, not with Gunnar and his family still so close to Ana. The plan included drawing Ashmedai away from Gunnar.

"I don't know how long it was there," she said. "When we went in, Mack stank so hard of alcohol I didn't smell it, but it must have been there to call the other."

Lily raised an eyebrow at her.

"I didn't, I swear. I just found him in the bar and carried him home for his own good."

"How does Ashmedai have enough resources to leave a demon at Mack's house?" Lily pondered, though Brie knew the question wasn't directed at her. "Let's see if we can bind it just for a moment to see what it is and then banish it."

Brie smiled as they stood up. She'd wanted to learn more of this from Lily, but she couldn't seem to stay around her mother long enough. It was too much of a strain on the two of them to carry between them what Brie was and how she needed to live. Even though Brie never blamed Lily for what she was, she knew that Lily blamed herself. The air was crisp with the smell of snow and it carried the tang of the demon easily.

"Over there." Brie pointed to a shed on the far side of the hotel parking lot, a good vantage point for the door.

"Keep its attention," Lily said and slid into the darkness.

Well, Brie was good with attention. She staggered into the pool cast by the parking lot light and looked down at herself, swaying like a drunkard.

"Are my buttons wrong?" she asked the night air. "I think they're wrong." And with that she unbuttoned her blouse and held it open, looking at the inside of the button strips. "I think they're sewn on wrong." She made a show of buttoning the wrong ones together and then having to undo it and do it over again.

While she worked she smelled the burning metal scent of the creature more strongly. It must have moved to the tip of the shed's roof to better look at her. Good to know the tricks that worked on men worked to some degree on these demons.

Lily came around the corner of the shed sprinkling a fine powder behind her until she returned to the spot she'd left from.

"There we go. Now. In the name of Solomon the King and of my own protectors, I bind you."

Was it really that simple, Brie wondered as the creature shrieked. It struggled, a patch of blacker darkness, seemingly pinned to the roof of the shed. Lily said a few more words in neither of the languages Brie knew and then held up her hand with a dark powder in her upturned palm. She blew it toward the demon and Brie felt it snap out of this world.

"That was kind of easy," she said.

"That one's not going to be our trouble. It's like being able to shoot down a squirrel when you're stalked by a tiger, so don't get overconfident. Let's go, we have to turn in this car and get another. I don't want to lead Ashmedai back to the hotel."

"What was the incantation?" Brie asked as they drove to drop off the car.

"Chaldean, but it doesn't have to be. I learned it that way. The important part is the intention behind the words. You could recite Jabberwocky if you could get your intention into it."

"Might have to try that."

"Now, do you mind telling me what you were doing with Mack?"

"Oh Mom, not what you think. I mean, I was out hunting, but for anyone else and then he was in the bar and he was so drunk I couldn't just leave him. I didn't have sex with him, honest. I know better than to feed from people who know me. Not that I wasn't tempted. Probably do him good."

"Brie!"

"Well, it would."

They drove in silence for a while and Brie's mind replayed the whole scene, from seeing Mack in the bar to leaving his house and smelling the sentry.

"That demon was bigger than I expected," she said at last.

Lily nodded. In the diffuse light from the streetlights, her face in profile was a collection of harsh planes, her strong nose almost knife-like. "You said there were two at Mack's house, one watching the house and one that followed you."

"Yes."

"Where did he get them from?" Lily asked, again more to herself than to Brie, but Brie answered anyway.

"Craigslist?"

Lily laughed. "That's not the craziest idea."

They left the car at the rental office and dropped the keys through the late-night return slot, then called for a cab to get them back to their hotel since they couldn't rent a new car until the place opened in the morning. Lily suggested they try to sleep for a few hours and then gather the others.

Brie was too on edge. She slipped out of the room while Lily slept and prowled through the halls of the hotel with no destination in mind. She'd fought strong demons before, maybe even stronger than Ashmedai if he was still as weak as Lily thought he was, and she looked forward to the opportunity to take him down. She felt surprisingly protective of Ana and Sabel considering she'd only known them a few days and Sabel seemed determined to get pissed at her at every turn. Even if she couldn't have them, it would be good to know they were safe and living their lives with each other.

* * *

Ana got up early and went running in the hotel gym while Abraxas explained to her that Lily and Brie had discovered that Ashmedai already had demon sentries in town watching Ana's family. She felt more exultant than angry. She wanted this fight. After a shower, she headed down to the breakfast room.

Lily and Brie were on one side of the breakfast table with Sabel and Gunnar facing them. Sabel had positioned herself to Gunnar's left, putting him across from Brie instead of her. Apparently the leash-removing attempt the other day hadn't changed her desire to stay away from Brie.

Ana had come into the room while Lily was talking and for a moment got to watch Sabel. The look on her face was pure concentration, her elegant brows drawn close, eyes intense, small, pink lips open slightly. Her face was longer than Brie's, her skin a cool, pale olive to Brie's warmer, darker tone, but to Ana there was no comparison. She wanted to put her hands on Sabel's cheeks and trace her lips with her thumbs and then kiss her until she couldn't speak.

Sabel looked up as if she felt Ana watching, caught her eye and smiled with a slight blush rising in her cheeks. Had she sensed what Ana was thinking? Did it show on her face? Or was Sabel having similar thoughts all on her own? Ana flashed her a quick grin and joined her at the table.

"Even if he has a dozen of those, we can still fight him," Lily was saying to Gunnar. "But we need to know we can get you and your family to safety. It might be possible to make it look like you're traveling with us back to Minneapolis and then send you out of another airport."

"One of us has to go with him," Sabel said.

"Explain it again," Gunnar said. "The airplane is safe but the airport isn't?"

"He could make an airplane crash, theoretically," Lily said. "But then he doesn't have you to use as bait, so he has to find a way to take you alive. The airport itself is also pretty safe because of the number of people there."

"Demons can't do magic in front of people?" Ana asked.

"Essentially no," Lily told her.

Sabel sighed and wrapped her hands around her tea mug. "It's the interplay of two factors—the first being the material world itself, which is moderately magic-resistant. It's much easier to do big magic in the Unseen World. And secondly, having a lot of people around, you have to work against their belief systems, and belief is a pretty strong force. Put those together and basically Ashmedai can't do anything significant in an airport."

"So we just have to get Gunnar from the funeral—that will be heavily patrolled by invisible demon spies—to an airport?" Ana asked.

"It's the demon spies part that's tough," Lily said. "I figured he would pick up a few allies, but he was so badly damaged that most big demons wouldn't bother to help him. They have nothing to gain. But from the look of that sentry, he has more help than I thought he would. He might have enough resources to follow both Ana and Gunnar from the funeral, so we have to make sure he can't follow Gunnar."

"Easy," Gunnar said. He'd been reclining but sat forward and put his hands on the table, fingers intertwined.

They all turned to stare at him.

"I don't go," he said.

"What?" Ana asked.

"I came to let Dad meet Sunny. Now he's gone. He doesn't care about his funeral. I've got to get my girls home safe, that comes first. I'll say goodbye to Dad when we're safe."

Ana reached across the table and put her hand over his clasped hands. "I'll say goodbye to him for you," she said.

He nodded.

"That does make it a lot easier," Lily said. "Ashmedai doesn't know where we're staying. We can get you out of the hotel and on the road as quickly as you can get ready."

"Give me an hour," he said.

"Maybe two hours," Sabel said quietly. "We need to get a new rental car, one that's not in your name, plus time to change your tickets."

"It's about a three-hour drive to Aberdeen," Ana said. "But that's better than taking the Sioux Falls airport now that Ashmedai knows that's the closest to where we are."

"I'll get tickets and the car," Lily said.

"And you go with them," Sabel told her. "Unless you're planning to send Brie."

Brie shook her head. "She's better at banishing than me, by a lot. And if Ashmedai comes after Ana..."

"I'll be back by then anyway," Lily said. "I'll go up with Gunnar today and drive back tonight. Then we attend the funeral tomorrow and get on the road by about five. Ashmedai should attack us sometime after that in the car. It's by far the easiest target."

"But is it too easy?" Ana asked.

"How so?"

"He's got to know that someone banished his demon spy dude, right? And the logical leap from that is that you're here with me." Ana pointed at Lily. "Unless South Dakota is known for its surplus of demon-banishers."

Lily shook her head. "That's not the popular local magic."

Sabel picked up her train of thought. "If Ashmedai knows we're here with you, he's going to be suspicious if we just all pile in a car, defenseless, to drive back to Minneapolis."

"Exactly."

"So what would we do if we were trying to get back without being attacked?" Ana asked.

"We sure as hell wouldn't take a car," Lily said. "He could just give us a flat at any point when he wanted to ambush us."

"You said airports are safer because what people believe limits the magic, right? Why don't we take the bus back?"

"It could put other people at risk," Sabel pointed out.

"But he'll try to get us away from the bus anyway," Lily countered. "It's a good idea. We can ward the bus well enough that it looks like we're really just trying to get away and he should still be able to make his move. If we all agree, I'll get us tickets for a time just after the funeral."

Seeing nods of agreement, Lily got up from the table and Brie went with her. Ana wondered if she could go for another run. She felt keyed-up, almost excited by the prospect of facing Ashmedai. With all of them prepared for him this time, she felt sure they could take him.

CHAPTER EIGHT

Lily drove Gunnar and his family up to Aberdeen and made sure they got on the airplane safely. He called Ana that night, when they were back home in San Francisco, and one of the tight spots in her chest relaxed. Without him to worry about, she could focus on Ashmedai and on Mack—surviving the one and defeating the other, or was it defeating both of them?

The funeral was scheduled for early Friday afternoon, so local folks could take a half day off work and the nonlocals would have some time afterward to start the journey home. Ana told herself that she was really going for Gunnar, to embody the respect he had for family, even if theirs hadn't remotely resembled the best family. That sort of worked.

She tried meditating, but that lasted for about a minute. Then she went looking for Sabel, who turned out to be reading in her room. Sabel gave her a long hug and went back to sit against the head of the bed, where she'd been propped up, fully dressed and on top of the covers, reading from her laptop. Ana paced a few times and then leaned against the desk.

"Nervous?" Sabel asked.

"Something like that. I haven't been to a funeral in a long time. I missed my boss's because of all the crazy stuff with the summoners and I didn't really know if I should go anyway. Heck, I haven't been to church in forever. Have you?"

"Witches don't go to church, at least not the Hecatines," Sabel said and then cracked a smile to show that she'd answered the wrong question on purpose. "Funerals...my grandmother's a few years ago, but that wasn't in the States and it certainly wasn't Lutheran."

"What was it?"

"Catholic, my mother's side. I do like their sense of ritual. I've never been to a Lutheran funeral, but I imagine it's going to be somewhat less dramatic." She paused and laughed a little. "You should have seen my father's sisters in that church. No one mourns like the Greeks. Even the priest was impressed."

"You don't talk about your family much," Ana observed. "How many sisters does your father have?"

"Five," Sabel told her. "All still living."

"Damn, how many cousins do you have?"

She paused, looking up as she counted mentally. "There are eighteen of us in total, counting my family, so that's fourteen cousins and three siblings."

"Seriously? I have, like, three cousins total. Do you ever have family reunions?"

"Every other year, opposite the Olympics."

Ana waited for her to grin again and show that was a joke, but she didn't. "You're not kidding?"

"I have to show up at least every other time."

"Are you going this summer?" Ana asked. "Do I get to come?"

Sabel sighed. "Sure, why not bring a girlfriend *and* a demon home to meet the family. At least it's in Greece, we can get some sightseeing in."

Talking about Sabel's family had been a distraction, but when she said Greece, Ana went back to feeling weird and anxious. How could she tell Sabel she'd never been out of the

United States—well, except to Canada—when Sabel talked about Greece like it was a close neighbor of Los Angeles?

Sabel must have seen the change in her face because she smiled softly and said, "Over there, everything is really close. You can just take the ferry from Greece to Italy or Turkey. You get used to hopping around to other countries like we go from state to state here. Remember, I spent my summers there until I was twenty. It would be fun showing you around some."

"I think I'd like that," Ana said.

Sabel got off the bed and stepped up to her. She placed her palm on Ana's cheek and rubbed her thumb across Ana's lips. She said softly, "This summer I'll have a lot of time off and hopefully I'll have this leash handled one way or the other."

Ana thought of images she'd seen of Greece, of the whitewashed buildings and the blue sea and sky, of the blowing gauzy curtains, and imagined herself and Sabel together under those skies, behind the curtains, in bed together.

"I'm in," she said.

Sabel rose up on her toes and kissed Ana high on the cheek, whispering, "And the Mediterranean is *warm*."

Ana wrapped her arms around Sabel and held onto her. A list of action items formed in her mind: survive the funeral; bind Ashmedai; get the leash off Sabel; find out if the Mediterranean was really warm enough to have sex in comfortably. It was a good list.

* * *

The funeral started off well enough, all the way up until Mack got up to deliver the eulogy. He looked bleary-eyed and pasty, and green enough that Ana knew his haggard appearance was more from drinking than crying.

Mack started by thanking the local folks who were there and saying how much their support had meant to his dad in his final months. "You all from the church, I know you were a godsend to my mom and that let Dad's heart rest light when he was in the hospital. He knew he wasn't coming out again when he went in that second time and it meant the world being able to see you all care for Mom.

"Dad always had a strong sense of family and community. I learned this working beside him these last few years. He always tried his best to do right by his people, even if the odds were against him."

In her seat, Ana ground her teeth and reminded herself that it was a eulogy and as such was supposed to be the good words about the dead. Never mind the years of her childhood during which her father never came home from the bar and when he did he was too far gone to help anyone in the family with anything. It was true about the odds though. One of those was his own alcoholism, but he'd also been undereducated in a poor town that didn't need any of his skills.

"Dad was loyal," Mack said. "He stuck by the church here and made it an important part of his life and he was always proud of his kids. He looked forward to news from the ones that moved away, even when it was scarce."

He glared at her as he delivered that last line. Ana tried not to take it personally. It was true she had moved away, not stayed in touch, not settled down to have kids, not made their father proud. As if she owed this family anything.

"He bore up," Mack went on. "He had a lot of challenges and he overcame them. I know some of you all think I'm the wild one of the family, but that's just because my sister never stuck around. She's the one who brought the cops to our house and Dad was ashamed of that for so long. It wasn't his fault he got unruly kids."

Ana wanted to get on her feet and ask him, if their father was so damned ashamed, why the hell Mack was bringing it up in the eulogy. But that would just peg her as being exactly as wild as Mack said she was. Her leg jiggled with pent-up energy, toes tapping frantically on the floorboards, and she pressed one hand on her knee to try to stop.

What is the wisdom in the heart of your anger? Abraxas asked.

Oh fuck the wisdom, Ana shot back internally. *Mack is just bitter because he never made anything of himself. He's trying to piss me off.*

He's doing a good job.
Shut up. You didn't have to grow up with him.

It wasn't even Mack's random bursts of anger that were the worst; it was the times in between when she sneaked around the house wondering when he'd catch her again and be in that mood and what he'd do. Though getting hit always made her furious, she could handle pain. It was the creeping, icy fear that she hated the most.

Once she got out of the house, she didn't even remember most of the incidents distinctly, only the worst of them. But she'd flinched when a girlfriend reached up to put away a dish because out of the corner of her eye, it looked like she was going to get hit. And then she had to explain and talk and try to bury her shame about being scared and try to sound like a good therapy graduate. At least with Sabel that never seemed to come up. She was sure Sabel had seen her flinch away once or twice, but she never showed it and she never asked.

Ana put her hand on the pew between her leg and Sabel's and felt Sabel entwine fingers with her and squeeze.

Mack went on speaking. "Whatever failings his kids had, I know Dad was happy to see his family all here with him again, real proud of his grandkid. As he got older, he told me he didn't care so much about money or fast cars, all he regretted was he didn't have more time with his family. Dad was a generous man, helped where he could, spent a lot of time and care with those who loved him."

Time with his family? Generous? Ana thought the rage in her gut would burn its way through her. It wasn't that these weren't true; in his later years he had been family-oriented and helpful. What pissed her off was the way Mack highlighted those features, not the other qualities—like her father's adventurous spirit and courage—that had been consistent even when he was drinking. Mack picked out the pieces meant to hurt her the most. It was like he was saying he got the father they all missed out on during the childhood years, implying she didn't deserve that father.

She felt the pain in her gut and chest. It was a mix of fury at Mack and the pain of loss, a strange feeling of being unanchored now that she'd lost a parent, even one who'd been troublesome. All the agony swirling around inside her reminded her of the attack from Ashmedai from inside her own mind and she wondered if she could get outside of it in the same way.

Ana took a few long breaths to steady herself and then stepped back mentally out of her body and looked at herself and the mass of feeling inside her. From a distance she saw it as colors and temperatures, varying from red to black and from very hot to a cold that also burned. She felt numb now, disconnected, and she welcomed it. Let Mack say whatever he wanted to now, she was well beyond his reach.

Your emotions are not the enemy, Abraxas said, but she ignored him.

CHAPTER NINE

From the funeral to the bus was a whirlwind of activity. Sabel watched Ana struggle through a goodbye with her mother, Mack nowhere to be seen, while Lily and Brie got all their luggage together. By the time they were settled on the bus, Sabel wanted to relax back into the seat. But she couldn't stop feeling on edge now that the time had come to deliberately be the bait for Ashmedai.

She and Ana were in two seats near the back of the bus with Lily and Brie across the aisle. They'd chosen the back so they could watch closely anyone else who got on. Already the bus was half-full with the kinds of people you'd expect on a Saturday evening: college kids going back to school in time to hit the Saturday night parties, a mother and her two children, a drunk asleep against the window with his hat pulled down over his eyes, two rough-looking guys probably headed to where they'd heard there was work, and a couple on vacation from the looks of their camera bags.

Next to her, Ana stared out the window. She seemed muted since the funeral. Sabel couldn't tell if she was trying to keep her temper regarding Mack or if she had steeled herself against grief so she wouldn't break down. Or maybe she just didn't grieve her father that much. Sabel held mixed feelings about her own parents, though she knew that when they were finally gone from her life and her own timestream she would mourn them. Still, it was never easy to spend time with them in their two-dimensional world of social status and family loyalty.

Across the aisle, Brie had her head back against the headrest with her eyes closed. She looked like a dark angel and her burnished skin glowed with an inner light. Sabel wondered how soft her lips would feel and shook herself. She reached across the aisle and touched Brie's arm.

"You were going to tell me what you did that reset the leash," Sabel reminded her.

Brie's eyes opened and focused on her. "I figured the leash was using the information level of things to scan for demon intrusion. I think it's the same way you can feel if I'm pushing you."

"Not always," Sabel said.

"I'm not always pushing," Brie replied with a coy smile.

Sabel blushed and mentally kicked herself.

Brie continued her explanation. "I'm not going to say this right, because I forget all the fancy ways witches have to describe how the world works, but basically the leash gets triggered if something comes at you with strong emotion or force magic, which almost all demons do, especially if they're trying to possess someone. Humans are pretty vulnerable to it."

"Makes sense," Sabel said.

"I skipped that way in and came in via the life force itself. Once I was in and matching your life force, I just sparked you up to see if it would trigger. But it didn't. Since it came from inside of you, the leash recognized it as you. So I used that method to send an all clear signal showing the leash that you were safe and relaxed, and that reset it."

It made perfect sense and it was one of the most frightening things Sabel had ever heard described—the idea that Brie, as a demon, could simply walk past all those carefully constructed defenses and blend in as if she were part of Sabel's energy body.

Brie must have seen the fear on her face because she reached across the aisle and put a gentle hand on her leg. "Almost no demons can do that," she said. "You need a body you're born with or you won't know how, and you need to be able to tap the life force. I've never met another demon who could do both."

"How did you learn to do it?" Sabel asked, incredulous.

From the other side of Brie, Lily leaned into the conversation. "That's a complicated question," she said.

A look passed between her and Brie and Sabel understood that Lily didn't want the Hecatine witches to know the answer. She filed it away for future investigation. It was beginning to make sense to her why Josefene had sent her and Ana on this trip. From the witches' perspective, it probably wasn't so much about protecting Ana as it was to gather information about Brie. Though maybe for Josefene it was both equally. She was more than capable of meeting varied motives at the same time. And Sabel knew Josefene liked the idea of she and Ana together, at least as long as she didn't think too much about the presence of Abraxas—but then Sabel often felt the same way.

Sabel changed the topic. "You think Ashmedai will try to take Ana before we get to Minneapolis? It's harder for him to come at her in any city, right? Even one not controlled by the Sangkesh."

"I hope so," Lily said and laughed, but the sound had no humor in it, just a release of tension. "You understand about cities in the Unseen World?"

"They're big, rambling, magical versions of cities in the material world, rooted in that same place. Each city in the Unseen World is ruled over by a faction that also has power in the material version of that city."

"Exactly," Lily said. "The Sangkesh demons hold San Francisco. They don't hold Minneapolis."

"Who does?"

"A god or maybe many gods."

From over her shoulder came Abraxas's voice, whispered from beside Ana: "Which gods?"

"Well, that's the strange thing. The god or gods of Minneapolis are hidden, no one I've asked knows who it is, but the power is apparent, and I've heard that it's powerful enough that other gods tend to gravitate toward the city," Lily said. "We should be safer there, and Ashmedai must know that, so his best bet is to get us out here on the road."

The next two hours passed smoothly. Sabel let the motion of the road lull her into a doze while Abraxas and Lily talked about magic and Ana chatted with Brie about movies and television. She woke up because she heard Brie gasp in alarm.

One of the passengers was standing and coming down the aisle toward them. When they'd gotten on the bus, he had looked like a drunk, sleeping it off with his hat over his face. Now, with the hat pushed back, she saw the small dark eyes and narrow chin of Ana's brother, Mack. He made his way, sure-footed, down the aisle of the bus and dropped into the empty seat in front of Brie.

She smiled, though Sabel saw the flicker of horror in her eyes before her flirtatious mask came down. "Hey baby," she said. "What are you doing here?"

"I wanted to see you again," he said. His voice was clear and that startled Sabel as much as the first sight of him. He looked like a drunk because he was wearing jeans and a crumpled shirt that stank of cigarettes and booze. He must have put on old bar clothes to disguise himself. He hadn't been sleeping it off in the front of the bus; he'd planned all of this sober and had waited for his moment.

He was still talking to Brie, "I know there's something between us and you feel it too. You took me home the other night, I remember that. I don't remember if anything happened. I think it didn't, but you wanted it like I did, I know."

Brie touched his cheek, still clean-shaven from the funeral. "It's not our time, baby. I've got a flight to catch."

"I got some time off work. I can come with you. Then we have time."

Brie's smile sweetened, but her eyes looked over-wide with fear. "Maybe," she said.

"Hi Mack," Ana said pointedly, her voice hard with anger.

"Hey," he said but didn't even turn to look at her.

"Is he possessed?" Ana asked Lily.

Mack laughed. "Good one."

Abraxas must have answered her silently because she nodded to herself. Sabel raised an eyebrow and Ana shook her head. So he was just under Brie's spell like the rest of them.

"How far?" Lily asked.

"Less than an hour," Ana said. "We're just past Belle Plaine. That was the last stop before the Cities." She didn't add that Mack must have known there was no chance of him being put off the bus for the next half hour.

"So, big guy," Brie purred at Mack. "Tell me about yourself. I hear you're good with your hands. What's the last bike you worked on?"

He began regaling her with tales of rebuilt engines and Brie kept pace with him. Sabel wondered, with a sick lurch, if Brie read motorcycle magazines just to seduce men, and if so, what else did she keep up on? Did she have real interests or did she only siphon hobbies from the most popular among her prey?

She leaned closer to Ana. "I'm sorry he's here. We'll get rid of him at the bus depot."

Ana shook her head. "Idiot," she said, but she didn't elaborate.

For the next few minutes the only sound in the back of the bus was Brie and Mack's light banter. Then, from the front of the bus, leather creaked and a chain rattled as three guys stood up. Two were dressed in biker leathers and the third in plain jeans. They'd all gotten on at Belle Plaine but looked completely uninterested in doing anything but talking about what they were going to do that weekend.

"All right," one of them said loudly. "Don't nobody move, this here's a hijacking. But we ain't no terrorists or nothing, so nobody act up and you won't get hurt."

They had guns. The closest to the front pointed his at the driver and the other two just held theirs pointed down at the floor. A mother sitting near them clutched her two kids close, and one of the college kids looked like he was going to pass out.

"Nice," Lily said bitterly. "He hired humans. We've got to get away from the passengers and away from these guys so no one gets hurt who isn't supposed to."

The one holding the gun at the driver told him to turn off on the highway onto a smaller side street.

"Where are we going?" Sabel yelled up to him.

But her question was answered as the bus turned onto the street and the farmland they'd been driving through gave way to trees. Some kind of state park, she guessed.

"Good enough," Lily said. "Let's not let them take us where he wants. Let's get out and find a place we can fight from. We're going out the back. Sabel, you have to take Mack."

"What?" Mack gaped at her.

Lily ignored him and kept talking to Sabel. "Keep him from getting hurt when he falls. The rest of us are tougher. Ana, get the emergency door."

Lily stood up and Brie stepped into the aisle. She moved toward the men near the driver, swaying with the motion of the bus.

"Sit down!" the nearest yelled.

"Oh, now don't be like that," Brie said. She flipped her hair loose around her shoulders and let her blouse fall open to show considerable cleavage. He stared at her, clearly not immune to her charm.

Ana slid out of her seat and ran, crouching, to the back of the bus and the emergency door. She cranked the lever and shoved it open.

"Brie!" Mack shouted and started up the aisle toward her. Lily lurched forward to grab him. Mack hit her in the ear, but she had her arms around his chest and dragged him backward. He tried to turn to hit her again and she rolled with him, bringing him facedown in the aisle. Sabel knew how strong Lily was, but would it be enough to carry Mack to the emergency exit while he struggled?

She spoke softly to herself using the Voice. *Strengthen*, she commanded and power flowed through her body.

She grabbed Mack's right arm while Lily took the left. He swore and writhed between them. If they hadn't been able to brace between the seats while they dragged him, he might have gotten off a good kick.

"Just throw him," Sabel told Lily as they approached the open door. "I can catch him."

"Are you sure?"

"Do you care?"

Asphalt sped by, rolling out behind the bus in an impenetrable, dark gray ribbon. Sabel didn't relish hitting it at any speed, but Lily was right to pick her to slow Mack's fall.

"I don't want to have to carry him if he breaks something," Lily said.

"I can catch him. Throw."

They both braced and hauled Mack to standing. Then Lily half threw and half shoved, and Sabel jumped with him, still holding on to his arm.

She stuttered out of time to look at where they were: five feet above the ground, moving about thirty miles an hour, Mack mid-flail, her body tightly aligned but hanging on to him. In her mind's eye, she sketched out the area she'd need to slow to keep them from getting hurt. To make sure, she extended it farther than she needed. Speed is distance over time, she reminded herself so slow time and she would slow speed. A factor of six should put them falling at about five miles per hour if her math was decent. That was doable.

She fixed the range in her awareness and the degree to which she needed to slow them. In addition, she ramped up her willpower because she was going to need to force this magic onto Mack, who would naturally resist it. Because it was invisible to him, she had a pretty good chance of making it work. Worst case it failed for him and he broke something—though she didn't relish the idea of having to carry a broken Mack anywhere.

When she snapped back into time, she had to slow it immediately, so she prepared everything and then let the present moment crash in on her. Fast turned to slow, but it still was a fall and now it included twenty seconds of tumbling through the air waiting for the ground to come up and smack her. She let go of Mack, tucked in and rolled just before she hit the asphalt. It still hurt, but on the level of modest bruising and a scrape across the outside of her left hand, nothing serious.

She pushed up to sitting. Her roll had carried her to the grass at the edge of the two-lane road. Mack was in the middle of the road on his hands and knees. He looked even less willing to stand up than she felt. She took a few more breaths and felt through her body again, making sure she hadn't seriously twisted or broken anything. Then she stood up and walked to Mack.

"Mack," she said. "You're in the road."

He looked up. A stream of blood ran down the side of his face, but his eyes seemed clear and focused on her easily.

"Fuckin' crazy bitch," he said.

She resisted the urge to kick him in the mouth. "Shut up and walk, you ungrateful prick. We just saved your life."

"You got a mouth on you," he said, but he got to his feet without insulting her again.

"You have no idea."

She walked away from him, along the side of the road, in the direction the bus had gone, trusting him to keep up with her. Ana, Lily and Brie must have jumped out a little farther along and shouldn't be hard to find if they stayed to the side of the road, where she'd be able to spot them.

She hoped Ana was okay. Her time slowing should have been saved for Ana, not her asshole brother, but Sabel understood that because he was the only person in the group without magic, someone had to look after him. Abraxas had done a decent job of protecting Ana the time Sabel accidentally threw her through a plate glass window, so hopefully that also worked with a jump from a moving vehicle.

Mack caught up with her. "That was a good fall," he said. "You didn't get hurt either?" His brain had already explained away the few seconds of magic, the way most modern brains could.

"Magic," Sabel said shortly. She paused and looked around, thinking they'd come far enough up the road.

"Over here," Lily called from a clump of trees.

Mack ran in her direction and Sabel wasn't far behind. She was so relieved to see Ana's bright hair in the shelter of the trees that she could have cried. Ana touched her cheek and then pulled her into a rough hug.

"You're okay?" she whispered.

Sabel nodded. "You?"

"Physically solid," Ana said and didn't elaborate. When they broke the hug, she kept one arm around Sabel's waist and Sabel leaned into her.

"Where's Brie?" Mack asked.

"She's leading the gunmen on a chase to somewhere they'll be safe. Don't worry about her. We've got to get somewhere we can fight from." Lily pointed at the sky where over the road dark shapes circled, too large for crows but close enough in size to be mistaken for birds by any casual observer. "Brie can handle the boys, but there are scores of sentries that followed the bus and somewhere in these woods, there's Ashmedai."

As she talked, Sabel heard the sentries wheeling above, crying out their location. Lily sniffed the air and pointed into the trees. "North, water. That'll work in our favor. Let's go."

Sabel was glad to see that Ana had grabbed Sabel's satchel, since her hands had been full with Mack. Along with her computer and a book, it held a large bottle of water and a couple of protein bars. Sabel slung it over her less-sore left shoulder and followed Lily and Ana. Mack took up the rear, still looking around for Brie.

"How will she find us?" he asked.

"First we need a defensible place for her to come to," Lily said. "Then we'll find a way to bring her in."

"How's she going to hold out against three guys? We gotta go help her," Mack insisted.

Lily rounded on him. Somewhere in the tussle and flight, she'd taken the caps off her teeth or lost them, and when she snarled at Mack her mouth was full of point-sharp teeth. "Run with us or away from us, but delay us and I will tear you apart," she snarled.

"Holy fuck! What the—"

Lily set off through the trees at a steady walk. Sabel pulled away from Ana for a moment and got Mack's attention.

"She's part demon," she told him, waving in the direction of Lily. "And your sister is hosting another demon. I need you to understand that, to believe it completely. If you can't do that yourself, I'll make you."

"Screw you," he said. "I know about demons."

"No, you don't," Sabel said.

"You don't know me."

"You just believe everything that's about to happen and then tell me if you know demons," Sabel shot back at him. "But I won't have your incredulity fucking up our magic."

"I don't think he knows what that word means," Ana said from behind her.

"Oh, fuck you both," Mack said and hurried to catch up to Lily. Sabel heard him ask her to show him her teeth again and she relaxed a little. If he was able to handle the magical aspects of what was about to happen, that would be one less thing for their side to deal with.

She zipped her jacket all the way up and kept pace with Ana's longer strides.

* * *

Brie didn't want to admit to herself how much she enjoyed the chase. She waited on the bus until the others were safely off. The three men wouldn't shoot her, she knew that, and after a minute of confusion they broke their line and came down the aisle to grab her.

"If you catch me, you can have me," she teased, sing-song, and jumped out the back. She'd wanted to land on her feet, but hadn't fully accounted for the momentum transfer between the moving bus and the unmoving pavement. Neither had her pursuers. They all ended up rolling on the pavement, though Brie had managed a judo roll and came out the better for it. She dusted herself off and waited for them to get to their feet.

Now they might start shooting at her, but they didn't. One came slowly toward her, hands out like he was trying to tame an animal.

"No," she told him. "I said you had to catch me." And then she was off through the trees.

At times in her strange life she couldn't tell if she was being cruel or not. Like now. These three men had been willing to hijack a bus and turn her friends over to a demon for money, but was it justice or malice to lead them into the woods like this? They weren't dressed for the weather, but hopefully she could leave them close enough to a town that they wouldn't freeze. They were certainly safer out here than they would be if they'd gone with Ana and Lily into a fight with who knows how many demons.

She led the chase for a good twenty minutes through the trees, always staying close enough that they could see her, and often calling back over her shoulder to taunt them. As she ran, she tried to recall the map she'd looked at on the bus. She remembered seeing the park land in green and the road ran to the east of it, so she continued in that direction until she started seeing the larger highway on the far side of the trees. These weren't men known to her or anyone she knew, and so she could treat them as she wished, but her wishes didn't include killing them.

She came into a clearing at the base of a hill and knew it was a good place. Ducking behind a tree, she shucked her clothes and stepped into the open just as they broke cover, her naked skin gleaming in the early dusk. She didn't feel the cold at all. The chase and the prospect of feeding warmed her thoroughly.

"Oh my God," one of them breathed. "Are you real?"

Brie walked up to him and stroked his chest with her palms. "What do you think?"

"I think you're some kind of crazy nymphomaniac," he said. "But I'm not complaining."

"Isn't it a little more wild out here?" she asked.

He nodded.

"Are you going to fuck me or what?"

That got the three of them out of their pants in a heartbeat. Was it cruel? she wondered. She could see she had their attention and moved from one to the other, kissing them for a moment, tasting their energy, touching their cocks until they were completely under her thrall. Brie felt she never really knew a man until she'd held his cock in her hand, and now she knew volumes about these three.

One was charismatic and too smart for his own good; he played the ringleader and if he'd made it through college he'd have been a great manager. The second was a straight-up hothead with no control of his temper other than his pot habit. The third was predominately gay and fighting it. Poor guy. She'd do him last so he could watch the other guys. Rural South Dakota was not the right place for him. Maybe after tonight he'd decide it was worth it to move to a big city.

She took Ringleader first on the gentle slope of the hill, wet grass cold on her back. He couldn't believe she was willing, Brie saw, but at least he wasn't disappointed about it. Men who wanted their partners fighting and trying to escape gave her the creeps. He tried to last more than a few minutes, but she dug her fingernails into his back and he spent himself with a cry. She could always tell what guys liked once they were inside her.

Hothead was jerking himself off and she shouted at him, "Hey, you don't touch yourself unless I say you can."

His mouth fell open. For punishment, she knelt at his feet and worked his cock with fingers and tongue, always stopping just short of his completion. The ringleader was already asleep in the grass, a smile on his lips, and the third man watched in fascination, his attention more on his friend's cock than on Brie, but she didn't mind. She just liked to feel the surge of pleasure in them, no matter what fed it, and then at its apex to drink some off the top. She'd learned how much to take to induce a stupor but stop well short of coma or death, usually.

She turned from Hothead to the third man. If he was imagining it was his friend's lips on his cock instead of hers, well, he fed her all the same. By now Hothead was whining with need and Brie brought him off quickly.

All three were semiconscious. Brie dragged them next to each other, like logs, so they'd keep each other warm. They should be up again in a few minutes. She hadn't taken too much from any one of them. If they didn't panic, they'd realize they were at the edge of the woods, within sight of the road.

Her body felt luminous with their energy, as if she could fly up into the treetops. She wanted to linger over them, but often when she drank life from a person she saw into their memories as well. Both Ringleader and Hothead had memories of meeting with Ashmedai to set up the highjacking. It was in Brie's mind now, hazy in the details, but clear enough that she could see the dozens of figures behind Ashmedai in whatever dim warehouse space he'd picked for the meeting. He had more help than they thought. A lot more.

She had to get back to Lily, to Ana and Sabel, to warn them that they weren't prepared for what Ashmedai had coming. Brie threw her clothes back on, checked her buttons and zippers quickly and got her bearings, then set off at a quick jog to the northwest.

Her mother would find a way to get a signal to her, she just had to get near them. After jogging back to where they'd gotten off the bus, she spotted the dark swirl of sentries overhead. Well, that was one way to find them. If the sentries were on them, it wouldn't matter if they signaled to Brie. She whistled piercingly in the direction of the dark cloud.

An answering whistle came a little to the north. Brie followed it, whistling when she needed, and after a few hundred more feet of picking her way among the trees, she broke through into a river valley. On a short strand of beach, the other five had made camp.

Mack was sitting against a fallen tree, looking unwanted, and she wondered if he'd pissed off both Sabel and Lily as well as Ana. The three women were bent together over a cloth spread with items and a map. Ana wore Abraxas's sheen around her head and shoulders.

"Heyas," Brie called down. "I nixed the guys."

"Are they dead?" Ana asked.

"No." Brie spat the word. Ana should know she didn't just kill people if she could help it. "They're taking a nap. I led them back toward the road so they can get out of here okay."

Mack loped over to her. "You're all right?"

"Baby, I can take care of myself. You look like you took a tumble."

He laughed, a rusty sound. "Ain't the worst I've been, and better now you're here."

"Date night in the woods," Brie snorted. She looked at the items in front of her mother: salt, bitumen, coal, sticks of incense, a roll of cord. "That's not going to be enough," she said.

"How many more?" Lily asked, not showing a hint of alarm, ever pragmatic.

"Three or four times what you planned for," Brie told her.

Now the lines around her mother's eyes intensified and her mouth turned down, lips thinning. "Abraxas and I will come up with a new plan. You get Mack as battle-ready as you can. We're going to need him."

Mack stood next to her, a crust of dried blood on his scalp. He wasn't a bad guy to have on her side in a fight. He'd fight regardless, so better they had someone for him to fight lest he start to pick on Ana.

"She said demons," Mack said, jabbing his thumb toward Sabel, who was looking at one of Lily's books.

"Yep, lots of demons, little dark ones like birds and big scary ones. Anything you see that doesn't look like one of us, you pound on it. You good with that?"

"More than good. I'll watch your back."

"Thanks," Brie said and patted his arm. At least she wasn't hungry anymore.

CHAPTER TEN

Ana reminded herself that the last time she'd faced Ashmedai, it had been so much worse. She was unprepared, Gunnar had been captured and was on his way to his death, and Lily's freakishly fast and attractive daughter wasn't on the team yet. But still the icy edge of fear rubbed against her nerves. The middle of the woods was not her favorite showdown location and she didn't want to have Mack to deal with, much less protect. For all the times he'd carelessly hit her, it was hard to believe he would now fight on the same side.

Lily described the updated plan. They'd create a big magic circle on the ground that wasn't active and lure the sentries into it, then invoke it. That was the easy part. Brie said she'd take on Ashmedai himself, but he would be bringing other demons and maybe humans with him. The other five of them would have to deal with whatever crew he brought while Lily performed the ritual that would bind him into the book they'd prepared. If he had as much help as Brie said, they'd need to bind more than Ashmedai into the book.

Ana watched Sabel unroll a supple piece of leather to reveal a set of tiny knives, each one the size of a finger. They looked as fragile as Sabel did. Lily and Brie might be shorter, but they were solid. Not for the first time, Sabel's build reminded Ana of a graceful bird or a gazelle.

She looked up and caught Ana watching. "These aren't the weapon," she explained. "They're the focus for it."

Ana remembered Sabel lying unconscious on the ground after Ashmedai tried to possess her and triggered the leash. Ashmedai had started breaking Sabel's fingers to get Ana to attack him. Kneeling on the ground now, she wrapped her arms around Sabel, who pressed into her.

"I'll kill him before I let him touch you again," she whispered.

"Same here," Sabel replied. "We're going to be okay." But her voice wasn't as confident as her words and Ana felt her shiver. With the sun down below the level of the treetops, it was getting cold in the woods, and dim.

"When you're done, come sit with me," Ana told Sabel and left her with the little knives.

She found a sturdy tree, sat against the trunk, and tried to conserve her strength and warmth. For being thin, the olive jacket was surprisingly cozy and she had a second jacket over it. When Sabel came to sit between her knees and lean into her the body heat of the two of them was more than enough to push back the chill. Ana didn't want to start a fight with cold muscles, and really she wanted the comfort of holding Sabel. Luckily fear wasn't one of the strong emotions that triggered the leash, so they could sit together easily.

Where is the fear in your body? Abraxas asked.

Ana sighed at him. This fear was the first clear, uncomplicated emotion she'd had in the last few days, layered as they were with sadness, disappointment, anger, rage, hurt, jealousy, pain, tenderness and passion. Now he wanted to test her. She thought she'd look in her body and find no fear and he'd tell her in his wise voice that fear didn't exist. But when she sifted her awareness down into her torso she did find it. Her solar plexus was stuffed with a cold, nauseating energy that radiated up the sides of her ribs. Where her awareness touched it, she flinched away.

It's in my solar plexus, she told him, certain he already knew.

Is it cold or hot?

Cold, very cold.

Is it tight or loose? he asked.

It's tight, Ana said.

What color is it?

Yellow, I think, or kind of white and gold and whatever color electricity is.

Is it anywhere else in your body?

Ana scanned down to her feet and up to her head, lingering in her limbs, in her pelvis, feeling the inner spaces of her body. *No,* she had to admit, *it's only there.*

Good, go more deeply into it. What's the source of it?

That was a stupid suggestion. Why would she go further into a sensation so uncomfortable? But what else was there to do with the cold of the ground seeping up into her butt and the agonizing wait for a battle she both wanted and dreaded? She sank again into the whirl of sharp-edged discomfort. What was the source of it? She had no idea. Maybe if she knew what it was, she could trace it back to a place where she could block it.

Fear had an energy of a particular taste and density. She kept feeling its coldness, the sharp edges, the places it ran into her lungs. She touched its sides and then its core, pushing her way in deeper. Inside the mass of fear, for a second she had the sensation that she turned and looked back into herself and there was a bright gold window, open, streaming into her chest. The flow from that window wasn't painful or nauseating, it was cold and clear like a mountain river.

Clarity rushed up inside her and when it hit her palate, her senses opened wide and perceived Ashmedai coming through the trees a quarter-mile distant. Her heart leaped and she fell out of the clarity back into her sickening fear.

"He's coming," she said. "That way. We have about three minutes."

She and Sabel stood up. Ana lifted the heavy tree limb she'd picked out when they first settled on this area as the location where they would fight. Sabel had the set of tiny knives in her left hand with a single knife between the fingers of her right. Mack also wielded a tree branch. Lily had a handful of powder and more in a bag at her belt, and Brie was empty-handed.

Brie moved in the direction Ana pointed and waited there near the edge of the circle Lily had drawn in the ground. Flashlights appeared through the trees and a party of men broke through the near line of brush and stopped.

"Oh, good," the one in the lead said. "You'll fight."

Ana saw a flash of fire in his eyes and recognized Ashmedai. This newest body of his was a big man but rough-looking, not attractive like the two Drake brothers he'd previously commandeered. Ashmedai now had the bulbous nose of a chronic drinker and scabs on the backs of his huge hands. He must have grabbed this body in a rush, choosing it for its size and power. Who had sold it to him and at what price? Was the man in it already gone or had he bartered away his body for some promise of future freedom or wealth? If so, where was he?

With Ashmedai were men and dogs, none of them really human or canine. The eyes of the four dogs burned with red fire. One of the men looked sculpted from clay, like Abraxas's spare body; many other figures were little more than clouds of black smoke, and four had human-like faces with an expression Ana had never seen before on a human: idiocy crossed with cunning malice. It looked like the demons possessing those bodies didn't know that a facial expression was supposed to involve the mouth as well as the eyes. Over their heads, dozens of sentry creatures wheeled and shrieked.

"Come on in," Lily said and threw a handful of powder on the fire. A smell like burning tar filled the air and the men flinched.

"Thank you, I will," Ashmedai said. He moved quickly toward the side of the fire where Sabel was standing.

"Hi, hot stuff," Brie purred as she intercepted him. "Is that a real human body you're wearing? How tasty."

He turned to her and his tongue slipped out to lick his lips.

"Go!" Lily commanded, and Ana felt Abraxas rocket up out of the top of her head. He swirled up into the sky and the sentries chased him.

The men closed in. Mack ran at one and tackled him into the dirt, pounding him in the head with his fist even as they fell together. A dog leaped at him and Ana swung her branch like a bat. It connected with a jarring crunch.

She tried to follow Sabel's motion, to make sure she was safe, but her darkly dressed body flickered like a shadow. It looked like she was running through trees, even in the clearing, where there weren't any. She moved next to one of the black smoke figures and spoke a word Ana couldn't hear. It vanished.

That was effective. Maybe she could spend less time worrying about Sabel and more time—she swung at the next dog to come at her and hit it a glancing blow. It turned and came back at her.

"You shouldn't have done that," it said with perfect clarity through its thin, black canine lips.

"I prefer Disney's talking dogs," Ana snarled back and swung again.

It flattened under the arc of the wood and launched itself at her face. She dropped toward the ground before it could hit, but claws raked her shoulder. Did it have cat claws? That was so against nature. She spun to face it, but Mack threw a leg over it from behind and grabbed its head in his hands. He twisted it sickeningly until the neck cracked. He was grinning like a boy at an auto rally as he threw the body aside and lunged at another demon in a human body.

A second man closed on him, but he seemed perfectly happy so Ana turned to find Lily struggling in the arms of the giant clay man. Two dogs snapped at her feet and she alternately kicked out and squirmed away. Ana ran toward her and saw that she was also drawing letters on the skin of the clay man as he held her in what had to be a crushing grip.

Ana batted the first dog back from Lily. The second froze in place with a small silver knife sticking out of its shoulder.

Ana reminded herself these weren't real dogs and brought the branch down on its head.

Lily completed a line of letters across the clay figure's forehead and it stopped moving. Slowly it tipped backward and shattered on the ground. Lily climbed out of the broken clay and dust, rubbing her hands on her jeans to clean them. She would start the greater binding that would place Ashmedai in the book as soon as they had the smaller demons bound and banished.

Above them, Abraxas flew in figure eights until all the sentries pursued him and then dove back down into Ana. For a moment she was engulfed in blackness, a hundred sharp beaks tearing at her, and then Lily shouted and the circle snapped into place around them. Pungent herbs danced in the fire and as one the sentries screamed and vanished.

Ana spun around to see who still needed help. Mack was holding his own. He had one man unmoving at his feet and the other circling him warily, fists up. Was it overconfidence that they didn't bring guns or did Ashmedai want to make sure they were alive? Probably both. He did seem to like to toy with her.

Lily was in her place by the fire, holding the book open in her hands, chanting. Sabel stepped in and prevented another of the smoke figures from descending on her. Another of the men was closing on her, so Ana charged him and tackled him to the ground. His head hit a stone with a loud thud which spared her the trouble of knocking him out. She rolled and looked for another target.

The shadowy forms were gone, most of the men and dogs were down, Brie still had Ashmedai's attention and they appeared to be wrestling on the far side of the fire. Lily was halfway through the incantation. Other than the fact that Ashmedai was still moving, it looked good.

There, look! Abraxas formed words in her mind and at the same time grabbed control of her body and turned her head toward the trees.

More figures moved toward them. Many more. That's why Ashmedai didn't bring guns—he had a small army. This was what Brie had warned them about.

"Lily!" Ana yelled and scrambled back, looking for a better weapon than a tree branch.

Lily finished a phrase and looked up. Her eyes narrowed. She looked from the advancing mass back to Ashmedai and then to the other demons. They came out of the trees, dozens of black-smoke creatures and blurred human and animal parts seemingly at random.

Lily turned toward them and held the book out so its open pages faced them. She shouted words Ana didn't understand.

Creatures were sucked forward into the pages. First just a few, then more, then over two dozen had been bound in the book. The pages flipped furiously. Lily's arms shook as she struggled to hold the book out to capture more of them.

The book's covers erupted into flames. Lily yelped and dropped it.

"Do the rest by hand," she shouted.

Sabel slipped up next to Ana and put a slender knife in her hand. "Drive it in until the thing vanishes," she said and moved away.

Lily had a set of longer knives and tossed one to Mack. That was the last thing Ana could focus on before the creatures were on them. She lunged at the nearest and drove the knife deep into its neck. As it dissolved, another grabbed her and she spun into it, stabbing as hard as she could. It was like trying to stab through thick tar, but when she got far enough in, its grip on her faded.

She made it through another and then got kicked in the shoulder and spun around. It hit her again and she stumbled across the clearing only to trip over one of the downed bodies and land hard on her wrist. She rolled over expecting to see the thing bearing down on her, but it was gone. Sabel gave her a wink from the empty space where it should have been and stepped away, stuttering across the open clearing toward the creatures pressing Lily.

By the time Ana was on her feet, those were gone as well and there were only two left. Then she spotted Brie and Ashmedai on the ground by the fire. He had Brie pinned under his huge body and was thrusting at her—Ana blinked hard—was raping her. Brie was screaming over and over, a raw, wild sound more like a battle cry than a howl of pain.

Ashmedai yelled in triumph, but the sound choked midbreath. He gasped, eyes wide, bulging, mouth working the air like a fish out of water. His hands let go of Brie's body and grabbed at his chest and throat. The skin of his face went from reddish to purple and then blue.

He fell forward over Brie and didn't move.

Brie clawed at the ground, trying to get out from under him. Ana ran to her, braced her feet solidly and heaved at Ashmedai's body. The dead weight rolled over twice from the force of her shove and ended up staring blankly at the sky.

"I'll destroy him. Find him, I'll destroy him," Brie was panting with fury.

Her blouse and bra had been torn open and bloody gashes marked her arms, chest and shoulders. Her pants were shredded in a pile between her and the dead body.

Ana took off her outer jacket. Brie saw her approaching and scrambled backward across the ground. Ana knew the feeling of panic and not wanting to be touched. She crouched and moved slowly toward her, holding out the jacket like an offering.

Brie's backward motion stopped when she hit the corpse of one of the men. In the fading light, her skin shimmered with a golden fire and gave off wisps of energy like steam. Ana wanted to wrap her up and take care of her, never let anything hurt her again. She wanted to touch every part of her and assure her she was all right. Her fingers brushed Brie's shoulder as she went to wrap the jacket around her and desire overwhelmed her. A moment ago she'd been in pain, disgusted, furious, and now she held only burning passion. Brie knew it too, her eyes locked on Ana's and her hand came up behind Ana's neck to pull her close into a kiss.

Brie's lips touched her everywhere as soon as they touched her mouth. Hot silk rested on her skin inside and out, the delicate pleasure against her own lips so intense that all her attention fled there and spilled over into Brie. She needed to be inside this other body, everything would be good forever if she could pour herself into Brie. She was falling forward into her, but some small corner of her mind knew it wasn't right.

Behind and above she heard Lily's shout, jagged with terror, and much too late, "Don't *touch* her!"

CHAPTER ELEVEN

Abraxas caught Ana from the inside, trying to pull her back toward her center. But if she could get into Brie it would be paradise forever. She could only pause, halt her forward motion and hang suspended between the two. Abraxas had hold of her, but he couldn't pull her back into her body, in part because she didn't want to go.

She tried to do what Abraxas had showed her with her fear, to go deeply into the sensation of Brie's lips on hers, how when they moved a fraction they spoke volumes of love poetry that went right to the base of her and lit her up from the inside with a glow of unsurpassed sweetness. What was all that? Where did it come from? Was it hot or cool? Where exactly did she feel it in her body?

She was on the surface now, suspended between her body and Brie's, no longer falling but not quite back to herself. It was too hard to go back, but she could stay here. She put her awareness down at that fire in her belly and kissed back, curious what else these inhuman lips could show her.

From near her left ear, she heard Sabel's Voice imbued with its terrible power.

"*Stop feeding*," Sabel commanded.

The pull toward Brie ended so abruptly that Ana snapped back into herself with physical force and landed on her butt. Lily had her hands around Brie's shoulders with white-knuckled strength, but it wasn't necessary now. Ana scrambled away a few feet and then touched her own lips gingerly with her fingers.

Having felt the full draw of Brie's power, she now understood how easily it was for her to kill someone and how happily they would agree to die for her. Terror and desire mixed sickeningly in her gut. Part of her still wanted to crawl across the space between them and kiss her again despite the danger.

As Ana stared at Brie with a maelstrom of feeling, Brie's gaze was fixed on Sabel's face and her lips parted in an "O" of wonder and surprise.

"Thank you," she breathed. She put a palm flat across her own lower belly. "You stopped me."

Sabel didn't seem to know how to react to that. Her face was an icy mask, tension showing in the iron set of her jaw. Fury coiled in the gray depths of her eyes and her chest rose and fell quickly. For all her careful control, Sabel was livid.

"Get away from her," Sabel grated in a low voice that carried no magic but plenty of power.

Brie pulled away from Lily and stood up so she could step farther away from Ana, but as she rose, Ana saw the tears gathering in her eyes. Brie turned away before they fell and walked toward the river.

From behind her Ana heard the sound of a body being moved and Mack's surprised, "Shit, you killed him with his pants down."

Lily got up and went in his direction. Ana didn't know how she was going to explain to Mack what Brie had done.

Sabel touched the side of Ana's face and turned her head gently so she could look into Ana's eyes. Her fingers quivered against Ana's cheek. Sabel's whole body was shaking.

"You all in there?" Sabel asked.

"I'm okay," Ana told her, hoping the words conveyed everything she didn't know how to say yet. Some part of her body and mind understood what had happened, but it wasn't the conscious part that connected to her ability to speak. She put her hand over Sabel's and pressed the palm hard against her cheek. She wanted to grab her and hold so tightly their bones creaked, but she was afraid of triggering the leash with all the magic in the air and in her body.

"Abraxas, is she…?" Sabel demanded.

"I was able to keep her from being consumed until you could break the draw of power," he answered from so close it sounded like he was talking in her ear.

"Thank you," Sabel said, and from the relief in her voice, Ana gathered he was definitely her favorite demon now and Brie was at the very bottom of the list.

She knew she should be more upset about what had happened. The lack of true fear for her own safety was disturbing. So this was what Sabel meant about Brie controlling emotions. She could have killed Ana and she would have only felt grateful to get to go into that glorious paradise of feeling.

To orient herself, she stood up and ran an inventory of her aches and pains. Her ass hurt from landing on it a minute ago, along with her pride. Her shoulders were sore, her wrist was pretty nearly sprained, and she had a half-dozen good bruises forming, plus the set of scratches across her back from the demon dog. Mack looked a lot worse. A black eye was starting to swell and a trail of blood ran from his nose to meet a similar streak coming from the corner of his mouth. He tried to go to Brie, who was now naked in the river and still facing away from all of them, but Lily bared her teeth at him and he backed away.

Mack went to the body nearest him and started searching it, pulling out weapons and anything else that looked useful. The clearing was scattered with bodies. A human-like creature lay near her with its head caved in from a series of blows. Two others were facedown in the dirt, and the last of them lay on its back with its lifeless eyes staring upward and no sign of damage on its body. There was also the body that Ashmedai wore into the fight, now blue-gray-skinned and cold with its pants around its thighs and no mark on him.

"What happened?" Ana asked, unsure if she was asking about him or about herself.

Lily shook her head. "There's no way he should have had access to that many demons at that level of power. The little sentries I can understand, they're easy, but the others should not be following him. He's not destroyed either, he just has to find another body. The book...He'll be back. Maybe I can make another."

"Is she okay?" Ana gestured toward Brie. "It looked like he was raping her."

Lily gave Ana the narrow-eyed, are-you-stupid look. "Brie can't be raped, at least not the way humans can, you should know that by now."

"She can't?"

Sabel's fingers brushed her shoulder. "She's not like us," she said. "Sexual union is how she killed him, or killed his body at least."

Ana looked toward the river, where Brie's skin glowed golden in the dim light of the moon. Water steamed off her bare skin and it seemed that a small, private sun shone on her while the rest of them remained in night. Ana still wanted to go to her and kiss her again, but she shoved the impulse away.

"I thought she was panicking," Ana said. "Or upset, or something."

"It wasn't an easy fight," Lily said. "But when you touched her, she didn't have her power back under control yet."

"I noticed," Ana said.

Brie stepped out of the water. The bloody gashes on her skin were closing. The wounds looked as if they'd been inflicted days ago, not minutes. Abraxas moved inside Ana's body and sped the healing of her own wounds, but nothing near that fast. Since Brie was a demon born into a human body, was it a similar energy that worked for her? Brie pulled on the sweatshirt Lily put out for her and shrugged into the jeans taken off one of the bodies, belting them tightly around her waist and rolling up the cuffs since they were a few sizes too big.

Lily joined Mack in the task of going through the bodies and in a few minutes they had a variety of coats, weapons and other implements spread out on the ground. In silence, they took what they wanted and packed it into their bags or onto their person. Ana noticed that a few of the bodies were already starting to crumble into dust. By morning, would they all be gone?

They were more magic than material, Abraxas told her. *And the material world protects itself from excessive intrusion by the Unseen...*

She interrupted him. *So yes, they'll be gone.*

Essentially, yes.

"You okay?" Ana asked Mack while they reassembled their bags with the additional items.

For the first time in...ever, she might be feeling something positive for him. Maybe respect or even a smidgeon of gratitude.

He shrugged and grinned at her. "This is some crazy shit."

When Brie was dressed he went over to her and talked in a surprisingly soft voice. Ana couldn't hear what they were saying, but Brie smiled at him and touched his cheek. The pang of jealousy she felt surprised Ana and she made herself stop watching them.

She turned to Lily. "That was a lot of demons," she said, which seemed more diplomatic than "What the fuck?"

"There is no way he had access to that on his own," Lily proclaimed. "He's found an ally, and one that's a lot more powerful than any ally he should've made. That first wave was a good showing for what he could reasonably drum up, but he just doesn't have the power for more—he doesn't have enough to offer."

"It's freezing," Sabel said. "Let's get going and figure this out when we're warm."

When they were out of sight of the clearing, heading northeast on the far side of the river, everyone seemed to relax. Mack retold his part in the battle to Brie, in excruciating detail, and Brie kept asking leading questions to prolong the conversation. Ana still hated watching them, but at least she didn't have to talk to Mack.

Abraxas went up to talk to Lily, leaving Ana and Sabel at the back of the quiet procession through the freezing night in the forest. Ana curled her fingers around Sabel's hand and felt Sabel's grip tighten around her fingers in response.

"Should I apologize for kissing her?" Ana asked.

"I doubt you could have helped that," Sabel said.

"I really understand what you mean about her ability to alter emotions now."

"Do you understand how close you came to dying? I couldn't get to you fast enough. If you didn't have Abraxas, you'd be lying on the ground back there right now too."

Ana thought about how Ashmedai's body died: clutching his chest with his face turning blue.

"Like a heart attack?" she asked.

"In the sense that your heart just stops, yes. She can reach into your body and pull all the life force out of you. All of it. And then you die."

In the dark it was impossible to see clearly, but Ana thought she caught the glint of a tear on Sabel's cheek before she impatiently brushed her free hand across her face.

Sabel continued quietly, "I have been trained for years to work with magic. I started when I was twelve. You've had Abraxas for just over six months. You scare me." She paused and the last words came out nearly inaudibly. "I almost killed her. I can't lose you."

Ana lifted Sabel's hand and pressed her lips hard against the cold, smooth skin over her knuckles. There was so much she wanted to say, but this wasn't the place or the time.

"No more touching strange demons," she said. "I promise."

They continued in silence for a while, the sound of Lily's and Abraxas's voices ahead soothing. Then Lily started asking Mack questions about how much he knew about hand-to-hand fighting. Brie fell back to walk next to Ana.

"I'm so sorry," she told Ana. "I didn't realize it would be like that. I should have told you in advance not to touch me if something like that happened."

Ana wondered how much of her conversation with Sabel had been audible to Brie whose hearing was undoubtedly more acute than human normal.

"What did you think it would be like with a prince of demons?" Sabel's voice was pitched low and held an edge.

"I thought he'd pull away when I started feeding from him, not push in. That fucker thought he could overpower me."

"The sex was the whole fight?" Ana asked. "He was trying to overpower you through sex too?"

Brie looked over with her head cocked to one side. "How else would two demons of lust fight each other? Slap fight?"

Ana laughed. Sabel didn't.

"He didn't really understand what I am," Brie said. "Well, to be fair, neither do I. Or most of the other demons. Almost all of the succubi are disembodied. If I didn't have a body, he'd have overpowered me easily. Even if I had a body I'd taken instead of being born with it. But he didn't realize that by being in a body he made himself more vulnerable to me. He just poured so much damn fire into me, I was out of control. I think he was trying to burn me out of my own skin. He's got a lot more inner fire than I do, maybe more than I could have taken in if he hadn't been in a human body. It was so much I couldn't think, all I could do was draw everything in as hard as I could."

"Including Ana," Sabel said.

"That was an accident. I just couldn't turn it off. I was trying to back away."

"I thought you were panicking," Ana said.

"Oh, I was. Just not for the reason you thought."

Ana remembered how it felt to have Ashmedai in her mind—his enormous presence grinding through everything she thought was hers. It wasn't the same for Brie, but she could understand somewhat the state that Brie must have been in as she killed his body.

"Thank you for taking him on so I didn't have to," she told Brie.

Brie grinned. "I'll kill him again if we get a chance."

"I'll be happy to let you."

The night sounds closed in around them. An owl hooted and night birds called out their territories. Their feet snapped branches and crackled the fallen leaves.

"May I ask," Brie said to Sabel, and hesitated. Then went on, "What's the power you used to stop me?"

Sabel was silent for so long that Ana wondered if she would answer the question. Then she said, "The witches call it the *marevaas*, the 'powerful voice' or 'dangerous voice,' depending on how you translate it."

"Did you learn it?"

"The talent for it is innate and then you learn first how to control it and second how to use it."

"It's fast," Brie said. "But it doesn't last."

"No, thankfully. If it's aligned with what a person would naturally do, it can last a few hours or more. If you're tired and I tell you to sleep, you'll likely transition into a natural sleep as it wears off. But if you're dead set against something, I can only force you for a few seconds. Long enough."

"I wanted to stop, I just couldn't. You don't know what that's like, do you? There's nothing in your life you can't stop doing."

Sabel didn't reply to that, but Ana knew Brie was right. After a while, Brie left them and walked back up to the front of the group.

"She's the most dangerous one," Sabel said.

"Of the three of us?" Ana asked.

Sabel stopped walking and gestured back the way they'd come. "Of everyone in that clearing. Everyone."

She started walking again. Ana held her hand tightly as they made their way through the trees.

* * *

By the time they came out of the woods and followed a one-lane track to a paved road, Sabel's chest was crossed with ribbons of pain. In the fight, she'd stuttered through time as much as she could to keep the heavy demon energy from triggering the leash to the point where it would knock her out, but now it was tight and burning against her ribs. There had been so much demon energy in the clearing it was impossible for it not to slowly constrict on her.

The temperature had been dropping steadily. Her toes felt like chunks of ice grating against each other inside her boots and she imagined there was a thin layer of frost over her skin. She was in a walking trance and the minute she sat down she knew she wouldn't be able to get up again.

Under the agonizing physical sensations, another pain pressed against her—the knowledge that she had nearly killed Brie. It was only at the last second that she'd changed to the command "stop feeding" rather than "stop breathing."

She leaned against a tree while Lily called them a cab. They'd just started getting cell phone service again. Ana looked at her, questions in her eyes, but Sabel shook her head. It was enough right now to focus on taking one breath after another. Finally, the cab appeared and pulled over to the side of the road. Sabel crawled onto the seat next to Ana, leaned into the back rest and Ana's shoulder, and passed out.

She woke to the sound of voices and the feeling of lying flat on an uneven but soft surface. Someone must have carried her from the cab to a couch or bed.

"What did it feel like?" Brie was asking.

"I was falling into your body," Ana said. "What did it feel like to you?"

Sabel kept her eyes closed and her breathing slow and even. Based on the distant sound of a highway and the stale smell of the room, she was in a hotel bed. And based on the fact that her toes were no longer made of ice, she'd been there for a while.

"Drinking," Brie told her. "Just drinking with my whole body. You're the only person I've ever felt resist and pull away from me inside. Was it the demon in you?"

"Partly," Ana said. "He steadied me and then I did some of the techniques he taught me and I found I could balance between the two of us."

"Damn, think you could do that again?"

There was a long silence in the room. Sabel barely managed to not hold her breath while she waited to hear the answer.

"Is it going to happen again?" Ana asked. Her voice sounded cautious.

"I never get to have sex with anyone who can resist me. Do you think she'd enjoy a threesome?"

Sabel didn't have to open her eyes to know that Brie was pointing at her. The awful part was how much she liked the idea. Ever since Brie sat her on the bed and ran that tremendous burst of sexual energy through her body, she'd wanted to do it again. She craved it and she hated that feeling. The craving only abated for the short time when she'd watched Brie nearly kill Ana. Then her anger had obliterated all other feelings. How could Brie, and Lily for that matter, have brought Ana into this situation saying they were protecting her and neglect to tell her the simplest steps to keep herself safe? They seemed to take it for granted that she should know these things when she just didn't.

Sabel tried to control the unruly feelings in her body. She heard the creak of a chair and the soft brush of Ana's feet on the carpet as she paced across the room and back again, the way she did when she was troubled.

"The leash," Ana said.

"I can hold it open."

"Can you get it off her?"

"I can try," Brie said. "I don't want to destroy it. It's no good to me if I can't wear it."

"Maybe if you ask nicely the witches will make you one."

Brie laughed. "That's not a bad idea. I've done better with witches than with the Sangkesh."

"They were that bad?"

"They starved me just to see what would happen. They don't see me as a real person. I mean the Sangkesh demon hunters, not the ones like my mom. The one time the demon hunters caught me, they put me in a cage and just let me sit with food and water that was useless to me and watched while I got colder and colder inside. After a while, every time I moved I could feel that it took energy away that my heart and brain needed. I started going in and out of awareness and every time I woke up, I felt my body fighting to keep living, but I couldn't do anything."

"Someone rescued you?" Ana asked.

"That was later. First they threw a criminal in with me, some guy they thought didn't deserve to live."

"Oh, shit."

A heavy silence filled the room and then Brie said in a whisper, "I killed him. It was fast. And then they started the whole thing again."

"I'm sorry," Ana said.

"It was years ago," Brie told her. For a while neither of them spoke and then Brie said wistfully, "Can I touch her?"

"Not unless she tells you that you can."

Sabel opened her eyes and sat up. She was in a queen bed in a shabby hotel room decorated in faded eggplant and tan colors. Brie sat in the armchair by the window, the farthest seat away from the bed. Ana was standing between the bed and the television, where she'd been pacing the length of the room. She sat down on the side of the bed and touched Sabel's shoulder.

"How do you feel?"

"How long was I out?"

"About five hours but I think some of that time you were just exhausted and sleeping. Brie loosened the leash as soon as we got into this room."

"Thank you," Sabel told Brie. Just looking at her curled up in the armchair, Sabel wanted simultaneously to run from the room and to crawl toward her. Or was it the other way around and the pull toward Brie was what made her feel like running? Every time Brie loosened the leash for her, the desire for her got stronger. She dropped her gaze to the bedspread and slowed her breathing.

Brie got up from the chair. "I'll tell Lily she's up," she said and went out of the room.

"We have about an hour until we head to the airport," Ana said. "Are you okay to travel?"

"I think so. I'd love a shower."

"Wake me up when you get out. Brie watched you for a few hours so I could sleep but I'm still wiped out."

Sabel nodded and went into the bathroom. She left the door cracked open, then stripped out of her dirt-spattered jeans and the shirt that was now missing two lower buttons and torn along one sleeve. A hinge creaked and she looked up to see Ana smiling at her from the doorway.

"I couldn't resist," she said. "I had to know if you were wearing the fight panties."

Sabel laughed and the release of tension through her chest and shoulders felt heavenly. Her collection of lacy underwear had been a running joke between them since the first fight with Ashmedai, and the first time they made love. She'd been wearing one of her more conservative black lacy pairs of panties, but they still struck Ana as incongruous and therefore as humorous as they were sexy. Sabel had described them then as her "fight panties" and the moniker stuck.

The current pair was a merlot color and started above her hips, but ended before the curve of her buttocks met the backs of her legs. She turned away so that Ana could see that effect and heard Ana swear quietly in appreciation.

"These are the new fight panties," Sabel said. "Very magical."

"I'll say. God, you're beautiful."

Sabel turned to face her and looked meaningfully in the direction Brie had gone.

Ana shook her head. "Don't," she said. She closed the distance between them and put her hands on Sabel's hips so that the lace rubbed roughly between Ana's palms and her skin.

"Abraxas is with Lily?" Sabel asked.

Ana nodded. "Tell me right away if the leash tightens."

Sabel ran both hands through Ana's short hair and pulled her. She leaned fully into Ana and Ana's arms enfolded her. They kissed until Sabel felt light-headed and then she rested her cheek on Ana's shoulder. Ana's hands stroked her back, her sides, her hips, and the feeling was more protective and reassuring than arousing, though of course that was there too.

There was a soft knock on the door and Lily's voice asking, "Are you two up?"

Ana kissed the side of her head and stepped away. "Take your shower," she said and closed the bathroom door behind her.

Sabel turned the water on as hot as she could stand, flicked on the struggling fan, and got under the spray. She crossed her arms over her chest and hugged herself tightly while water pounded on her back. Soon they'd be home in San Francisco. She had to…she couldn't even finish that thought because there were so many things that had to happen but it all ended the same way: she needed to curl up with Ana for days and shut out everything else. She needed to cry and scream, and have orgasm after orgasm in Ana's arms. But she couldn't.

She grabbed the shampoo bottle and turned her face to the water. It was hard to admit to herself, but in a way the familiarity of the feeling of needing to open up and being unable to do so was a lot more comforting than the raw emotion she'd experienced the time she and Ana had been alone with no limits on them.

Some minutes later the door opened again and Ana said, "New clothes," before leaving again.

A bag from a big box store was sitting on the lid of the closed toilet. She didn't have much hope for its contents. The jeans fit, but not in any way that was flattering, and there was a gray T-shirt and dark red sweatshirt. They would do. The underpants were exceedingly mundane, but Sabel preferred that to the idea of Lily knowing what she liked to wear.

Ana was in a similarly plain outfit and had a duffel bag open on the bed. "Toss anything you want to keep in here and we'll wash it when we get home," she said. Then explained, "Lily called the bus line. They'll ship our other luggage to her store address. She told the cops a lot of 'I don't knows' about the hijackers and that Mack's PTSD got triggered and he went out the back so we had to follow. That took care of it. It's about a half hour to the airport, so we've got to leave in ten. You ready?"

"Very," Sabel said.

They met up with the others in the hotel lobby. Lily had picked up a pair of khakis for Mack, probably at Ana's suggestion. She was clearly intent on tormenting him if he persisted in accompanying them, and he kept shifting uncomfortably in the starchy pants. Brie looked like Wonder Woman's alter ego Diana Prince after a too-speedy transformation, her hair escaping the loose knot at the back of her neck, her pants too new and pressed, the light blue sweater overly country club. Naturally it all looked great on her.

They piled into the cab, with Mack in the passenger seat and the four women in the two rows of van seating. It was good that Abraxas didn't take up space. Next to Ana, Sabel closed her eyes and leaned her head back. The underside of her eyelids still felt gritty from exertion and too little sleep.

The cab was approaching the "Welcome to Minneapolis/ St. Paul International Airport" sign when Ana gasped. She sat up straight and told the driver, "Stop! Right now, pull over, turn around, do something!"

The cabbie veered to the side of the road and ground to a halt, turning to glare at her.

"Just stay here a minute, we'll pay you for it," she said. "Brie, Lily, come with me. You two stay here with this guy."

Sabel watched them climb the grassy rise between the car and the view of the airport. Brie was sniffing the air and shaking her head. She cracked the window so she could hear them.

"...I can smell them on the wind," Brie said. "But I can't tell if they're all the way around."

"How do we get in?" Ana asked. "I thought he didn't have power this close to Minneapolis."

"It's his ally," Lily said angrily. "Dammit. Who with that much power would help him?"

"We don't know how long they've been here," Brie told her. "I could draw them off."

"No, he won't fall for that again," Lily said. "For all we know, he posted demon sentries here days ago to try to catch us going into the airport. We need to know who lent him their power for this."

The cabbie didn't seem inclined to immediately call them in as a terrorist threat, probably because they were mostly youngish, attractive women, so Sabel got out of the cab and walked up the hill to the rest of them. Mack was capable of not letting the cabbie drive off, no matter how crazy they all seemed, so she wasn't worried.

"Since they can't act in front of humans, can't we just drive in?" she asked the group.

"The cab will break down," Lily said. "That's what I'd do. Then we'd be stranded on the side of the road within their sphere and probably whatever help came for us would be hired by Ashmedai. We know he likes to hire humans, he clearly still has some of his wealth. I could ward the cab, but they'd still feel Abraxas when he passed close to them and then they only need enough magic to stop us. What do you think your range is?"

Ana answered, "He says...well it translates to about twenty feet. So I guess we can't just smuggle him in."

"So they'll know we're in the airport and I'll bet he's got humans in there waiting for us," Lily said. "For all we know, he'd have called us in as a security threat to delay us until his guys can pick us up."

"Devious," Sabel said. "Can we use a similar technique? If we know who his ally is, we could see if anyone in Minneapolis isn't particularly happy about having intruders on their doorstep. Can we essentially call the local magic cops on him?"

Lily grinned. "It's the best plan we've got. Anyone feel like demon hunting with me?"

"You're going to catch one of them? Won't that alert him?" Ana asked.

"Not if I do it right," Lily told her. She rolled her shoulders to loosen them.

"Where's the nearest one?" Sabel asked. She didn't see anything out of the ordinary.

"There."

She followed the line from Lily's pointing finger. The welcome sign to the airport sat on a small rise surrounded by a border of stone. A black trash bag had blown across the highway and wedged itself against the base of the sign. As she watched the garbage bag blow in the wind, a pattern formed. It blew the same way, as if more than the sign held it in place, as if an invisible form stood behind it. There was the head and shoulders.

She shivered. "It's the bag?"

"Yes, simple misdirection, most of the noncorporeal ones can do it."

"I don't suppose we could just walk over and grab the bag then, can we?"

"We should be so lucky," Lily said.

"Let me and the big guy take this one," Ana suggested.

A shimmer like a heat mirage moved out of Ana's body and down the hillside. Sabel couldn't follow its progress but could only infer where Abraxas was from Ana's position and the speed he'd been moving. The garbage bag fluttered up as if hit with a strong swirl of wind. Then it dropped to the ground.

After a moment, Sabel felt more than saw Abraxas pass her again and Ana doubled over with a gasp. "Bitter," she said and spat into the grass.

"So it's too much to ask him to do all of them that way?" Lily asked with a wry smile.

"Yeah," Ana gasped. "But he's practicing. He says it came from the east, from the lake and the wind...oh, Chicago. Chicago? Is that right?"

"Likely," Lily said. "Let's go and I'll make some inquiries and confirm it."

They piled back into the cab and, under Lily's direction, had him take them away from the airport and into downtown. Lily checked them into another hotel there. Apparently she had a small store of assumed names. Sabel didn't know what she'd use them for but when she saw the pale expression on Brie's face, she assumed it was for demon hunting.

The Marquette Hotel was a nicer hotel than the Holiday Inn Express and that made Sabel worry about exactly how long Lily thought they would be in this city.

CHAPTER TWELVE

They went to their rooms to nap, bathe, research and settle in. Ana fell across her bed and slept for about three hours, waking near lunchtime. She had that moment of complete disorientation that sometimes accompanied waking in a strange place. Her eyes focused on tan wallpaper and a long navy blue drape and she couldn't remember what city she was in.

Minneapolis, Abraxas said quietly in the back of her mind. She remembered the funeral, bus ride, fight and long trek through the woods all at once. It made her not want to get out of the bed.

Can he find us here? she asked.

Only by chance, Abraxas told her. *The airport was an easy guess, but no matter how powerful his ally, he can't have enough sentries to cover the airport and every block of this city. And each of them would have to be able to recognize not only demon power but also human faces. That takes a high level of competence.*

What about covering all of downtown? she asked.

That's more possible, if he had reason to suspect we came here rather than staying near the airport or leaving the city altogether.

Why don't we just leave? Lily has other names, we could rent a car and just drive back. He can't cover all the possible routes back.

It's an option and maybe the best one. If I were him, I'd set sentries on all the major routes, so we would have to plan carefully to avoid those. You should ask Sabel if she has magic that would increase our chances.

You think she does? Ana asked.

He didn't answer, but he didn't need to. He wouldn't have suggested it if he didn't already suspect something like that could be done.

Did you know witches before…? Ana asked.

She didn't know what to call that time in Abraxas's existence, but he understood. Nearly a thousand years before, he'd traded places with a human, giving that person his immortal body of fire and taking the human body. Still, he couldn't exactly be killed, so when the human body died, he was able to use it to travel into the realms of the dead. When Ana asked him what those were like, he said that he hadn't yet found a way to put it in words. She considered asking if he could just show her, but she was afraid of what she might see.

His long sojourn in death meant that he'd been out of the human world for centuries. Ana didn't exactly remember how long and she had trouble calculating the human years from the demon calendar. It was something like the year 1000 something or maybe 1100ish that he left the waking human world that she knew, and he'd only made it back a few months ago.

He met her question about having known witches with a strange, long silence and finally answered by saying only the word, *Yes.*

Because her brain was also his home base, though, she felt all kinds of emotions resonant in that single syllable: love and loss, grief, joy, admiration.

You loved someone, Ana guessed. *A witch? Wasn't that all Romeo and Juliet style forbidden?*

It was secret, he said.

Who was she?

She felt rather than heard his negative response, like seeing a person shake their head, but from the inside. He only said, *Lily and Brie are talking about how to leave the city if you care to bring Sabel and join them.*

Ana shoved herself off the bed. *Can you eavesdrop on them from here or are you a little in Lily's head too?* she asked.

Eavesdropping, he said.

Not polite to hang out in your girlfriend's mind?

Would you? he asked.

I'd miss the surprises, she admitted.

He didn't answer in words, but she felt the warm pressure of his amused agreement and the relief that she wasn't asking him more about his past love. That topic was filed away for future questions.

She went into the bathroom and splashed water on her face. Then she stepped into the hall and knocked on Sabel's door. Sabel looked better than Ana felt.

"You're up," she said. "I was going to order room service and wake you in a bit, just so you wouldn't sleep through to four a.m."

"Let's get it sent to Lily's room. I hear she and Brie are talking about how to get out of here."

Lily and Brie's room was the largest of the four and included a sitting room. When Lily opened the door, Ana saw that she and Brie had two maps spread out on the coffee table. The bottom map was the western United States and the top map was a city, presumably Minneapolis.

"We thought we'd order room service and eavesdrop on your plans," Ana said.

"Come on in."

Sabel went to the phone and called in an order of salmon for her and a burger for Ana. Ana took the far end of the couch and Sabel settled into the armchair by the large window. Ana couldn't tell if she was trying to position herself away from Brie or from Ana. Maybe both. Since Sabel had been in so much pain the night before from the leash constricting on her after the fight in the woods, Ana found it hard to blame her, but she wanted her closer.

"Where's Mack?" Ana asked, though the question made her mouth bitter. He was good in a fight, but she still hated having him around. The fact that he thought he could just hitch a ride to the Cities with them to spend more time with Brie was more of his bullying crap. He never asked for anything before just taking it. He never took "no" for an answer. The sooner they could leave him behind, the happier she would be.

"He went to walk around the skyways," Brie said. "He's the safest of all of us with no magic. He's basically invisible. I think he's trying to find a club he can take me to later."

"Ugh," Ana said, but then hastily added, "thanks for keeping him busy." *And away from me.*

"What are we looking at?" Sabel asked.

"Back roads," Brie said.

Lily explained, "We're trying to see how many routes out of the city are unlikely to be guarded. But we don't have a good sense of how much support he has. Chicago is pretty big, but I doubt Ashmedai had access to the city's entire standing army."

Ana felt Abraxas flow out of her and she didn't need to look to see that he was standing behind her.

"Who holds Chicago?" he asked, his whispery voice just loud enough to be audible throughout the room.

"Ashtoreth," Lily said.

Sabel looked thoughtful. "She's not the same as the god Astarte?"

"She's a distortion of Astarte," Lily answered. "When men became afraid of the power of women's fertility and saw those gods as negative, a lot of Shaitans stepped into those fears. Ashtoreth is one of those."

"Why would she help Ashmedai?" Sabel asked.

Lily turned and looked pointedly at Abraxas. "I've been thinking about this since the fight and I've come up with only one possible answer. If Ashmedai is desperate enough to capture Ana, he may have offered Abraxas as payment."

"How much is he worth?" Ana asked.

"A lot," Lily said. "And I'm not just saying that. Abraxas is at an age where most demons can't be absorbed into another, but he's still weak enough that he could be. If Ashtoreth needs to bolster her power, and she probably does because Chicago is a really big prize for a single Shaitan prince to hold, the offer of Abraxas would be very tempting."

"Way to go," Ana said. "I thought you were supposed to make us safer, not bankroll the opposition."

Abraxas would know she was teasing. She appreciated the augments to her body that made her stronger and more resilient, and she knew that he tried to keep her safe in every way that he could. He wasn't the one who'd pissed off another demon prince.

"How many resources would she offer in exchange for me?" Abraxas asked.

"Ashtoreth has held Chicago for years, she would have hundreds of sentries to spare, maybe thousands."

"Enough to cover all the routes out of the city?" Brie asked.

"Maybe," Lily said. "We have to choose carefully. I think we should go north or east first, maybe even up through Canada."

Room service arrived. Sabel lifted the lid of one of the plates, revealing salmon in a maple glaze.

"Looks good," she said. She glanced over her shoulder to where Lily, Brie and Abraxas were bent over the map. Quietly, only to Ana, she added, "I can improve our chances of getting out of the city, but I don't want to talk about it here."

"We'll meet in your room after this, or mine, I'm flexible," Ana told her.

"Mine," Sabel said with a half wink. She picked up the plate of salmon and went back to her armchair.

Ana took her burger to her side of the couch and dug into it. The perks of being in a nice hotel: it was cooked medium and juicy all the way through with savory cheese dripping down the sides and the bacon on top was actually crisp. She tuned out the other voices for a few minutes so she could enjoy the flavors. When she was half finished with it, she started listening again.

"Yes, I like that one too," Abraxas said.

"We could double our chances if we can make a decoy," Brie suggested.

"We'd need another demon for that," Lily said.

"Or a powerful, diffuse magic," Abraxas said thoughtfully. "Like the power of a god."

"You're thinking the god of the city might help us?" Lily asked.

"You can feel the power of this city," Abraxas replied. "It's not hostile or angry. It's calming. The god might have an interest in turning away conflict, if we can figure out how to approach the god. It's not as if we can go up to a door and knock."

"Don't the gods of a city, or whatever, hold court somewhere?" Brie asked.

Lily looked at her like she had two heads. "How many of my lessons did you ignore?"

"It wasn't like I ignored them, but there's just more interesting stuff out there. In the movies they'd all be holed up in some really posh nightclub. Is that too much to ask?"

"There might be gods who hang out in nightclubs," Lily admitted. "But I'm not sure they're the ones who would be helpful to us. Gods are even less like humans than we are."

"You should tell Ana more about them," Sabel said.

Ana wasn't so sure she wanted to know, but if Sabel thought it would be useful, she'd better listen. She wasn't any kind of practicing religious person, but her Lutheran upbringing had instilled in her the sense that there was some great, benevolent power out there and she could rely on it in times of need. She didn't know what to think of the idea of many gods all running around in the same world.

"The gods are vessels, like all of us, only much larger," Abraxas said.

Brie held up a hand. "Vessel doesn't translate," she said. "Think of computers and mobile devices. Humans and demons, we're like smartphones—we have certain abilities given by our hardware and software, and then we connect to fields of signals that make us who we are. Gods are like…well, more than computers really."

"Internets," Sabel said. "If you think of each god as a mini Internet and compare that to your smartphone, you get a sense for the scale of things. I'd say that regular people are like smartphones, they run their programs and they're tuned into some signals and that creates their personalities and their habits. Demons, witches, other magical types are like computers. We have more access, we can do more, we can change faster. And gods are Internets."

"Can my computer access a god's Internet?" Ana asked.

"Of course. That's why we picked this metaphor," Brie said. "What do you think prayer is? When you pray, you log into that god's network and ask to access some of its data or power or whatever."

Ana rubbed the side of her head. The scary thing was that the analogy made sense to her. She could easily see her relationship with Abraxas as two closely networked computers, or maybe a complex program using her hard drive to run itself. That's why he couldn't stay away from her body for long. She was his hardware right now. And it helped her understand why it was so hard for him to find the right "vessel" for himself—he wasn't looking for something like an empty vase, he was looking for a very precise, complex environment to run his program from. If he didn't have the right hardware, did that mean he couldn't access parts of himself?

"Essentially," he said, answering her unspoken question aloud. "It is a much better metaphor. In a limited vessel, or the human equivalent of an old computer, I'm not all here."

"But those parts of you are still somewhere, you just can't get to them, right? Like memories?"

"Yes."

"So do we just pray to the god holding Minneapolis or are they located somewhere, like a server room or something?" Ana asked.

"There will be locations where it's easier to access them," Abraxas said.

"Research break," Brie declared and stood up. "I need to go work out or something, I'm all tight from yesterday. Anyone want to check out the gym with me?"

"I will," Ana said. "Let me go see what the closest thing to workout clothes I have is."

"Come knock on my door when you're ready."

"I'll stay here if you don't mind," Abraxas said. She felt him flow out of her and into Lily and now she could perceive more clearly through the computer metaphor as if he was transferring some of his processing from her body over to Lily's.

* * *

"I'll be in my room doing my own research if anyone needs me," Sabel said.

She got up and followed Ana out into the hall and gestured Ana into her room. It was the mirror image of Ana's, but the bed looked less rumpled.

"How do you feel?" Ana asked, gesturing vaguely at Sabel's torso and hoping all the pain from the leash was long gone.

Sabel smiled and put her arms around Ana, leaning against her. Ana returned the embrace, holding Sabel close. When she felt her own level of desire starting to rise, she kissed Sabel's hair and pulled away.

Sabel settled into the chair by the desk while Ana sat on the end of the bed.

"There's a kind of magic I can try," Sabel said. "But it's very unpredictable."

"Like throw a person through a window unpredictable?" Ana asked.

Sabel rolled her eyes. "You're never going to let that go, are you?"

"It made you really stand out among the women in my life."

"I'd better stand out," Sabel said roughly.

"Oh, you do."

There was a long silence in which they stared into each other's eyes. Ana could tell that Sabel, like herself, was aching to close the distance between them again.

Sabel looked away with a sigh. "The Hecatines divide magic into eight fields," she said. "Most of us, myself included, usually work in the field of information, which can include time. But time also extends into the field of probabilities and I can..."

She paused and gazed upward and Ana could all but see her organizing her thoughts. Whenever Sabel tried to explain time magic to her, it scrambled her brain. Demon magic was pretty simple: you had a lot of power or a little and you could use it to do things; you could combine your power with others, or maybe consume their power. That was pretty much it. On the surface it wasn't so different from physical strength except that different kinds of powers did different things and you could add to your own power by taking someone else's.

But the magic of the time witches...She understood that Sabel could stutter her own place in time so that she was ahead of the present moment or was running time slightly faster around herself than in the world at large. But when Sabel started to talk about how her future self could send information to her present self, it all began to unravel.

"From the perspective of the present, the future is unknown," Sabel said. "But not completely. There are attractors at varying temporal distances from now, like San Francisco. You and I are being attracted to San Francisco because we want to get there. But we're also being attracted toward Ashmedai because he wants us. At any given point in the present there are billions of attractors of varying strength that pull us into the future. I can try to shift some of them. I can make San Francisco more likely and Ashmedai less likely. I can change the probability."

"But?" Ana asked.

"Probabilities aren't events. I can't make us get to San Francisco. I could increase the probability and we might still never make it back to the city."

"Can't you just ask your future self if we did?"

"Ana, she can't tell me. Literally, if she tried to tell me, I would not be able to hear it. She can only send me the messages I can hear. Well, unless I really force it, but then if I see the future I'm locked into my course of action in the present, which is pretty insanity-inducing."

"Because they already happened to make her who she is, so that she can talk to you," Ana said to show that at least she understood that much. Or maybe it would be better to say she'd heard it when Sabel explained it—she wasn't sure that she understood it. One thing she knew for sure: every time Sabel started talking about this complex, crazy, future stuff, she just wanted to throw her down on the bed and make her forget every moment except the present.

"You know what future attractor I want you to make more probable?" Ana asked. Leaning forward from her spot at the end of the bed, she could just reach Sabel where she sat in the desk chair. With the tips of two fingers, she lifted a lock of Sabel's dark hair that had fallen across her forehead and cheek. She pushed it back and ran the underside of her thumb down Sabel's cheek.

"Is it a future in which you're on top and I'm saying 'please'?" Sabel's eyes were lit with the rare mischief that showed when she let herself tease Ana.

The thought made Ana's body heat suddenly and she beamed. "I don't think you can catch your breath enough to say anything in *that* future."

"Oh gods, stop that or I'm going to throw myself at you and we'll have to call Brie over here after I pass out."

Ana dutifully got up from the edge of the bed and paced between the door and bed to walk off some of the energy surging through her. She pulled them back to the original topic, saying, "You were telling me that you can't make future stuff happen, you can only make it more likely."

Sabel cleared her throat and looked down at her hands clasped between her knees. She was still smiling. Ana wanted to tip her head up and kiss the edge of her mouth, where her small, full lips came together in a delicate upward curve.

"Exactly," Sabel said and her voice wavered between a serious professor voice and a humorous lilt. She cleared her throat again and her voice settled toward the serious. "I can't see all the probabilities, all I can see are the major attractors, so I don't know if I'm opening up a path that leads to some really crazy stuff. When we were back in San Francisco fighting Ashmedai the first time, I kept pushing away the attractors for death. I pushed away the one in your future and it opened up attractors for everyone around you. It may be that my pushing led to him kidnapping Gunnar."

"He would have done that anyway," Ana said.

"I think he would have thought of it, yes, but you have to understand that changing probabilities may have made it easier for him to just pick up Gunnar. If I push attractors now, we have no idea what will happen."

"What are you going to push?" Ana asked. "Just San Francisco?"

"I can't make Ashmedai less probable, because his own will is stronger than my ability to push him away. But I can make all routes out of Minneapolis more likely."

"Is it hard? I mean, does it hurt you?"

"It's just draining," Sabel said. "You think I should do it?"

"Yes."

Sabel nodded. "I'll need most of the day."

"Tell me how it goes," Ana said. She walked up to Sabel and kissed her on the top of the head, then moved away before it could get more intense. "I'm glad you're on my side," she added.

"Me too," Sabel said.

Ana let herself out of the room and went to find something she could wear for a workout. A long workout and then a cold, cold shower.

* * *

Sabel went around the room and put everything in order. It was already pretty tidy, but touching the different elements of this strange place helped to make it more conducive to her magic. She straightened a lamp, arranged the pillows on the bed, pushed together the hangers in the closet, and folded a washcloth in the bathroom that she'd used that morning. She wasn't a neat freak, but she needed to know the space around her before she could do magic in it. It wasn't as good as being home, but it would do because it had to.

She picked a spot on the far side of the bed, putting the bed between her and the door, and set down an extra blanket.

Then she sat on it. Kneeling was better for questions, but for probabilities and pushing attractors, sitting was preferable. She drew in her feet and sat with them close together so that her butt and knees made the three points of a triangle.

Her breathing slowed and she slipped into a light trance until her body was settled and grounded. Every witch had to create her own interface for working with the layers of reality and the powers available in the world. Some preferred a shamanic overlay of jungles and animals to translate information and probability into something they could understand. Others preferred warrior archetypes with weapons and battles, or shapeshifting, or growing a garden.

Josefene explained that she could use anything she wanted and over the years her interface, or workshop as she liked to call it, had changed and modified itself. When she was ready, she turned around inside her body and stepped through the door into her workshop in the Unseen World. Her body stayed in the hotel room, but her consciousness was now in this other space. It looked like a large room inside a villa, furnished in the Greek style with a clean wooden floor and low tables at one wall but little else. Sliding screens covered two other walls and the fourth was made of windows that looked out over a peaceful ocean to a vast horizon.

She slid aside one of the screens to reveal a set of stairs going up. The stairs were narrow and metal like a lighthouse, and at the top was an observatory with a giant telescope. She sat in the chair and put her eyes to the viewer. Her consciousness followed her vision so she didn't stay in the chair but instead soared up into the sky past the atmosphere and into space. This was her metaphor: the vast open reaches of the galaxy with its swirling arms and billions of stars.

No human mind could directly perceive attractors in the future. You could see your own, but not other people's. How would you know what they were? It frustrated Sabel when she was a little younger, but now she liked to work with this enormous, strange landscape. She was comfortable in it—

sometimes more comfortable a little way into the future than in the present.

Everyone lived in the future as well as the past, but most didn't know it. It was so easy to see how past actions caused the present situation. If you were driving your car and you crashed into a signpost, clearly the crash caused the damage to the car. People weren't used to seeing how the future attractors also caused the present. The destination you were driving toward also caused the crash as much as the fact that you got in your car in the first place. You wouldn't be in your car at all if you weren't being pulled toward a future destination. People just weren't used to looking at all the future destinations causing events in their present moment.

Sabel understood the reasons—it was a lot harder to look at attractors and possible paths than to consider a single line of cause that led to the present moment. In the present, the past collapsed but the future remained splayed out in possibility. She chose to see the landscape of attractors in the context of the galaxy itself. As her consciousness went up from the telescope, it zoomed out until she could see a massive spiral arm of the Milky Way. It wasn't the real galaxy; it was her mind translating millions of probabilities into something that looked like stars. But it worked.

She saw the cluster of them—Ana, herself, Abraxas, Lily, Brie, Mack—as a dense system through which stars streamed. She'd long ago accepted that her vision wasn't astronomically accurate, it just used the metaphor of stars and space to show her what was going on. It was based on the astronomy lessons her father gave her when she was a kid, so it might even be outdated.

When she focused on them closely, Abraxas looked like a huge golden mass with pulses of glowing waves around him like a nova or small nebula; he was untouched by many of the probability streams. Brie, on the other hand, was a blue-white mass swirling with patterns of dust comprised of small stars. Ana was a smaller, duller blue but still large and heavily interactive.

Lily shone steady and yellow like the sun, thoroughly connected but not overwhelmingly interrelated like Brie. She and Brie were in a close orbit but Sabel could feel the energy radiating from them as Brie pushed away as much as she was drawn in. And Mack burned a hard red with as little interaction as Abraxas but for different reasons. Many paths didn't include him.

Sabel couldn't see herself, only the position where she would be. She thought this was because her mind couldn't place her there and be the viewer at the same time.

She looked out across the arm of the galaxy. There was a repeated white-yellow pulse from various parts of the star field that had to be Ashmedai and she saw his gravity interacting with a white-blue power. She looked along the drifting lines of stars to find the ones that didn't contain him. She needed lines in the star field that didn't contain Ashmedai and did contain San Francisco. That took her a long time to find. With the thousands of cities in existence, she had to keep narrowing by characteristics until she found San Francisco in the future. Then she put anchors in those future San Franciscos that did not also include Ashmedai.

Already fatigue was dragging at her. She wanted to look through the futures to find the ones that stretched into her not wearing the leash, but there were so many futures that included San Francisco and not Ashmedai that she didn't know where to start. There were at least an equal number that did include Ashmedai and an infinite number that didn't include San Francisco. Her mind was aching from looking at all of them: stars on top of stars in patterns that shifted, made sense, stopped making sense, shifted again.

She looked closely at their solar system. There was the absent space that marked her place and there was the blue-white intensity of Brie. She saw crossing paths as trails of stardust and energy fingers prying at the leash. Could she find a future where Brie got the leash off of her by following these paths from the present? She looked forward, trying to spot an attractor along a line with no leash.

She followed one line of probability but it seemed to overlap a no-San Francisco future too often, so she went back and followed another. Another dead end. Drawing back, she looked across the enormous pattern again to find another line of stars to follow.

And then she saw it.

A super massive nebula of towering dark gas clouds blotted out half of the galaxy arm where she was standing. In her years of working with this interface, she'd never seen clouds like these that flatly obscured so much of the future. A moment ago she'd been big enough to walk across the galaxy and suddenly she felt tiny and exposed.

The smoky blue-black-gray clouds churned—and looked back at her. A dozen eyes more vast than solar systems stared and blinked out of synchrony with each other. It was alive and sentient. It watched her with a keen curiosity. Although the visual impression didn't change, she thought it smiled. Not a kind smile. Not benevolent. It was pushing the probabilities as if they were nothing, shoving the future around like a child's game of marbles—and the path it opened led cleanly back to San Francisco with no leash and no deaths.

She should be happy but she was terrified. The nebula exuded overwhelming pride and mirth at her, as if it was saying: see how easy this is for me?

Sabel fled backward along the line of sight that she'd followed up from the observatory, feeling that monstrous gaze on her as she went. Even in the observatory, it was watching her. She rushed through her villa and back to her body, desperate to get away from it. Back in her body in the tiny hotel room on a tiny planet in the middle of nowhere, she doubled over, crying in fear.

She was afraid to look up, afraid that it would still be looking down at her.

A fist pounded on her door and Brie's voice called, "Sabel, do you need help?"

She clasped her hands over her mouth and swallowed the sounds. It was only fear. Fear she could manage. Maybe. She rose to her feet but her balance was off and she fell toward the bed. Pushing off the bed, she staggered in the direction of the dresser, bounced off that, caught the doorway to the bathroom and managed to unlock the door before her legs gave out and she dropped to sitting in the doorway between the bathroom and bedroom.

Brie knelt in front of her. "Are you hurt?" Even with her brow creased with worry, she looked gorgeous. Her hair held a perfect, curling wave that fell beautifully over her shoulders.

Sabel shook her head and looked away.

"Is it okay to touch you, regular human style?"

Sabel nodded. She wasn't sure if she wanted Brie to touch her or not, but when she put her arms around Sabel's shivering shoulders, Sabel found that she needed that contact more than anything.

"You're shaking," Brie said. She sat and leaned against the bathroom door holding Sabel tightly.

Sabel pressed against the comforting familiarity of another body and the soothing presence of Brie in particular. Even if she didn't like her artificial attraction to this woman, Sabel appreciated the way her presence was turning down the distress in her body.

"Magic," Sabel managed. She was still trying to get her racing heart and shallow breathing under control. *It was only panic*, she told herself. She'd felt panic before—but it never felt quite this legitimate.

"Trying to influence our future?" Brie asked.

"Probabilities," Sabel said, surprising herself with that admission. She wondered how much Brie knew about her and about witches in general to be able to guess that the future would be involved in this kind of magic.

Brie nodded, the motion brushing against the side of Sabel's head. "My stepfather said he could never get the hang of that. He's very good in the near future, but that long-term stuff, not so much. What scared you?"

"Something looked at me from…I don't know where. It must have been a little outside of time but also in the present or the near future. Or maybe both. I think it spanned time, like people do, but much bigger."

"Demon?" Brie asked. "Maybe the one in Chicago who's working with Ashmedai?"

Brie's hair smelled like chocolate and sweet musk with a clean, clear top note like lemongrass. With a distant pang of horror at herself, Sabel buried her face in the shelter made by Brie's curls and her shoulder. Brie's hand rubbed a gentle circle on her back. The traitorous leash did nothing.

"No," Sabel said. "It was really massive. When I see Abraxas, he's bigger than we are, but what I saw now was a million times more massive. It pulled all the probabilities aside like they were nothing and cleared a path home. But I don't trust it." She shuddered again and the arms around her tightened.

Brie's head moved as she looked up. Then Brie said, to someone other than Sabel, "This isn't what it looks like."

"I'm not sure what it looks like." Ana's voice came from the doorway. "What happened?"

"I was going out and I heard her...It sounded like she was upset. Something happened with the probability magic."

Sabel pushed herself away from Brie, which took a lot more effort than she wanted it to. Ana was standing in the open doorway looking perplexed. Brie got up and moved into the room so Ana could kneel and peer into Sabel's face. She touched Sabel's cheek gently and Sabel leaned into her touch.

"You're okay?" Ana asked.

Sabel nodded. It was too hard to explain all of it. She still had a feeling of dread, but the panic was gone and some of the feelings caused by Brie that had taken its place weren't worth mentioning.

"This was from the stuff you said you were going to do? Did it go wrong?"

"It went fine until the end and then there was just this... creature looking at me from the present and the future. It was just so huge. I've never seen anything like that before."

"Can it hurt you?"

"I don't know. It seemed to be trying to help, but I'm not sure it's a kind of help that I want."

She hadn't seen if there were others like it in that infinite space. Maybe it had its own limitations or others of its kind that stopped it from just toying with people any way it wanted. She hoped it did.

Ana closed her hand around Sabel's arm and helped her to stand and walk to the end of the bed, where they both sat.

"I should eat something," Sabel said.

"I was coming to see if you wanted to go out for dinner," Ana said. "But maybe we should just order in again."

Ana got the menu off the desk and Sabel picked the honey-glazed salmon again. Ana called the order in and came back to sit on the bed. Brie was standing by the window, looking out over the city in the fading evening light.

A knock sounded on the door.

"That was awfully fast for room service," Ana remarked.

The man at the door was easily over six feet tall and beautiful with dark olive skin and long, straight black hair held back in a short queue. With a slight bow of his head and shoulders, he presented a sealed, cream-colored envelope.

"An invitation," he said.

Ana took it and turned it over but there was no name or address on it. "From who?" she asked.

"She will introduce herself," he said and walked away down the hall.

Ana shrugged and tore the envelope open. "Club Bliss," she said. "Tonight, ten p.m., the Cyprian."

Brie crossed the room and held out her hand. "I want to see it," she said and Ana gave her the invitation. She turned it over a few times and rubbed her fingers on the paper. "It's nice," she said finally. "I'm in."

"Wait," Sabel said.

Ana gave her a questioning glance.

"Working the probabilities, how sudden it is—something doesn't feel right about this. Probability magic is never this blunt," Sabel explained.

"We're not the only magical people in the city," Brie said. "Let's go check this out. Maybe she could tell you were here and doing magic."

"You know that implies she was the thing looking at Sabel," Ana said.

"Did it look female?" Brie asked. "And clubby?"

"I don't know what clubby looks like, but if this is that creature, do you have any idea the kind of power it would take to be able to locate us in a city?" Sabel asked, exasperated. "In the material world, the physical presence of the city makes magic almost impossible to see. There's no one I know who is capable of something like this."

"That might be even more of a reason to meet her," Brie pointed out. "You said it looked like she was making a way for us to get home."

"You just want an excuse to go out clubbing," Ana said.

"Absolutely. I so volunteer to go. If it's part of that probability stuff it could totally be our ticket out of here. You can thank me later. Now what am I going to wear…"

She left the room and Ana turned to Sabel. "You think that's a bad idea?"

"Yes, but I don't have any other ones and whatever she is, she could get us home. I'm just not sure we're going to like how she does it."

CHAPTER THIRTEEN

For once Brie could go out dancing like a regular girl. She was so well fed from the three guys in the woods and the energy of Ashmedai's borrowed body that she felt energetically stuffed and in no danger of giving in to Mack's overt come-ons. She just wanted to go out and dance and be part of a crowd; large, happy groups gave her a light buzz. Mack was more than happy to oblige her.

They still had a few hours before the ten p.m. invitation time, so Brie made a quick trip through the skyways to find something more suitable to wear. She found a fitted peach dress featuring a suggestive mesh panel down the front and paired it with red pumps with modest heels. Then she took Mack out to dinner and listened to more stories of motorcycle engines and bar fights. They arrived at the club a little before ten.

On the dance floor, Brie let herself go, confident that Mack's hovering proximity was enough to keep other men at bay. She danced, but she only pretended to drink. She wasn't going to be that careless. She could still feel the body Ashmedai had worn fall over the edge of life into death and it made her shiver. If she got the chance, she would kill him just for making her feel that again. Well, that, and for all he'd done to her new friends. She wasn't going to be bloodthirsty solely for herself.

But for Ana and Sabel—how strangely she felt about both of them. She wanted it to feel the way she thought she would when she first met them, to like Ana and dislike Sabel.

Her feelings for Ana were strongly positive—so much so that she wondered if they were some shadow of how people felt when they were around her for a while. If so, no wonder they'd follow her from town to town if she gave them the chance. She felt that she'd fight for Ana, take care of her, stay around her—but not obsessively like her own lovers, just sweetly.

Ana had tremendous strength about her and an almost crazy heedlessness—a counterpart to the core of rage that Mack carried around with him. Brie wasn't surprised that Sabel felt protective of her. But who was looking after Sabel?

Ever since Sabel's implacable voice had cut through her out-of-control feeding and stopped her cold, she'd wanted to feel that again. Once she understood that it was as easy for Sabel to kill by accident as it was for Brie, she saw Sabel differently. All that control, those layers of discipline, they weren't just there to protect her from the world; they were there to protect others from her—and for that Brie envied her. She'd never had anyone who could really teach her to control her powers. She didn't want to end up as bound up as Sabel, but oh that binding was so compelling. It was not just the leash itself. Sabel's whole character begged to be let out of its constrictions.

What was she like in bed? If the experiment running energy through her body was any indication, she was glorious.

When she'd heard Sabel whimper in panic that afternoon, her heart had sickened with dread. She'd started pounding on the door before she knew what she was doing. And the memory of Sabel curled against her lingered like honey on a burnt tongue: sweet and stinging. She didn't just want to get inside the energy leash, she wanted to be inside Sabel and understand what made her. She wanted to take her apart and put her back together again and she wanted to lose control of herself knowing that Sabel's voice would keep her safe.

To distract herself, Brie looked around the club. If she got too far into those thoughts, it was all kinds of trouble. Already the longing was stirring a deep hunger.

The massive space had been divided into a main floor that hosted a substantial dance floor and four bars. The second floor was two huge balconies overlooking the main floor. Above those at the third-floor level were two more balconies, one the DJ booth and the other held couches, pedestals on which dancers gyrated, and a small bar with no clear way to get up there.

"Come with me," Brie yelled in the vicinity of Mack's ear and he nodded to her.

In the far corner a muscular man stood in front of an elevator blocked off by a rope line. She went up to him and held out the invitation envelope.

He glanced down at it and pressed the button for the elevator.

"What's up there?" Mack asked, not quick to drop his suspicious mien.

Their guard didn't answer, so Brie put in, "Does she own the club?"

"Yes," he said.

It was a very modern, spartan elevator with a mirror along both sides so that Brie could make sure that her hair was perfect—it was—and that her dress draped the way she wanted it to.

The doors opened on a quieter space than Brie expected. The music was still audible, the bass shook the walls, but something up here absorbed most of the loudness, like hearing the club from outside its walls. Across from the short bar, three large couches created a sheltered semicircle. The pedestals with the dancers were at the open end of this shape, so that the people sitting had a very good view of the lithe woman and man who danced up there, mirroring each other.

Eight people sat around the couches, with room for as many more. They sat mainly on the side couches and all attention was focused on one woman in the middle of the longest couch. She looked more real than the other people there, more real than Mack and, Brie feared, more real than she did. She was so solid that the room seemed to bend toward her. Her skin was a shade darker than Brie's mixed Arabic-Spanish-demon heritage, and her onyx black hair was pulled up in an elaborate coiffure held by silver netting. She wore white pants that flared below the knee, a white tank top with a V-neck open halfway down her chest and a semitransparent, shimmering bronze jacket. The clothing accentuated the fact that she was a large woman, heavy and thick in her thighs, wide-hipped and—Brie couldn't think of a better word—stacked.

She rose when Brie stepped off the elevator and crossed the room, carrying her weight easily, as if it was a natural extension of her power. Those plum lips would be ideal for kissing and a person could lose herself in that cleavage. Brie shook herself mentally. The woman had a glamour that was part of what she was, as Brie's was part of her.

"You are very beautiful," the woman told her.

Brie brightened. "I thought so too, until I saw you."

The woman inclined her head. "They call me the Cyprian. What do they call you?"

"Brie, if you please."

"I do. And your friend?"

A muscle tensed in the side of Mack's jaw but he didn't respond. Brie had made him promise to let her do the talking.

"This is Mack, he's human," Brie answered.

"I see that."

"But he's the only human up here, isn't he? I thought magic folks didn't keep clubs. At least that's what my mother said, but then, she owns a bookstore, so I don't know why we wouldn't have other businesses. Thank you for inviting us up, it's really lovely here."

Brie realized she was babbling and shut her mouth. She was not some schoolgirl to be taken in by a glamour of attraction. Though how fun would it be to pit her powers against this woman's?

The Cyprian guided her over to the couch and set her at her right hand with Mack on Brie's other side. Someone put drinks in front of them, and though Brie knew better than to drink hers, she touched it to her lips to be polite—it was too easy to conceal powerful magic in food and drink. The other people up here had moved off, cleared a space for them to talk in private.

"You're not a demon are you?" Brie asked.

"Oh, that's what you are," the Cyprian said. "I haven't met many demons with bodies. There were others with you. They didn't come?"

"They're a little less adventurous," Brie told her. "They mean no offense."

"Tell me about them, and you." The Cyprian's fingers toyed with a lock of Brie's hair where it fell over her shoulder and she grew hot inside.

Brie leaned into her, the Cyprian's heavy breast pressing deliciously against hers, close enough to be sure that no one else could hear. "I'm not a safe person to flirt with," she said.

"Oh, really?"

"I just don't want anything bad to happen between us, since we just met," Brie said and blinked up at her, sweet smile and wide-eyed. This woman, whatever she turned out to be, didn't seem to be any more immune to Brie than Brie was to her.

The Cyprian breathed in and pulled her hand away from Brie's hair. "You'd make a good little toy, wouldn't you?"

"I always do," Brie said, sitting back again. "Until it's over."

She let her energy sense extend into the Cyprian's body. It didn't feel like a normal human body. With humans, she felt the tree-like structures of their energy channels all connecting in to the spine. The Cyprian was a single mass of energy. There was no part of her that was more or less dense with power.

"You're not even a little human," Brie said. "What are you?"

"I am The Cyprian, goddess of love…" Her voice trailed off and Brie waited, thinking there was more. Love and what?

When it didn't come, she digested the first part. "And here I thought gods didn't hang around in nightclubs."

The Cyprian laughed, a sound like deep wind chimes. "I'll admit this wasn't my first choice, but I've been biding my time and this amuses me. I suspect we have similar interests. When I saw your companion pushing the Fates, it seemed we wanted compatible ends."

"That was you, then. You scared the daylights out of her."

"She's not a demon either, is she? She seemed human."

"She is."

"But she has that much power to move the Fates? Tell me about the others."

Brie knew the Cyprian's power was still on her. She'd already said more than was probably wise, but at the same time, if this goddess was willing to help them, they could really use that kind of power. And as much as the Cyprian was manipulating her, she could manipulate in turn. The base of the Cyprian's power was still the raw power of the universe itself, which was a kind of vitality and therefore the kind of power that Brie could consume.

"Will I disappoint you if I admit I'm here with my mother?" Brie asked mischievously.

The Cyprian laughed. "That depends on who invited whom."

She responded seriously. "She asked me to come help protect our group against this other demon. He's a nasty sort. I'm totally going to take him out one of these days. But now he's got help from Chicago and he's blocked our routes out of the city."

"I've had my eye on Chicago for a few years now," the Cyprian said. "And you say that your enemy is now allied with my enemy. The enemy of my enemy appears to make a lovely friend. If you can help me move against Chicago, I can help you with your problem."

Brie raised an eyebrow.

"Chicago is held by the demon prince Ashtoreth," the Cyprian said. "I don't have expertise with demons. I could use someone with knowledge and the right techniques. I don't even know why they call themselves princes. Why don't they call themselves kings?"

"There's only one king of demons," Brie said reflexively. Any child of a demon lineage knew that.

"Oh, and this king of demons is not in Chicago, I gather?" the Cyprian asked. Brie didn't bother to answer and after a moment the Cyprian continued, "This prince, Ashtoreth, took the city a few years ago and when I looked at all the cities I might like to call home, Chicago suits me best. I enjoy the water and the wind. But I don't have as much traffic with demons as would serve me in this circumstance, so I need information about how to unseat this prince. I have a small army at my disposal and I think you and I share some other avenues of entré into a stronghold." Then she laughed, "Listen to me sounding all high and mighty. You put me on my guard, little gem. Will you come see me tomorrow and bring your people? I promise no harm."

At the Cyprian's signal, one of the men seated around them set a small square of white on the table in front of Brie. It was a business card with an address and a time.

Then, since she'd begun the night feeling sated and had long since tipped into recklessness through the proximity of this beautiful creature of power, she laid her hand along the Cyprian's cheek. Brie's thumb traced the lower edge of her lip, not as full as Brie's own mouth, but wider and more supple. The Cyprian's mouth parted with the quickening of her breath.

"You are an interesting one," she said, the silk of her lip tickling Brie's thumb as it moved. It took all Brie's strength not to slide her thumb into the Cyprian's mouth, because she knew if she did, she'd be lost on the rising wave of her own desire. That was one move she could ill afford.

Brie pulled back her hand, feeling that she'd just been given a dare and then lost it. "Tomorrow," she managed, roughly.

The Cyprian inclined her head and then she and Mack were shown out. She didn't pause on the first floor—any desire to drink or dance was gone—but pulled Mack out into the street and went straight back to the hotel. With a chaste kiss on his cheek she sent that bewildered man to his room and hurried into hers, eager to tell her mother that goddesses apparently did hang out in bars.

* * *

Ana woke up because she was cold. Sometime in the night, she had kicked off all the blankets. And she was alone. Sabel slept in her bed in the adjoining room and Abraxas was across the hall sleeping both beside and a little inside of Lily. Not that he needed much sleep, but he anchored himself in her body instead of Ana's while he did his nightly thinking and roaming in the Unseen World.

It made it easier for him to pull Lily into a dream with him when they wanted private time. More than a few times, Ana caught pieces of their shared dream and woke feeling both aroused and disturbed. She didn't mind the feeling of being in Abraxas's male body: she enjoyed the sensations as long as she remembered she wasn't going to be stuck with them, but she didn't appreciate dreaming about having sex with Lily. Not that Lily wasn't attractive, but it just irritated Ana because it reminded her how much she wanted to be with Sabel all the time.

What did that feel like to Lily to have her lover residing partly inside of her? To Ana, now that she was used to hearing someone else's voice in her mind, Abraxas had become a comforting presence, but in a way it was a lot easier because he was male. She'd feel a lot less comforted by having Sabel in her mind. Not that she had anything to hide, but she'd finally stopped worrying what Abraxas thought of all her stupid little thoughts. It would be different with someone she was in a relationship with.

Plus she had the impression that Abraxas was no stranger to violence. It wasn't what he chose, but that was because he'd worked through it, not because it didn't occur to him. Ana had seen Sabel drop a man into sleep with a word, but she couldn't imagine Sabel taking him out in a more brutal way, for example by smashing him in the head with a pipe wrench. What would Sabel think if she had access to Ana's darker impluses and to everything she thought about Mack and Ashmedai?

Speaking of people she wanted to smash in the head—Ana changed into the shorts, sports bra and T-shirt she'd picked up for working out and made her way down to the hotel gym.

There was no heavy bag. She really wanted a heavy bag that she could hit and imagine was Mack's face. Instead she got on the climber and set herself a steep route that she tried to run as much as possible. He needed to go back to South Dakota soon. Having him around made her feel jumpy, like she was in one of those scenes in a horror movie where you couldn't see anything ominous, but the scary music had just picked up volume and you knew any second one of the secondary cast was going to get it—and she was part of the secondary cast, and the music never stopped playing.

She ran until sweat dripped from under her breasts down the sides of her belly and trickled down her back between her shoulder blades, replacing the crawling feeling she had from thinking about Mack. Then she stretched halfheartedly and looked at her phone. There was a text from Sabel saying that she was heading to breakfast if Ana wanted to join her. Ana thought she should probably go up and shower and change first, but the message had come in twenty minutes before and she might miss her opportunity.

In the hotel's restaurant it was still early enough on a Sunday morning that most of the tables were vacant. She could easily spot Sabel sitting in a booth with her e-reader propped in front of her. She took a sip of her coffee and then tucked a loose strand of her dark hair behind her ear.

Sabel looked up, scanned the room and saw Ana. Her eyes widened and her mouth formed a half-open smile.

Ana walked up to the booth and slid into the open side. "Stop grinning at me like that, I smell like a monkey."

"I could not care less," Sabel said.

"You say that now…"

"You shouldn't be allowed to wear those shorts in public."

Ana laughed and ordered a coffee and breakfast number two. When the waiter left, she said, "I'm just lucky you like your girls tall and padded."

Sabel rolled her eyes. "You have the quads of a Greek god."

"With the extra strength Abraxas is building into me, I'll bet I could deadlift you."

"I would literally faint," Sabel said.

"Literally?"

"Absolutely."

Ana didn't want to pressure her about Brie and the leash, so she just took an overlarge gulp of hot coffee and ended up spitting it back into the cup with a yelp. Laughing, Sabel shook her head and handed her an extra napkin.

* * *

After breakfast Sabel went back to her room and sat for a few minutes to let all the aspects of their current situation settle and sort themselves in her mind. Then she moved to the desk to check and respond to any important school emails.

She'd planned to have the second half of April off anyway to travel out to the witches' archive to see what she could learn about the magic that created the leash, and about historical cases of humans sharing their bodies with demons. Plus there was something Abraxas had said: that he had switched bodies with a human once so that he could travel through the death of that body into the realms of the dead. Her understanding of demon magic wasn't that extensive, but the more she thought about it, the more it sounded like witch magic and she wanted to see what precedents there were for demons to use the witches' magic.

Maybe if they got home in the next week she could still make it out east to the archive and get Devony working on her query. She wanted to take Ana, if Ana would let her spring for their plane tickets and hotel, since her stash of severance money had to be running low at this point.

Material world details complete, she took the next hour for magical preparation. She reinforced the usual magic she carried on and in her body to protect herself and she sent a carefully worded update to Josefene in case the woman had any help for her on the nature of the Cyprian. That reminded her that she wanted to ask Abraxas the same question and she went to look for him and Ana.

She knocked on Ana's door and heard steps come to the door and pause. When it swung open, she was looking not at Ana but at Brie.

Sabel took step back.

"Get in here," Brie whispered. She was barefoot in jeans and a peach-colored shirt that made her warm skin seem to glow.

Sabel brushed past her into the room and looked around for Ana, but Brie was there by herself.

"What are you doing here?"

"I'm hiding from Mack," Brie said. "Ana went to get some nonhotel food and whatnot, and he was being all clingy this morning so she said I could stay in her room since it's the last place he'd look."

"You don't have some way of handling him?"

Brie crossed the room and flopped down on the bed next to an open magazine.

"None of them are really applicable to this situation," she explained. "I could feed off him and knock him out, but when he woke up, he'd just want to hang around me more. That's not a great idea since we have to spend the next few days together. I don't have any way to repel someone."

"What do you do at home?"

Brie flipped a page of the magazine, not really looking at it, but not looking at Sabel either. "I make sure I drive at least three hours away before I feed and I never give anyone my real information."

Sabel imagined Brie driving for hours only to find some random stranger to hook up with and then never see again. She knew Brie wasn't human, but still, that seemed like a crappy way to live if you didn't have a choice about it.

In her early twenties, away from the consistent pressure of her family, Sabel had her own wild times and one-night stands, but she always knew she had the choice to stay with someone she cared about. At the time, having one person around all the time was too high a price to pay because it would interfere with her studies. But now, what would it be like to know that Ana existed in the world and she couldn't be with her—not just couldn't touch her for long, they'd work that out—but that she would have to stay away to protect her? If Brie fell in love with someone, she'd have that dilemma, or had she already fallen in love and discovered this?

"When Lily called you, why did you come to help us?" Sabel asked. "Did you think we might be able to fix your situation?"

Brie's head came up quickly, her eyes hard. "My mom asked. That's all there is to it. Or was."

Sabel raised an eyebrow at her.

"I think you know I'd die to save Ana, and you too, arrogant witch that you are." Her dark chocolate eyes held Sabel's, unblinking, and Sabel had to force herself not to look away.

"But I don't know why," Sabel said.

Brie pushed up off the bed and stood in front of Sabel. In her socks, she was an inch or two shorter, her kissable lips nearly level with Sabel's. They were only a handbreadth apart and Sabel's breath quickened.

"If you haven't figured it out," Brie said, "I'm not telling you."

She reached up and tangled her fingers in Sabel's hair in a painfully tight grasp, then gave a playful tug as if she were a kid yanking a girl's ponytail.

"You two drive me crazy," Brie said.

"Me too," Sabel admitted. "Can you get this thing off me?"

"I'd love to try again."

Sabel looked around the hotel room. A T-shirt was thrown over an armchair, the only sign that this was Ana's room, and it made her smile. She remembered how consumingly sexual the process had felt the last time Brie ran energy through her to loosen the leash. It was hardly an act of infidelity to try to get the leash off herself, but at the same time it wasn't something she wanted Ana to walk into unaware.

She took out her phone and called Ana.

"Hey, I'm on my way back, you want to get an early lunch?" Ana asked.

"Grab a snack and get back here, and drop off Abraxas with Lily. Brie and I are in your room and we want to try removing the leash."

"Be right the—" Ana hung up so quickly she cut off the last part of her own sentence.

Sabel smiled to herself and put her phone back in her bag. Brie had stretched out on the bed and was watching her.

"If you weren't with her?" Brie asked.

"It wouldn't work between us," Sabel told her. "We both essentially like the same thing."

"We do?"

"Being told what to do, having to surrender, or being allowed to surrender."

"Oh?" And then more emphatically, "Oh! Do you think Ana would…?"

"I can tell I've been around you too long because that doesn't sound like an awful idea."

Brie grinned and Sabel sat carefully in the chair at the desk across the room from her.

"You know, I'm pretty flexible about that," Brie said. "I tend to adapt to whatever a person wants."

Sabel didn't reply because she couldn't find a polite way to point out that Brie simply wasn't Ana and that's what she really wanted: impulsive, hot-tempered, messy, trustworthy Ana who was sometimes brave because she didn't know better and courageous when she did.

Ana threw the door open and slid through the doorway like she'd run the whole way back from whatever store she'd been in when Sabel called. She locked the door behind her and put the security latch in the locked position as well. Then she stopped and looked at them.

"Are you sure you want me here for this?" she asked.

Sabel got up and crossed the room to her. She kissed her without reservation since if the leash triggered she could just have Brie reset it. Ana held her tightly and kissed back gently at first and then with increasing urgency. Both of them were breathing quickly when they pulled apart.

"I think I need you to be here," she said, standing in the circle of Ana's arms. "Otherwise it feels sneaky."

On the bed, Brie was sitting up and watching them with unconcealed hunger.

"Down girl," Ana said with a grin. "Play nice."

"Always," Brie purred.

Ana stepped out of the shared embrace with Sabel and crossed the room to the armchair in the corner. Brie moved up to the head of the bed and piled pillows against the headboard. She sat back and opened her legs. With a deep breath, Sabel climbed onto the bed and sat with her back against Brie. This time she was hyperaware of the other woman's full breasts against her back.

She tried to remind herself that this attraction was manufactured; it was a byproduct of the energy work they did together and of the time they'd spent in each other's presence. After all, look at Mack. He'd been around Brie a day less than Sabel and he was already stalking her.

Still, it was only her residual cold fury at Brie for almost consuming Ana after the fight with Ashmedai that kept her from turning around and kissing Brie. She looked across the room and met Ana's eyes.

"It's okay," Ana said, though Sabel had no way of knowing which unspoken question she was answering.

She clasped her hands together and wedged them between her knees to keep herself from stroking Brie's legs where they lay outside of hers.

"I need to touch you," Brie said and quickly added, "for the magic."

"Go ahead."

Brie's hands came around to the front of her body. Her right hand rested over Sabel's solar plexus and her left covered her throat. That touch of bare hand on the vulnerable skin of her throat rocked her control. Her head tipped back and she pressed into Brie. On the energy level, she opened.

Brie was inside her in an instant. The touch didn't begin tentatively like the last time. Her energy flowed in quickly and filled Sabel from the base of her spine up to her throat. It felt like the moment before orgasm with no physical location and no peak to the energy. The mix of pleasure and desire made her moan.

In front of her, Ana was at the edge of the chair, her hands clawing its overstuffed arms. Her knuckles stood out under whitening skin and the tendons were taut cables across the back of her hand.

Brie's hands pressed hard against Sabel's throat and body as energy pushed through her skin to the level of the leash. Invisible fingers touched the many places it connected to Sabel's energy. From the inside, Brie filled her more completely and she felt how the leash backed off the more energy she had. If she could get through this without losing her mind, she understood that Brie could push the device open from the inside while she disconnected it from Sabel.

She focused on Ana's eyes. "Please," she gasped.

Ana left the chair slowly and climbed onto the bed. "Can I touch?" she asked Brie.

"Baby, you can touch anything you want to," Brie said.

Ana wrapped her hands around Sabel's. She put her cheek alongside Sabel's and whispered in her ear, "I want you to give in to her, can you do that for me?"

"Yes," Sabel breathed and the last reticence of her body gave way. A flood of energy poured in and the leash pulled away.

Brie's fingers seemed to tuck around it and disengage it in one place and then another and another. Sabel knew what she felt wasn't Brie's physical hands, but it felt as if she were being touched inside her skin in the most amazing ways. Along with the unceasing flow of pleasure, Sabel felt a tenuous clear thread of hope.

The bands came loose from her chest and her throat. In one quick move, Brie pulled up and it was over her head.

Sabel threw herself forward into Ana's arms. Her body felt airy and jangling with energy that wasn't hers. Every cell danced in a pool of light. She was higher than the last time, so blissed out of her mind that she could barely focus her eyes. Thankfully, the witches had trained her for intense pleasure as well as intense pain. She wondered for the first time how much of this they'd foreseen and how many years ago.

She turned in Ana's arms and looked at Brie, who was curled against the headboard with her arms around her chest.

"Did you get it?" Sabel asked. The words came out slightly slurred, but comprehensible.

"Yes," Brie gasped. "How can you even talk?"

"Discipline," Sabel said.

"Fuck." Brie breathed out the word in a tone of awe. Her skin looked ashen and she was shivering even though the room was hot. Sabel remembered Brie telling Ana about the time the Sangkesh demon-hunters starved her—how she'd become colder and colder.

"You gave me too much of your energy," Sabel said. "Take it back."

"You really want me to feed on you?" she asked, her teeth chattering lightly.

Ana shifted behind her. "You can't feed on anyone else in that state," she said. "You don't know if the leash will shut you down and it doesn't look like you have a lot of control right now."

"I don't," Brie said. "But feeding is more…direct than what I've been doing."

"Better that than risk killing someone out there," Ana said.

Sabel turned far enough sideways that she could see Ana's face. Ana nodded to her, but there was a question in her eyes. Sabel returned the nod and smiled a little.

"Brie, shut up and feed," Ana told her.

Sabel might have the powerful Voice magic, but when Ana gave a command in her normal tone, it carried its own kind of weight. Brie was out of her curled position in half a breath and across the bed.

Her hands gripped Sabel's face and their lips connected roughly, but it wasn't exactly a kiss. Brie inhaled with her whole body. Energy streamed out of Sabel's mouth and someplace much lower. This time the orgasm was very real, completely localized and overwhelming. Her shocked cry was muffled against Brie's lips but still resoundingly loud in the small room. The cresting wave of intense pleasure was so strong that her joints went weak and she'd have fallen over if Ana hadn't been holding her tightly.

It felt so good to be awash in pleasure and in Ana's arms that she could almost overlook how it all happened. She kept her eyes tightly shut and pulled away from Brie, pressing back against Ana's chest. Ana tightened one arm around her, but her other arm was stretched out. Sabel cracked her eyes open.

Brie was crouched in the middle of the bed with a feral look on her face as she stared at Sabel. Ana's left hand curled around the base of Brie's throat, holding her back the full length of Ana's arm.

"No more," Ana said.

Brie blinked and her face exchanged some of its wildness for pleading. "Please, her energy is so clear. Everything I gave her came back so sweet."

"Are you still hungry?" Ana asked.

"No."

"Then maybe it's time for you to go shopping or help Lily, because Sabel is mine."

Brie sighed but her face looked human again. "Sorry," she said, but the look she gave Sabel was all desire and no apology. She made a visible effort dragging herself off the bed. The door shut softly and the only sound in the room for the next minute was the quiet rush of their breathing.

"You okay?" Ana asked.

Sabel tipped her head up and smiled. "What benefits package comes with being yours?"

"Anything you want," Ana said. "Considering I just about died from wanting you a few minutes ago. But if you're not—"

She didn't get the last words out because Sabel kissed her and the momentum carried them both off the side of the bed and onto the floor. Sabel thought it would be smart for them to get up and climb back onto the bed, but Ana rolled over so she was on top, pressing Sabel between her body and the floor, and that was the last thought Sabel had for a long time.

CHAPTER FOURTEEN

"We can't…keep having…sex…on the floor," Sabel said and the words came out in little clumps because she was still breathing hard.

After the first, rushed and hard coupling on the floor, Ana had rolled them over so she wouldn't bruise Sabel too badly. Now Sabel moved off her to lie beside her, leaning up on one elbow, still touching everywhere she could. Ana stroked Sabel's hair.

"Bed next," Ana said. "Then…other side of the bed."

"Then shower?"

"Mmm, yes. Unless we can't make it that far."

Sabel laughed as she pictured them on the floor of the entryway outside the bathroom, and she could so picture it.

Ana sat up, found her balance and then deadlifted Sabel, who threw her arms around Ana's neck and laughed.

"You're not fainting," Ana said.

"Too much adrenaline in me," Sabel told her and kissed her.

The momentum of Sabel leaning into her for the kiss pushed her back a step and she staggered, then found her balance again.

"You're a lot stronger," Sabel said.

"The hosting-a-demon workout is very effective."

Ana didn't add that she was at the stage where her physical strength was a little frightening to her. The other day, at home, she'd easily broken a jar she was trying to open. But here she had little doubt of her ability to not hurt Sabel. She carried her to the side of the bed and lowered her gently, sealing the gesture with a long kiss. Then she stepped back to pull off her shirt and the bra that was riding up around her collarbone since Sabel had unhooked it and shoved it out of the way.

Sabel's shirt and bra had already come off. Her pants were down around her calves and she kicked free of them. She hooked her thumbs around her white lace and satin panties, but Ana shook her head and said, "Not yet. I like those."

Ana stepped out of her underpants and crawled onto the bed. She ran her tongue along the lace edging of the panties and traced the curve of Sabel's hip and upper thigh. She worked her way slowly down to the wet satin between Sabel's legs, and put her lips there, inhaling deeply through her nose and then blowing gently through the satin.

"Oh gods," Sabel said. "Every single one of the gods, thank you, thank you—" Her breath caught and turned into a sound of desire.

Ana kept teasing around the edges of the panties with her teeth and tongue, running her tongue across the material and then pulling away. She thought Sabel deserved it for wearing these, and for what she wore most days. Whether Ana saw it or not, she always knew Sabel was wearing something beautiful and provocative.

Sabel was saying "Please" repeatedly and Ana asked, "What is it you want?"

Sabel told her in great detail and included many words Ana was surprised to hear her say out loud.

"Dr. Young, you have the vocabulary of a sailor," she said.

"If I say it all again, will you *please*..."

"Oh, yes," Ana said, and she was more than happy to oblige.

It was a long time before they made it to the shower.

* * *

The meeting with the Cyprian was at dinnertime but Lily said they should eat either before or after so Ana consumed a handful of nuts in the room while she waited for Sabel to finish getting ready. She'd thrown on the designer jeans and olive jacket—they'd come through the fight in the woods in reasonable shape and had been sent out to the hotel's laundry service. Under the jacket she wore a golden-tan shirt that Sabel had picked up for her at one of the nearby shops.

She sat in a warm glow of satiety and watched Sabel getting her outfit and jewelry and makeup together. As soon as she had herself put together, Ana wanted to take it all apart again. She contented herself with shoving Sabel against the wall by the door and kissing her hard until her lipstick was thoroughly ruined and she had to go wash it off and reapply it.

"You go wait in the hall," Sabel told her sternly, with her eyes dancing and lit with pleasure. Ana growled at her but obeyed.

Sabel joined her a moment later. Standing next to her purple silk blouse and dark pants, tiny pearl earrings, matching necklace, and dramatic eye makeup, Ana felt underdressed. It was both worse and better when she saw Brie come out of her room across the hall. Brie had managed to get her wild mass of hair into a knot behind her head from which an array of curling tendrils fanned out. She wore a simple black dress that gathered behind her neck and fell in two bands, barely covering her breasts, to join at the level of her bellybutton. It was also backless. For evening shoes, she wore low sandals made of a dozen tiny straps in sparking silver chains.

"Trying to impress someone?" Ana asked on their ride down the elevator.

Brie actually blushed. "She has a power like mine, to evoke desire."

"Seriously? Who doesn't have that power on this trip? Next time someone should warn me that I'm going to be attending the annual demons of lust convention. How helpless are we going to be?"

"You and me, moderately, everyone else...I don't know."

They took a cab to the address on the card, a shimmering new condo construction, all glass and metal. The Cyprian's suite was the top floor. They were ushered into a white room walled on two sides with panes of glass that looked out over the city. The carpet, the couches and chairs, the leather-topped tables, were all the same shade of white. But here and there among them, like birds in a forest, were flashes of blue. A robin's egg-blue vase on a table with a single white lily soaring up from it, a sea-blue pitcher set out with matching cups, a painting of white houses and blue water.

The Cyprian entered through the far door wearing sky blue capris and a white blouse whose first button occurred a third of the way down the front. Ana's initial thought was: *she's heavier than I am, and prettier. How is that fair?* Then she wondered if as a goddess the Cyprian got to choose her appearance, and if so, why she had chosen the plus-sized model. Perhaps Rubenesque was in fashion in her part of the world. How often did Ana wish it were more in fashion here?

"Welcome," the Cyprian said. Her eyes regarded each of them and stopped on Brie. Ana could have taken the sexual tension between the two of them in her hands like a rope. They played a dangerous game, and she wasn't positive for whom it was more dangerous; she feared for Brie.

"Please make yourselves comfortable," the Cyprian murmured, her gaze still on Brie.

She didn't offer anything to eat or drink, but Lily had said that was polite since some of the gods and goddesses of old had gotten a bad rap for enchanting humans with food. By not offering food, the Cyprian indicated that she didn't want them to feel threatened or have to choose between social convention and personal safety.

"As you know, I am called the Cyprian and am a goddess of love and..." she waved her hand dismissively, "related emotions."

She also didn't try to shake anyone's hand, another nod to their feeling comfortable and secure with her, since some magics worked better with touch. She simply settled into a large chair facing the couch and gestured broadly for them to choose their seats.

"Lily Cordoba," Lily said. "You've met my daughter Gabriella."

The Cyprian nodded. All of her gestures seemed to have a power about them. It was hard not to stare at her.

Brie sat at the end of the couch closest to the Cyprian and Lily took another of the chairs arranged in a semicircle to face the couch. Ana opted to sit next to Brie, which put her in the middle of the couch.

Ana said, "I'm Ana Khoury and I'm also host to the demon Abraxas."

"A demon prince, yes?" the Cyprian asked.

Abraxas shifted out of Ana just enough to appear as if he were sitting beside her on the couch. "Not anymore," he said. "I gave up my title before I left this world and have not sought to take it back."

"Do we share a homeland?" she asked. "When were you made?"

"The year 419, that is 551 BCE by the Roman calendar, near Susa in the Persian Empire."

"And 419 is dated from…?"

"Solomon," he said. "The Great King."

"Captivating. Why do you count from him?" the Cyprian asked.

"He gave us bodies," Brie told her. "He chose us from among the spirit beings to have a closer relationship with humans. Sometimes very close."

"I see that." The Cyprian's teeth shone between her plum lips. She looked back at Abraxas. "So we missed each other by a few hundred years."

"But your title is Mediterranean," Abraxas pointed out.

"I traveled. The Cyprian is an appellation I earned, not my original name." She paused and looked at Sabel, who had chosen the chair on the far side of Lily away from the Cyprian. "And you are?"

"Dr. Sabel Young, professor and Hecatine witch."

"Yes, and there's something else about you."

Sabel's smile didn't reach her eyes and Ana saw the tension in her jaw. Her choice of seats put her farther from Ana, but at an angle where they could easily see each other.

"There's a lot else about me," Sabel said evenly, "but maybe we should talk about why we're all here together."

"Yes," the Cyprian said. "Let's share our troubles and see if together we can find a resolution. Then maybe you'll tell me a little more about yourselves and the demons' *close* relationship with humans."

Lily briefly sketched out the problem: that Ashmedai had blocked them from the airport and by using the support he had from Ashtoreth in Chicago could possibly watch all of the roads out of the city. If their group passed within twenty feet or so of one of the sentries, it would sense the presence of a demon as large as Abraxas. As he'd been gaining power, it was harder for him to hide himself completely within Ana. Even if they did find some way to hide him, it was possible that the sentry demons knew their party by sight or even by smell.

Ana said, "It seems to me that he's not going to stop until he has me and Abraxas. Well, Abraxas at least. I think he'd be happy to kill me and be done with that. I want to know how to stop him for good. We came out here to trap him—and I don't want to go back until we figure out how to do that. I want him finished, one way or another."

The Cyprian nodded. "My help isn't free. These accomplishments will cost you. I have had to live in this city carefully these last few years to stay unnoticed by the local god. I want a city of my own. I want Chicago."

"Why Chicago?" Sabel asked.

"I like it," the Cyprian said plainly.

"It is the third largest city in the country and it is the least strongly held," Abraxas contributed. "My guess is there's some reason you can't move on any city in Texas. New York and LA are much too powerful to take, and Philadelphia..."

"Too many factions there," Lily said. "No way to cleanly grab power. Chicago is simply the biggest available prize on the map."

"As I said," the Cyprian stated with a tilt of her head, "I like it."

"What kind of help do you want from us and what are you offering in return?" Brie asked.

The Cyprian flashed her a wide smile. "Let's discover the details of what we'll need to do and then we'll see what it's worth. I have at my disposal a small army willing to move against Ashtoreth, plus one of her own commanders will turn on her and aid me. But that's not enough to assure my victory. In addition to the raw power of the city itself, Ashtoreth has a much larger army and I must know that she cannot bring its force against me. Tell me more about your opponent. Why would she aid him? What is his aim?"

"He seeks to bind me," Abraxas said. "As long as I'm without a body that's fully my own, I can be bound and thereby compelled to do his bidding."

The Cyprian looked at Abraxas for a long time. Then she nodded. "Yes, you're old and capable of power. How much power, I wonder? Why didn't Ashmedai simply take you the first time he saw you?"

"He tried," Ana said. She didn't know what else to say, where to start the story, but Abraxas elaborated for her.

"He thought he could separate me from Ana by going after her first, but she fought him," he explained. "He left the body he was using, thinking he could take hers. She essentially turned the technique he was using to try to get her out of her body against him and stripped him of a great deal of his power."

"So he's bodiless too," the Cyprian said with a gleam. "That's rich. You only need to bind him as he would bind you and that problem is resolved."

"That was the plan, actually," Ana said. "The reason we left San Francisco was so we could draw him out and trap him in a book. But then he had a lot more help than we expected."

Lily added, "I didn't think any other prince would ally with him as weak as he was. He must have promised Ashtoreth something very valuable—maybe all of Abraxas's power."

"Are you worth that much?" the Cyprian asked. He didn't respond and after a moment she continued. "How did you lose your body? Or did you say you gave it up willingly?"

"I did. Some time after I gave up my title, a human friend was dying and we exchanged bodies so that I could travel into the realms of the dead spirits."

"How did you know you could come back?" the Cyprian asked, curious.

Ana saw Sabel's head jerk a fraction of an inch and she looked from the Cyprian to Abraxas. Because he was beside Ana, she had a clear view of Sabel's face as she stared at Abraxas, but Ana was at a loss to decode the emotions that passed across it. Shock? Fascination? Fear?

"I gambled," Abraxas said. "As it was, it took me nearly a thousand years to find a way back here."

"You've been worshipped as a god," the Cyprian said. "Did you draw on that power to come back?"

"It may have contributed to the effort," he said in a tone that even Ana could hear was too careful.

"Ah, it doesn't work like that, does it?" the Cyprian mused.

"It wouldn't," Sabel said quietly.

"I thought you witches made magic unnecessarily complicated," the Cyprian said.

"Everyone thinks that," Sabel replied. "Until it works."

"Before you all get completely esoteric, can we talk about the part where we actually get Ashmedai off my case?" Ana asked, in part from impatience, but mostly because she felt a pulse of discomfort from Abraxas. Whatever magic they were obliquely talking around, it made him supremely uneasy.

"You help me remove Ashtoreth from power in Chicago, and I will take care of Ashmedai for you," the Cyprian said. "It's that simple. Without Ashtoreth's power, he's nothing to me."

"How do we take care of Ashtoreth then?" Ana asked.

"We could try a banishing or even bind her," Lily suggested. Then she looked up thoughtfully and shook her head. "But first we have to break her bond with the city. The city functions like a body for her, only better, so she can't be bound while she holds it. And we'll have to use surprise if she has superior force."

Brie interjected, "They won't expect us to come after them in Chicago. Last they saw, we were running."

Ana thought there was far too much she didn't know or understand about how these battles worked. Apparently the Cyprian's powers had more limits than Ana expected from a goddess. She couldn't help but ask.

"Why can't you just blow in there and take what you want? Being a goddess and all."

"I could easily overpower Ashtoreth one-on-one, but with the power of the city behind her, I can't be sure. I prefer to be sure of the outcome before I start a war."

"So we really need to disconnect her from that city. How does that work?"

"That *is* our core problem," the Cyprian said. "It's not as simple as disconnecting or I'd have done it already myself."

Sitting beside her on the couch that faced the Cyprian, Brie slid her fingers the few inches to where Ana's hand rested on the cushion and wrapped her fingers around Ana's. Ana felt the other woman quivering with strain. Ana had expected that two women with similar powers would cancel each other out, but apparently they magnified or aggravated each other. Was that the solution of how to get into Chicago? After all, didn't Ashmedai also have similar powers which had made him vulnerable to Brie once before? She wouldn't be able to take him with that trick again, but maybe the Cyprian would know how to use their combined power to come up with this binding.

"Ashmedai is a demon of lust and he's also vulnerable to lust, as we discovered," Ana said. "Is it the same for Ashtoreth? What's she a demon of?"

"War," Lily said. "It's another reason it's hard to go head-on against her."

The Cyprian shook her head. "Poor Astarte. To have her shadow fall so far from her glory."

"You know her?" Ana asked.

"The goddess Astarte is the Aphrodite, like me." Seeing the confusion that statement caused, she went on, "We're not like humans, not like you little singletons. Some gods are part of larger gods. The Aphrodite contains all of us who are some aspect of love."

"Like smaller computer networks connected to a huge network—intranets and the Internet, or something like that?" Ana asked.

The Cyprian blinked. "Yes, that's quite apt."

"But the others who are part of the Aphrodite aren't going to sweep in and help you take a city?" Sabel asked.

"No." Her tone was as short as the word.

"If we had another demon of war, could they take out Ashtoreth?" Ana asked quickly to head off the dark look coming over the Cyprian. Then silently inside herself to Abraxas: *What are you a demon of? You've never told me.*

There isn't a word for it, not like 'lust' or 'war.' You could say I am the duality that unifies, I am synthesis and liberation.

Trust you to not be anything simple, Ana told him.

"We can work around the war aspect," Lily said. "What needs to happen with the city?"

"If we can remove Ashtoreth from the heart of its power, I can begin to redirect its energies to me immediately," the Cyprian said. "It will take a few days to completely absorb the power flowing from the city, but with Ashtoreth bound, I should have all the time I need."

"So we don't need to kill her or anything like that," Lily mused in the halting voice she used when thinking aloud. "Demons are pretty hard to kill, but if we could bind her outside of the city's heart of power, I think that would work. It's a cycle we need to interrupt. Knock her off the power for an instant and start a strong binding, then she can't connect back to the city. Even if she eventually got loose from the binding, you would have the upper hand. Would that be enough for you?"

"It would."

"Then we're left with the problem of Ashmedai," Lily continued. "Assuming we can find a way to get around the city's power and bind Ashtoreth, she can call on him and her army to come down on us. You said your army is much smaller than hers. I imagine we'd be overwhelmed. You would survive that, but I doubt we would."

"Run," Brie said thoughtfully and all eyes turned to her. She looked around the room with her dark gaze like a child seeking approval. "If we run…"

"Ah yes!" the Cyprian exclaimed. "Ashmedai will chase and he'll bring some of Ashtoreth's army with him. The hare draws the hunter and we come in behind, I like it."

"Easy for you to say," Ana told her. "I'm the hare."

Lily shifted in her chair. "If we pursue this plan, and I'll say now it's not my favorite, how will we get him to chase and still stay ahead? He'll have to know we're running and then lose us for a while."

"Not 'we,'" the Cyprian said. "Ana runs. I need you with me to bind Ashtoreth."

"I'm going with Ana," Sabel said.

"No." Brie didn't have to raise her voice for it to cut across the room. "I am. You invited me here to be her bodyguard and I'm not done. I'm the only one with a chance against Ashmedai."

"Both of us, then," Sabel insisted.

The Cyprian turned to Lily. "Are you certain you have the power to bind Ashtoreth on your own?"

"No," she admitted.

"Who else would you need?" Ana asked.

She looked from Brie to Sabel and back again.

"Remember," the Cyprian said and her voice was soft but heavy with power, "if we fail in Chicago, everyone dies. Ana only has to run and not be caught. We cannot get to Ashtoreth and fail or she and Ashmedai will surely destroy each of you. Now, what do you need to bind her?"

"Ideally, Abraxas and one other person, either Brie or Sabel. Actually Sabel would be best. If we use your powers properly, I'm pretty sure we can't fail."

"I am not leaving Ana," she said.

Brie stood up and went to Sabel, leaned over and whispered in her ear. After a moment, Sabel got up from her chair and walked away from Brie. She stood in front of the glass windows looking over the city. Her narrow shoulders slumped and she tipped her head down.

"Lovely," the Cyprian said quietly, as if to herself.

Her voice sounded appreciative, but Ana didn't like it. She joined Sabel in front of the windows. The view of the expansive city light in the darkening evening was spectacular. She put her hand lightly on the small of Sabel's back, and Sabel leaned toward her.

"I can't go with you," Sabel said in a whisper. "I'm a liability."

"You're safer with Lily anyway. I don't want to have to worry about you while I'm running," Ana told her.

"What about me worrying about you?"

"Don't. I'll be okay."

"I hate this," Sabel muttered.

"I can offer Ana and Brie considerable protection on their run," the Cyprian said. "The farther they go, the more resources he'll take on his chase and then we'll attack him from behind."

"Plus," Brie added, "Mack will come with us and he's a pretty effective shit-kicker if it gets physical."

Ana shook her head. "No, we drop him off somewhere. I don't want to have to think about him."

"He can hold his own," Brie said. "He demonstrated that."

"I'm not worried about Ashmedai getting him. I'm worried about him...Just leave him."

"I don't think we can," Brie told her. "I've altered his energy and he's been around me too long. If we leave him, he'll just follow us and either alert Ashmedai or get himself caught."

Ana wasn't sure she cared whether Ashmedai caught Mack, but she certainly didn't want the demon to be able to cull through Mack's memories of her for ammunition.

"What's your plan for after this is over? How are you going to get rid of him?"

Brie shrugged. "Take a long vacation in Canada. Don't worry, I can lose him once I'm not around you."

"Perhaps," the Cyprian said with a languid smile, "when this is over you could offer him to me. Regardless, Lily said she needs both Sabel and Abraxas. How does Abraxas travel if not in Ana?"

"We've been working on having me host him," Lily said. "But never for very long or at a great distance from Ana. He can't completely disconnect himself from her."

Sabel turned to the Cyprian. "He doesn't need to disconnect, does he? You can shorten the perceived distance to almost nothing. I saw you do it in the probabilities."

"I can," she said. She leaned forward and looked at Sabel closely. "You're a perceptive little thing, aren't you?"

"Insight without power isn't all it's cracked up to be," Sabel said.

The Cyprian laughed.

"All right, this is by far the least bad of all the plans I've heard," Ana said.

"Good, take the night, sleep on it," the Cyprian ordered. "I'll need a day or two to prepare anyway. Make a plan for your route back to San Francisco and then plan alternative routes. I'll have some of my people take the alternatives to throw him off."

As they were heading to the door, the Cyprian brushed her fingers along Ana's arm in a subtle gesture for her to wait.

The Cyprian's eyes had been dark but now they were fully black, empty as space, and as Ana looked into them she saw infinite depths. They reminded her of the moment in the woods when she felt through her fear into an open state that allowed her to feel Ashmedai approaching. For a moment, her mind was as empty and open as the space she looked into.

"That is what he's trying to show you," the Cyprian said.

"Who? Abraxas?" Ana asked, but the Cyprian had already turned away and the others were waiting for her in the hallway.

"What did she want?" Sabel asked.

"Nothing," Ana said, puzzled. "She just showed me… nothing. But she said it's what Abraxas is trying to show me. No, wait, she said 'he' so maybe it could be anyone. Abraxas?"

Yes and no, he said.

"Wow, just when I thought nothing couldn't get any nothingier." Ana rolled her eyes and got into the elevator with the others.

* * *

Sleep came late because Ana and Sabel were enjoying the absence of the leash and so Ana let herself doze in the morning, wrapped around Sabel's warmth. Only when Sabel slipped out of bed to use the bathroom did she push back the covers and contemplate getting up and finding some breakfast. She heard the shower and debated joining Sabel, but she was starving and if they were in the shower together it would be a while before she got breakfast.

She wondered if Abraxas and Lily were up. They probably were, and had fresh coffee. Abraxas felt her thinking about him and came across the hall to settle into her.

What do you think of this Cyprian? she asked him.

You have a saying for our situation with the Cyprian, he told her. *'Like using a sledgehammer to kill a mosquito.'*

Just because we visited where I grew up doesn't mean you have to start using the local jargon. Is Ashmedai really a mosquito, relative to the Cyprian?

Perhaps the analogy doesn't hold, but the scale isn't completely off. The few gods I've met could neutralize a demon prince with no trouble at all. The issue is that prince's allies. It's one reason the Sangkesh hold together so strongly—on the greater scale, any one of them isn't the most powerful being out there, but together they are formidable.

And Ashtoreth together with Ashmedai? Ana asked him.

I don't think she's lying that she could use the help. Ashtoreth has been sunk into the heart of that city for a long time. The Cyprian is fighting two or more demon princes with the power of a large city behind them. That might truly be beyond her. But dispensing with Ashmedai is not.

He paused for a time and she got out of bed and found some reasonably clean clothing. Sabel came out of the bathroom wrapped in a robe and kissed her. Ana grabbed the sides of the robe and used it to hold Sabel close, but after a minute Sabel pulled away.

"I'm going to get dressed," she said. "And then we should meet up with the gang and talk about this Cyprian situation."

"Did we skip dinner? I'm starving."

Sabel grinned. "You just burned a lot of calories last night. Back in a sec."

Ana went down on hands and knees to see if her shoes had been kicked under the bed. One was there and the other had somehow ended up under the dresser along with Sabel's bra. She hung the bra over the lamp for effect and put on her shoes.

So you're for siding with her and doing this? she asked Abraxas.

In a war between two demon princes and a god, I'd rather be very far away, but if that's not possible, I prefer the side of the god. And yet, I will be surprised if she has revealed her entire end game to us.

Ana went back into the bathroom and rubbed wet fingers through her hair to even it out from where she'd slept on it. She could use some gel but she didn't have her usual brand. Traveling without luggage sucked.

Sabel came back wearing another pair of hastily-bought jeans and a light tan sweater. She laughed when she saw the bra but left it there while they headed down to breakfast.

Lily, Brie and Mack were in the restaurant. Ana took the seat farthest from Mack. She was already sick of being in this building and doubly sick of having to share it with Mack. Brie was glowing a little, but Ana couldn't tell if that was some kind of power or just self-righteousness. Lily looked harried, and Mack, well, she didn't bother to look at him. Being on her side for a single fight against Ashmedai was only a tiny dent in the years she'd spent hating him and the fear he'd infused into her.

"I'm torn," Lily was saying. "Ashtoreth is one of the Shaitan demons, so there's no reason from the perspective of the Sangkesh not to help. On the whole, the leadership is likely to be pleased that we helped unseat a powerful Shaitan. And I get what Abraxas is saying that the side with a god on it is usually the side to be on. But we certainly have to be very careful. Once the Cyprian has the power of the city of Chicago behind her, she'll be much stronger than she is now."

"And she's already too strong for us to go against her," Sabel said. She handed Ana the coffee carafe. "Assuming we help her, will she be bound in any way to protect us?"

"We can request that," Lily said. "The Cyprian's oath should be as binding as anyone's, maybe more so."

"Weren't you doing magic to get us out of the city? Then she shows up to get us out of the city. I thought that's how it's supposed to work," Brie said.

"The probabilities didn't pull her to us," Sabel told her. "She contacted us because she saw me doing the magic—there's a difference."

"I'm not seeing it."

"Probabilities can be unexpected and go in strange ways, but they're also nonpersonal. They don't do favors and they don't hold grudges. A goddess taking a personal interest in us—I don't trust that," Sabel said.

Brie looked helplessly at Ana, who shrugged and waved down a server so she could order breakfast and more coffee.

"You think we should disqualify her because she offered to help?" Brie asked.

"I'm just saying we should wait and see if other opportunities arise," Sabel said.

"How common are these kinds of fights over cities?" Ana asked while dumping cream into her coffee.

"They're not common, but they're not exactly rare either. Let's say there are about ten thousand reasonably large cities in the US. Probably in a given year at least fifty of them are having some kind of dispute from outside or from within. A lot of the largest cities are actually more stable because the city itself gives power to whoever owns it, so it's easier to keep."

"And it sounds like we're talking about a lot of power here," Ana said.

"The third most powerful city in the country," Lily told her. "I'm fairly certain she's not interested in it for the scenery."

CHAPTER FIFTEEN

After the meal, they all gravitated up to Lily and Brie's suite. Ana went to the minifridge that Lily had stocked with juice and poured glasses for herself and Sabel. Sabel took hers gratefully, still dehydrated from the night before. They settled around the table, with Abraxas's form standing between Ana and Lily. Sabel sat across from them, where she could look at them and contemplate whether she was going to argue more strongly that they should wait and not just jump at the Cyprian's offer.

Sabel couldn't find any specific fault with the direction they were all about to take, but that didn't stop her from feeling uneasy about trusting something as vastly powerful as the Cyprian. If only Abraxas hadn't been valuable enough to draw the attention of Ashtoreth. She thought back to the conversation of the night before and previous conversations. It was clear that Ashmedai wanted Abraxas to absorb as raw power, or at least that's how the chase had started, but why would Ashtoreth, who already owned a powerful resource in the city of Chicago, also want to absorb Abraxas? Was there something beyond his raw power that these other demon princes wanted from him?

Sabel looked at the slowly shifting cloud shapes that formed his face and the dark recesses of his eyes. "How *did* you get back here?" she asked. "From the lands of the dead, I mean."

He turned and paced a few steps away in an odd copy of one of Ana's gestures. On him it looked less coiled and more pensive.

"I'm not prepared to say," he said finally.

Lily pushed her chair back and looked at him, her dark eyebrows pinched together.

"It was the magic of the summoning circle, wasn't it?" she asked. "And your history of being worshipped like a god, right?"

"How could it be?" Sabel asked her and then looked to Abraxas again. "You were fully gone, through death, into those places beyond. That's not where summoning reaches."

"Okay, I know I'm the newbie here," Ana said. "But don't people talk to ghosts and spirits and stuff all the time?"

"Ghosts are here in this world when we see them. Spirits, not so far off. And sometimes you can reach through the information level of the world to contact someone who's really far away, but you're not pulling them to where you are. It's like you can call Australia, but you can't teleport someone from there to here."

"But they can just get on an airplane."

"It's an imperfect metaphor. Let's just say there are no airplanes but suddenly someone shows up in your living room and says they just came from Australia."

Ana looked at Abraxas. Sabel couldn't hear the question she was asking mentally, but after a moment she shook her head at him. Then, out loud, she said to him, "Are you sure it's not because she's a witch and you just don't want the witches to know?"

"I don't want the Sangkesh to know either," he said. "It's not good knowledge to share."

A phrase came to the forefront of Sabel's mind—the one Devony used to describe the magic of the galla-demons: "a bridge across life and death."

"Abraxas, did you meet any of the galla?" she asked.

His gray-white form turned stormy and dark. He swirled into a whirlwind, swept across the table and poured himself into her body.

There was no leash.

Nothing stopped him, but her own defenses triggered so that he couldn't immediately change her in any way. Still he hit her with enough force that he threw her consciousness out and away from her body.

She found herself standing on an oppressively hot beach of white sand, a roiling storm front turning the Mediterranean green-black. A tallish, well-built man with tawny skin and fire for eyes glared at her.

"No more questions!" he thundered.

"How?" she yelled back at him. "How did you come back?"

He grabbed a handful of her hair and jerked her face up toward his. His breath was like fire on her cheek. "Do you want all of your secrets revealed, witch?"

She put one hand on either side of his face, thumbs under his eye sockets, pressing lightly but firmly—pulling closer, threatening. She knew pain, she didn't care about his fire, let him try. He might think she was ice he could melt, or metal he could liquefy, but at the end of it all, she was pure information and will. Fire could not burn her.

"If your secrets harm Ana…I will bind you to that torment all your days."

"You don't have the strength."

"I will learn it." She spat the words in his face.

Enough time had passed in this place that she had her bearings. It was an eddy of the Unseen World, like the time eddy she'd once pushed herself and Ana into, given form by her internal expectations and not connected to anything other than her consciousness and Abraxas's. She could feel his connection back to Ana and oriented herself along it so she had access to her full power.

She gathered her will and used the Voice. "*Tell me*," she said.

His face jerked back from hers. He must have thought her Voice was connected to her body. His mouth moved of its own volition.

"The magic of the galla—" he started, and then the connection to Ana pulled hard and he was gone.

Sabel stared out over the storm-wracked water. She picked up a stone and hurled it, following it with a shout of frustration and rage.

Then she turned the Voice on herself and commanded, *"Return to your body."*

Her eyes were already open and they focused on a room that was much calmer than how she felt. She was still sitting in a chair at a small round table in a hotel room, with Ana leaning across the table and staring into her eyes.

"Are you okay?"

Sabel took a long, slow breath and then another. She felt like she should be shaking, rippling with adrenaline and anger, but none of that had penetrated her body.

"Yes," she told Ana. "We just needed to have a little talk." Her teeth clenched around the last few words.

Ana straightened up and addressed Abraxas, who was once again to the side of and a little behind Lily. "What the hell did you do?"

"No leash," he said in an oddly flat tone.

He was right, of course: he'd just demonstrated that not wearing the leash put her at risk again from Ashtoreth and her minions. But his choice of now as the right time to point that out was a clear attempt at distraction.

"You know, I didn't understand why Ana swears at you and about you so much," Sabel said. "But now I do. You're maddening. You think you always know best."

"You should hear what she thinks about you," he replied.

"Oh my god, you two are like giant magical babies," Ana said. "Cut it the fuck out. I can't even follow what you're fighting about anymore. And I do not swear at Sabel in my head; I'm using the word 'fuck' in an entirely different context there."

The humor mixed with suggestiveness cleared away some of the icy rage building in Sabel. She had to laugh, and then stand up and put her arms around Ana, who pulled her even closer and held on to her tightly.

The hotel room door lock clicked open and Sabel heard Brie say, "Um, hi. What did I miss?"

Lily stood up. "We're going for a walk," she said and gestured toward Abraxas. He poured himself into her body and she passed Brie into the hallway.

"I'm getting that you-don't-want-to-know vibe," Brie said. "Should I be clearing out too?"

"This is your room," Ana said. "We'll go back to mine."

"We're going to need your help, though," Sabel said. "We transferred the leash too soon. In Chicago, we're up against another demon prince. If Ashtoreth or one of her minions possesses me…"

"But how would they even know what they could do with your Voice?" Ana asked.

"If Ashmedai knows, it's a good bet that Ashtoreth does too."

"Fuck," Ana said.

Sabel kissed Ana's cheek and pulled away from her.

"You want me to put it back on you?" Brie asked.

"Want? Not really. But I think it's what's smart. Can you?"

"Oh, yeah. It's pretty easy for me to pull it off myself. It's still fitted for you anyway. I was going to take it to my stepdad to get it tweaked for me because I don't know how to mess with all this lacy witch magic."

"Lacy?" Sabel asked.

"Do you prefer frilly?"

"Intricate, perhaps?"

"I was thinking girly, maybe with a hint of princess," Brie said.

"Princess?" Ana asked with a raised eyebrow.

"Don't you forget it," Sabel said. "It's late, and we've got at least a day before the Cyprian said she'd be ready. Why don't we revisit this tomorrow?"

Ana grinned at her.

"You're swearing at me in your head, aren't you?" Sabel asked.

"You know it."

Brie rolled her eyes and flopped backward onto the bed farthest from the door. "You two are awful. Get going. Nobody cares about the poor succubus."

Sabel paused in the doorway and looked back at Brie, who winked at her, but there was a touch of pain in her smile.

* * *

For the rest of that day, Ana and Sabel were indisposed. And maddening. If Brie stayed on the hotel floor near them, she could feel the waves of energy coming out of Ana's room, but she couldn't put her hands on it and feed from it the way she wanted to. Even if she stood right outside the wall of their room, she wasn't quite close enough to drink the power. And even if she could, it didn't feel right to feed from them without asking first.

She went out shopping, but nothing held her interest so she just walked. The forecast promised a snowstorm in the next day or two, so while she could still walk around outside easily, she explored back and forth across downtown. She wanted to try to feed with the leash on, while she could still play with it, but she knew she couldn't do that alone. She'd have to bring Sabel with her in case the leash didn't work, because she'd have to try to feed to the point of killing someone, and if it didn't work there needed to be another way to stop her. But it had to work. She wanted what Ana and Sabel had.

She headed back to the hotel at dinnertime to see if Lily wanted to hit one of the local restaurants with her. The elevator doors opened on the golden hallway, lit only by the overhead lights because the sun was already over the horizon, and Brie took the two left turns toward her room.

Mack was sitting on a chair outside the door of his room. She stopped, but he saw her and got up.

"Thought maybe we could get dinner," he said.

He kept walking until he was a few inches from her. He smelled clean, freshly showered and shaved, anointed with crisp aftershave. She saw a lock of his rust-colored hair still damp at the back of his neck and she wanted to touch it. It wasn't fair that she couldn't have Sabel, or Ana, or even Mack. Someone should be hers.

"I was coming back to see if Lily wanted to go," she told him, hoping that would quash the asking-for-a-date vibe.

"We have something, don't we?" he asked. "You're dodging me."

Brie backed up a half step. He'd placed himself in the middle of the hall so, this put her back to the wall. He advanced and flattened one hand on the wall next to her—between her and the route to her room.

"It's just not a good time for me," she said. "Back home… something bad happened not long enough ago, you know?"

"Yeah, I get that," he said, but he didn't back away from her. He was close enough that he could kiss her easily if he wanted to.

She pressed her palms against the wall behind her to keep from grabbing him or shaking with the effort not to. He smelled like anger, gunmetal, hot grease, disaster. She wanted to put him in her mouth and taste all of it.

The elevator chimed, doors swished open and then walking footsteps turned to running. Brie glanced to her right in time to see Ana grab Mack by the back of his shirt and swing him into the far wall. He staggered when his shoulder hit but didn't go down.

"Fuck you," he snarled and threw a tight punch at her.

They were close to the same height but Mack had about twenty pounds on Ana, most of it muscle. She stepped sideways and toward him, his blow grazing the side of her cheek. Her left fist caught him in the gut. He bent forward and she hit him in the side of his head hard enough to knock him to his knees.

"Fuck," he spat, and this time the word was edged with shock and worry. He shuffled back and got to his feet, holding his hands in a guard position in front of his face.

Ana had her own fists up, white-knuckle furious but with good form. Abraxas must have been training her, Brie thought with appreciation before her better sense grudgingly fought its way to the front of her brain.

"He wasn't hurting me," she said. "Ana, I'm okay." But her voice sounded small and breathy. It took most of her attention to keep from grabbing one or both of them and turning their anger into lust.

"You want to fight?" Mack asked. "Come on. You never could beat me before."

Ana's voice was low and crisp. "I grew up," she said.

He came toward her in a balanced stance, feinted with his left arm and watched her reaction. He'd clearly boxed before. Whatever Abraxas was teaching Ana, it wasn't boxing. She stood with her hands up and waited. He took another step toward her, bouncing a little, gaining confidence. He feinted slightly right and then heavily left, punching hard with his right.

Ana's strike was faster. Brie missed it, but she saw Mack's head snap back and his punch went wide. Ana hit him again and again, backing him down the hallway with the force of the punches. His ankle hit the leg of the chair outside his door and he fell, arms tucked tightly in front of his face.

Ana sidestepped his kicking legs and dropped to kneel over him, her fists coming down on the side of his head and then his upper chest. It was enough. More than enough, but she didn't stop. Brie knew on some level that Ana would hate herself for putting Mack in the hospital, but if she kept going, that's where this was heading.

"Ana, stop."

Even she wasn't convinced by her words. She ran the few steps to Ana, locked her arms around Ana's upper chest and dragged her backward off Mack. Ana fought against her grip and Brie felt her fingers slipping. She let her inner sense flow into the mass of Ana's rage and push it back along the spectrum of emotion and a bit sideways into lust. Ana stopped fighting and Brie stopped trying to hold onto her.

Ana turned and grabbed her, locking their bodies together and kissing her hard. Brie's awareness flowed through both of them. She opened her mouth and her will to Ana, drawing her in.

Ana's lips tasted of blood and adrenaline and triumph. But behind that, Brie felt another presence come up sharply and for a moment she was kissing two people. Atop Ana's soft mouth, she felt the firm, rich lips of Abraxas.

She stepped back at the same time that Ana pulled away, fighting to catch her breath.

"Gross," Brie panted. "You're totally banging my mom."

"What?" Ana gasped.

"Abraxas put his energy over yours to remind me not to get carried away."

"Yeah, nice save."

"Not nice," Brie insisted. "Not nice at all."

She looked down the hall away from Ana. Lily was kneeling next to Mack, trying to get a good look at the bloody mess of his face. Sabel stood in the open doorway of her room, her face expressionless. When her eyes met Brie's for a moment, they were as hard as granite.

She came down the hall with her mouth a thin line. Brie stepped away from Ana and moved over to where Lily was looking at Mack. Peripherally, she saw Sabel take Ana's hands and turn them palm down so she could examine the bruised and swelling knuckles.

"How bad is he?" Brie asked Lily.

"He'll need stitches. Hopefully there's no concussion."

"M'fine," Mack grumbled.

Brie put her hand on his upper arm and warmed him lightly so that he'd be more amenable. "Come on, big guy. Let's get you looked at and then we can get dinner on the way home, okay?"

She got a hand towel from their room to slow the bleeding from gashes on his cheek and forehead, and then she and Lily helped him stand and walk carefully down the hallway past Ana. Brie glanced back over her shoulder and saw Ana watching Mack walk away. She was smiling.

Sabel stood by the elevator, scooping ice into an ice bucket. She didn't look up as they waited for the elevator, but before it arrived, she turned her head slightly toward Brie and said, "When you get back, come see me."

CHAPTER SIXTEEN

Sabel put the ice bucket gently down on the dresser and went into the bathroom for washcloths: three dry, one damp. Ana was pacing on the far side of the bed. Sabel dropped the washcloths on the foot of the bed and said, "Let me see your hands."

Ana held them out to her. The knuckles were bruising blue-purple. The middle of her left hand had swollen so that the second and third knuckles were no longer visible under the puffy lump of skin. On her right hand, the skin was split and crusted with blood across her first and second knuckles. Sabel picked up the damp washcloth and reached for Ana's hand.

"Have you asked Abraxas if you broke anything?" Sabel asked.

Ana shook her head. "It's fine. My hands are tougher than Mack's soft fucking head."

The angry words sent a ripple of longing through Sabel. Ana moved toward her and caught her chin in one battered hand, pulling her closer still. She opened her mouth to Ana, pressed against her, wanted to drag her to the bed. Wanted Ana to take her, throw her on the bed and use her bloodied hands on her.

Somehow Sabel got a hand between them and pushed so that Ana had to break the kiss and let go of her. Confusion and hurt in her eyes, Ana pulled the washcloth out of Sabel's clenched fingers. She sat in the armchair and began slowly working loose the drying blood on her fist without looking up.

Sabel moved away from Ana, picked up two dry washcloths and carried them to the ice bucket to fill. When she set them down, her hands were shaking.

This was so clearly not the time. Filled with desire formulated from rage, courtesy of Brie, Ana would be eager to oblige Sabel now. And she would hate herself as soon as she cooled down. Ana wasn't comfortable with the line between anger and lust; she'd never said it aloud, but Sabel saw in the way she contorted herself in their daily lives to avoid ever hurting Sabel with the leash, that she was deeply afraid of her own anger allowing her to hurt another person.

Brie could play with Ana's emotions and the edges of what she could tolerate, but Sabel would never let her act in ways she'd only regret later…no matter how much she wanted right now to crawl across the room and press her face into Ana's hands.

She'd taken much too long putting ice into the washcloths, so long that when she took them back to Ana, Ana was staring at her in puzzlement.

"She was just trying to get me to stop," Ana said.

Sabel put the ice packs on the table next to the armchair. She knelt in front of Ana and gently pulled the wet washcloth out of the fingers of her swollen hand. She placed the hand on Ana's thigh and settled an ice pack on it. Ana's other hand was already resting on her other leg and Sabel placed the second ice pack over the bruised, bloody knuckles.

She looked up at Ana. "Take me with you tomorrow," she said. "Don't go with Brie and Mack, send them to Chicago."

"Nothing's going to happen," Ana said.

"That's not what I'm afraid of."

"I can choose who I sleep with," Ana insisted.

The words stung. As if she was a jealous girlfriend. Like she wasn't trying to avert a variety of magic-related disasters. Sabel pushed up from kneeling at Ana's feet and walked halfway across the room from her.

"It's not the sex part that worries me," she said. "It's the choosing. When you kissed her in the hall, didn't it feel like you chose that?"

The words came out with a harder edge than Sabel intended and she heard her fear in them even if Ana didn't. Seeing Ana so easily manipulated by Brie—it wasn't that she'd kissed Brie, it was that her energy could be used like that and she was helpless to prevent or stop it.

She could trust Ana but only as far as Ana was fully herself. What happened when Ana couldn't tell the difference between her own desires and the emotions Brie pressed upon her, or Abraxas, or any of the other demons she seemed so fond of?

"It's just magic," Ana said. "It's not like it's real."

"Of course it's real," Sabel snapped at her. "You think this is real?" she said and slapped her hand on the dresser. "Doesn't Abraxas teach you anything?" The words spilled out, the volume rising until she was yelling. "The Unseen is what's real. This is just things. You think Brie evokes some kind of fake lust in you, really? Does it feel fake?"

Ana was on her feet, the washcloths falling from her hands to scatter ice across the carpet. "What the hell? You let her inside your body to take the leash and you're pissed off that I kissed her?"

"It's not about the kiss. Gods, you think I'm just some jealous girlfriend. You don't understand."

"Then tell me."

Sabel shook her head. How could she explain? Ana couldn't see that Sabel was trying to say that her lack of understanding was the problem. It wasn't some double standard Sabel had about magic and demons and kissing, it was that she didn't understand at some fundamental level how the powers around her worked and because she didn't understand, Sabel couldn't trust her—couldn't trust Ana to protect herself against them but also couldn't trust Ana to take care of her.

She felt alone suddenly, a million miles from Ana who was only a few feet away. Tears welled up and fell and she turned quickly toward the door before Ana could try to comfort her and end up making her feel worse. She didn't want Ana to touch her and show her how separate she could feel even in Ana's arms.

"Sabel—" Ana said, but she opened the door quickly and stepped into the hall, letting it close behind her and shut out whatever Ana was going to say.

She went into her room and locked the door with the bolt and the chain. The room was too big and empty, so she tucked herself into the corner between the bed and armchair. She put up every magical defense she could think of and then bent her legs to her chest, wrapped her arms around them and cried silently for a long time.

* * *

Did you still want to see me? Brie texted.

Yes, now is fine, Sabel replied.

A moment later Brie knocked on the door. She came into the room and carefully sat on the foot of the bed. Brie stared at her, and Sabel wondered how bad she looked. She should've checked herself in the mirror before answering the door, but she just couldn't care right now.

"What's the deal?" Brie asked. "Ana says you yelled at her."

Sabel raised an eyebrow. "That's not why I called you here."

"Yeah, well, it's why I showed up. What's up with you? You know I had to get her off Mack before she wrecked him. What do you think I should have done?"

"It doesn't matter," Sabel said.

"How can it not?"

"Sooner or later you'd have done something like that regardless of the context. It's what you do. You'll make her want you."

"And that's what you're pissed about? That I can do that to her?"

"No," Sabel said coolly. She looked at Brie's pretty face and her warm, dark eyes, and because she did want to say it aloud to someone, she told her the truth. "I'm not upset because you can make her want you. That's just who you are. I'm upset because she doesn't know the difference."

"Come again?"

"She can't tell the difference between her feelings for me and the feelings you can give her for you."

"No one can," Brie said. "Because it's the same thing."

Sabel sat in the desk chair, crossed her legs and looked at Brie in silence for a long time. It was hard to explain and she wasn't sure she wanted to try. It wasn't jealousy or envy. Of course Brie was lovely in a way Sabel could never compete with, but she didn't need to. She was pretty enough and women generally wanted her for her brain as much as her body; in that department, Brie was outmatched.

And it wasn't that Brie could make Ana want her—it was that once Brie started mucking around in Ana's emotional world, it got hard to tell what was trustworthy. Plus it reminded Sabel that Abraxas could do the same thing to Ana and he lived inside her. The fact was that Ana could be pushed so easily one way or the other without realizing it, and that she had no ability to know if she was or wasn't being pushed.

"I can tell the difference," Sabel said.

"Yeah." Brie grinned and Sabel thought she also saw a slight blush rise in her cheeks. "But you're not actually doing that through the emotion, you're using magic that tracks the source of it, right?"

"Essentially. Ana could do that too if Abraxas taught her, but he hasn't."

"You think he pushes her too?"

Sabel shook her head but without conviction. "I don't know. Anyway, I didn't ask you here to psychologize with you. You need to give me the leash back."

"Oh, yeah, thanks for asking nicely."

"If you want, I can ask much less nicely than I did," Sabel said.

"Bitchy much?"

"Just do it."

"You're not the fucking Queen of Everything," Brie said.

She got up from the foot of the bed and grabbed Sabel by the front of her jacket, hauling her up from the chair. She pivoted and shoved Sabel toward the bed. A couple inches shorter than Sabel, Brie still had the strength of a demon and it was a strong shove. Two unbalanced steps back, Sabel's knees hit the bed and she fell backward onto it.

With inhuman speed, Brie leapt onto the bed and knelt over Sabel so that she straddled her pelvis. She put one hand on either side of Sabel's head and kissed her roughly.

Sabel understood the gesture. Brie wanted her to get angry and fight, so she was implying that Sabel had a double standard when it came to Ana kissing other women, or demons. And if Brie wanted her to act rashly in the heat of anger, she'd do the opposite. She'd spent years learning how to feel manipulation on any level and how to avoid it.

She returned the kiss and at the same time took a long breath in through her nose, slowing her heart rate, opening her awareness into the larger, magical space around her body. She mentally undid the catches on her defensive lattice and opened it to Brie. Then she drew energy up through her body and opened herself down to the most primal levels.

Brie's head jerked back. "Holy fuck, you can do that?"

"You have something for me," Sabel said.

"Oh, yeah, I do."

She kissed Sabel so hard that she tasted blood. The first time, when Josefene put the leash on her, it had taken hours and left her dizzy and weak from all the places it tapped into her energy system. Brie's energy came up inside of Sabel, grabbed the leash where it was snug inside of Brie's body and slammed it back into Sabel.

It was like having a dozen large needles stabbed through the most tender points of her torso, and at the same time Brie's energy radiated pleasure through her like an orgasm that originated everywhere and had no peak and no decline. Pain and ecstasy rolled through her, threatening to drag her down into unconsciousness. She let her head fall back, pushed the last of her breath out of her lungs and surrendered to it.

She didn't exactly pass out, but for a long time there was no conscious thought in her, only keen awareness and waves of sensation too intense to name. She let the pain carry her back to full wakefulness, since it was the more reliable conduit. The leash was back in its place and she felt shaky and slightly ill. Brie was still sitting across her pelvis, staring down at her, mouth open in amazement.

"Thank you," Sabel said.

Brie shook her head. "Baby, between you and me, I'm not the scary one."

Sabel smiled serenely up at her. "Of course you are."

"I've never seen a human who could do that," Brie said. "Not even close."

"By your own admission, you only know one other witch. Also, you're sitting on me."

"How did they make you like that?" Brie asked.

"I could tell you, but then I'd have to kill you."

Brie laughed. "All right. Can we do that again when I take the thing off you after this is all done?"

Sabel thought about it and told her, "The open part, sure. Maybe not the painful part."

"Yeah, sorry. You just piss me off sometimes."

"Likewise."

Brie moved sideways off her and asked, "Are you going to talk to Ana?"

"I can't yet," Sabel told her.

"You need to."

"Just let me figure out how to say...I don't even know what."

Brie got off the bed and stood next to it, looking down at her with a worried crease in her forehead. Then she nodded and left the room. Sabel stayed on the bed, slowly putting all of the pieces of herself back in their proper places. It took a long time and when she was done she slipped roughly into an exhausted sleep shot through with painful dreams.

* * *

In the morning, Ana regretted everything. Mostly she wished she could have spent the night with Sabel in her arms and she desperately wanted to know what was going on that made Sabel push her away so abruptly and completely.

She also regretted that she hadn't hit Mack enough to discourage or disable him from accompanying her and Brie on their run west. She tried to cheer herself up by thinking they could use him as bait. Ana had seen the way Mack had been leaning into Brie in the hall, the way he thought his will was the most important and that she'd give in to whatever he wanted. Sure, Brie could more than handle it, but Ana didn't trust that she'd handle it harshly enough. Mack shouldn't be allowed to get away with behaving that way.

And so what if she had been looking for an excuse to hit him. It felt good to make him hurt and it had scraped the top off her fear. She felt almost ready to start a mad dash cross-country with him and Brie.

Other than leaving Sabel, the part of the plan she disliked the most was transferring Abraxas into Lily's body and leaving him behind.

Are you sure you'll be okay that far away from me? Ana asked him while she was in the shower.

The Cyprian is lending me support. It should be enough. In the worst case, I simply return to you and leave them.

Do they really need your help that much? She didn't add "more than I do," but because it was in her thoughts she knew he heard it anyway.

You will need my help only if the efforts in Chicago fail, he said. *I don't want to leave you on this run without me, but I trust you to use what you've learned.*

She wanted to yell at him, but how could she argue with him when he was saying that he trusted her?

Out of the shower and dressed, she went to Lily's room. It was a straightforward process to let Abraxas cross the short distance to Lily's body, since they'd done it so often in less complete forms. Lily said a few words to help him settle himself in her and Ana was on her own. She went back to her room for her two small bags and then knocked on Sabel's door.

Sabel looked tired, her eyes more gray than blue and shadowed with worry, and her forehead creased. Ana reached out for her and Sabel didn't turn away, but when Ana hugged her close, Sabel didn't relax either.

"You're going to tell me how to make this right, aren't you?" Ana asked.

"When this is all over...when it's over, maybe it will just be right."

"Maybe?"

"It will. It will," Sabel said. "And I'll tell you whatever you want to know when we're home again."

Ana saw the fear in Sabel's eyes and it stopped her from pushing for more information now. Instead, she kissed her and Sabel's hand rose to the back of her head, fingers playing in the short hair at the nape of her neck. Ana took Sabel's hand and kissed each finger.

"Let's go home," Ana said.

"I'd like that. I hear they have some nice flights out of Chicago."

"I'll meet you there in a few days. I promise."

She shouldered her backpack, picked up the other bag and backed down the hall toward the elevator, watching Sabel as she went. Sabel waved and tried to smile, and Ana wanted to drop everything and run back to her, but she kept going. Until she met Brie and Mack in the lobby.

Mack's face was swollen along one side and he had a black eye, along with a few long gashes that had been stitched and taped over, but he looked at her expressionlessly and acted like it was no big deal. The three of them got into the back of a cab, with Brie in the middle, and went to the train station. Ashmedai should have spies here. Brie nodded to Ana as they walked up the steps and touched the side of her nose to show that she smelled the invisible demons watching for them.

They already had tickets for the train, bought online under names provided by Lily, and they had only minutes to cross the station and board. They got on the train in silence and settled into seats with Ana facing Brie and Mack. She and Mack ignored each other.

"How many are there?" Ana asked as the train pulled out of the station.

"Can't tell, a few. They're here for sure," Brie answered in a strained voice.

She and Lily had worked out a way for her to give off enough demon magic for a short time that it would seem, to a casual, magical observer that Abraxas was still with them. Whatever the technique was, it seemed to take most of Brie's concentration.

"Crack the window," Brie told Mack and he did. She leaned across him and sniffed the cold air.

After a minute she said, "I smell fewer than I did when we walked into the station. I think they sent a few with the train and some to alert Ashmedai."

"I hate this part. How long until he gets to us?"

"Depends on how far away he is and what he's using for a body now."

The train sped through the bare landscape and Ana tried to get her muscles to unclench, but she expected an attack to come any minute.

In St. Cloud they had to get out and run to the car the Cyprian had waiting for them. Ana was glad to see four identical cars side by side in the parking lot. That would make it tough even for a human observer, and the demon sentries employed by Ashmedai might not know details, like the importance of license plates. This plan could actually work. They got into the second car and were off again.

The Cyprian's driver took them on a circuitous route out of town and then headed south toward Iowa. Brie fell asleep in the back of the car with her head on Mack's shoulder. Ana sat in the passenger seat and tried to pretend he wasn't on the trip with them.

After a few hours, the driver pulled over at one of the thousand identical rest stops throughout the Midwest, where a rental car waited for them. Ana took the first shift driving. It was three hours to Kansas City.

When they got to that city, they sat down for a meal that was either a really late lunch or an early dinner. Ana figured the latter since they'd gotten fast food on the way to Kansas City. After eating, they bought four bus tickets heading southwest, using Ana, Brie, Lily and Sabel's real names, but they didn't get on the bus.

Back in the rental car, Mack drove them north for a while. Brie sat next to him, chattering away about the Midwest and sports teams and a collection of subjects so inane that Ana stretched out on the backseat and dozed. She woke when it was dark and her cramping legs felt ready to hop off her body and make a run for it.

They pulled into a roadside hotel at ten p.m. Brie booked them rooms using an identity from Lily: one room for her and Ana, and another down the hall for Mack. Ana was relieved when the door closed behind him and more relieved when Brie locked their door.

"You look worried," Brie said. "He's not going to hurt either of us."

Ana shrugged. She wasn't much afraid of Mack hitting her anymore. She was afraid of the copy of him that lived in her that grinned every time she saw the damage she'd done to his face.

CHAPTER SEVENTEEN

Sabel hated letting Ana go without her, and she hated that she was such a danger to Ana that she couldn't go along. When she was younger and first heard about the *marevaas* power, she thought it would be wonderful to develop the ability to give unbreakable commands to people. But in truth the power had caused her so much more grief than it was worth.

She kept telling herself that Ana would be fine, that all Ana had to do was run, using all the resources the Cyprian made available to her, and keep ahead of Ashmedai for long enough that this group could assail the city. Then they could come to her rescue with a truly impressive cavalry. She looked forward to seeing Ashmedai crushed by the Cyprian and she had no doubt that she could do it.

That didn't make it any easier to let Ana leave without her—and with Brie. What shape would Ana be in when she came back? Would she be changed in some way that she didn't know? Or would she seem exactly like her usual self, maybe even *be* her usual self, and all that would have changed would be Sabel's doubts about her, the insidious lack of certainty?

After Brie and Ana reported in from Des Moines, the Cyprian announced it was time to move. She had a white car waiting. Lily got in the back with the Cyprian, so Sabel ended up in front with the driver, an ebony-skinned guy with brilliant white teeth and a shimmer to him as if his skin were being broadcast onto a screen. By simply driving into the city in the material world, they could settle in and gain a foothold without alerting Ashtoreth that they were there. Given time, maybe a few days, she'd feel a change in the city that suggested the presence of magical others as powerful as the Cyprian, but they weren't going to wait long enough for that to happen.

Sabel stared out the window and thought about the feel of Ana in her arms. The image of Ana leaving the hotel haunted her. She wished she could have figured out how to talk to Ana—about magic and manipulation and her fears—but she was so used to setting aside her feelings in the midst of a crisis that she couldn't figure out how to give voice to them.

They arrived in Chicago in the late evening, having stopped in Madison for dinner. Sabel made herself lie down in this latest hotel bed, determined to sleep a little. Her resolve must have worked because when her phone buzzed, the morning sunlight was forcing its way in around the blinds. She rolled to one side and looked at her phone.

Ana's text read: *Heading north again. All clear so far. Miss you.*

Sabel texted back: *We're in the big city. I miss you too. Stay safe.*

She wished she could talk to Josefene, but her concentration wasn't great and she worried that the Cyprian could somehow overhear them the way she'd seen Sabel working with probabilities. Instead, she sent a carefully worded message to Josefene, updating her on all of their actions as the Cyprian already knew them. It was easier to craft her information in a written message so that Josefene would understand what was going on without Sabel having to explain it all. In person, she was afraid Josefene would start asking questions in a way that would reveal Sabel's suspicions that the Cyprian wasn't as good an ally to them as she seemed.

She put on something new and unremarkable. Then she went across the hall and knocked on Lily's door, thinking that the bland tan walls and carpet of the hotel hallway felt like déjà vu. Lily invited her in and she saw that the room's small desk was covered with pieces of paper with symbols on them.

"Is that the binding?" Sabel asked.

Lily nodded.

"Do you want my Voice for all of it?"

She looked down at the sheet in front of her. "Just this part right here. I'll teach you the syllables."

"Ana says they're heading north again."

"I heard," Lily said. "They should be in Fargo before dinner, then I think they're going to try to sleep a little because they pick up the train at three a.m."

"Do you think they'll actually make San Francisco?"

Since last night, it started to seem reasonable to think that Ana might really get back to their city and its protection. That would make this task a whole lot easier.

"It's a lot of travel on the same train," Lily said. "And it's too soon to know. I think if they make it to Washington they should definitely switch to a bus and then it's pretty possible as long as Ashmedai expects them to be coming in from the south."

"Are we going in tonight?"

"Tomorrow. The Cyprian said she needed more time to confirm Ashtoreth's troop movements out of Chicago. Let's go up and have a look."

She and Lily went up to the top floor of the hotel where the Cyprian had a four-room executive suite that took up a corner of the building. Sabel expected to see papers strewn around, like in Lily's room, or perhaps computer monitors with reports and maps. The Cyprian welcomed them and brought them into what looked like an empty sitting room.

"It's going well," she told them. "Ashtoreth is devoting considerable effort to helping your enemy. Abraxas must be quite the prize."

Lily laughed. "He says he's pretty much useless, but I think he's being modest."

With Ana not around, Abraxas didn't have the power to project himself out as a ghostly image and Sabel found she almost missed the guy. It was probably an extension of her worry about Ana; for once, she'd feel a lot better if Abraxas were with her.

"We're attacking tomorrow?" Sabel asked. It seemed like an unnecessary delay to her, but then, she'd never waged a battle in the Unseen World before.

"At dusk," the Cyprian said. "My army is still getting into position and I'm waiting on contact from one of the insiders."

Sabel felt movement brush across her left arm and turned to look but saw no one there. Still, there was something in the room with them. She couldn't evoke the full trance that gave her access to her otherworldly workroom, but she slipped a little way into the state that let her see more than the obvious world around her.

The actual beings weren't visible to her, but she could see the traces of them in the timestream. It was like watching fish move through water without being able to see the fish.

"Who's here with us?" she asked the Cyprian.

"Can you see them or not?" the Cyprian asked in return.

"Yes," Sabel said with a half smile and the Cyprian chuckled.

"Ah, you can't see them in the Unseen World, but you can tell they're here? Is it the same magic that let me see you?"

"A version of it. I can see beings bounded by time pushed by their pasts and pulled by their futures, but not the beings themselves."

"They're too fully in the Unseen for you," the Cyprian said. "I can grant you sight into it."

Many traditions taught that there was a material world, where humans lived, and a spirit world, Sabel mused. Quite a few of them failed to mention that the unseen spirit world and the material world existed in the same place—on top of one another. The Hecatine witches knew enough about the Unseen World to be able to teach each other how to perceive when spirit beings were around them, but Sabel never thought she'd have the opportunity to see them with her own eyes.

She bowed her head as the Cyprian approached her. Hot fingertips touched her cheek and the touch itself held more gravity than a normal human's. The Cyprian put her hands on either side of Sabel's face and it felt rather like being caressed by a mountain. The Cyprian's breasts pressed heavily on hers and the flower and honey smell of her filled Sabel's head like alcohol. She closed her eyes.

The Cyprian kissed one of her eyelids and then the other. Then she laid her mouth over Sabel's and blew a soft breath into her. When she stepped back, Sabel opened her eyes.

Where there had been only the four of them, now there were a dozen other people in the room, but not human people. Semitransparent creatures came in and out, some of them speaking to the Cyprian in words Sabel couldn't hear, others just moving up to overlap their hands or faces with her form and then turning away. When she looked at them directly, they seemed as transparent as a dusty window, but in her peripheral vision they looked as vibrant as stained glass.

Most of them were humanoid, either shaped like people with elongated bodies or bodies made of dark smoke. A few had extra limbs or tails, and one resembled a six-legged lion.

"What do you think of them?" the Cyprian asked carelessly while the lion overlapped its face with her leg. "Is this more what you hoped to see?"

"Yes," she answered truthfully in surprise, and then to Lily, "Can you see them?"

"No, but Abraxas can. He's been telling me who's here."

"Now, I must continue my preparations," the Cyprian said. "Excuse me."

Sabel watched the semitransparent figures move around the room, most of them coming through to speak to the Cyprian and then leaving again, though a few stayed. Some of them glanced at her, but she noticed that most of the looks were directed at Lily—or Abraxas.

* * *

Even as she slept, Sabel saw people come and go from the hotel in preparation for the morning's battle. The sight was so much like dreaming she couldn't tell where one left off and the other began. Her second sight wasn't clean-edged like normal eyesight and often what seemed to be individual forms would blur into groups, or something that appeared to be a single large entity would suddenly break apart into distinct figures. She saw figures through walls and on other floors in dizzying visions.

Sabel got up and checked her phone but there were no new messages since the one from Ana at three thirty a.m. reporting that they were on the train headed out of Fargo. She wanted more information about how Ana was doing in close proximity to Mack, but Ana's silence on the subject said enough to give her some idea. She did have a message from the archive in her email and when she opened it she saw a simple line from Devony herself: *When you're alone, call me.*

Sabel glanced at the clock. Six a.m. in Chicago was seven in D.C. Maybe she could catch Devony before she went to bed. She threw on jeans and a sweater and hurried down to the lobby. The front desk clerk pointed her to a courtesy phone. Many of the beings who lived primarily in the Unseen World, like the Cyprian, didn't have an up-to-date grasp on modern technology. Some of the demons, who had an affinity for metal, could work wonders in the online world, but Sabel was betting that at most the Cyprian would have bugged her room phone and maybe hired a specialist to clone her cell—and that she had no magical capacity to listen directly to all of the conversations happening on all the phone lines in the hotel at once. Even gods had their limits, especially when they were partially corporeal and caught up in a war effort.

She dialed the Archive general number and said, "Sabel Young for Devony." She was on hold for a half second and then Devony answered.

"Good morning," she said cheerfully and Sabel laughed.

"I was hoping to catch you before bed."

"You know it's not really a bed, but yes, you've caught me. Josefene forwarded your message to me. Listen, does she call herself Cypris or the Cyprian?"

"The latter," Sabel said.

"Little bird, tell me you have an escape planned."

"This is the escape."

"No, it isn't," Devony said.

Sabel blew her breath out. On some level that was what she expected to hear and yet it sounded so much worse than she wanted it to. "What interest would she have in us?"

"It could be her nature. She's a goddess of love and betrayal. But it's best to assume there's more to it than that."

"That's the second half of her nature?" Sabel asked. She wasn't exactly surprised. She'd heard the Cyprian say "love and related emotions" and then trail off as if there was more left unvoiced, but there were so many variants of love goddesses and so many incarnations of the Aphrodite that it really could have been something less dangerous.

"You were hoping for love and puppies, weren't you?" Devony asked.

"True story. Do you think she wants us for my Voice? Will the leash keep out a goddess?"

"I'll ask Josefene," Devony said. "I'd better do that now, I only have a few minutes."

"Thank you," Sabel said as the line disconnected.

Love and betrayal—not her first choice. Still, better than love and pestilence, right? How early had the Cyprian's power begun to affect all of them? Had it been influencing her and Brie and Ana during all that turmoil at the hotel? It would explain some things, but she wasn't ready to hand over responsibility that quickly.

She picked up the courtesy phone again and dialed Ana's number. It clicked into voice mail immediately. She had to be out of cell phone range.

"Get off the train," Sabel said. "The Cyprian is going to betray you if she hasn't already. She's after me and Abraxas. You need to get away from any of the routes she knows about. If you need help, have Brie call the witches' archive, use my name."

She paused, unsure how to put her feelings into words. There was so much she wanted to say to Ana, but it would have to wait. She added, "Please...You mean the world to me."

She went back to her room to meditate, shower and eat some breakfast. Then there was another briefing with the Cyprian, in which they were given no new information. Sabel felt certain she was stalling them, probably waiting for Ana and Brie to be too far away to come back and help. It was all starting to make sense now, her suspicions that this was still too easy, the way the Cyprian had split their party, the delays she was creating.

After the briefing, Sabel followed Lily back to her room. Whenever she turned her head away from Lily, she could see Abraxas around Lily like a ghostly man, slender and muscled, unadorned white cloth wrapped around his middle, his dark hair bound back in a club at the base of his neck. It made her uncomfortable to have him here—in part because it meant he wasn't with Ana, but there was another piece to it that she still couldn't put her finger on. Hadn't the Cyprian seemed overly interested in getting him into Lily's body and having him come with them? With Sabel's Voice, Lily could do the binding without Abraxas. They didn't really need him.

Maybe it was the love between Lily and Abraxas that made it so compelling to bring him? She discarded that idea. Plenty of people loved each other. Maybe it was the fact that it took him away from Ana and made her more vulnerable.

She sat in one of the chairs by the windows in Lily's room and Lily took the desk chair, pulling her feet up in a way that made her look much younger.

"How do you think the trip is going?" Sabel asked.

"As well as I hoped," Lily said.

Sabel had considered many ways of getting a message to Lily before settling on just going back to her room and telling her. The magical ways were probably the easiest for the Cyprian to eavesdrop on. She could have texted it or emailed it—the Cyprian didn't seem to be the most tech-savvy, but that didn't mean she wasn't employing humans to monitor electronic conversations between Sabel and Lily. And then it occurred to her that from the Cyprian's perspective, it probably didn't matter. Even if she did overhear a conversation between Sabel and Lily, at this point when they were so locked into this course of action, she wouldn't care if Sabel knew her full identity.

She had to be fairly certain there was nothing Sabel, Lily and Abraxas could do to her. If they refused to bind Ashtoreth, the Cyprian could turn her full fury against Ana and Brie. And Ashtoreth, who was already allied with Ashmedai, had no reason to help them, so they'd simply lose one ally and put themselves in a worse position. At best, Ashtoreth would try to take Abraxas while the Cyprian vented her displeasure however she chose.

"We have a problem," Sabel said. "The Cyprian is the goddess of love *and* betrayal."

"So she'll betray us," Lily said. "She has to if that's part of her domain."

"I believe she already has. I left Ana a message this morning and I haven't heard back."

"They're out of cell range most of today, but still, do you think she would tell Ashmedai where to find them? You think she already has?"

"Yes."

Lily was silent for a while and then said, "Abraxas says Ana seems to be all right. He can't get details, but she's not hurt in any way. Still, that doesn't mean they're not riding into an ambush. The Cyprian wants our cooperation, so she'd have told Ashmedai a point that Ana and Brie will be at after we start the attack this evening. If they get your message first..."

"That's what I'm hoping. They'll get off the train, run, take some other route we didn't plan."

"Brie has money and alternative identification," Lily said. "Depending on how far out from the ambush they get the message, they could be in pretty strong shape."

Sabel nodded. "I hoped that was the case. That leaves me worried about us. She's going to try to keep us. Can Abraxas leave you and get back to Ana?"

Again a long silence and then Lily shook her head. "No. He says he should have wondered about it, but the Cyprian's power bound him pretty strongly to me. He can only get back to her if she's close to us...or if I die."

"Then she won't kill you. I think she wants him at least as much as she wants me." Sabel looked at the air just above Lily's head, where she could occasionally see Abraxas's face. "Why does she want you?"

"He says because he's old," Lily said.

"How old is Ashtoreth? Four, five thousand years? Older than Abraxas, but the Cyprian doesn't seem to care whether she gets Ashtoreth or not. Why would she want Abraxas more than that? There's something about you, isn't that it? Something that makes you valuable to Ashtoreth too? Is it because you've been to the realms of the dead?"

"Yes," Lily said slowly, looking perplexed and cocking her head. "Why…?" Her voice trailed off.

"He won't tell you, will he?"

"No."

Sabel had a growing feeling of dread. She almost knew what it was; she suspected, she just wasn't quite ready to let herself believe it was true, because if it was—it was so much worse for all of them.

"Let's just figure out how to get out of here after the fight and then we can talk about that other thing," she said. "The best plan I've got so far is to run like hell as soon as we get Ashtoreth bound and pray that the Cyprian's oath not to kill us also applies to her people."

"It does," Lily said. "But that doesn't mean we'd make it by them. Maybe we should go on pretending ignorance and wait for her to be preoccupied. From what I've read, the process of taking the power from the city should take most of her attention for a few hours."

"So maybe we'll get lucky and be able to go for dinner and just take off?" Sabel asked.

"I want that to be true," Lily said. "But we'd better keep thinking of alternatives."

CHAPTER EIGHTEEN

Ana was thoroughly sick of moving. They'd gotten on this train around three a.m. in Fargo and it took her a good couple of hours to shake off the chill. Then she slept for a while, but now she couldn't get comfortable in her seat. She checked her phone but she still had no cell service. That was the downside of taking the route across northern Montana—the reception was crappy at best.

If they'd done their job well and the Cyprian covered their tracks thoroughly enough, Ashmedai should be following multiple routes across the southwest into San Francisco, all very far from where they were now. Brie had talked to Lily in the middle of the night while they were waiting for the train and they thought it would be best to take this train to Washington State and then catch a bus south for San Francisco.

Ana wondered if she'd actually make it home. It wasn't as exciting a prospect without Sabel next to her. Plus Brie would have to leave her at the city limits since it wasn't safe for her inside San Francisco. Ana still didn't understand everything that happened at the hotel after she'd beaten up Mack and she wanted to ask Brie if she could explain it, but she wasn't eager to have that conversation in front of Mack. He'd hardly said a word to her on this trip and she was glad of it. He seemed to be sleeping now, so perhaps it was time to talk to Brie.

She reached over and touched Brie's hand lightly. The skin felt feverish to her, demon blood burning hot in those veins. She was growing used to the subtle tug Brie exerted on her, even enjoying it. Mack still hung on Brie's every word, poor jerk. It was disorienting to see him in this light—the man she'd feared her whole childhood, the mean bastard—how needy he was now, how uncertain of himself and the way he covered it up with his loud voice and rough manners.

Brie's eyes fluttered open and for a moment burned with inhuman blue light before she blinked them muted again. Ana's hand was half raised toward that entrancing fire and she dropped it into her lap quickly where it crinkled the map she'd been studying.

"Plotting?" Brie asked. She leaned too far forward to examine the map and displayed an extraordinary view into her cleavage.

Ana rolled her eyes. Was there any move this woman made that wasn't also a flirtation? She put her hand on Brie's shoulder and pushed her back into her seat, but not forcefully. A flare of lust blazed up in Brie's eyes. She laughed, then sobered.

"Sorry, I'm getting hungry." Her gaze wandered over to where Mack slept wedged against the wall of the train with a baseball cap down over his eyes.

"Don't tempt me, I'd turn him over to you in a heartbeat," Ana said. "I wanted to ask you about Sabel. You talked to her back in the hotel. Do you know what's going on with her?"

Brie looked out the window. "I can't read her," she said and added, "I mean, I can't read her energy like I can with most people. Especially not after, you know, she just totally shut herself away until I went to put the leash back on her and then it was like…I don't even know what it was like. Do you know what they did to her?"

"Who?" Ana asked.

Brie turned to look at her full on, surprised. "I thought you'd know. She didn't tell you?"

"Tell me what?"

"That's the thing, I don't know what. Just that a person doesn't get to be like that through normal means."

"Like what?" Ana's voice was rising with each question she had to ask.

"It's all on the energy level," Brie explained. "But it would be like if someone broke all of your fingers in a bunch of places so they could put in extra joints and some extra muscles. She's got a strength and flexibility in her energy that just, frankly, shouldn't be there. But it's amazing."

Ana understood that it was a metaphor, but not one Brie chose carelessly. Whatever had happened to Sabel must have been extremely painful, if not physically then in some other way that Ana was only beginning to understand. She wished Abraxas were there so she could ask him.

"Would the witches do something like that?" Ana asked.

Brie shook her head. "My stepfather's the only witch I know other than Sabel and he'd never do anything like that. I don't think he could. You'd have to be almost completely inside her energy to break her up like that. But the witches might be the ones who put it all back together for her."

Ana looked over at Mack. There was one way to get inside someone's energy that she knew all too well—be related to them and have access to them when they were too young to defend themselves. She always assumed she was the broken one in the relationship, but now that she thought back, Sabel rarely talked about her childhood. She mentioned it even less than Ana did. Had something happened to her when she was young that rendered her broken in the way Brie described?

"You think you know," Brie said.

"No. But I think I'm understanding why she might panic if she felt she couldn't trust me." She looked at her phone again. "Shit, still no service."

"We should get some here," Brie said and touched a point on the map just to the side of a large patch of green.

Ana stood up and held the phone toward the ceiling of the train. What was she going to say? She wanted to turn around and run back to Sabel, and to Abraxas, so she could both protect Sabel and have the power to do it. She sat and stared at the phone, wanting to send a message but not sure what to say.

She had thought Sabel was just jealous or angry that Ana had kissed Brie. Now she felt stupid that it hadn't occurred to her there could be a deeper issue triggered by the whole incident. For all she knew, it could have been Sabel seeing the bloody mess of Mack's face and his blood all over Ana's hands. She doubted it. She still felt a tug of nameless emotion when she thought of Sabel kneeling in front of her, carefully putting the ice packs on her hands. It was like a benediction, like Sabel was letting her know she could handle the physical part of what had happened.

Sabel only got angry after Ana had said that magic wasn't real, or something like that. She rubbed her forehead where a headache was starting over her left eye. This didn't feel like a problem she could work out on her own. She had to talk to Sabel.

The phone in her hand pinged to indicate she had a voice mail message. She hit the voice mail button but the call wouldn't connect. The service was flickering like a candle in an open window. She got up and walked to one end of the train car but it was no better.

Finally the call went through to her voice mail and she heard Sabel's voice: "Get off the train. The Cyprian is going to betray you if she hasn't already. She's after me and Abraxas. You need to get away from any of the routes she knows about. If you need help, have Brie call the witches' archive, use my name. Please... You mean the world to me."

Ana played it again, listening closely to the end and hearing the words catch and then rush out. She wanted to call back and say "I'm sorry" and "I love you" about a hundred times each, but neither had said that to the other yet.

She walked back to her seat, still staring at her phone.

"You have the weirdest look on your face," Brie remarked.

"When is it too soon to say 'I love you'?" Ana asked.

"Sabel said 'I love you?'"

"No, she said that we're headed into a trap."

Brie shook her head in disbelief. "Oh, so she said, 'It's a trap,' and you want to reply, 'I love you'? Yeah, that makes total sense. What trap?"

"She says we can't trust the Cyprian, who apparently is after Sabel and Abraxas, and that, yeah, trap. Plus you're supposed to call the archive if we need help, do you know how to do that?"

"Not a clue," Brie said. She grabbed the map and spread it across her knees. "What time is it?"

"Six thirty-three."

"We're here," she told Ana and pointed at a huge, dark green spot on the map. "Just going into the national park. With this cold snap, we can't get off the train until we're near Whitefish or we'll just freeze to death out there."

"So we get off at Whitefish and run for it. Missoula doesn't look too far and if we can hop a bus we can start heading east again. We have to get back to Chicago before anything happens."

Ana kicked Mack lightly and his head came up, pale eyes glaring at her. "What?"

"Trap," Ana said.

"We jumping?" he asked without skipping a beat.

"We can't until after we leave the park, but then it's probably a good idea not to roll into the Whitefish station."

Mack pulled the map out of her hands without asking and she let him. He tapped at it. "What about this here? Columbia Falls. Looks big enough."

"It's not a scheduled stop," Brie said.

"Works," Mack said. "You girls ever jump off a moving train before?"

"Uh, no," Ana said and Brie just grinned at him.

"They're going to slow down coming into town. Wait till we've got a clear patch of dirt or grass, don't overthink it, roll when you hit, don't try to land solid."

Ana wished for Abraxas to be there to help break the fall. Ironic, for all the times Mack had shoved her, tripped her or knocked her down the last few steps of a flight of stairs, she was now about to voluntarily throw herself off a train with him.

While the train rolled through the wilderness, they looked over the map and thought about ways to get back to Chicago. Ana called up the texting app on her phone, opened a message to Sabel and stared at it for a long time. She wrote: *I love you.* Then she erased it. She wrote: *You mean the world to me too.* She erased that.

She wrote: *I want to give you everything.*

It was what she'd said to Sabel the first time they'd made love, outside of time with their possible deaths hanging over them. It was a memory Ashmedai had taken from her and that Sabel restored to her and she trusted that the single sentence would convey everything she wanted to say about how important Sabel was to her.

Brie announced when they were getting close to Columbia Falls. They got their packs and headed down the aisle to the emergency exit. As Mack predicted, the train slowed at the city limits and then at a sharp turn slowed again. He thrust the door open, setting off a loud, repeating buzz, and leapt through it, tumbling into the slope of scrub brush beside the track. Ana told her panicked brain to shut up, and followed. The ground leapt up and smacked her so hard her teeth jarred against each other. She was spinning and then her shoulder cracked into the trunk of a small tree and the world stopped moving. Her inner sense of equilibrium took a few more gut-wrenching circuits and then settled.

A soft, hot hand slid behind her neck, delicate fingers running over her scalp. "Looks solid to me," Brie whispered from nearby. Her lips brushed Ana's temple and a surge of energy lit up the inside of her skin. She could feel her body turning the energy into healing, the way Abraxas had trained it.

"I'm okay," she said, pushing up on her nonbruised arm.

"Then let's go," Brie told her. She hooked her arm under Ana's and helped her up the rest of the way, and a good thing because apparently her balance hadn't recovered as fast as the rest of her. With Brie to steady her, they set a rapid pace down the line of the tracks.

Within twenty paces they met up with Mack, grinning like a boy and covered in dirt. "Good jumps," he said.

Brie put her nose up like a hunting dog. "Demons," she announced. "Must've been on top of the train."

"Do they see us?"

"Let's assume they do. We need to get among people or someplace else where we can hide."

They jogged along for a few minutes, moving south of the track toward where they could see houses. The area they'd jumped into was a new construction site, mostly dirt and open spaces.

"Smell that?" Mack asked.

"No, all I smell are demons. What is it?"

"Road tar," he said. "Isn't that one thing your Ma uses to drive 'em away?"

Brie grabbed his arm and planted a kiss by his ear. "You're wonderful. Lead on!"

Ana ground her teeth but didn't say anything.

Mack turned north again and led them to a garage that housed road paving equipment. It was almost nine p.m., so the whole place was closed down. But they were able to shove through a gap in a back fence. Then Mack tried the windows until he came to one that hadn't been latched and shoved it open. They climbed into a big, cold space with hulking machines.

"So if we're really lucky, the demons lose track of us because the smell drives them back?" Ana asked.

"That's the idea," Brie said.

"And if we're less lucky?"

"We can't stay here," Brie said. "Sooner or later there's going to be a small army showing up. We've got to find a way to get moving again."

Ana looked around at the various pieces of slumbering machinery. "Maybe we could ride the tar truck out."

"I could drive it," Mack offered. "But it tops out at, what, ten miles per hour?"

"It only works if he doesn't have humans working for him," Brie said. "They'd just pull us off the truck. Anyway, the smell wouldn't keep demons back forever. We should stay here for a bit, maybe ten minutes, then I'll go out and see if they've cleared off. If the demons are gone and there's no human pursuers, we can call a cab. Maybe we can find one willing to take us all the way to Missoula."

They stayed by the back wall of the garage, rubbing their arms and shifting from one foot to another to stay warm. Ana had had more than enough of the cold on this trip. If Sabel had been serious about her offer to take her to Greece in the summer, she was absolutely going to take her up on it. And then lie on the beach for about ten years in the blazing sun until even the memory of this cold was baked out of her. She wondered if Sabel owned a bikini and if it had little bits of lace around the edges, and that set her on another path of memories that warmed her much better than the hopping around.

At the front of the garage a lock rattled and Brie stood up from where she'd been crouched against the wall, dusting off the seat of her pants. "If we're lucky, that's a facilities guy who saw us sneaking in. Maybe I can get him to lend us a car." She walked around the machinery between the window they'd come through and the front doors.

From the far side of the room a man's voice called, "Don't touch her, use the ropes."

Ana dashed around the trucks between her and the voice. There were a dozen men with various weapons, a few guns, a few clubs, and four of them held long poles with loops at the end, the kind that dog catchers used. She kept moving forward until she was in front of Brie and held out her empty hands. She wanted to prevent a fight, which would only get them hurt and she couldn't stand the idea of Brie being bound like an animal.

"Don't fight," she called back over her shoulder, but the rumble of an engine told her she was too late.

With comic slowness, the road roller edged around the side of another truck and headed for the door. "Jump on!" Mack yelled down from the driver's seat.

Ana couldn't help but remember a clip from some action movie that employed a steamroller as a weapon. This was nothing like that. The massive thing rumbled slowly for the open door and the men in its path moved quickly out of the way and flanked it. One tried to scramble up the side and got Mack's boot in his mouth, but another was already halfway up the far side.

She couldn't stand by and watch. Ana ran around and grabbed the back of that man's jeans, but before she could even pull, two others wrenched her arms away. One elbowed her in the jaw. She kicked at him and got a club across the back of her shoulders, knocking her forward and down. Above and past her, Mack was hollering insults.

The road roller cleared her line of vision and on the other side of the garage Brie had been backed against a wall by three men with long poles. They poked at her when she tried to cut around one way or the other, working her back toward the corner. When she had nowhere to go, one man struck her in the stomach with his pole and as she doubled over, another looped the rope at the end of his around her neck. It tightened and her hands flew to her neck too slowly to remove it, fingers clawing around the rope, eyes wide with panic.

Ana lunged toward her, but the man behind her clubbed her across the shoulders again, knocking her back to hands and knees. Outside the building, a gun fired once, then again. She rolled forward away from the men behind her and gained her footing, running toward the sunlight. A pole swept her feet out from under her, sending her sprawling onto the concrete. The rope fell over her head and tightened.

* * *

Chicago's downtown streets were dark but still crowded with people leaving work. A light snow driven by the wind scoured

Sabel's cheeks. Others had their heads down and hurried to get out of the cold. She and Lily got into the car the Cyprian had provided for them and it took them to just outside of Willis Tower, where the Cyprian was standing with hundreds of nearly invisible gossamer bodies moving around her and around the oblivious people making their way home for the night.

"Time to go," the Cyprian said cheerily. Six huge men fell in with them, along with two dozen nonmaterial beings in various kinds of armor. They were laughing and goading each other, but Sabel couldn't hear the words. The Cyprian had touched her eyes and her mouth, but hadn't opened her ears, and Sabel wondered if that was because there were conversations the Cyprian didn't want her to overhear. If so, what was in those conversations?

Sabel paused and touched her index finger to her right ear. "I can't hear anyone," she said. "That could be a problem in the fight."

"Ah," the Cyprian said, as if she'd forgotten, though Sabel thought that was unlikely. She leaned toward Sabel and casually blew across her ear.

The words of the beings around them immediately became clear. The warrior creatures were teasing each other and boasting about how many victories they would win. It wasn't anything particularly useful and Sabel couldn't help but feel that whatever the Cyprian hadn't wanted her to hear had been said already.

"Thank you," she told the Cyprian, who gave her an oddly human wink.

They walked down Canal St. to Adams and turned right.

"How do we get in?" Lily asked.

"You will remember," the Cyprian said evenly, as if walking at this brisk pace took no effort from her, "that one of Ashtoreth's commanders will betray her to me. Today he is responsible for the defenses of her tower. One-third of her army is moving west to find Ana, the other two-thirds are now engaged with my small force, which leads them away from this tower. So, defended only by a traitor and her personal guard, she will be easy to access.

The difficulty will be to bind her while she still draws this city's power, which I trust you to handle for me."

The tower loomed in front of them, 110 stories of metal and glass reflecting the jewel lights of the city and the vast black sky. They didn't walk up to the front doors, but around to the alley and the receiving docks. One plain gray door was flanked by shadowy figures, who stood aside for the Cyprian. She opened it and walked in.

In front of the freight elevator stood a pillar of black smoke, eight feet tall with white-hot eyes. It bobbed toward the Cyprian.

"Lady," it rasped. "The way is clear to the ninety-fifth floor. I trust your people will allow us the illusion of a good fight."

"Of course, Zamosz, it would be their pleasure. You serve well," the Cyprian said.

"Don't say that to me, Lady," he replied with force. "I serve you very poorly and intend to go on tasking you in a way you find reprehensible. You will consider my work here barely tolerable."

She laughed. "You are very clever. For your sake pray you don't fail."

In the elevator, Sabel said, "He seemed outstandingly humble for a demon."

The Cyprian didn't respond, but she didn't need to. Sabel knew what was going on: he was trying to keep the Cyprian unhappy with him. He didn't want her favor or her affection because if love and betrayal went hand-in-hand, then having her favor opened the pathway for her betrayal. The more she loved anyone, the more she would betray them, and likely the stronger anyone around her felt love, the more vulnerable they were to her power's dark side.

What was the range on that? Brie and the Cyprian clearly had affection for each other. She'd likely already betrayed Brie halfway across the country, but could she also force Brie to betray Ana?

Sabel followed Lily off the elevator. They were in a narrow hallway that ended at a metal door. The Cyprian and her people led the way. They blew the door wide and stormed into an expansive room with windows looking out on the city.

The room looked like a conference room, with a heavy wooden table in the middle and richly carved chairs all around. Armed guards ringed the walls, but when the Cyprian and her people pushed in and fanned out in the room, some of them turned on the others and fought alongside her.

Ashtoreth was as tall and slender as an aspen tree. She looked almost human but elongated, though Sabel could see that the elongated effect was only visible through the enhanced sight that allowed her to perceive the Unseen World. In the material world, Ashtoreth was a lean, elegant, middle-aged woman in an expensive gray suit.

The Cyprian made a beeline for her. Next to the solidity of the Cyprian, Ashtoreth seemed even more tree-like. Sabel expected the Cyprian to grab Ashtoreth, maybe even to hit her because she was moving at her so quickly, but she stopped short. Power crackled in the air between the two of them and her second sight caught more movement than she could understand.

A normal human would only see two women staring intensely at each other with expressions of fury and hatred. Although Sabel could see more than that, she knew she only perceived a fraction of the levels on which the fight took place. They fought each other in the Unseen World and into the future and even some distance into the past. It hurt to watch but she wished she could see all of it.

"Move," Lily hissed at her.

She went to the left, sprinkling salt and drawing in chalk on the floor a copy of the symbols Lily had shown her. She made herself stumble and smudge one, though she knew how dangerous it was to make mistakes in magic. But she had to both serve the Cyprian poorly to protect herself against being completely betrayed, and leave them an opening to escape when the time came to use it. If she'd done it right, the binding would take initially, but it would have a weak spot in it. They could use the weak spot to draw the Cyprian's attention while they got out.

Two of the massive, armored creatures that had come in with them stayed at Sabel's back and fought off anyone who would interfere. Lily was on the other side of the room performing the same ritual as Sabel. When she chanced a look up, she saw Lily hunched and busy, her guards defending her against three assailants.

The Cyprian had fallen to her knees while the fight with Ashtoreth raged around her and now the other woman's hands were at her throat but she wasn't trying to choke her, the gesture was just the surface symbol of the dominance she exercised with her will. Without their ritual to bind Ashtoreth, she would win over the Cyprian.

Lily had finished her side and in another minute Sabel was next to her and the circle was complete. Lily's words rose with the depth and power of Abraxas's voice behind them. She laid the groundwork for the circle. It was a delicate lattice of information and power. The symbols they made began to glow with light in the Unseen World.

Lily looked at her and nodded.

Sabel breathed down to the depths of her belly and drew upon the power of the Voice. Then she spoke the words Lily taught her. They rang in the air like thunder. She let the *marevaas* power falter as she called the last syllable, so that it sounded only with her normal voice. The circle snapped shut but it was weak and shaky.

Ashtoreth's long body jerked back. She clawed at her own throat and choked on the words caught there.

The Cyprian stood up. She brushed her hands together as if knocking off dust.

When they'd come in, Lily had set a stone box on the conference table and now the Cyprian moved it closer to Ashtoreth and opened it, revealing a mirrored interior for this demon of war. Ashtoreth screamed, but the sound died in her throat. Her energy streamed into the box and the Cyprian slammed the lid down on it. Ashtoreth's human-like body fell to the floor, shattered, and dissolved into dust.

The Cyprian walked slowly around the table, looking at the box, instructing her men in the cleanup, and then Sabel felt the usual pace of the world fall away from her as the Cyprian pushed them out of sync with material time. She realized too late that this was the perfect start to the Cyprian's betrayal of them—to use the time magic of the witches against them. The weakness in the binding would do them no good if they were too far out of sync with the timestream to use it, but there was nothing Sabel had that was powerful enough to stop the Cyprian.

CHAPTER NINETEEN

Ana lay still and sucked a ribbon of air through her half-closed throat. Her vision darkened almost to the point of passing out, but she focused on her breathing, slowing the attempts at gasping until her sight cleared. The rope released slightly.

"Get up slow," a man's voice said. "We're going out to the truck."

She did as he said, turning gently onto her right side and pushing up until she stood. In the corner of the building, Brie was doing the same and all the men watched her languid movements. From the way their faces were layered with lust, awe and fear, they must have been threatened with death itself not to go near her.

Once on her feet, she walked as if nothing touched her, as if the rope around her throat were a diamond choker and the men trailing behind her were part of her entourage. Outside the building was a van, its back doors thrown wide. Mack was on the floor clutching a bloody thigh. The blood appeared mostly on the outside of his leg and low, as if someone aimed for his knee and missed, not up by the femoral artery where the shot might have killed him.

Brie climbed up first and sank down gracefully by his head. It was strange how the more afraid she was, the more elegant she became. Brie stroked Mack's sweat-slicked hair back from his temple, oblivious to the rope being lifted from her neck. "I never had anyone take a bullet for me," she said.

The pain in Mack's eyes diminished enough to let him look clearly at her. Ana got in on his other side and lifted the rope off her throat as soon as it loosened. Their captors slammed the doors shut and locked them from the outside. Ana leaned against the side of the van, sitting cross-legged so that her knees and calves would brace Mack's torso and prevent it from shifting too much as they drove. Brie did the same on his other side, still stroking his face.

"They'll get you bandaged up," she told him. "We're no good to them otherwise."

They drove for about twenty minutes, with Mack deathly silent, and then Ana felt the hum of power around them.

"Demons?" she asked Brie.

"Lots," Brie said.

"Do we have a plan?"

"I figure we do that thing we did in Minneapolis. You know, when they surprised us at the mall."

Ana searched her memory, but all she remembered at the mall was having to hit the GAP store twice because Brie decided she had to have the short periwinkle jacket. Was she trying to tell Ana to do something twice? What could they do twice here? Or maybe she had no plan at all and was making it sound good for Mack, who looked like he was trying not to cry from the pain.

The second visit to the store, Brie had insisted on another salesperson, avoiding using the first again because he'd been too enamored of her. If she didn't mean that they should do something twice, was she trying to tell Ana they had to get someone out of the way? Why not just say that out loud?

Ana looked down at Mack. Brie was hiding her meaning from him, not from any guards who might be listening; she wanted him out of the fight.

"You're right," Ana said. "Mack gives us the opening for the mall gambit because he's shot."

"Exactly," Brie agreed, her eyes wide and hopeful.

I don't have a plan either, Ana thought, but she wasn't going to say that. Let them think she'd come up with something. Her best idea was to buy time and pray that when the Cyprian took Chicago they could get someone here fast enough to rescue the three of them.

"What do I have to do?" Mack asked through gritted teeth.

"You have to act like you're hurt worse than you are," Ana said. "I know you could still take a couple of them, but we need to play dead weight, to slow things down, okay?"

"Yeah." He gave her a thin smile. "I can fake unconscious pretty good."

"Perfect. We need them to concentrate on you for a bit, give us some room to move. And if you see civilians or anything, play up the blood, see if you can get them to send help."

"Got it," he said.

The doors to the van opened and Mack's eyes fluttered shut so convincingly that Ana wondered if he'd really passed out now that he had permission. She climbed out of the van first, wanting to hit whatever trouble awaited before Brie could.

They were in a big, underground parking garage nearly empty of cars. A man in an impeccable navy suit stood a dozen feet away. His face was unfamiliar but his eyes held Ashmedai's familiar glare. He looked badly formed, like a hastily sculpted image of a man, face and hair all one color of tan-gray. Next to him stood a woman, her graying amber hair pulled back in a ponytail, sandstone-colored skin rich with fine lines, dressed in worn jeans and an oversized flannel man's shirt. She wore a lot of silver and turquoise jewelry, but faded and worn and authentic, not bought from a tourist shop.

In a semicircle fanned out from those two were at least thirty human-like people, including the men with clubs and the dog-catching poles, and behind them stretched ranks of demons that Ana couldn't see without Abraxas but could sense like a thunderstorm before it broke. Brie stepped up beside her.

"These are the ones?" the woman asked Ashmedai's new body.

"Yes, quick work."

"We're effective in my state," she said. "You'll go now."

So she was the god or demon or whatever held Montana and she sounded none too pleased with Ashmedai and his gang invading her turf. An idea was coming to Ana.

"Ma'am, I don't believe we've met," she said with a bow toward the woman. "I'm Ana Khoury. This is Brie Cordoba and in the truck is my brother Mack. Before we have to go, may I ask you a question?"

The woman's face loosened, some of the lines around her mouth disappearing, and her right eyebrow climbed as she took in Ana and Brie. "Call me Kay, little one, and ask away."

"Well I...I admit that I slept through some of the demon history lectures, but there's different kinds, right? And Ashmedai is a Satan or Shaitan, isn't he? Oh, wait, that's not my question, don't answer that. My question is this: if Ashmedai is a Shaitan, then isn't it true that anyone who can defeat him in a straight fight gets his turf?"

Kay laughed, a rolling sound like water over rocks. "Yes, it is. Will you be challenging him yourself?"

Ana didn't know that she had a chance against him herself, but she wasn't sure that Brie could take him either—not in this new body that looked like clay instead of flesh. Her goal was to get him to agree to fight them both at once.

"I don't know if it should be me or Brie here," Ana said slowly. "She's got a real beef with him and we've each already beaten him once."

Ashmedai's chuckle held a deep, harsh tone. "You did not beat me and you're just trying to goad me into a fight."

"That's obvious," Ana said. "You come with this whole army to attack us—how dangerous do you think we are? You're what, some hundreds of years old and a demon prince and me and Brie together don't add up to sixty."

"Eight hundred years," he said.

"I rest my case. I think if you can't beat us you should just let us go and we'll call it a draw."

"Ridiculous," he said.

Kay raised one delicate, weathered hand. "She makes a valid point. That is the custom among your people, isn't it?"

Ana was prepared to make a chicken clucking sound to get this going if she had to. But then what? She knew neither of them could defeat him the way they had in the past.

"It's not a clean fight," Ashmedai said. "She carries a demon prince inside her."

"Actually I don't at the moment," Ana admitted. "He stayed in Chicago."

"Chicago? Why?" Ashmedai's face turned a paler shade of tan.

"Wouldn't you love to know. Look, it's your chance, it's just me and Brie, if you can take us, you can have us."

"Absolutely," he agreed.

"Do you want to fight them one at a time?" Kay asked.

"No." He laughed derisively. "Without her demon she's just a human, and this other half-breed has already used up her surprises on me. Let's be done with this."

Ana looked to Kay. "Is there a ceremony or something?"

The other woman shook her head. "Not among Shaitans. It's more of a street brawl."

Already the others were drawing back to the sides of the vast indoor garage. Ana had been hoping for more time, and maybe an arena, and a chance to escape. She remembered how she'd trapped Ashmedai last time, but felt certain he wouldn't let her do it again. For all she knew, he'd just catch her and break her neck.

Ashmedai removed his jacket and rolled up the cuffs on his white button-down shirt. "Give the start when you're ready," he said.

Brie stepped up next to Ana and whispered to her, "You have a plan?"

"Wing it?" she suggested.

"Any time," Ashmedai said. "Ready when you are."

Ana sighed. "Go ahead. Bring it."

"So soon, you catch me unprepared," he said, kneeling down to take off his shoes. At first his feet were normal human feet, but as Ana watched, the skin swelled and changed until he was standing on powerful talons, similar to Lily's but much bigger. He put one hand to either side of his head and pulled the skin out like taffy. One side formed into a bull's head, the other a ram's. The bull head snorted gouts of flame and smoke trickled up from the ram's nose.

"Would you like to run?" he asked from all three mouths simultaneously.

"Not really," Ana said.

Part of her did just want to take off, but another part, the part that reminded her uncomfortably of Mack, was more than ready to do as much damage as she could before he killed her. What would Abraxas say to her now that her whole body was filled with anger? Should she feel into this? Would it give her the leverage she needed to hit him a little harder and make him hurt the way she wanted to?

Ashmedai laughed and closed the distance between them, grabbing her throat in his powerful hands. Maybe she should have run. But there was Brie at his side, stroking his shoulder. He backhanded her across the face, knocking her away hard enough that she staggered and fell. Then he threw Ana in the other direction and turned back toward Brie.

"All right, succubus!" he bellowed. "You dare seduce the lord of lust! I'll tear you apart!"

Ana pushed herself up, shoulders aching from the beating of earlier, tailbone bruised and pain shooting down her legs. She couldn't get her mind around standing up all the way, so she crawled across the floor toward Brie. Brie had landed on her knees, but was up again when Ashmedai reached her. She cocked one hip and flipped her hair back over her shoulder, lips pouting. Her whole body radiated life, health, sexuality, invitation. Only Ana knew that meant she was terrified.

Ashmedai paused in front of her, licking his lips. He raised one heavy fist and drove it toward Brie's head. Her arm spun up and deflected it, but his other fist was already swinging into the space she ducked into and that one smashed into her face. Brie's head jerked back and her body followed, dropping to the ground, hands to her nose. Blood streamed out from between her fingers.

Ana rocked back on her heels and forced herself to stand, get her balance. She pulled her arms in and tucked low, spun all her force behind her right leg in a jab kick to Ashmedai's lower back. It connected with a satisfying shock and he staggered. Brie swept one leg across the floor, connecting with his ankle and toppling him forward onto his hands.

He roared with laughter and was standing again before Ana could see how he'd come upright. "This is not your Tae-bo class," he spat at her. "You can't even hurt me."

The bull's head turned toward her and blew a gout of fire. Ana scrambled back from the heat. Then the ram's head came around and from its mouth was a blast of wind so sudden it lifted her off her feet and threw her against one of the garage's support columns. Her body struck the concrete and slumped, the breath knocked out of her.

Ana's still open eyes registered Brie moving, holding one hand to her bleeding nose and using the other to push up, circling around Ashmedai toward Ana. All Ana could do was gasp like a landed fish, straining to draw a full breath into her shocked lungs. She had to do better than physical violence, since that was proving useless against this new body of his.

The body was clay. If she had water or a hose or something, maybe she could wash him away. But she'd seen nothing like that in this space. Could she make a circle on the floor and trap him in it? She didn't know the right things to do, Lily was still teaching her about bindings. Even if she did, he had a body which made him immune. Yet he said she couldn't hurt his body. Was he really invulnerable?

Ashmedai walked up to Brie and grabbed a handful of hair at the back of her head. His other hand turned her shoulder away from him as he pulled her toward his chest so she had to back into him.

"You think you can eat me, that you could consume me?" he murmured into her hair, only loud enough that Ana and the few onlookers nearest her could hear. "Why don't you try?"

Brie moaned and rubbed back against him. To Ana it looked like Brie was as enthralled by Ashmedai as he was by her. Which one would prove stronger? With a trail of blood from her nose down over her lips, Brie appeared more vampiric than wounded, but Ana knew she turned fear and pain into self-preserving attractiveness. Brie's hands were behind her now, struggling with Ashmedai's pants.

He laughed and threw her forward onto her knees. "Stay there," he growled. "It suits you."

Brie tossed a glance over her shoulder at him that was pure hunger. She undid her pants and shucked them, waiting for him, daring him. He dropped his own pants, knelt and grabbed her hips, pulling her toward him.

"You will lose," he panted at her. "This body is not human."

He entered her from behind with force and Ana saw the first flash of panic in Brie's eyes. Ashmedai was telling the truth, because he wasn't in a human body, Brie didn't have the kind of power over him that she was used to. Brie's hands clawed the concrete as he thrust into her over and over. The sounds that came out of her alternated between cries of ecstasy and groans of pain.

Ana crawled toward her, crossing the few feet between them to touch Brie's cheek. It burned painfully.

Ashmedai glared at Ana over Brie's arched back. "Watch her die," he said.

"He's crushing me," Brie told her. "He's pushing himself in…all fire…too much…help."

She had nothing with which to help, neither weapons nor strength nor magics, not even Abraxas, not even a good idea, only the horror that filled her. Reflexively, she pushed into her horror and anger, searching for the core of it. She thought she felt something cold and electric but made herself push further in. There was a place in there, incredibly small and yet vast. Dark and open.

It reminded her of space, of looking into the Cyprian's eyes and seeing the infinite reaches of space itself, of seeing nothing. The glimpse that the goddess had shown her married itself with the lessons Abraxas had been giving about her emotions.

Ana sank into herself like a bird diving for prey. She found the deep roots of the horror in her heart and plunged in. It was nauseating and thick, painful like burning tar. At first it overwhelmed her and she could breathe no better than when she'd hit the wall. She kept at it, pressed in, refused to come up. Through darkness and darkness, and then it began to open completely.

At the heart of emotion was energy. Each emotion a different energy, but each energy came from a source, from the same source, from this Place that was everywhere and nowhere. From this vast open nothingness that contained everything.

She took Brie's bloodied face in her hands and kissed her. Instinctively, Brie parted her lips and began to draw on Ana's life energy. She felt so soft Ana could fall forever but here she had to balance. In front of her this temptation into all pleasure. Behind her horror. But on the other side of that seething mass there was…everything. Ana pressed her lips against Brie's and felt the sexual energy rising up her spine toward her heart.

When the energy drew close to her heart, Ana inhaled. Then she stepped back through the door that had opened there. She turned and went through the open portal at the heart of her horror and fell into the nothingness.

* * *

When Ana kissed her, Brie was already out of her mind with pain and lust. She kept trying to draw Ashmedai up into her body, like a reflex, and each time he came further in and crushed her more. She felt her own orgasm drawing close and tried to push it away, knowing he would kill her when she opened that fully to him, but she wanted the release so badly she couldn't stop herself from riding him.

Then cool lips touched hers, drew her attention forward for a moment. She felt Ana come toward her, caught in the terrible maelstrom, and then pause as she had once before. There was something else in Ana's body, not a demon or any creature Brie could identify, just a seed of something or a crack of light in a dark room.

Ana's inhale drew in much more than breath. It opened the channel between them so wide that on his next push, Ashmedai fell forward through Brie. The momentum of his energy body didn't crush her as he'd planned, because now he had so much further forward to go. He would never fit in Ana, but she had opened herself. Ana wasn't there in her body anymore. Her whole body was only a portal to a dark universe woven through with indescribable brilliance.

Ashmedai's power washed through Brie like the wind, touching her everywhere but unable to grab or hold any part of her. The momentum was too great; he'd been using all his strength to drive in and crush her and now that he had so much further to go, he tumbled onward.

She imagined him screaming, though his body made no sound. His energy flared out, sought anything to catch on to and found nothing in the pure channel that had been Ana. Fear contracted him, curled his energy inward, speeding up his fall into nothingness.

Brie must have passed out because the next sensation was one of being smothered. She was facedown in Ana's lap with three hundred pounds of dead stone on top of her. Brie set her arms and pushed back, harder with the left than the right. Ashmedai slid out from inside her and off her in the same heavy roll.

Sitting up she looked at him. The body was empty and inanimate. A thick fissure started across his chest and with a thundering crack, the body split in two jagged pieces.

Brie hurt in every joint and her pelvis felt crushed, but the whole part about still being alive made up for it. She grabbed a clay arm in both hands, braced her bare feet on his torso and pulled until it cracked at the shoulder. Pushing up to her knees, she swung the arm up and smashed it down into his face. The demon Ashmedai was destroyed, fallen into the void and dissipated into nothing, but Brie wanted to see the same thing happen to his body.

The clay arm was cracking as fast as his lifeless head. After a few swings, Brie held only a cold hand in hers. The animal faces on the side of the head had cracked off like masks and the human face was pulverized beyond recognition.

Light fingers brushed the back of her shoulder, a gesture rich with the kind of power she'd felt from the Cyprian.

"Your friend will follow him if you don't call her back," Kay said.

Brie looked at Ana, who sat cross-legged, eyes half-shut and looking at nothing. She crawled over and waved a hand in front of her face with, no response.

"Don't go," she whispered. "Come back. We need you." She brushed a lock of golden hair off Ana's forehead.

Her eyes didn't seem to see anything, not Brie's face in front of hers or the motion of her hand. But Ana's body still breathed.

She laid her hand along Ana's cheek. "Ana, you have to come back here. Abraxas and Sabel will kill me if I don't bring you back whole."

Nothing.

Brie looked up at Kay, pleading. "I don't know how."

Kay shrugged. "You didn't know how to kill him either, I gather." She pointed at the cracked pile of clay pieces that had been Ashmedai.

"Wing it," Brie said.

She kissed Ana and tried to draw energy up through her, but it all leaked out behind at the level of her heart. She thought about the feeling of Sabel's energy, the clever construction of it, the patterns, how unlike Ana's it was. In Ana now the part that would be like a cathedral had been blown open to the night sky.

Brie thought about the leash and the kinds of magic she'd seen her stepfather do. Small movements, delicate, without the wild power of demons.

Ana's energy wasn't like a cathedral though, not like anything manmade. An untouched glade or wild plant. Brie put her hands over Ana's heart and thought of clouds covering the sky. No, better yet, a plant closing in on itself one leaf at a time.

"I think you have it," Kay said. She rested her hand on the top of Brie's head and the leaves began to curl in faster.

The energy stopped streaming out of Ana's body and collected inside her again.

Ana blinked. "Oh," she said. "I'm alive."

Brie threw her arms around her shoulders and felt Ana's arms encircle her waist in response.

A staccato sound started on the far side of the garage and Brie jerked up in alarm before she realized it was applause. Kay held Brie's pants out to her.

"We have not seen the likes of that in many centuries," Kay said. "Will you be my guests here before you return to your city?"

"We have to go," Ana said. Her voice still sounded spacey, as if she were picking out the words from a great distance away. She gathered herself to stand up and then seemed to think better of it. She still seemed unsteady and not completely back from wherever she'd gone. "Chicago," Ana managed to say and then had to think for another moment. "The Cyprian. It was a trap."

Kay's eyebrows drew together and Brie tried her luck at explaining their situation since Ana didn't seem to have made it back to complex sentences yet. "My mom and Ana's girlfriend and, um, demon are in Chicago in what's probably a trap because we were offered help from the Cyprian but it turns out she's a goddess of betrayal or something like that, so we need to get back there and rescue them."

"There are early morning flights out of Missoula. I'll get you on one," Kay offered with supreme practicality. "You have a few hours. Perhaps you'd like to clean up and eat. I'd enjoy hearing the long version of that story over a late dinner."

"Sure thing," Brie said. "Thank you. And Mack, her brother, he was shot…"

"We're already mending him," Kay told her. She gestured at the prone body that had been Ashmedai. "You must take a trophy of your victory."

Brie considered it, but really, what part would she take as a trophy? And if she did, how could she explain that to her mother?

"I think it would be best to burn that, if it burns. Or crush it," Brie said. She slid her pants on, mortified that she was sore for once. It might have been a nice feeling if she didn't have to think about the source.

Kay reached into the cracked chest of Ashmedai's body and pulled out a golden seal, about the size of Brie's palm, on a chain. "I could keep this, but I don't want such a weight." She handed it to Brie. "Give it to Ana when she's fully returned to herself, unless you plan to keep it as your prize."

"She did the killing," Brie said.

"Then it is hers."

Brie weighed it in her hand. It was the seal of the office of the Ashmedai. She'd never touched a demon prince's seal before, but she'd seen pictures. How was she ever going to tell Ana that she'd become a demon prince? Maybe she could just hand over the seal and let Lily do the explanation. Brie wasn't sure a human could even hold the office or access the power that came with it.

The parking garage, it turned out, was the lower level of a luxury hotel. Brie gathered from the three people assigned to escort them to a suite that Kay didn't live in the city, but when she came she stayed on the top floor of this hotel. Ashmedai's sudden appearance on her territory with a small army had been enough to draw her down from the mountains. She and Ana would be invited to dine with Kay, but for now they were to bathe and rest.

Ana still seemed shell-shocked. Brie had her lie down on the bed and drew a bath in the three-seat hot tub that their palatial bathroom featured along with a shower that could have hosted a small party. She lay back in the water and tried to let the burning memory of Ashmedai's touch dissolve in the water.

The sound of cloth on cloth made her open her eyes. Ana was standing in the middle of the bathroom pulling off her shirt. She put one foot in the tub, winced at the temperature and set about slowly lowering herself into the steaming water.

"There are bubbles if you want," Brie offered.

"This is fine," Ana said. She opened her arms and Brie crossed the tub to rest her head on Ana's shoulder. They sat together until the water had gone tepid and then washed each other.

When Ana stood up and climbed out of the tub, Brie saw the bruises darkening all across the back of her shoulders, at points along her backbone and at its base. She hissed through her teeth in sympathy.

"Looks bad, huh?" Ana asked.

"Very," Brie said.

"Your nose cleaned up well. I thought it was broken."

"Oh, it probably was, but my body puts itself back together pretty quickly when my beauty is at stake. It's just sore now."

She rubbed herself dry with the thick white towel and slipped on one of the plush hotel robes. Ana did the same. When they went into the main area of the suite, they saw that someone had dropped off new jeans and sweatshirts for them in roughly their sizes.

"We have to go," Ana said when they were dressed. She was still sounding vague.

"We will, but you really need to eat and rest some more. You don't really seem okay yet."

Ana held a hand out in front of her face and waved it in a general semicircle. "I keep seeing through it," she said.

"Your hand?"

"Everything. It just falls away. The floor is a piece of paper spread over nothing, the walls are like shadows, my body is a line drawing and behind it all is this presence."

"Like a person?"

"Just Being, big capital B Being. But the is-ness of it is so... real. Is that what Sabel meant when she said magic is what's real?"

Brie shrugged. "I never know what she means. But sometimes when I feed, if I feel along the line of energy, I touch something like that, that just Being."

Ana's eyes focused on Brie's face for the first time since the fight and she grinned. "Oh, good, I'm not losing my mind."

"Baby, you lost it the minute you let Abraxas into you. No sense worrying about that now. Let's go get some dinner and then we can ride into Chicago like the cavalry."

"Yeah, all two of us."

* * *

Ana expected Kay's dining room to be as fancy as the bath had been, but instead they sat at a small table in a modest hotel suite in front of windows that looked out on the mountains. She guessed this was breakfast, although it was three thirty a.m. They'd gotten a few hours of exhausted sleep and would leave for the airport in an hour.

Brie told most of the story while Ana explored how much coffee she was going to have to drink to start feeling normal again. There was a great spread of eggs, bacon, sausage, pastries, a few flavors of juice, lots of fruit, and some kind of fried bread that she thought she could eat for days. Brie was only nibbling, but Ana ate heartily and Mack heaped his plate and dug in. He'd taken the seat next to Brie and looked a lot better than he had in the van. Ana wondered if Kay had magically fixed him up somehow.

When Brie got to the end of the story, Kay asked, "What do you plan to do when you get to Chicago?"

"Bust them out and run for it?" Brie suggested, looking to Ana.

"That's what I was thinking. Unless you have some kind of superweapon." Ana directed the latter statement to Kay.

"I do not," she said. "I'm only powerful on my own land."

"You have guns or something?" Mack suggested.

"Yeah, that we're going to fly into Chicago with?" Ana asked caustically.

He hadn't really helped at all on this run, other than telling them how to jump off a train and locating some paving equipment. She'd expected, coming back from the space of great emptiness and openness, that the next time she saw Mack, she'd feel peaceful about him. She didn't. She still hated him. More to the point, her body still reacted with fear to him. When he reached across Brie for the jam, Ana felt herself flinch.

Beating on him hadn't changed that. Dissolving into emptiness at the source of her emotions hadn't changed that. Maybe nothing would but time and distance.

"You're not coming with us," she said.

"What the fuck? I've come this far."

"You got shot and we could've done this whole thing without you," Ana told him.

"I was looking after Brie," he said, turning toward her. "Right?"

Brie didn't answer. She pushed a cut strawberry across her plate, leaving a pink trail.

"She's not for you," Ana said.

"Oh, and she's for you, you fucking whore."

Ana was on her feet, fist raised, but Kay's voice thrummed through the room, soft and heavy with power. "Sit," she said.

Ana sat. Mack looked smug for an entire second.

Kay turned to him and watched him for so long that his fingers started to twitch nervously.

"She defeated a demon prince who thought he could hunt with impunity in my mountains," Kay said slowly. "And you sit at my table with your shallow and disrespectful words. What should I do with you?"

He didn't look up as his fingers turned the fork over and over again. "Ma'am, I apologize…you don't understand how she is…she just takes everything good."

Ana's throat tightened, her eyes stinging. Maybe he would never change. There was some part of her that remembered being really little, three or four years old, and loving Mack. Before she was old enough for him to bully and shove around, she thought he was the strongest, bravest person she knew. She felt the last flicker of hope that he could become that person again sputter in her heart and go out.

Kay glanced at her, eyebrows raised in a question.

"If it's not too much trouble," Ana said, "could you send him home?"

"Is that all you want?" Kay asked.

Ana was about to say yes, but from the building pressure in her head and chest, she knew that it wasn't.

"Can you heal his bullet wound?" she asked. "I see you did something to make him feel better already, but if it's not completely healed, can you do that?"

Mack's head came up in surprise.

"I can," Kay said.

"Can you even get rid of the scar? So no one ever knows this happened and no one will ever believe him if he tries to tell them. And then send him home. Let him live knowing there's magic in the world and it's not for him."

To Mack she said, "You made your bed years ago, go rot in it."

He opened his mouth to protest but Kay made a dismissive gesture. An older, lean man with leathery skin who'd been standing by the door came forward and took Mack's arm. He pulled him up and shoved him roughly ahead of him out of the room.

Ana wanted to feel triumphant. She didn't. But she did feel clearheaded and safe. Now all she had to do was fight a god.

CHAPTER TWENTY

Time bent around Sabel. It was the opposite of the technique she employed when she stuttered time. Usually she made time around her run a little faster than the timestream, but now an immensely powerful effect dragged at her and Lily and Abraxas. The power was so vast she couldn't tell how long it took for her to realize she'd been slowed down. The windows had already been dark and the sun wasn't up yet, so part or most of the night could be passing.

Figures moved around them with blinding speed. It was hard to pick them out, but when Sabel realized she'd been slowed, she stepped a little outside the timestream and spread herself across a broader present moment. It was hard for her human brain to see and it took intense concentration until she could read the trails of activity—then she saw what the Cyprian had done.

While she, Lily and Abraxas were standing outside the top arc of the circle that bound Ashtoreth and made it possible to catch her in the mirrored stone box, the Cyprian had her people redraw another circle, a copy of the first, so that it included them. She had had everything she needed from Lily's work to bind Abraxas the same way they'd bound Ashtoreth. Except for Sabel's Voice.

Around her body, Sabel felt the slowed time speeding back to match the present, but she kept her mind a little outside of the timestream. She had enough consciousness inside the timestream to function but with another part of her mind, she went through the steps to get into her interface with probabilities.

The Cyprian let the slowed bubble they were in snap back into the present, and then she started the binding.

Sabel didn't waste breath on curses or threats. The Cyprian had to know Sabel was furious with her and seeking a way to destroy her—she was further into the future than Sabel herself and could see it clearly. Sabel's wish to ruin her shone like a beacon in the future, and with seemingly little effort, the Cyprian reached with some part of her being and snuffed it out.

Sabel clenched her jaw as a shockwave traveled back from the future to land in her body with a sickening impact. Her hatred of the Cyprian flickered out and in again taking another form.

"What are you doing?" Lily asked, but she couldn't move quickly enough to stop the Cyprian.

A new circle flared up on the floor, a smaller repeat of the one she and Lily had made. Lily choked and doubled over. Sabel caught her before she hit the floor.

"Abraxas," Lily gasped.

He rose above her towering to the height of the ceiling. "You would bind me," he thundered.

"Yes," the Cyprian said coolly.

"I cannot be bound."

"Don't be ridiculous," the Cyprian said. "The only reason I can't put you in a box is because your Ana is still living, for the moment."

"You told Ashmedai where to find her," Sabel said.

"I did, but that's not all. Can you see it, little witch?"

The Cyprian waved her hand and behind it Sabel saw part of a pattern become clear.

When they'd first met her, the Cyprian did something to Ana, gave her the means to defeat Ashmedai because that defeat would lead to Ana betraying herself. Defeating Ashmedai made Ana the inheritor of his power. There was something about winning against him—Sabel couldn't make out the details—but there was a path that led to Ana becoming a prince of the Shaitans, becoming the new Ashmedai. She had just enough demon blood for it to count. Sabel had to warn her, but she couldn't see how, or what she had to warn her against doing.

"I see it," Sabel said. "But how does it benefit you?"

"Betrayal always benefits me. And she'll come to rescue you," the Cyprian said. "She'll put herself in my power. One way or another, she'll give me that demon." She gestured toward Abraxas.

"She won't," Sabel said, though she was afraid of all she didn't know.

"You think that. Do you know who he really is?"

Abraxas made an inarticulate sound of pain.

Sabel voiced the conclusion all her research had begun to point to. "He was in the archive," she said. "He's the prince of the Sangkesh who took the tablet of the galla."

The Cyprian's face lit up. "Yes, you know this already."

"No!" Lily protested. "There was no Sangkesh prince. Abraxas was gone before that."

"Gone from his title," the Cyprian said. "Not from this world. As I remember it, he stepped down from his title willingly." She grinned broadly at the curled-in, smoky form of Abraxas. "You fell in love, didn't you? I could feel it. But she wasn't someone you could have as a prince of the Sangkesh, as The Abraxas, so you stepped away. But that didn't change what you were. The witches still read your energy true when they searched the burned-out husk of the archive."

Abraxas didn't uncurl, but his voice was clear. "She told me to take her and the tablet of the galla and run. The attack was from the Shaitans and the galla. I was rescuing her."

"Not a very good rescue," the Cyprian observed. "She was found dead the next morning. Mortally wounded in the escape, I assume. What did you do with the tablet?"

"I hid it," he said.

She roared with laughter. "Terrible lie. You ate it, didn't you?"

He didn't answer, but Sabel knew it had to be true. She could see clearly now what must have happened. In 1138 when the archive was attacked, Abraxas had been in there, secretly, with the woman he loved. She was the head of the archive itself. The same witch found dead outside the archive the next day with the energy of the Sangkesh around her body.

As head of the archive, she must have tried to get Abraxas to take her and the tablet to safety. He couldn't save her, but he could keep the knowledge on the tablet from falling to the Shaitans or the galla who opposed the witches, so he made the tablet part of his being. But then he would have to flee somewhere that no one could find him and force the knowledge from him. The only place he could be completely safe was death itself.

He should never have come back.

As soon as the other witches knew, they'd be after him. The Sangkesh would be after him, and the Shaitans, and the galla. All of them wanted that knowledge because whoever held it could control the living galla, many of them thousands of years old. And the tablet's owner could turn humans into immortal creatures.

"Now you see it," the Cyprian said, her arms crossed. "Nowhere is safe for him and for your Ana. Here, in the heart of this city's power, I can protect them. Ana will come back here and stay because I am the least of her problems now."

No, Sabel thought, she'll never stay here. We'll leave and I'll find a way to protect her, no matter the cost.

The Cyprian turned and swept out of the room. Two human guards with guns stayed just inside the door.

Lily appeared to be having a long, silent conversation with Abraxas and Sabel didn't interrupt. She hoped Lily was doing a lot of mental yelling. Why had he come back? Why now? Why Ana?

She wanted to hope that if they escaped, the Cyprian would tell no one about Abraxas. But that was a stupid hope to cling to. Considering how easy it had been for the Cyprian to betray them to Ashmedai, Sabel had to assume that the minute they left Chicago, the Cyprian would declare open hunting season on Abraxas.

Still, it was hardly safe to stay with the Cyprian. Even if she intended to protect Ana, if Sabel understood her power correctly, she would eventually betray her, whether she meant to or not. First they had to get out of this tower and then they could find someplace safe for Ana and Abraxas. She had the money, she could send them anywhere in the world to hide until she could talk to Josefene and Devony and find a way out of this.

Her cell phone was in her front jacket pocket. It was too much to hope for, but she pulled it out, the view of her action shielded from the guards by her body. It had reception and a mostly charged battery, plus a series of messages from Ana. The first one came from the day before and said simply: *I want to give you everything.*

Sabel blinked hard and willed the tears out of her eyes. Ana had gotten the intention of her last message, the veiled apology and her awkward attempts to find the right way to express how she felt while they were so far apart and caught up in all of this. She'd understood and sent the perfect reply. They had to find a way out together.

The rest of the messages started just after midnight and were more pragmatic:

"You were right. Caught in Montana—Cyprian tipped off Ashmedai. We took care of him. You safe?"

"Driving to airport in Missoula, arriving O'Hare midday, can you get out and meet us?"

"I'm on the plane. Where are you?"

The last message had been sent almost two hours ago. They should be landing soon. Sabel wanted to text her back and tell her to run, to go anywhere that no one could find her, but she was afraid that the Cyprian was right and that Chicago was the safest place for her now.

She typed: "*Trapped. Willis Tower floor 95, SW corner conf. room. Abraxas bound. 2 men with guns. And some other problems. Call me.*"

"Ana and Brie are coming here," Sabel said. "Should I tell them to run?"

"Yes," Lily said at the same time that Abraxas said, "No."

Sabel sighed and hit Send. Even if she told Ana to run, she knew Ana wouldn't listen.

* * *

When they landed, Ana found a series of messages from Sabel:

"*Trapped. Willis Tower floor 95, SW corner conf. room. Abraxas bound. 2 men with guns. And some other problems. Call me.*"

"*Abraxas's binding isn't complete because he resides in you. You must stay out of the circle, but come break it and take him.*"

"*Two guards with semiautomatic guns here. More in the hall. They're giving me dirty looks because they can't step into the circle to take my phone.*"

"*Lily says tell Brie to use the fact that it's a workday to your advantage. Even gods have to be careful in the material world.*"

"*If something bad happens, there's an envelope in my right desk drawer at home with your name on it. Read it. All of it.*"

Ana hated the contents of the last message, and she wasn't sure what they were going to do about a bunch of armed men, but she and Brie had formed the bare bones of a plan and since she couldn't come up with anything better, she was ready to follow through on it.

They caught a cab from the airport and got out a few blocks from the Willis Tower. It was just after the lunch hour and the streets were awash with people heading back to their offices.

She felt like she hadn't slept in days and in a way that was true; a few hours last night, the night before that she'd caught snatches of sleep on the train, and before that it had been a short night in a Lincoln hotel. Three days she'd been on the run, longer if you counted from her father's funeral. That seemed a year ago now.

They paused on the corner, Brie shading her eyes and looking up at the Tower. "Wish me luck," she said. She looked as worried as Ana felt.

"Be safe in there," Ana said.

"Take care of my mom," Brie said and then she was off across the street toward the Tower.

Ana pulled on her tourist wear: the "I Love Chicago" T-shirt, a Cubs baseball hat under which she tucked her hair, and the awful, large sunglasses. She headed for the front of the Tower, taking time to stare up at the windows and let Brie get enough of a head start for this to work.

CHAPTER TWENTY-ONE

Brie walked up to the information desk. "Hi there, I'm Brie Cordoba, here to see the Cyprian. I have something she's looking for." The woman stared at her blankly, but a man stepped up next to her.

"I'll take you up," he said.

He looked like a Secret Service agent in his olive suit, with the little communications earpiece curled over his ear. It was so cute, nestled against his skin like a pet. She smelled his pride and strength, and the undertones of insecurity. She could balm those if he gave her the chance. She could show him such a good time. Brie felt the habitual flirtation rise to her lips and kept them shut. *Save it*, she told herself.

There were rooms near the top of the Tower that looked exactly like the rooms in the Cyprian's condo building in Minneapolis. That was power, Brie thought with a snort, the ability not just to move furniture, but the whole setup. And she bet the Cyprian hadn't used a truck to do it.

The Cyprian came in through the same door by which Brie had just entered and she actually looked harried. A lock of her hair had come loose and curled down the side of her neck and her eyes were tight. Brie wanted to rub the lines of worry from her forehead, soothe her and take her mind off these troubles. She let that feeling rise up in her, go to her head like alcohol.

"Didn't expect to see me again, I'll bet," she said with a radiant smile.

"I am surprised to see you," the Cyprian admitted. "But not disappointed."

"I'm glad. I thought we had unfinished business." She took the seal of Ashmedai out of her pocket and tossed it lightly in her hand so the light from the windows flashed off its dull gold surface.

"Ashmedai," the Cyprian said without surprise.

Brie nodded. "Mine now. And I have Ana."

She gave Brie a smug smile and shook her head. "No, you don't. And that," she pointed at the seal, "is bound to Ana, not to you. But you did bring me something I want."

Brie raised an eyebrow and the Cyprian beckoned to her to come close. She stepped up to the Cyprian and kissed her. Energy flared in her, but no desire. Was she so full from Ashmedai or so raw from him that she actually no longer wanted this? She steeled herself and faked it.

The Cyprian kissed back and Brie could sense both passion and curiosity from her. She could borrow the Cyprian's passion for this. The Cyprian drew her toward another door that opened on a bedroom, white as anything else in that place. What was her thing with white? Brie wondered if she'd really bed a goddess between those snowy sheets. She was starting to get into it, her usual fire returning with the desire to taste this incredible creature.

Gunshots sounded on the other side of the building as they reached the door to the bedroom. The Cyprian smiled.

"Ah there they are," the Cyprian said in a voice much colder than her body. "Now, let's see how much your friends love you."

* * *

Sabel's phone rang and the loud, clear sound echoed in the room. She stared at it in surprise and then clicked it on.

"You ready to go?" Ana asked.

Just hearing her voice gave Sabel confidence. "More than ready," she said.

"Good. Create a distraction."

Ana hung up and Sabel turned to Lily and Abraxas. "That's Ana, she says get ready to go and we need a distraction."

"The box," Abraxas said.

The stone box holding Ashtoreth was still on a meeting table in the middle of the room and the large binding circle. This soon after the binding, Sabel could understand why the Cyprian was afraid to move the box. She didn't want to chance Ashtoreth getting loose—and she knew that Lily and Abraxas couldn't leave the small binding circle to get to the box. There was a chance that she didn't know, given how much else was going on now, that Sabel had smudged the binding circle on that side as she drew it and that its power had been leaking out all night. If she could just get the box open, the circle would no longer be powerful enough to hold Ashtoreth.

Sabel wasn't bound by the small circle the way that Lily and Abraxas were because she had no demon magic in her. But she was bound as effectively by the men standing on either side of the doorway with their guns. She had to get to the box without being shot, and then she had to pray that Ashtoreth was more interested in her own freedom and revenge against the Cyprian than turning on Sabel and her group. If she did turn on them, they'd be torn apart before they could react.

The top of the table was thick wood covered with stone inlay. It looked heavy but not impossibly so. Sabel inhaled deeply and opened her throat. Using the Voice, she commanded herself, "*Be strong.*"

Then she stepped across time a half second into the future and stuttered across that future and the shared present. The effect was that when she sprinted for the table, she seemed to be a half second behind where she was.

Shots exploded into the air behind her as she dove for the table. A searing line of pain cut across the side of one leg. She ignored it, braced and heaved the table over on its side so she was behind it.

The stone box fell to the ground and cracked open as more bullets shattered the inset stone of the tabletop. Sabel scrambled backward, keeping the table between her and the guards, until her hand could reach the blur in the chalk of the large circle. She erased it.

With a howl of wind, Ashtoreth was out of the circle. Sabel heard the sickening crunch of many bones shattering at once and the gunshots stopped. Then came the crash of the metal door being blown open. When Sabel hazarded a look over the edge of the table she saw the two guards broken on the floor and through the ruined door a whirlwind of chaos.

"She's headed somewhere to heal and amass power," Lily said. "She won't come back after us yet."

Now that the guards were down, Sabel could open the small binding circle and let Abraxas out and Lily with him. Lily helped her to her feet and they limped through the door into the hall.

Ashtoreth was moving down the hall, breaking guards as she went. She went through an open door and Sabel heard the sound of breaking glass as she blew out the windows and fled into the open air.

A familiar figure ran around the corner, hat falling off to reveal spiky golden hair. "Sabel! Abraxas!" Ana yelled.

A serpent of fire shot down the corridor and dove into her chest as Abraxas returned to his home in her. She looked brighter with him back inside her, and a touch larger than she had before. Sabel worried a little less about her now, and more about the rest of them.

The hall was empty of guards, which was good from a not-being-shot perspective. It also allowed Sabel to have most of her awareness in the space of her workshop and look out over the probabilities streaming backward into this major event.

Lily went toward the bodies Sabel couldn't bear to look at and came up with a gun. Ana rushed to Sabel's side and put an arm around her, taking Sabel's weight off the burning pain in her calf. Leaning against her heavily, Sabel pushed her mind further out from her body, roving back and forth across the probability lines. The Cyprian should have been on them already. She could easily slow them all again, but her mass of power was occupied, focused on the city itself and on one much smaller bright star.

"Is the Cyprian just going to let us walk out?" Ana asked.

"She has Brie," Sabel told her. On the probability level, every future seemed to pass through Brie.

"Brie was just supposed to distract her and get out."

The dense patterns of energy around Brie's pulsing star made sense now. "She can't get out," Sabel said. "She's the most vulnerable to the Cyprian because she loves everyone."

"What?" Ana asked, her voice rising with alarm.

"The Cyprian's power is love combined with betrayal. The more you love, the more she can make you betray everything you love."

"Where are they?" Ana insisted.

Sabel pointed down the hall at the door behind which she could see the most energy converge. Ana kicked the door and with her Abraxas-enhanced strength, it flew open and tore half off its hinges.

The Cyprian was standing in the middle of a comfortably appointed room. The center had been cleared and around it was a range of couches. Handsome young men reclined on most of them and Brie was crouched over one of them. She looked up as they came in, her expression a mix of grief, horror and hunger.

"See what your daughter is," the Cyprian said to Lily. "How many will she kill before you stop her?"

Sabel couldn't tell how the Cyprian was forcing Brie to feed, but from the intense power flowing between the Cyprian and Brie, she knew that was the case. The Cyprian could force her to kill every person in this room and she would still be hungry. It was the greatest betrayal of herself and of Lily and Ana, so it was easy for the Cyprian to do.

Lily leaped across the room and knocked Brie off the man, whose lifeless body fell back on the cushions. Mother and daughter fought with a combination of wrestling and thrown physical blows. Leaving Sabel to brace herself on the end of a couch, Ana tried to move toward them, but she was immobilized. She couldn't take an action that wasn't a betrayal, and to stop Brie and Lily fighting betrayed no one.

Sabel's attention was drawn to the Cyprian, who stepped to her side.

"Do you know what she was doing while you were trapped here?" the Cyprian asked and pointed to Ana. "Off playing with the pretty one. Kissing, caressing, caring for each other while you were here, in mortal danger. But you could stop it all, bind her to you, command her never to leave you. You could make her yours forever. Or maybe it would be better to stop the little succubus. Just end her and save all these people and your love."

The forces pressing on Sabel were too strong to resist so she didn't try. Head-on resistance wasn't her strong suit anyway; she took the path of surrender. She let the drive to betray wash over her and as it swept through her psyche, she tapped it slightly one way and another.

She had to betray someone in the room, preferably more than one person, but she could choose the betrayal. She drew on her Voice and turned it on Lily and Brie.

"*Stop fighting,*" she commanded. She limped between the couches to get to where their momentum had carried them.

Kneeling down beside Lily's shaking body, she commanded, "*Run away from her.*" Her face twisting in anguish, Lily got up and ran. It worked because to leave her daughter in this kind of danger was a clear betrayal.

The Cyprian laughed. "Oh, beautiful, little gem, go on!"

Brie was up again and moving toward the closest man on the couch. Whatever the Cyprian had done to her, it made her need to keep feeding. Still kneeling, she turned toward Brie.

"*Feed on me,*" she commanded.

Brie turned on her in an instant. Sabel's power was magnified with the compulsion provided by the Cyprian. In the blink of an eye, Brie had her pinned on the floor and was drawing her life force out of her body.

Sabel slowed time for the two of them. She focused on the probability space and pushed away the probability that Brie would kill her, but the Cyprian tapped it and easily knocked it back into prominence. Sabel could hear the Cyprian laughing. She hadn't considered how overmatched she was amid the kinds of power the Cyprian held not only over probability and time but over these master patterns, like betrayal.

What she'd failed to see when she let the power of betrayal into her mind was that to die was also to betray Ana. Now there was a very real possibility that she had just engineered her own death.

Sabel looked for any place she could put her energy to keep Brie from consuming it, but there was nowhere. She couldn't use any of the larger probabilities. She couldn't resist physically because Brie was so much stronger than she was. She couldn't stop Brie from feeding because letting Brie kill her was also a betrayal of Brie and the probability of that just kept coming closer.

Sabel made herself look away from that near future and her own death. She sought out the smallest strands, the dark and shadowy options. What was likely but just out of reach from this moment? What could possibly halt the Cyprian's overwhelming power to make them all turn on each other until none of them were left alive?

She saw a glimmering silver trail of stars and touched it with a small corner of her mind. The bulk of her will and power she directed at holding off her death. It was what the Cyprian would expect and she hoped it was enough to keep her attention away from the other probability Sabel was increasing.

Ana's stiffly moving form came into her peripheral vision. She looked like a person walking against an impossibly strong wind. For the last few feet, she dropped to hands and knees and crawled. Sabel was on the verge of losing consciousness to Brie's relentless draw on her energy. Ana grabbed a handful of Brie's hair and dragged her sideways off Sabel. The feeding paused.

"You can only betray," Sabel gasped at Ana, then took a quick breath and tried again. "Only actions that betray someone you love."

Ana shook her head. She was holding Brie away from Sabel, but her grip was slipping.

"Betray me or yourself," Sabel forced the words out. "You must."

Jaw clenched, tears rampant in her furious eyes, Ana raised her right hand in a fist. Sabel thought she was going to hit Brie with it, but it came down hard in the center of Sabel's chest. A wave of demon energy flowed into her body and triggered the leash with a crack.

Because time was slowed for her, Sabel didn't pass out instantly. She hung for a moment between consciousness and oblivion and pulled herself further out of her physical body and into her probability space. Now her body was out cold but her mind could operate for a short while until the limitations of her body caught up with it. The threads around her told her that Ana and Brie were trying to kill each other and the most likely outcome was that Ana would win. Brie couldn't kill Ana by drawing her energy as long as Abraxas was in her, but Ana could kill Brie by strangling her as she was trying to do.

She could talk to Abraxas, Sabel realized abruptly. With the leash already triggered, she had nothing to lose. She found his probability sphere and pushed at it with her mind. She wasn't good at any kind of mental communication, but as soon as he felt her near him, he could open a channel to her.

Can you call Ashtoreth back here? she asked him.

I can send a message, he replied. *But where is here?*

He was right. Ashtoreth could find them eventually. It might only take her a few minutes if she decided to take them up on their invitation, but even that was too long. Sabel needed a beacon to call her to. There was no way in this nonphysical space to indicate a location in the material world. Whatever message Abraxas sent would be the equivalent of telling a friend, "Meet me at four p.m." and hoping they could guess the right location.

She and Abraxas and the Cyprian all spanned a number of probabilities spread across multiple moments in time. She needed to pick a time and place that occurred before someone died, not concurrent with any of the near future deaths she was seeing. But there was nothing with enough magic to be on the probability level and simultaneously at a single point in time, because objects in the material world didn't have that kind of magic. Man-made objects, like the couches and tables in the room, were particularly bad for having any kind of probability associated with them. If there had been a tree in the room, she might have used that, or a stone or any kind of naturally made thing or even a magical artifact.

Oh, but there was one: the leash itself. It crossed all kinds of magic but was bound completely in one present moment.

Sabel grabbed it mentally and held it out to Abraxas. *Call Ashtoreth to this*, she said before her body's unconsciousness caught up with her mind.

CHAPTER TWENTY-TWO

With Sabel unconscious, Brie stopped feeding on her. Triggering the leash must have prevented Brie from drawing any more energy, because she paused and stared at Ana. Her body tensed, preparing to jump. Ana moved first, closing the distance between them and fixing her hands around Brie's throat. She constricted hard enough to make Brie claw at her hands and focus on survival rather than hunger.

A little help here? she asked Abraxas.

His voice, inside her mind, sounded strained and distant. *Calling Ashtoreth back to fight her.*

Call louder, Ana told him. To Brie she said, "You can only betray those you love." She pointed her chin at the Cyprian. "Haven't you been admiring her since you met her?"

Brie's eyes glinted with understanding. She still looked like a feral creature, but now there was a hint of light in there. She made a low growl of agreement that vibrated against Ana's hands.

Carefully, she let go of Brie, who took two long, shuddering breaths. "The seal," Brie said.

She pulled the flat golden metal disc out of her pocket and shoved it at Ana so hard it knocked her back. Brie crossed the room to the Cyprian.

Ana moved away from Sabel, though she ached to touch her, because she didn't trust herself not to somehow hurt her. Bad enough that she'd hit her. She had to find a way to get Brie and Sabel out of the room. Her impulse was to drag Sabel to the door, but Sabel had said only actions that were a betrayal, so she had to get Brie out first.

The Cyprian had Brie pinned against the wall, or had Brie pulled her close and refused to let her go? Their hands stroked and clawed each other, tearing clothes and skin, more violence than passion.

Ana's hand closed on Brie's wrist and the skin burned like hot metal. She tightened her grip against the pain and dragged at Brie.

"We need to go," she insisted.

Brie turned her face to Ana for a moment, lips bloody. "Use the seal," she hissed.

The cold disk was inscribed with signs. As she looked at it, the signs moved, drawing her in. It terrified her. The Ashmedai had been a demon not only of lust, but also of destruction. She didn't want to put her will into this thing. It was chaos and yet it was familiar. It was anger itself.

In front of her, Brie let out a gasp of pain and sagged against the wall. Ana held out the seal toward the Cyprian and pushed everything in that direction. *Away*, she intended, with all her heart behind it.

The force blew the Cyprian across the room where her impact smashed a side table. She got up and shook dust from her hair.

"You don't learn," she said. "You can't hurt me."

Ana looped her arms under Brie's shoulders and dragged her toward the elevator, which she seemed able to do only because of the terrible feeling caused by leaving Sabel where she lay.

"I don't need to hurt you to stop you," Ana said.

The Cyprian shrugged the shoulders of her jacket level again and walked toward them. She was halfway to them when the whirlwind came howling around the corner and engulfed her. The force of it knocked the Cyprian through the wall into the adjoining room.

How long can Ashtoreth hold her? Ana asked Abraxas.

Minutes, he said. *The Cyprian is stronger now.*

The elevator chimed and its doors opened. Ana tried to push Brie through them, but Brie used her momentum to reverse the gesture. Ana staggered backward. Brie lifted a foot and kicked Ana solidly in the chest so that she hit the elevator's back wall hard. She dropped to the floor, struggling to catch her breath as Brie hit the button for the first floor and stepped back into the hall, leaving Ana alone in the descending elevator.

* * *

Sabel felt the leash loosen and she was back in her body and awake. Brie leaned over her.

"Kiss me," Brie said. "And mean it."

A quick glance showed the room being torn apart in a whirlwind of glass and debris. Brie had bleeding gashes across her cheek that were healing as Sabel watched. She'd taken in so much energy that even as a shard of glass tore across her shoulder, the wound closed behind it. Her body shielded Sabel from the worst of the storm.

Even though the Cyprian was occupied with Ashtoreth, the field of her power still dominated the room—narrowing all actions to love and betrayal. Sabel looked into Brie's dark eyes and understood what she was asking.

She focused on the feeling of Brie in her energy body, loosening the leash, filling her with pleasure in the midst of all this pain. Any criticisms or negativity she shoved to the side. She made herself want Brie and love her. She grabbed Brie's face in her hands and kissed her deeply.

Brie's arms went around her shoulders and under her legs, lifting her effortlessly. She carried Sabel to the bank of elevators and held her while they waited for one of the cars to return to their floor. Her lips were hot and tasted like blood and sugar and sex. Sabel felt terrible and exultant. When this was well behind her, she swore, she would go home and enjoy feeling no strong emotion for weeks.

They entered the elevator and Brie set Sabel's feet on the floor. A shock of pain traveled up from her calf. She wavered on her feet but managed to hit the button to the first floor. Then turned back to kiss Brie again. Brie's back was against the elevator wall, her hands grabbing Sabel's hair, crushing their mouths together. Her tongue was nimble and searing and maddeningly perfect.

The farther they descended through the building, the weaker the field of the Cyprian's power became. Sabel had the impression that not only did it lessen with distance, but that the Cyprian was having to marshal more of her strength to fight Ashtoreth.

The elevator stopped its downward motion with a smooth settling and the doors opened. Sabel stepped away from Brie, who grabbed her elbow and pulled her out into the lobby. Ana was pacing between all the elevators and turned to them.

"Go," Brie said. "Too close."

Ana reached toward Sabel, but she shook her head. "Just run," she told her.

Run was overstating it though. Sabel could manage a limping walk. Her inner defenses were in ruin and she couldn't completely block out the pain that lanced up her leg with every step.

They went to the front doors together and out onto the evening street. Sabel heard sirens coming closer. Someone must have heard the breaking glass on the Cyprian's floor and probably the gunshots and called the police.

"You're bleeding," Ana said.

"Betrayal," Sabel warned. She stripped off her sweater, leaving only a thin shell against the chill wind. Wrapping it around her calf, she used the arms to tie it as tightly as the pain allowed. She took a few more dragging steps.

"Let Abraxas help," Ana told her. "He can betray you and touch you."

It was Ana's arm that wrapped roughly around Sabel's shoulders and helped her get the weight off her calf, but it was filled with Abraxas's energy. She could feel the burn of his anger at her for figuring out who he was and his mistrust about what she would do with that information. There were a hundred ways their mutual survival would lead to future betrayal and that was enough to keep them together and moving away from the Cyprian.

They walked in silence for a few blocks. Tears streaked slowly down Sabel's cheeks from the pain but she focused on just taking the next step, putting as much weight on Abraxas as she could.

When she felt the remaining strands of the Cyprian's power weaken sufficiently that she could shake them off, she said, "Stop."

Abraxas, still dominant in Ana's body, helped her sit against the side of the building.

"We're out of her field," Sabel said. "Should still leave the city though, and fast."

Brie dropped down next to her. "I feel like I'm going to hurt for a year," she said and Sabel just shook her head because Brie didn't seem to have a scratch on her.

Ana grabbed her hand. She looked afraid to do more than that, and Sabel remembered the pain in Ana's face right before she hit her to trigger the leash.

"I'm okay," Sabel told her. "I'm shot and bruised and sore in a hundred different ways and I never want to fight a goddess again, but I'm okay."

"We need bandages for you," Ana insisted. "And maybe a hospital. And coats."

"We have to figure out where Lily went," Sabel said. "My command wasn't that strong, but with the Cyprian's power behind it, there's a chance she's still running."

"She isn't," Ana said. "I texted her from the lobby. She's got a cab and is coming to pick us up so we can blow this town."

Sabel leaned against the building behind her and crossed her arms over her chest, trying to stay warm. Ana put an arm around her again, but this time it was all her energy and not Abraxas. Sabel leaned into her.

"So much for running away together," Brie said with a glint of humor in her smile.

"You thought the betrayal had to go that far?" Sabel asked.

"Why did you think you were kissing me?"

"Kinky succubus power thing," Sabel said and smiled lightly at her. "I'm kidding. I knew as soon as you told me to kiss you that we could only get out of there if we were running away together."

"You didn't *have* to kiss me the whole way down in the elevator," Brie said.

"It was strong magic," Sabel replied. "I thought we shouldn't take chances."

"That's why you drop-kicked me into the elevator, so you could make out with my girlfriend?" Ana asked.

"Best escape ever," Brie told her. She pressed against Sabel's side and Sabel didn't begrudge her the warmth or the contact.

"She drop-kicked you?" Sabel asked Ana.

Brie answered, "It was more of a side kick, my dropkick would break your face."

"Oh, yeah, keep trash-talking, I can take you," Ana said, leaning around Sabel to glare playfully at Brie.

"I know you can," Brie replied and pressed harder against Sabel's side.

Ana looked down at her and Sabel nodded; Brie put her arm around Sabel, over Ana's, and the three of them huddled together until Lily arrived.

CHAPTER TWENTY-THREE

Ana expected they'd exchange the cab for a rental car, but Lily told the driver to take them all the way to Gary, Indiana, and he was happy to oblige. In the backseat, Ana sat in the middle with Sabel on her left and Brie to her right. Lily sat in front and Abraxas remained quiet in Ana's mind. He hadn't said much and when she sent a wordless question his way she was met with a dense cloud of shame and discomfort, so she backed off.

Before her mind had time to fully adjust to the fact that she wasn't fighting or running, they arrived at a hotel near the Gary airport and Lily was checking them into another set of rooms. Once she got home, Ana resolved to avoid hotels as long as she could. She no longer had good associations with them.

Lily had picked a hotel with room doors all facing to the outside. Despite Sabel's protests, Ana carried her from the cab to their room. At least this time she didn't have to worry about Mack staying in a room down the hall from her; he was back in South Dakota and texting Brie every ten minutes.

In the room, Lily had Sabel strip out of her torn and bloody jeans and sit on the edge of the tub while Lily examined her leg. Ana stood in the doorway with her arms crossed because there wasn't room enough for three of them in the little bathroom. Brie had thrown herself across one of the made beds and was staring up at the ceiling.

A bullet had torn across the side of Sabel's calf leaving a bloody gash about a half-inch across. After a quick glance at the wound, Lily's gaze shifted somewhat higher and she stared at Sabel's underpants. They were a beautifully rich shade of purple, at least where there was any fabric at all.

"When you got up yesterday morning and decided to get dressed for a magical war, that's what you put on?" Lily asked.

"Well, yes," Sabel said. "I picked them up in Minneapolis for just such an eventuality."

"And so from here on out, I dub them the war panties," Ana said.

Lily looked at her and cocked an eyebrow. "I don't even want to know," she said. But added, "Tell me that's not a witch thing."

"It's a Sabel thing," Ana said.

Lily shook her head and returned her attention to the gash. "That's going to need stitches."

Sabel sighed. "I figured."

"I'll clean it and bind it up as well as I can," Lily said. "And I could do the stitches for you, but I think it would be better if you have a doctor do it."

"Of course you know how to stitch a wound," Ana said with a dry chuckle.

"I started as a hunter in the nineteen fifties," Lily said. "It required some self-sufficiency. Brace yourself, this is going to hurt."

"I can turn off the pain as long as I can concentrate and I'm not fighting a goddess or anything," Sabel said.

Lily cleaned the wound while Sabel sat very still with an intense look on her face. Her breathing was slow and measured, but she didn't seem to be in pain even as Lily ran water over the bloody gash. Then Lily produced some gauze from the hotel's first aid kit and wrapped it tightly around Sabel's leg.

"That should hold you for now," Lily said. "You should get in to see your doctor as soon as you get back. I'm not up on how to treat modern bullet wounds."

"When can we fly out?" Ana asked.

"I'll see if I can get us tickets for tomorrow afternoon," Lily said.

Sabel looked up quickly, her face going from pale to paper-white. Ana heard Brie hop off the bed and walk across the room.

"Wait," Brie said.

At nearly the same time, Sabel said, "You can't."

Ana looked over her shoulder. Brie's expression was worried at best. "What?" she asked.

Brie craned around Ana in the doorway and addressed her answer to Lily. "She killed the Ashmedai and took his seal," she said.

"If she hasn't used it yet..." Lily began, but faltered mid-sentence as she saw Brie slowly shaking her head. "You used it. Okay, we can work with that. It doesn't mean you won't be allowed in San Francisco ever, but for now the binding that's on the city to keep Ashmedai out will keep you out."

"I can't go home?" Ana asked plaintively.

Brie's hand was light on her shoulder. "You're the new Ashmedai," she said. "Prince of Lust and Destruction."

"What the hell. Abraxas, why didn't you tell me?"

He pushed out of her body like a man reluctantly rising from a long sleep and stood in the foyer of the room, behind her.

"I didn't know you were going to use the seal until you did," he said. "But the investiture hasn't fully happened. You can transfer the office to another."

"Can I give it to you?" she asked.

"I'd rather you didn't."

"Yeah, well, I'd rather be allowed back in my own city."

"It doesn't matter," Sabel said, her voice bleak. "You couldn't go back anyway."

"What else did I do?" Ana asked, angry but not at anyone in particular, yet.

"It's not what you did, it's Abraxas," Sabel answered. Her face looked gray with exhaustion and pain that went beyond the physical. Ana pushed into the bathroom, beyond Lily, and went down to one knee on the bath mat so she could put her arms around Sabel, who leaned gratefully into her and rested her head on Ana's shoulder.

"Remember when I told you why the Sangkesh demons and the Hecatine witches have been at each others' throats for about eight hundred years?" Sabel asked the question quietly with her lips near Ana's ear but Ana had no doubt that everyone in the small space of bathroom and foyer could hear her words.

"Roughly," Ana said.

"The important part is that when the archive was attacked, the tablet for making the galla demons was taken," Sabel said. "The tablet that describes both how to make and how to control them. It's incredibly powerful. Whoever gets hold of that tablet can essentially control a small army of immortal humans."

"And you're about to tell me that Abraxas found it in the Cyprian's attic?"

Sabel's voice lightened for a moment as she said, "Essentially, yes. But not in her stuff." The humor went away again. "Abraxas has it. He was in the archive when it was attacked and he took the tablet but apparently he thought there was no place safe for it, so he consumed it. Now he *is* the tablet. That's why the Cyprian wanted him so much. She doesn't care about a single demon prince, but the power to make humans immortal? Everyone wants to get their hands on that."

"Abraxas?" Ana asked.

"It's true," he said.

She thought he would say more, but he didn't. Now she understood the strange emotions she'd been feeling from him.

"But we got away from the Cyprian," Ana said.

"For now," Sabel said. "What happens when she tells the Sangkesh, and the Shaitans, and the Hecatine witches that you're holding something they all want?"

"Why would she do that?"

"She has to," Brie answered. "It's her nature to betray us any way she can."

"Well, shit," Ana said. "So I'll get rid of the Ashmedai thing and then go back to San Francisco and Abraxas can give it to the Sangkesh."

"I can't," he said. "Or I would have done it eight hundred years ago. The Sangkesh in the area weren't strong enough to defend it. It's the same now. Leaving aside the question of whether they're prepared to handle that kind of power, it will make them the target of the Shaitans and the witches."

Lily added, "And other Sangkesh. It's not like we're all unified globally. Factions within us want that knowledge, like the demon-hunters. And even if the Sangkesh of San Francisco had the whole power of the Sangkesh around the world behind them, it could simply start an all-out war with the Shaitans in which San Francisco is ground zero and everyone you care about is a potential target."

"What if we give the tablet to the witches? Are they strong enough to protect us?"

"Doubtful," Sabel said. "The current Hecatine leadership isn't any more powerful than the Sangkesh, probably a good bit less. But I do know someone who might be able to help us figure out what to do with it."

* * *

"This time I want to travel with luggage," Ana said, trying to keep the hurt out of her voice.

The bathroom floor was hard against her knees, and having Sabel's arm around her shoulders was creating a painful reminder of the many bruises there, so Ana gently pulled away from Sabel. She got to her feet and helped Sabel up. They moved into the other room and Sabel sat on the bed, then pushed herself backward until she could sit against the pillows at the headboard. Lily grabbed two more pillows and used them to raise and bolster Sabel's leg.

Ana climbed onto the bed and sat cross-legged next to Sabel, not ready to lean back against anything until her shoulders stopped throbbing.

"So where are we going?" Ana asked.

Sabel looked at the cloudy form of Abraxas in the hallway and Lily standing next to him, and then at Brie, who was perched on the edge of the desk across from the bed.

"The witches' archive in Washington, D.C.," Sabel said. "But we don't all need to go and we probably shouldn't go straight there."

"I'll meet up with you," Brie said. "Just tell me where."

"I don't think you can get into the archive," Sabel told her. "I'm going to have enough trouble trying to get Ana and Abraxas in."

"Well, then, maybe I'll play the distraction."

Lily sighed at her and then turned to Sabel. "I'll meet you there as well. You might need someone to host Abraxas for a bit if you can only get Ana in. But it sounds like you had another stop in mind first."

Sabel reached across the bed and entwined her fingers with Ana's. "This time of year, Greece is a lot warmer than the Midwest, and I know some very small villages where it would be easy to hide you for a while until we know more about who's going to come looking for Abraxas."

"I could definitely use some time in the sun," Ana said, though the idea of going all the way to Greece still made her nervous.

"Speaking of luggage," Brie said. "You going to take that leash with you?"

Sabel looked up and smiled. In a clear voice, she said, "No, I'm not."

Ana squeezed her fingers and ducked her face so that her wolfish grin wouldn't be too obvious.

"But not right now," Sabel added. "None of us have slept in a day and I'd rather we not screw this up. Let me contact Josefene and see if we have an allied doctor in the area who makes house calls, or hotel calls. The leash can come off tomorrow."

Ana knew she had to be bone-tired because she didn't feel nearly the sting of disappointment that she should have. She stretched out on her stomach next to Sabel and muttered, "Okay, wake me when something's happening."

Before sleep closed over her, she felt Abraxas slip fully back into her body. Shame still radiated from him and she was almost tempted to tease him about working with his emotions. That didn't feel right. She was pissed at him for not telling her everything, but he was already more upset with himself.

Was it possible that in her short life she'd fucked up more things than he had in his very long one? Did she know more about screwing up and recovering than he did? Maybe she could be the teacher for once.

She pushed her mind against his presence and he pushed back lightly, like two people sitting side by side with their shoulders touching.

* * *

Lily ended up scheduling an extra day before everyone was due to fly out, and Sabel appreciated having unrushed hours around the hotel room. While Ana and Brie went off to get food, she limped in to take a bath. The witches' doctor had been efficient with the stitches and generous with extra bandages. Thankfully, because despite propping her leg on the side of the tub, Sabel got the current bandages soaked.

By afternoon she felt rested enough to try handing the leash over to Brie. When she mentioned it to the room at large, Abraxas jumped from Ana to Lily and they left hurriedly. Lily said something about a movie but Sabel got the impression she and Abraxas wanted to be far away from Brie's magic.

Sabel was sitting on the bed with Ana and Brie in armchairs, but a moment after the door shut, Brie climbed onto the bed. She moved slowly and sinuously, like a cat just waking up, and crawled up the bed to Sabel, careful of her wounded leg.

"How do you want to do this?" Brie asked.

Sabel remembered how Brie had crouched over her and slammed the leash back into her body before she left for Chicago, and shivered. In the last few years, she'd tried to stop vilifying herself for the amount of force and even pain that she liked in bed. Not that she'd come anywhere close to broaching that topic with Ana. If only Ana could be the one to reach into her body like that…but at least she could be close and hold Sabel while Brie took the leash back.

Sabel rubbed her leg lightly above the bandages. The side of her calf still burned lightly through the pain medicine she'd taken. Although some kinds of pain could be sexy in bed, Sabel felt certain that an accidentally jostled gunshot wound wasn't that kind of pain.

"Ana, would you sit behind me?" Sabel asked. "And Brie, you can do this from the front, right? Like when you put it back on—but not like that."

"Not hard and fast?" Brie asked. She was grinning but Sabel saw the tightness around her eyes, the concern.

Ana climbed onto the bed and put her legs around Sabel, holding her against her chest. The feel of Ana's heavy breasts against her back made Sabel want to turn around and kiss her, and to lean back farther and let herself drift into a doze. She didn't understand how she could find Ana's body simultaneously arousing and soothing. No one else had ever made her feel so deeply relaxed and razor-edged with need. It shouldn't work like that, but it did and now that she'd had it, she didn't think she could want anything else.

"Good," Ana said, words close to her ear. "Just relax."

Ana's voice and her demon-hot breath made Sabel want to sleep and to orgasm at the same time. Impossible and maddening, but wonderful. She nestled back against Ana and tried to remember what sort of magic helped with the leash transfer.

Brie snagged one of the pillows from the head of the bed and rested it next to Sabel's wounded calf, pushing Sabel's legs open in the process so she could kneel between them. She sat back on her heels and took Sabel's chin in her hand.

"You look half gone," she said.

"I'm still pretty worn-out," Sabel said. "I burned through everything in the last few days."

"Let me take some from Ana and give it to you, okay? I don't want to hurt you."

"It's okay."

Brie laughed. "You like it when it hurts?"

"Sometimes," Sabel said, the drowsy, comfortable space with Ana making her careless.

"I can oblige. Can you do that cathedral thing where you open up inside?" As she talked, Brie moved her hand from Sabel's face to trail down the front of her body until her fingers tucked between her legs.

Waves of energy trailed up inside her body from Brie's fingers. Sabel thought she'd be used to it, but she wasn't—like getting turned on, being in the middle of sex, but all her clothes were on and Brie's fingers hardly moved.

Brie put her mouth on Sabel's and she opened her lips, feeling Brie draw in a breath that pulled more energy up through her. She reminded the nagging, worried part of her mind that this was okay. Ana was here and she could protect her from anything Brie would do.

Brie pushed the leash open from the inside and tugged at it. She was going slowly, being gentle. The leash didn't move. It felt stuck.

More energy streamed up through Sabel, warm and languid. The leash relaxed a notch. Brie gave it a stronger tug. Still no movement.

Brie pulled away. "We might have to try hard and fast," she said. "I hate to say it, but the leash doesn't feel like it's in a mood to be played with."

Sabel thought that a magical thing shouldn't have moods, but she wasn't opposed to the method. She gave a little shrug and nod. "Sure."

Brie pushed her hand further by an inch so that her palm was completely under Sabel. Despite two layers of fabric between Brie's skin and hers, the gesture felt more intimate, not less. Kissing her hard, mouths open, Brie pushed a dense wave of energy up into Sabel. From Brie's body a heavy gravity yanked at the leash.

Instead of pulling free from Sabel, the leash's thick bands of energy clenched around her. It felt like a hand grabbed her spine and yanked it into her ribs. Muscles spasmed, pain exploding through her. Sabel's body jerked hard, a yelp of alarm forced from her lips.

Ana's arms went around her, pushing Brie away. Sabel saw the shocked look on Brie's face for a second before she faded into semiconsciousness. In the darkness, she felt the years of defenses on her body closing and trying to repair the damage.

She wanted to tell Ana she was okay, but a few minutes must have passed before she came fully conscious again. Brie was standing all the way across the room from the bed, near the door, her empty hands held up.

Ana had pulled Sabel back to the head of the bed and laid her down. She was just getting off the bed, her face a mix of worry and anger.

"Not her fault." Sabel forced the words through a throat still constricted with the shock of whatever the hell that was.

Brie came back to the bed in a flash. Ana moved to stop her, but Brie dodged around her with a burst of speed and crouched on the bed next to Sabel. Her fingers brushed the sides of Sabel's face and she felt a featherlight touch under the skin, just feeling the limits of the leash.

Ana whirled and grabbed Brie by the shoulders. Brie ducked, twisted, came up holding Ana's hands in an Aikido-style wrist lock.

"I'm not hurting her," she said.

"Ana," Sabel said, coughed, caught her breath. "It's true."

The muscles across Ana's shoulders relaxed, which was a very good thing since Sabel figured she could probably throw Brie across the room even from a wrist lock.

Brie dropped Ana's hands and came back to her position by Sabel. "It changed. Something altered the structure of the leash."

"Fuck," Ana said.

"The fight," Sabel explained, because that had to be it. Her muscles were unlocking more and she pushed herself up a few inches on the pillows. Swallowing hard, she went on hoarsely, "Battling the Cyprian, I had Abraxas use the leash to call Ashtoreth. Because I was outside of time but the leash wasn't. She could follow it back."

"Do you think Ashtoreth changed its structure? Or the Cyprian?"

"They must have but I don't understand how. It still feels like witch magic, there's no demon energy in it," Sabel said. "Can you hold it open for me, just for a moment?"

Brie nodded and put her hands around Sabel's ribs, using the attraction in her hands to hold the energy open. Sabel felt down into its structure in a way that would have triggered it in the past: the branches that Brie once described as lacy were fused and thick now, organic like a tree's roots or a human system of sinews, tendon and muscle.

There was new magic in it. But it was still the magic of the witches and it felt older than anything Sabel had ever experienced. Thousands of years old.

Sabel closed her eyes. She knew what had happened. Tears of frustration ran down the sides of her face. What was the good of working with time if she couldn't go back and undo this? And what if she could? They'd have died from the Cyprian if not for Ashtoreth's return.

If she could have warned Abraxas, would that change anything? He couldn't have known this would happen. He didn't understand witch magic—even as he carried it inside himself.

Abraxas *was* the tablet of the galla. In addition to being a demon, he was also a six-thousand-year-old spell that turned humans into immortal servants of the witches. Some part of the spell had applied itself to the leash. Sabel wasn't even sure what part of the spell had activated and what it had done, but the thought that echoed in her mind was: *Who am I bound to now?*

If she couldn't figure that out or if it turned out the answer was no one, the leash might never come off.

No, she couldn't accept that. There had to be a way. She'd go to the archive, she'd talk to the leadership, she would find a way to get this thing off her so she could be with Ana freely.

Brie's hands moved off her ribs and she felt Ana beside her, pulling Sabel against her chest, brushing the tears off her face.

"Her energy is really low and kind of fucked up," Brie said.

"Is that what's wrong?" Ana asked.

"The leash is different," Brie told her. "I don't think I can get it off her now."

Ana's lips brushed Sabel's forehead. "Is that why you're upset?" she asked.

Sabel nodded. She didn't want to have to tell Ana that this was because of something Abraxas had done. She didn't even understand all of what had happened herself, and that was reason enough not to speak of it.

"We'll figure it out," Ana said. "I'll get this demon prince power transferred to someone else and Abraxas can spend more time with Lily. We'll figure it out."

"She's losing energy," Brie explained. "A bunch of it leaked out when I tried to take the leash."

"But you can give her more, right?" Ana asked.

Brie shook her head. "Not mine, but yours. I can still hold the leash open and you're basically an energy volcano right now."

"How?" Ana asked.

"I'd recommend the slow way with the kissing and all that."

"I'm not making out with you while Sabel's hurt and upset," Ana said. "What's the other way?"

Sabel pushed herself up just enough to see Ana's eyes, narrow with worry and anger. Even that gesture took too much energy. Life force was still leaking out of her from the leash where it had jerked in place and wasn't sitting right. She could almost understand the kind of hunger Brie must feel all the time.

"Please," Sabel said. "She's right."

"I don't like this," Ana told her.

"Okay, now you're just hurting my feelings," Brie said.

Sabel had to laugh at that. She leaned into Ana. "Help me prop up on some pillows and go kiss the nice demon for me."

She didn't have the energy just then to fully explain to Ana that she wasn't possessive like that. As long as she knew that Ana was hers, that Ana adored her and would be there when she needed it, she didn't care about sexual exclusivity. Someday, if they'd had enough to drink and more than enough time in bed together, she'd tell Ana about her rebellious twenties that made a threesome look tame by comparison.

"Well, if it's for you…" Ana said.

She piled three pillows by the headboard and leaned Sabel back on them so she was mostly sitting. It scared Sabel that she didn't have the vitality in her own body to even sit upright on her own, but she tried not to show it.

Ana got up and Brie met her at the foot of the bed. Ana's side of the kiss was careful, Brie's hungry. Sabel wondered how much energy Brie had lost in the effort to take the leash. Too much. Ana had her hands lightly on Brie's hips, but Brie was holding Ana's head tightly, crushing her mouth against Ana's. Sabel felt the force of Brie's kiss in her gut. A sigh slipped out of her lips.

The kiss went on long enough that Sabel wanted to get up and join them, but she was still hovering at the edge of passing out. When they broke apart, Brie crawled up the bed to her and brushed her fingers across Sabel's mouth.

"Open," she said.

Sabel opened her lips. Brie's mouth came so close that she felt a feather-soft brush of lips on hers and then exhaled breath like fire rolling down the back of her throat, down her spine, into her belly.

The passing-out feeling dissipated but the energy wasn't enough. She still felt off-center inside, like her bones weren't in their proper places.

Brie pulled away and smiled at her. "You want more, don't you?"

"I think we need to reseat the leash," Sabel said.

"So what you're saying is, we're going to need *a lot* more?" Brie asked, raising her eyebrows and smirking.

The thing that was so insidious about her, Sabel thought, was that she didn't have any ill intentions about her. After a while, you couldn't help but like her. Or maybe that was still the magic and she'd been too worn-out and preoccupied to see if Brie was pushing her emotions. She'd sort that out later.

"She says we're going to need more," Brie repeated to Ana, as if Ana hadn't heard it the first time.

Ana came around the side of the bed and sat next to where Sabel was lying against the pile of pillows. She reached across and brushed her fingers down Brie's leg, then turned all her attention to Sabel.

Ana leaned close, bracing herself on her hands. She kissed Sabel's cheeks, forehead, mouth. Then she moved back just enough so they could look at each other.

"Do you want this?" she asked.

"Am I yours no matter what happens?"

Ana's smile gleamed as she nodded. "You're mine."

"Then please, yes, I need so much more energy and I'd rather we do it the nice way."

Ana grinned at her and shook her head. "Professor Young, you surprise the hell out of me."

"Someone has to."

"Gods and powers, you two are going to kill me," Brie said. She got off the bed and Sabel wondered if they'd offended her. Instead of leaving, she stopped in the middle of the room and pulled off her overshirt, undershirt and bra. Her body was a miracle of curves, from her full breasts to the muscled and lush contour of her belly. She shucked her jeans and got back onto the bed.

"Plain cotton?" Sabel asked, gesturing at Brie's underpants.

"I didn't know it was war panties day," she said.

Sabel expected her to crawl across the bed to Ana, but instead she moved gently over Sabel and kissed her.

Brie's energy brushed the outside of her skin lightly, settling over her like a cool sheet. Where it sank into her skin, a gentle euphoria spread out. The lingering pain in her leg vanished.

At any moment, Sabel figured, Brie would stop and turn her attention to Ana. She kissed back and let herself enjoy it. Her fingers trailed along the sides of Brie's body until she felt the rise of her breasts. She cupped one and let her thumb toy with the straining nipple.

Brie's fingers found the zipper on her sweatshirt and tugged it down. She pulled back enough to murmur, "Take it off."

Two thoughts hit Sabel at the same time. The first, that if she wasn't careful, she could end up taking orders from Brie and liking it. And the second, which canceled the worries about the first, was that Ana was loving this. As Sabel shrugged out of her sweatshirt, every movement drew Ana's gaze, her caramel-brown eyes wide open with wonder.

Sabel raised an eyebrow at Ana. "Shirt too?" she asked.

"Oh, yes."

Brie caught the hem of her shirt before Sabel could. Sabel raised her arms and Brie pulled it off.

"Of course there's a matching bra," Brie said with a sigh. She bent and kissed from Sabel's collarbone down to the lace edges of the bra. Her hands played with Sabel's breasts while her lips teased her through the bra.

Ana's fingers brushed a lock of hair back from Sabel's face, tucking it behind her ear. "Take off the bra," she said.

Sabel sat up again, but Brie did the work of unclasping and removing her bra before she could even start to think clearly. Brie moved between Sabel's breasts, touching everywhere with her lips, tongue, teeth and the soft curls of her hair. She kept her face turned toward Ana and Sabel realized that Brie was teasing her intensely.

Ana watched Brie licking and playing with Sabel's breasts. Sabel let the moan she'd been suppressing slip through her lips, let herself show Ana how good Brie's mouth, hair and fingers felt on her. Ana's hands clenched and unclenched on the coverlet. Sabel reached over and touched one, pushed the fingers to uncurl. She lifted it to her mouth and sucked on Ana's thumb.

Ana groaned and rocked forward to kiss Sabel. Her thumb, still in Sabel's mouth, held her jaw open while Ana's tongue danced around her lips.

Brie was kissing her way down Sabel's belly, fingers working at the stiff button on the new pair of jeans.

"I don't want to hurt you," Ana told Sabel.

She meant the bullet wound, Sabel knew, but so much more than that. And Sabel had a hundred things to say in reply, but this wasn't the time. She looked at Ana's warm, dark eyes. "I trust you," she said.

Ana kissed her as Brie pulled off her pants and the newly-dubbed war panties. She almost protested that this wasn't quite

what she'd had in mind when she suggested the three of them...
but then she couldn't finish the thought because Brie's tongue
slid across her clit.

Ana pulled away from the kiss and watched Sabel squirm
and gasp and extend a hand toward Ana but not quite manage
to reach her. Ana tangled one hand in Brie's hair and pulled
roughly. Brie sat up, eyes wide. Ana kissed her deeply.

Sabel felt the energy of Ana's arousal streaming from her
into Brie like a river of fire. When Ana paused to catch her
breath, Brie leaned up Sabel's body to put her mouth on Sabel's
and breathe most of the energy into her. Sabel smelled herself
on Brie and Ana's scent of vervain and musk. Her body soaked
in the energy Brie offered.

"You know," Brie said. "It's more effective if I put the energy
in your body from lower down."

To illustrate, she moved back down Sabel's body, parted
Sabel's lower lips with her tongue and pushed energy up.
Tongues of energy licked up inside of her skin.

"Is she right?" Ana asked.

"Very," Sabel gasped out as tendrils of energy extended
across her pelvic floor and up.

"So if I can give her more energy, she can pass it along to
you," Ana murmured, half to herself as she moved down the bed.

She put herself behind Brie, stroking her back and ass and
legs. Slowly, watching Sabel, Ana pulled Brie's white cotton
panties down. Sabel could feel the moment Ana's fingers
entered Brie because she moaned with her lips against Sabel's
clit, sending tremors of pleasure up her body. Sabel gasped,
hands clutching the blanket on one side of her and the pillow
on the other.

Ana watched her and grinned. She fucked Brie with a deep,
thorough rhythm. Sabel felt it inside her body, from the memory
of what Ana's fingers felt like inside her and from the energy
that echoed up into her. As Ana thrust into Brie, Brie drew Ana's
energy through her body and thrust it up into Sabel.

The effect of Brie taking energy like that pushed Ana closer
and closer to orgasm.

Ana was still fully dressed in her jeans and soft, heather-gray button-down shirt, its sleeves rolled up. Being the one clothed person in a room with two naked women, being the one effectively fucking both of them, gave her an aura of power that Sabel wanted to hold in her mind forever.

And at the same time, she loved that Ana was slipping in and out of control. Sabel could see it in the way her eyes kept losing focus and then finding Sabel's face again.

"Please," Sabel said.

Relief flashed in Ana's eyes. She thrust harder for a minute and then her head rocked back.

A wave of exquisite force hit Sabel. Her body transmuted that power into motion and snapped the leash fully back in place. The jarring, almost painful sensation merged with the pleasure arcing through her and pushed her over the edge.

Brie's hands gripped her hips, tongue still playing with her as she came, pushing her higher. Her eyes had closed, but she felt Ana moving up the bed, strong arms around her while she was still rising on the energy. She pressed her face to Ana's chest and Ana tightened her grip.

Afterward, she thought should be exhausted but she felt vibrant.

When she opened her eyes, Brie was crouched midbed grinning at her. "Good job on the leash," she said. "I couldn't have resettled it in the midst of all that. Do you think the witches would make me one?"

It took a bit for Sabel to parse Brie's words into sentences again. Sudden topic change? No, deflection and fear. Brie had just found the only two people in the world she could safely have sex with and now they could walk away from her.

"Come here," Sabel said and patted the empty side of the bed next to her. She brushed her fingers down Brie's cheek. "Thank you."

"Hey, anytime."

"I'll ask when we get to D.C.," Sabel told her. "We'll figure it out."

Brie beamed at her. Then she hopped smoothly off the bed. In the darkening light of the room as she moved around finding her clothes and putting them on, she seemed to glow.

"I love you guys," she said. "I'm going shopping."

Before they could respond, she was gone.

Ana's low chuckle vibrated against Sabel. "She's such a punk," Ana said.

"What?"

"She knows we haven't said that yet, to each other," Ana explained. She wrapped a lock of Sabel's hair around her finger. "I do, you know. I love you like crazy. I wanted to tell you on the train and it wasn't the time, and then later, but this whole time—"

Sabel put her fingers on Ana's lips and then replaced them with a kiss.

"I love you too," Sabel said. "Demons and all."

Bella Books, Inc.

Women. Books. Even Better Together.

P.O. Box 10543
Tallahassee, FL 32302

Phone: 800-729-4992
www.bellabooks.com

Printed in the USA
CPSIA information can be obtained
at www.ICGtesting.com
JSHW082153140824
68134JS00014B/208